BRIGHT FAMILIAR

BONDS OF MAGIC
BOOK TWO

BY

JEFFE KENNEDY

He wanted her with consuming passion… and so did the monster within.

Lady Veronica Elal has been freed from her tower—and entered a life of servitude. It doesn't matter that her wizard master has odd ideas about circumventing Convocation tradition and making their relationship equal. Nic prides herself on her practicality and that means not pretending her marriage is full of hearts and flowers. Besides she understands that, despite her new husband's idealism, they face obstacles so great the pair of them could be crushed to nothing, even without dashing themselves brainless trying to fight the Convocation.

Lord Gabriel Phel has come this far against impossible odds. He was born with powerful wizard magic, the first in his family in generations. He's managed to begin the process of reinstating his fallen house. And—having staked his family's meager fortune to win a familiar to amplify his magic, a highborn daughter to be mother to his children, his lady, and lover—he rescued Nic in a distant land, successfully bringing her home to House Phel. Though she's cynical about their chances of success, he's certain they can defy their enemies and flourish. Together.

But, the more Gabriel discovers about working with the fiery Nic, attempting to learn the finer points of wizardry and marriage, the more illicit fantasies plague him. His need for Nic—and the dark cravings she stirs in his black wizard's heart—grow daily. Though Nic has reconciled herself to being possessed by Gabriel—and indeed yearns for even more from her brooding and reluctant master—creating a new life for herself isn't easy. Especially when Gabriel seems determined to subvert the foundation of her world. Starting with her father.

DEDICATION

To all of you who embraced, gobbled up, and recommended
my Dark Wizard.
This series lives because of you.

ACKNOWLEDGMENTS

Many thanks to Emily Mah Tippetts and Darynda Jones, who read this book literally as I was writing it, to the point of vetting the final chapter the night before I sent it to the proofreader. Emily gets credit for suggesting Nic's alternate form and Darynda gets love for saying that she loved the book and found it engrossing even though she didn't understand why.

A round of coffee to the Writer Coffee peeps—Emily Mah Tippetts, Jim Sorenson, Trent Zelazny, and J. Barton Mitchell—for long-ranging conversations and sympathetic nods.

Hat tip to Jennifer Estep—I believe this is the Yoda scene you were looking for.

Thanks and love to Carien Ubink for All The Assisting, drawing the Elal crest, and weeding out hundreds of images of Spirit: Stallion of the Cimarron.

Love to my mom, who is a pillar who holds up my personal sky. See? I finished the book on time anyway!

Love to David, who is there every day, and who makes everything possible.

~ I ~

THREE MESSAGES ARRIVED at House Phel, all before breakfast, all bearing bad news.

"I told you so," Nic said, taking in Gabriel's frown as he read the missives.

Lifting his wizard-black gaze, he cocked his head at her. "No doubt you did, but which thing are you referring to this time?"

"That they wouldn't leave us alone for long."

"I thought we'd have at least a day to settle in."

She snorted at his optimism. The morning had dawned fair and mild, so they'd decided to breakfast near the balcony overlooking the river. It wasn't much of a breakfast, as apparently the minimally livable manse did not yet include a working kitchen. Instead they were eating the cold supper left over from the welcome-home picnic from the afternoon before. As Gabriel had asked his mother when he and Nic had abruptly left the party so as not to fight in front of his entire family, the food had been left outside the master suite doors. What with resolving their differences, discovering the arcanium, and finally—finally!—completing the bonding ceremony, they'd never gotten around to eating an actual supper.

The cold fried poultry was a bit disconcerting as a breakfast meal, but *something* to eat was welcome, as she was starving. She would kill for a hot cup of coffee with cream and sugar, but the hot, subtly floral tea would do. At least the view was lovely, the several sets of glass-paned doors open to the breeze that ruffled Gabriel's raggedly cut hair. Without the weight of its previous length, the white strands curled in the humidity, glittering bright in the morning sun—except for the streak at his right temple, black as night, black as his eyes. She wanted to run her fingers through the surprising waves, but she and Gabriel had been observing a somewhat formal distance this morning. After the crashing intimacy of the bonding in the arcanium the night before, not to mention the life-altering sex, they'd barely made it back to the master suite before falling into bed and into instant sleep.

Waking to their dramatically altered relationship had been somewhat awkward.

Gabriel kept giving her searching looks, as if uncertain of her. She wasn't sure what to say to reassure him. When he'd gone downstairs to determine the possibility of something for breakfast besides leftovers and returned with the missives, she'd been almost grateful for the distraction. Even though she was experienced enough in the ways of her people to know they wouldn't say anything good.

"News travels fast in the Convocation," she told him. "Now that they know where to find us, they have. No doubt they've been chomping at the bit to scold us. May I?"

"You don't have to ask," he replied almost testily, pushing

the letters toward her, the formal stationery rustling crisply over the polished wood.

She restrained a similarly tart comment to that, also. As his familiar, she *did* have to ask permission for such things, but Gabriel didn't follow any Convocation customs—to the point of obstinately insisting on subverting them—so suggesting anything of the sort would only lead to yet another argument. Still basking in the glow of the bonding, and the exceptionally good sex, she was unwilling to disrupt their tentative peace. They were traversing uncharted territory, however, and she disliked not knowing her footing. Gabriel might detest Convocation law, but at least she knew where she stood with the Convocation.

Gabriel seemed to think that everything would just fall into place for them, whereas she knew their struggle was only beginning. And these missives were the opening salvo in the coming war. With a sigh, she raked back her hair, feeling that odd jolt of surprise when her fingers immediately sprang free. It would take a while to get used to being without her own formerly waist-length tresses, particularly given how unkempt she now looked.

Gabriel's assessment that she'd need a trim following the abrupt shearing during the bonding ceremony had been a massive understatement. One look in the bathing chamber mirror had confirmed that much. Without the weight, her dark locks were also curling—and with such uneven and wild abandon that they stood out around her head like a deranged halo. She would have gotten her grooming imp to try to tame the mess, but Gabriel had already returned from his fruitless breakfast quest—well, not entirely fruitless, as he'd found the tea and also brought some fresh oranges—and she hadn't wanted to make him wait on her. Maybe she could find time later.

Setting aside the irritating but arguably frivolous concerns of vanity, she picked up what should be the easiest missive to deal with: the demand from House Iblis. It was exactly what she'd expected. Gabriel's impulsive "liberation" of the aged familiar Narlis had been taken amiss. She sighed for that unnecessary complication.

"What do you think?" he asked, peeling an orange and giving her half.

She took it, the scent bright as sunshine. "I thought the orange trees drowned when the levee broke."

"Leaked, not broke," he corrected. "And just the new saplings. We have mature orchards, too. What do you think about the demand from Iblis? You have to admit it's not as bad as you predicted."

"Do I?" She decided not to point out that she was sensitive to Convocation nuance that he wasn't. The missive was disturbingly condescending. "I don't suppose you're willing to return Narlis?"

Gabriel sat back, giving her a disappointed glare. "How can you even suggest such a thing?"

"I'm not suggesting it," she replied mildly, not pointing out that he'd asked for her opinion—which she would have withheld, like a good familiar should, had he not requested it. "I'm ascertaining your position on the matter."

"Hmm." Unconvinced, he chewed a wedge of orange.

"This decision, at least, is easy. Iblis asks that I return Narlis or pay for her. I'll send the money, and we can knock House Iblis off our list of potential enemies."

She nodded, giving every appearance of agreement.

"What?" he demanded.

She raised a brow. "I didn't say anything."

"Nic." He bit back a sigh and took his irritation down a notch. "I'm relying on you to give me advice in navigating the arcane etiquette of the Convocation houses. If you see a pitfall that I don't, I hope you'd tell me."

She supposed she should try; she *had* harnessed her fortunes to his, after all, which meant this would be far from the last custom she'd disregard. "They're asking for a ridiculous amount of money."

"It's not that much. House Phel may be far from wealthy, but we're not beggars either. I can pull those funds together."

Nic set her teeth. "That is not the point."

"It's exactly the point."

"No," she nearly growled at him. "An elderly familiar, well past her prime, who almost certainly won't live a handful of years more, who will be only a mouth to feed and a consumer of expensive healing if you're unwilling to let her suffer, which I'm sure you will be, and—"

"Of course she'll have healing. We may be provincials here in Meresin, but we're not monsters."

"*And* who provides zero value in return," Nic continued remorselessly, "is not worth any amount of coin, much less this absurd price. If anything, Iblis should pay you to take her off their hands."

"We're talking about a human being here," he said tightly.

"Not in the eyes of the Convocation, we're not," she shot back, annoyed enough with his naïveté to abandon the circumspection she'd previously resolved upon. Which always seemed to happen in her interactions with Gabriel. "You want my opinion? Fine. To the Convocation, there are wizards, familiars, and nonmagical commoners." She ticked off the points on her fingers. "The first have value. The second have value in respect to the first. The third are irrelevant. By demanding a price for Narlis that is beyond all reason, House Iblis is testing you. They've figured out who you are, which means they're well aware you're from a fallen house and were not trained at Convocation Academy. You revealed yourself as being weak by showing sympathy for a dried-up, worthless familiar to the point that you went to the trouble of exposing us by abducting her, which—as I told you at the time—is an act of war. Now they're determining just how inexperienced you are by seeing if you'll meet their absurd demands."

Gabriel regarded her thoughtfully. "So, we have three options: pay the price, return Narlis—which, you are correct, I refuse to do—or refuse altogether."

"Four options," she corrected. "You could counteroffer."

Though he remained apparently relaxed, his jaw tightened. "It doesn't sit well with me to haggle over a human being." When she opened her mouth, he shot a finger at her. "And don't tell me a familiar isn't a human being. I don't care what Convocation law dictates. She is a person, as are you."

"We're not talking about me," she replied, aware of the bitter edge to her voice. Hoping to sweeten it, she added honey to her tea.

"Nic," Gabriel said, far more softly, and set his hand on the table, palm up. Always giving her the invitation rather than the demand that was his right. When she relented and laid her hand in his, he squeezed it gently. "I don't believe either of us is capable of having a conversation about familiars and their second-class status in the Convocation without both of us being very aware that everything we say also applies to you."

She sighed for the truth of that. Much as she'd rather have it otherwise, she'd been doomed to the life of a familiar long before Gabriel Phel applied to participate in her Betrothal Trials. None of it was his fault. So, she squeezed his hand in return. "Fine. Given that, I'm going to suggest that you'll do better in dealing with other Convocation houses if you can set your emotions aside and view familiars—Narlis and me, both—the way they do. Otherwise they'll discern your weakness and use it against you."

Holding her hand, he rubbed his thumb over the back of it, the caress both soothing and arousing, as he gazed steadily at her with those wizard-black eyes. "I would argue," he said softly, "that having feelings for the woman who is my lover, my wife, and the mother of my child is not a weakness."

Her heart wriggled at the words, and the heat behind them, but she sternly told it to behave. "I'm your familiar first. In the eyes of the Convocation, I'm *only* your familiar, and I'm one who broke a number of laws. If you want to restore House Phel, you'll have to deal with the Convocation, like it or not. They will be searching for ways to bring me—and you along with me—to heel. If you're going to fight them, you'll have to meet them on their terms."

He gazed at her a moment longer. "And to think just yesterday afternoon you told me I wouldn't have to become like them."

He started to withdraw his hand, but she held on. "You won't become like them. I don't think it's in you, frankly, though it would make this quest of yours far easier. But you *will* have to fake it at times."

"What is the difference," he mused, "between appearing to be a thing and becoming it? I suspect if I act the role long enough, the clothes will begin to fit so well that I'll forget I was ever pretending."

She just had to land herself with the one ethical wizard in all of existence. "Gabriel…" she replied helplessly. "Can we forgo philosophy until we at least survive the threats piled on our breakfast table?"

He followed her glance to the missives, then met her gaze again, turning their joined hands so their fingers interlaced. "Isn't that how these things begin, though? You abandon a bit of integrity to survive the moment, exchange what's right for another day, another hour of security, telling yourself you'll make it up later, but by then you're midway down a slippery slope, gaining momentum for the chasm below."

With a groan of frustration, she pulled her hand away, seizing her eating utensil and stabbing it into a cold piece of fried poultry. No one would blame her if she imagined stabbing something else. "It's a bit late to be worrying about that slippery slope. The time for that was before you applied to acquire me in the Betrothal Trials." She pointed her utensil at him. "And cheated in order to win, I might add."

That was the absolute wrong thing to say. His expression darkened, black eyes going broody as he gazed at her, jaw set. "Believe me, I'm well aware of my offenses against you."

Good going, Nic. She mentally kicked herself. Putting down her utensil, she levered her elbows on the table—how Maman would cringe at the inelegant manners—and briefly buried her face in her hands, willing herself to think. When she met Gabriel's gaze again, she caught the anguish in his eyes before he banished it.

"Lord Phel," she said with deliberate formality, "you acted in the best interests of your house and the people of Meresin, who depend on you. More, what's done is done. I'm yours, and you wanted me because I would be the best possible asset in the struggle ahead. Don't throw away your best weapon because you're squeamish about its provenance."

"Squeamish," he echoed, smiling without humor. "A benign word for a grave transgression." But he held up a hand to stop her argument. "Still, I take your point. We're bonded now, and we must move forward. A counteroffer, you suggest?"

"Yes." She named a figure so low it had his dark brows rising. "It gives you room to *haggle*," she added with asperity, hoping to make him smile—to no avail. "No matter what, refuse to apologize. You are a high-ranking wizard and lord of your house. You took Narlis because it pleased you to do so. Now you're willing to pay a pittance to resolve their petty claim, but it's worth no more of your attention than that."

He inclined his head, taking the missive from Iblis and

setting it aside. "I'll draft the reply after breakfast."

"And send it via Ratsiel courier."

With a slow blink, he assimilated that as if she'd suggested they fly to the moon. "No one was around to retain the Ratsiel couriers after they delivered the missives."

She chewed another wedge of orange, slowly, to kill the urge to roll her eyes at him. "One doesn't retain Ratsiel couriers," she explained. "House Ratsiel wizards wield communication magic like you do your water and moon magic. Use your magic to notify Ratsiel of your need, and they will supply it."

"For a price."

"Of course. I assume House Phel hasn't set up an account with Ratsiel yet?" She sighed mentally as he shook his head. On top of everything else, she had a monumental effort ahead of her as Lady Phel in simply putting her new house on a basic footing of a minimal standard of living. Until Gabriel had manifested as a highly rated wizard—out of nowhere, generations after the last wizard Phel had produced—the people of Meresin had lived like wild creatures in the swamps. The house itself had fallen into ruin. Indeed, all but the section they occupied was suspiciously damp, if not actually underwater. They enjoyed none of the conveniences that made life in the Convocation comfortable. "That will be my first job after breakfast. I'll draft the proper documents to set up an account with Ratsiel, and also with Refoel for healing, and a few others to get us started."

He frowned blackly. "I don't like the idea of being beholden to the other houses, especially the High Houses."

"First of all, we'll be paying for services, or bartering with them for House Phel's, so there will be no debt incurred. House Phel will not go into debt under my management." Maman had taught her that much. House Phel might be foundering financially as well as in its physical foundations, but Nic could and would fix that much. She hadn't grown up as the eldest child of the wealthiest house in the Convocation not to use those skills. "Second, you're going to need allies among the other houses, *especially* the High Houses—and establishing mutually beneficial financial relationships is one of the best ways to do that. If they need what House Phel produces, then they'll reconsider before trying to crush your efforts to reestablish Phel to its former position in the Convocation."

Gabriel regarded her with some bemusement—which was at least better than the black displeasure. "Need I remind you House Phel has no products to export or barter at this time?"

"You do too, and you'll have more soon. I'll be working on that, also." *Add it to the list.* "For now, I'm going to promise only what I *know* you can deliver." She gave him a bright smile, and he held up his hands in surrender, laughing a little.

"It occurs to me that this is part of why I thought it would be a good idea to marry the daughter of House Elal," he commented wryly. "I don't know why I'm arguing."

"I don't know why either," she agreed pertly, then hesitated.

He narrowed his eyes. "What?"

"May I—would it be possible for me to have access to the house ledgers?"

"You can just *have* them," he replied fervently. "Please take over the house accounts. And stop asking me for permission."

Instead of explaining, yet again, why asking his permission was necessary, she picked up the missive from the Convocation, setting aside the one from her father to do so. Gabriel made note of her choice, black eyes studying her. Yes, she was more afraid of what her father had to say than the Convocation enforcers. What of it?

Gabriel ate steadily as she read the extensive list of her crimes and the Convocation's detailed terms for when and how House Phel would relinquish her for punishment and retraining. Though some of the promised treatments to subdue the rebellious inclinations she'd demonstrated and to ensure her future obedience turned her stomach, they were also nothing new. She'd been a star student at Convocation Academy and hadn't needed to undergo the more brutal methods of rendering a familiar pliant to their wizard's will, but she knew of other familiars who had. Those treatments weren't fun by any stretch, but they also wouldn't kill her. Or permanently harm her. After all, she was a highly rated familiar, far too valuable to injure, and she carried the unborn child of her and Gabriel's propitious blending of magical potential scores. The Convocation might not want House Phel to reclaim its former status among the High Houses, but they absolutely would want this child.

If she couldn't persuade the Convocation that she'd been duly tamed, they'd simply take the child, and her own chances would turn sour rapidly. They wouldn't kill her, but they'd make use of her in distasteful ways.

Feeling Gabriel's steady gaze on her—his moon magic

glinting silver-sharp in the air—she essayed a measuring glance at him. Oh yes, he was bubbling with quiet fury.

"Before you say a word," he said coolly, "I am not complying with the Convocation's insane demands. Not even the least of them."

"Gabriel, if—"

"No."

She took a breath, staring him down. "I'm just saying that—"

"No!" He slammed the meat of his fist down on the table, raising his voice in a rare shout, their breakfast dishes rattling in counterpoint. A few silver needles formed in the air and showered to the floor in a chiming rain.

Taking note of them, and that their appearance meant Gabriel had lost control of his moon magic, she raised a brow. "Can we have a conversation, or are you simply going to bellow at me?"

"I'm not having any conversation that involves turning you over to the Convocation for punishment and retraining." He spat the words with profound distaste. "I chased after you, deprived you of your freedom, and brought you here—against your will—entirely to prevent them from doing exactly that. I bonded with you last night, against my better judgment, because you persuaded me that they couldn't take you away if I did. I have become more of a monster than ever, all to prevent *this!*" He seized the Convocation missive and tore it into shreds.

Nic poured herself more tea—handy that her water wizard could heat it for her—added honey, stirred, then sat back in her chair, politely waiting.

"What?" he ground out.

Pleased with herself for outlasting him, she cocked her head. "Am I allowed to speak now?"

"I told you that you don't—" He caught himself and raked both hands through his waving silver hair. "Point taken. Though I didn't mean that you shouldn't speak. Just that—" He broke off with a rueful sigh.

"It's in a wizard's nature to be commanding," she replied sweetly, noting the flinch as her barb hit home.

"This is probably not the best time for you to needle me," he said with a brooding glare. "I am not... the most rational where you are concerned."

The magic—and sexual tension—hummed between them, so thick in the air that Nic nearly forgot what points she'd been hoping to make. She didn't know what to make of his protectiveness. All wizards were possessive of their familiars, but Gabriel actually cared about her feelings. He truly wasn't like any other Convocation wizard, with his odd obsession with making her a partner in all things.

"Go ahead," he prompted ruefully. "Say your piece. I promise to keep my temper. Though I don't promise to agree."

"The Convocation intends to send my Betrothal Trials proctor to evaluate our bonding, along with my physical and mental health. Remember that they regard me as valuable and will want to confirm that I haven't been damaged." The proctor would also want to assess her tractability, but she didn't mention that, as Gabriel was touchy on the subject.

"It's a firm no if the proctor wants to travel in the company of hunters," Gabriel cut in. "I won't allow those things near you. I won't allow them anywhere on our lands."

"Then tell them so," she replied with considerable exasperation. "Play arrogant Lord Phel, say that you have no agreement of reciprocity with House Tadkiel—true—and that you won't allow Tadkiel magic on your lands until you do. But that you will welcome the proctor so—"

"I don't welcome her. I met her at House Elal after you fled, remember? Her and that vile oracle head. I don't want either of them near you."

Nic pressed her lips closed and waited quietly, sipping her tea.

Gabriel growled, deep in his chest, and folded his arms. "Fine. I'll stop interrupting."

"I'm far from fond of the proctor," Nic continued agreeably. "She can, however, attest to the successful bonding. If I appear sufficiently contrite and utterly enchanted with being your familiar, slavishly devoted to my wizard master..." That grinding sound must be Gabriel's teeth, but to his credit, he didn't interrupt her. She gave him a warm smile. "Perhaps we can get the Convocation to give me a probationary period to demonstrate that I've changed my ways. After that, they might leave us alone for a while."

"I want them to go away forever," Gabriel ground out forbiddingly.

"You might as well wish the sun from the sky," she retorted. "The Convocation rules the world and—"

"Not *all* the world," he countered.

"All of *our* world, they do. I tried to escape the Convocation, remember? They sent the hunters after me anyway. You want to restore House Phel? Then we need to be in good status with the Convocation."

He gazed at her, sensuous lips slightly parted, black eyes opaque with dark thoughts. "I'm not sure I care about that anymore."

"Then start caring again," she replied briskly. "Because to all those people who welcomed you home yesterday, you are the sun of their universe. They need you."

"Meresin survived before I manifested as a wizard."

"Gabriel," she said softly, "you tried to deny your nature. It didn't work. And now that we know your sister, Seliah, is a familiar, you can't go back to paddling about the swamps and pretending these things don't affect you. She's already losing her sanity. If we don't get her Convocation training—and eventually a wizard to tap her magic—it will kill her."

He grimaced, nodding reluctantly. "But I don't want that proctor going near Selly."

If Nic's brief introduction to Gabriel's sister was any indication, Seliah wouldn't be capable of a conversation with the proctor. It made sense that she had manifested as a familiar, as far as any of the strange happenings made sense in the sudden, unprecedented resurrection of House Phel. The family, including all extended branches, had failed to produce anyone with measurable MP scores for generations—thus losing them their house status—and then Gabriel appeared. An adult wizard, self-taught, with MP scores of the highest levels.

Of course his sister just had to be talented, too. Because

familiars couldn't work magic on their own, their manifestation tended to be less dramatic. With no one trained to recognize magical potential, Seliah had lived with untapped magic well into her twenties. It was a miracle she was still alive, let alone able to string two words together. Though Nic hadn't wanted to upset Gabriel by putting it that strongly.

The best place for Seliah was Convocation Academy, but Gabriel wouldn't agree to that at this point. If Nic could demonstrate to the proctor that her training was intact, that she'd happily bonded to Gabriel and was indeed fascinated by her wizard master, the proctor would relax considerably. Perhaps at that point, Nic would be able to show Gabriel that the Convocation wasn't all bad.

Of course, she'd have to explain to the proctor why she fled rather than marry Gabriel, but she had time to think up a story.

"So, you'll reply to the Convocation and invite the proctor to confirm our bonding?" she asked, a bit tentatively, as Gabriel still looked apt to explode. For a wizard of the quieter water and moon magics, he was fierce when pushed. In truth, the man couldn't be pushed, which was a large reason for her flight. Before she met Gabriel, she'd hoped the upstart rogue wizard would be malleable enough for her to manipulate. Ha to that.

She also hadn't counted on the Fascination, that will-sapping desire that drove her to do anything to please him. Even knowing he wanted her opinion, she had to focus to go counter to his stated desires. Knowing that he wasn't being reasonable, or thinking like a truly ambitious wizard should, only helped her resolve to a small extent.

"I'll draft a reply and you can look it over," he conceded.

"All right." She'd call that a successful negotiation.

Unfortunately, that left only the missive from her father still to read. It lay between them on the small table, like a snake coiled to strike. Her stomach chilled at the prospect of reading of Papa's furious disappointment in her, she who'd once been his golden child. The one he'd trained to succeed him as the head of House Elal. Until she turned out to be a familiar instead of a wizard. When she'd made the decision to flee, she'd known she risked losing his respect and love forever. She'd also thought she'd be so far away that she wouldn't have to face it.

"You don't have to read it," Gabriel said gently.

"I think I do."

"At least finish your breakfast first."

She glanced at the remaining piece of cold poultry, her stomach revolting. "Is it awful?" she asked in a small voice, feeling ridiculously like a child.

"He's obviously not happy," Gabriel replied slowly. "Though most of it is directed at me for interfering in recovering you, against his specific orders. He wants you to come home."

She met Gabriel's black gaze, taking in his oh-so-neutral mien. He'd let her go, too. Had offered to before. "This is my home."

"I won't keep you against your will."

"My will is to be with you," she answered with perfect honesty.

He winced, understanding all too well. Perhaps she shouldn't have explained the Fascination to him, how she would follow after him no matter how he treated her, how she wouldn't be able to help herself. He wanted her to love him, and she did. But he had ideas that somehow her love wasn't offered freely enough. She didn't know how to give him any more than that.

She reached for Papa's letter, and Gabriel once again put his hand over hers. "I can reply to it, Nic. You don't have to put yourself through this."

"Are you telling me not to read it?"

"No," he answered, holding her gaze. "You are an adult who can decide for herself. I'm offering to shoulder this burden for you."

She slid her hand and the missive out from under his. The Fascination might be beyond her control, but she didn't have to lean on Gabriel more than it compelled her to. Her relationship with her family was her problem.

Opening the folded letter, she began to read.

And her heart sank to join her stomach.

~ 2 ~

GABRIEL WATCHED NIC read her father's letter—and as her dusky skin paled to the point of having a greenish tinge. The missive hadn't seemed all that terrible to him, but families had a way of slicing to the bone so subtly that those not in the know wouldn't even see the blade.

"Maman," Nic said, almost soundlessly, slowly lowering the letter to her lap.

"She sends her love, yes?" Gabriel asked. "That's good."

Nic lifted her gaze to his, the deep emerald green swimming with tears. Mutely, she shook her head, the rioting curls bobbing unevenly. He'd done a poor job of cutting off the long tail of her glorious hair. Not that he'd have expected differently using an athame in the middle of an overwhelmingly potent magic ritual. Still, he regretted not doing better by her.

On so many levels.

Getting up, he went around to Nic's side of the table, easing the missive away and setting it aside. Crouching down, he took her clammy hands in his. "Tell me," he urged.

Nic turned a look of profound misery on him, the tears spilling over to run down her cheeks. "Maman would have written her own note. She always did when I was at Convocation Academy. There's only one reason that she wouldn't have penned her own message."

Gabriel closed his eyes briefly, unable to bear the pain in hers—and to hide his revulsion from her. He'd been in Lord Elal's study when the wizard had forced Nic's mother to take her alternate form. Lady Elal had begged to be allowed to have a voice in the conversation, but her husband had exercised his authority over his familiar and compelled her to change into a cat. The casual display of tyranny had repelled Gabriel then, and if anything, affected him even more now. "She's still in feline form," Gabriel said quietly, ordering himself to meet Nic's gaze.

She nodded. "And he wants me to know it. Punishment for us both." Pulling her hands away, she scrubbed furiously at her tears, then lightly slapped her cheeks. "Do you know, I never saw Maman weep? Not until the day I tried on my wedding dress—and Papa made her cry in front of me."

Aghast, Gabriel swallowed against his dry throat. The image of Nic in the wedding dress she would've worn to marry him if she hadn't escaped nearly crowded out his other thoughts, and he had to sternly order himself to focus. "Why do you think he did that?"

Canting her head, jaw firm, Nic gave him a hard look. "To remind me that a familiar is subject to their wizard master's rule. Maman had raised the concern that you might not be able to restore House Phel, that I'd belong to a no-tier house with little fortune and meager prospects."

"A valid concern," Gabriel admitted, folding himself to sit cross-legged on the floor, keenly aware of the warped boards beneath the antique rug.

"I told you before, I don't care about that. Besides, with me on the finances, House Phel won't be impoverished for long." She smiled thinly, and he took heart to see her fiery nature reemerging. "But the implication that I might try to evade being tied to you made Papa angry. Remember, I told you before that Papa likes you."

"It didn't seem that way to me at our single"—and singular—"meeting."

Nic looked sympathetic. "He was in a rage, no doubt." Her gaze strayed to the discarded letter. "He still is."

As worry clouded her gaze again, Gabriel sought to distract her attention. "What did he say about me to make you think he liked me?"

"Fishing for praise?" she asked, clearly amused.

"I'll take any I can get from you," he replied lightly, abruptly aware of how much he craved that assurance of her regard. He had no illusions about their relationship, not with how he'd taken away her one chance for freedom. He also understood that she didn't love him, possibly never would—and he frankly didn't blame her—and that the Fascination would always complicate her feelings for him. Still, from their first meeting, he'd discovered the uncomfortable sensation that her good opinion mattered to him. He wanted to be worthy of her admiration, for himself, not because the magic demanded it.

"When he first approved your application for the Betrothal Trials," she replied, "Papa told me that you deserved a chance to rebuild your house, same as any other man, and more than the soft, indulged, barely talented scions of established houses." Her smile deepened. "He said you had balls even trying for me."

Wasn't that the truth? More than once, Gabriel regretted the ambition that drove him to try for a wife and familiar as talented and high ranking as Nic. Before he knew her, and before he understood how the wizard–familiar dynamic worked, he'd been sanguine about the gambit. Why not go for the very best? All of it had been a risk—and a lot of it had felt like a game. He hadn't had much to lose. Yes, the fate and fortune of House Phel had rested on him, but in the end, the worst that could happen was they'd let the rotting structure sink into the marshes again, and his family and people would return to the living they'd been scraping out before that.

Now he knew better. He'd seen how the people of the Convocation lived, which was leaps and bounds ahead of even the easier life they enjoyed at House Phel since his wizardry took him by violent storm.

But Nic… Without realizing it, he'd ruined her life by tying her fate to his.

If he'd known, he'd go back and change it. At least, he liked to tell himself that. In the darkest corners of his heart, however, the knowledge lurked that he was savagely glad he couldn't change the past. Nic was his now, and he wouldn't let her go. *It's in a wizard's nature to be commanding,* Nic had said, only half because she liked to tease him. Before this, he'd have said it wasn't in his nature to be dominating, but Nic changed everything. Her magic called to his with a siren song, seductive, sweetly tempting, and part of him hungered for her with an unslakable need. Even now, that silver bed in the arcanium, with its chains and whispers of erotic anguish, called to him. *Monster...*

Thrusting that image away, he shook his head, bewildered that he could feel such tender affection for her, could want to protect her with every fiber of his being, and also brew such dark sexual fantasies.

"You don't agree?" Nic asked, canny green eyes studying him with alert interest. He had to think back to what they'd been discussing before his thoughts took him down such dark, twisting paths.

"That I had balls to try for you?" he asked, going for a lighter tone. "I suspect it was more the bliss of ignorance. You, more than anyone, are aware of how little I understood—and still fail to understand—about the Convocation. You called my applying for you in the Betrothal Trials a fool's gambit, and you are likely correct."

"We agreed last night: no regrets."

He weighed arguing that, knowing full well how bitter and heavy her many regrets were. With her shadowed side of the coin, it would be beyond callous to express how profoundly he relished his success, how much he savored having her here with him, how very much he... well, that he loved her. He hadn't admitted that to her, even when she'd baldly asked if he was in love with her. He'd equivocated, saying that he thought he could be, and then took refuge in honesty, trying to explain how wrong it felt to love someone the Convocation regarded as his possession. How could he love her when she had no choice but to be with him, when she was forced to be depend-ent on him in every way? Even his horse, Vale, had more autonomy, the ability to leave him if Vale didn't like how he was treated. Nic, eternally bonded to him—chained to him by her own nature, by the magical force of the Fascination—had no freedom to walk away, no matter how he made her suffer.

He scrubbed his hands over his face, feeling supremely unable to rise to this challenge.

Nic slid off the chair and onto the floor before him, the robe he'd bought her in Ophiel billowing in bronze velvet folds. It should be comfortable for her while the morning air remained cool, but he should get her something lighter. As spring waxed into summer, it would be far too heavy.

"Gabriel." Nic cupped his face in her hands, nails scratching lightly over the beard stubble he had yet to shave that morning. "You must banish this guilt. You've done nothing any Convocation wizard wouldn't have done, and—"

"That's not exactly a high standard," he pointed out wryly.

"*And* you've dealt with me far more kindly than any of them would." She kissed him lingeringly, the taste of fresh oranges bright on her lush lips. The craving in him leapt to the touch and taste of her, wanting to seize her and push her to her back, spread her slim thighs and plunder her luscious sex.

He groaned into her mouth, viciously restraining himself even as his cock rose, hard with greedy desire. "Again, not a high standard," he ground out.

Breathing a laugh, she pressed light kisses over his face while he kept his hands firmly off of her, wrapped tightly around his drawn-up knees. "You're not going to go back to refusing to bed me, are you?"

He'd strongly considered it. If he were any kind of gentleman, he wouldn't take advantage of her magically induced willingness. But the sexual frenzy of the bonding ceremony the night before had uncorked a bottle that could not be stoppered again. On all the long journey from Wartson, he'd managed to restrain himself, thinking that perhaps they'd find a way to come together as equal partners. Or, failing that, that she could go back to her life. Neither was possible any longer. Nor was it possible for him to stop wanting her with all the savagery of his black wizard's heart.

Nic growled, pushing him onto his back and straddling him. With him pinned under her slight weight, she deftly unlaced his sleep shirt, spread it open to bare his chest, and scraped her nails over his skin. His self-control frayed under her caress. Helpless to resist her, he drank in how glorious she looked, even with her lopsided curls, glossy black and catching the morning sunlight. As much as he'd loved her dramatically long hair, the shorter cut showed off her strong face, the high, sculpted cheekbones, her green eyes dominating with the force of her intelligence and potent charisma.

"You made me a promise," she reminded him, gaze raking his body along with her avid touch, lips curving wickedly as she toyed with one of his nipples, making him shudder. "Remember? One of the happier benefits of this relationship we find ourselves locked into." She bent to replace her fingers on his nipple with her mouth, laving it tenderly, then nipping with kitten teeth so he jumped.

Trying to focus his thoughts, he nevertheless combed his fingers through her thick curls, savoring the tensile silk of them. "I am quite certain I made no such promise."

"Fidelity," she purred, drawing hard on his nipple so he arched his back. "You said you wanted us to be faithful to each other. A marriage in truth, despite our startling lack of marriage vows to reference."

They needed to take care of that, have an actual wedding, no matter how much Nic might declaim the need for one. She'd transferred her avid mouth to his other nipple, and his mind had lost all ability to think logically. A bright haze of need obscured the conversation from the evening before, but he was sure they'd ended the argument with him agreeing to the bonding. Certainly he'd formed a plan to establish an equal footing between them so he wouldn't feel quite so predatory with her. "I will be faithful," he gasped, her scorching sex grinding against his erection. "But I refuse to take advantage of you."

She paused, lifting her head, a gleaming black riffle falling over one eye as she gazed at him in shrewd amusement. He tucked it back behind her ear, using the recess from her determined seduction to catch his breath. "You do realize," she purred, "how ridiculous that sounds given our current positions?"

"The power imbalance is larger than this moment," he replied quietly, "and exceeds the physical." He gripped her wrists, moving them easily with his greater strength. "I could do anything to you and you couldn't stop me. Worse, you wouldn't even try." And how terrible was it that the words aroused him further even as he spoke them?

Proving the point, Nic yielded utterly in his grip. "That's true. Better, I want you to." She rubbed her groin against his, eyes half closing in sensual surrender. "Do your worst, wizard."

As if her words snapped some desperately eroding grasp on his better nature, he lost all reason and flipped their positions, pushing her onto her back and pinning her wrists to the floor as he straddled her. "Is this what you want?" he snarled, her magic filling him with the heady scent of red wine and hothouse roses.

"Yes." She undulated in his grip, body writhing with need, hips lifting as she attempted to spread the lovely thighs he'd pinned together with his knees. "Please, Gabriel. Please."

It shouldn't be so exciting to hear her beg, but it was. Taking both of her slender wrists in one hand, he stretched her arms over her head, opening her robe to reveal her lushly naked body beneath. Her deep-rose nipples were taut, tipping her full breasts, her narrow waist a contrast to her generous hips. Tracing her curves with his free hand, he slipped his fingers into the sweet vee at the crest of her rounded thighs, the curls at her mons as glossy thick as her hair. Feeling as if he'd starved for her, he cupped that enticing mound, fastening his mouth on one delicious nipple, exulting in her strangled cry of desire. Turnabout was fair play, so he bit her nipple lightly, stretching her arms tighter as she thrashed beneath him, and parted her swollen nether lips. He groaned as her slick heat met his questing touch.

"Please, Gabriel," Nic chanted the pleas. "I need you inside me. Please, oh please."

He needed no further urging, any vague thought of going slowly fleeing in the face of the grinding need to bury himself in her. Releasing her wrists, he spread her knees wide, taking a moment to savor the sight of her open sex, an even deeper rose, unbearably erotically lovely with the twinned curves of her ass beneath.

Positioning his cock, he thrust into her, not going gently at all. And Nic screamed, full-throated, digging her nails into the rug as her back bowed, thrusting her full breasts into glorious profile. She was so beautiful, magic emanating from her skin like a mist that warmed the coldest, dampest, and loneliest corners of his soul. Burying himself in her felt like coming home to the place he'd longed for all his life and hadn't known how to find. And as she wrapped her long arms and legs around him, her seeking mouth finding his and drinking him in, he felt embraced, somehow loved and accepted unconditionally as no one else ever had.

A great irony there, as he was the worst person in the world for her.

"You're thinking too much," she said throatily, then sinking her teeth into the side of his neck, galvanizing him with overwhelming need. "Stop thinking. Take. Have."

She'd said that to him on the floor of the arcanium. And he'd obeyed. He'd taken everything she offered and more.

He took again.

Thrusting into her, pushing ever deeper, as if seeking out and devouring every drop of her being, he was barely aware of her incoherent cries in his ear, her nails digging into his ass as if trying to pull him even deeper. He flung himself into the frenzy of it, her magic flowing into him thick and hot as blood, nourishing and heady, filling him with power.

She convulsed under him, her thunderous climax seizing him by the throat and dragging him after. Helpless in her grip as her sex clamped on his phallus like a fist, he spent himself in her welcoming depths, then collapsed in a bloodred haze, momentarily dizzy from the utter loss of self. Nic's essence of wine-infused roses filled him so thoroughly he didn't know where he ended and she began.

Lying there, their skin slicked together as the sun grew ever brighter with the warming day, her body lush and yielding as a bower of rose petals, he wondered blearily if this happened to all wizards. The Convocation made much of the familiar submitting to their wizard's will, but did other wizards also discover this drowning influence of their familiar's aura?

Nic laughed hoarsely, her full breasts shivering with her amusement, crushed under him. Chagrined, he levered himself onto his elbows, shifting the bulk of his weight off of her. Her legs still vised around his hips, holding him tightly sheathed in her still. She gazed at him, sultry green eyes half lidded, full lips curving with sensual satisfaction. So beautiful, even with the half-healed abrasions and purple-green bruises mottling her collarbones and throat from the hunters' collar. He felt as terrible about them as if he'd put them there himself. Observing his perusal, Nic raised a brow in inquiry.

"Why do you laugh?" he asked instead of voicing those thoughts, finding he had to clear his throat to get the words through.

"I should time your busy brain," she replied, "from the moment I can get you to stop thinking until you start up again." She wriggled beneath him, digging her heels into his ass to keep him swallowed in her. "It could be an interesting challenge, to attempt to beat my personal bests."

Charmed and amused by her despite himself, he allowed a grudging smile. "I don't think I'm quite that bad."

"You aren't always," she conceded. "You weren't the night of our Betrothal Trial, canny as you were about seducing me."

He lowered his head to kiss her, thinking to make it a kind of apology but unable to resist tasting her, sweeping his tongue inside her delicious mouth, feeding on her lush lips like the sweetest of fruits. She sighed, her languid body melting further, her fingertips lightly and lazily caressing his spine. That night had been a more innocent time, at least for him, when he'd believed her willing to wed him and only needing some gentling to grow used to him. Regrets, indeed.

"That night was also salient," he murmured against her lips, enjoying the brush of them as he spoke, "in that we actually made it to the bed. Something we should consider for the future."

"The future," she echoed in a dreamy voice. "That sounds promising. Though the floor serves well enough, here or the arcanium. I'll put acquiring a mattress for the arcanium bed on my list. Don't tense up."

He closed his eyes against the images that wanted to roar up. Nic, chained to that bed with silver glinting against her dusky skin, spreadeagled and helpless to stop him. He started to withdraw from her even as his cock immediately hardened at the thought, but Nic held him tight.

"And don't run from this," she said in a harder voice, winding her fingers in his hair.

He opened his eyes to meet the green glitter of hers. "Nic…"

"You could have me on the arcanium bed without a mattress," she noted in a helpful tone, not fooling him for a moment, "but those silver coils will abrade my skin. If you choose to draw blood from me, there are—"

"Stop," he barked out, far more harshly than he intended. "Let me go."

"You don't want to go," she murmured, moving her hips to stroke her slick inner muscles around his phallus.

He groaned, meeting her movements despite himself. "I want to be gentle with you. I don't want to hurt you."

"Then be gentle." She smiled, feathering her fingertips over the shells of his ears, making him shiver. "All ways can be ours. Have me any way you want me. It's good and right. All of it."

He doubted that, but he was too far gone to deny himself. Or her. Or whatever she was up to with these seductive games. Determined to last longer this time—and able to, with the savage passion slaked for the moment—he made love to her, showering her face, throat, and breasts with kisses. Nuzzling and licking those bruises as if he could erase them from her otherwise flawless skin. Finding the depth and rhythm that best pleased her, he brought her to climax twice more before releasing himself into her.

This time, it felt like a benediction, and like an offering. A small repayment for his many crimes against her.

She sighed and stretched, at last unwinding her legs. "A personal best," she decided. "Except you're already thinking again."

He rolled onto his back beside her, gazing up at the tongue-in-groove pattern of their bedroom ceiling. "I was only thinking that we need to have a healer see to your throat, and the hunter's bite on your arm, too."

"True. Also your injuries, though you're healing well. The nice thing about magical healing is making it all go away immediately. Let's do that today." When he cleared his throat, she turned her head and narrowed her gaze. "You said you have a healer here in Meresin."

"We do," he replied defensively. "Of the regular variety. Not a wizard."

She groaned, beating her head lightly on the floor. "Silly me. What was I thinking?"

She'd been thinking that she still lived in the Convocation, where people had easy access to magical healing. "Will you go?" he asked.

"Go where?"

"Home, to House Elal, as your father bids."

She rolled her head to look at him, losing the dreamy softness. "*This* is my home."

"But if you wish, I—"

"Gabriel." She levered up onto one elbow, the robe she still wore sliding off one smooth shoulder, golden and delicately muscled. "More precisely, *you* are my home now. I'm bonded to you. Even if you sent me away, I would find my way back to you. I thought you were clear on this."

"But your father—"

"Papa doesn't know we completed the bonding ritual. He's

simply probing, guessing, testing for your response. That letter was addressed to you, wizard to wizard. Lord Elal wants to determine whether Lord Phel has taken his familiar in hand."

He winced at her phrasing, certain that she employed those terms with deliberate ruthlessness. Probably she thought she could inure him to what she believed were the immutable realities of the Convocation. Something he intended to fight, even if he had to go down doing it.

"No, he doesn't know, does he?" Indulging himself, he stroked a finger along the velvet skin of her shoulder, taking in the sight of her gloriously nude, voluptuous figure, so enticingly framed by the bronze robe. "Nobody knows that we made the bonding ritual reciprocal, that I'm as bound to you and you are to me." Likely that's why the very concept of parting from her felt impossible, striking him with a physical ache.

"We don't know that it made any difference," she warned him, but she returned his caress with a tenderness at odds with her forbidding tone.

"We'll have to experiment, to find out."

"Something else for the long list of tasks we're not getting to by lying here on the floor, ravaging each other."

It pleased him—and perhaps salved his conscience—that she phrased it as a mutual ravaging.

"If there *is* a difference in the bonding, we should disguise that fact from the proctor," she added.

"Wouldn't the Convocation be interested to know that the bonding doesn't have to be so one-sided, though? Maybe we should show the proctor the truth." Maybe familiars wouldn't have to be so dependent. They could enjoy more freedoms, even choose the wizards they partnered with.

"You *cannot* be serious." Nic sat up, drawing her robe around her and scowling at him, her tone scathing.

"It could change a great deal." He sat up also, then pushed to his feet and offered her a hand up.

She took it, then faced him, her expression deadly serious. "Gabriel, I know you're an idealist, and I also know that you've had very little experience dealing with the Convocation, but you cannot imagine that they would take this news well."

"Yes, it would shake things up at the academy, but—"

"Gabriel!" She interrupted him so sharply, with real fear in her face. "It would turn the Convocation upside down. Do you really think the wizards would stand back and let you do even the slightest thing to erode their grip on the power they enjoy?"

He shook his head. "We can fight them on it, then."

"Fight them?" She threw back her head and laughed. "Who—you, me, and the barely talented water mages of the Meresin swamps?"

"If necessary," he replied stubbornly.

She set her teeth, jaw flexing. "Do you have any concept of how vast the Convocation is? We're talking twelve High Houses, thirty-six second-tier houses, and at least a hundred lower-ranking houses. All of them have more than a single wizard leading them."

"Yes, but I have the most powerful familiar in the Convocation," he countered with a smile that she didn't return.

"They will crush us," she said implacably. "This is not a

fight you can win, Gabriel."

Maybe not, but it sat ill with him to simply give up without even trying. "Wouldn't it be worth it?" he asked her softly, stroking the back of her fine-boned hand. "We could change the world, so no familiar ever has to endure the Betrothal Trials again, so no other brilliant young woman like you feels forced to escape to another country to avoid losing her very will."

"Gabriel…" Her eyes gleamed, luminous with emotion, but she pressed her full lips together into a firm line. "People only change the world in novels. It's a romantic idea, but not a practical one. The stories don't tell the real tale because it's short and boring: someone tries to buck the system, fails, and dies."

"You said once before that when you read my dossier that you knew I would be the sort to dash myself brainless trying to fight the Convocation," he offered, still hoping to make her smile. No luck there. She only gazed at him with that look of panic and despair.

"I know it," she spat, but without any real fire. "I should've filed my summary refusal right then."

"Why didn't you?" he asked, genuinely curious. "I mean, besides the fact that you also recognized I was naïve and desperate and thus a good bet to be easily manipulated—why didn't you give the rogue wizard from a fallen house a hard pass?"

"Clearly a major lapse in judgment on my part. Temporary insanity, perhaps," she replied haughtily, jerking her hand away and tying her robe firmly.

"I think you liked that I was outside the Convocation's rigid structure," he speculated, amused by her. "You're a rebel at heart, Lady Veronica Elal."

"There's no need to resort to name calling," she retorted, then sobered, giving him a very serious look. "Gabriel, please don't try to fight the Convocation. You'll only lose. Your status, your house, and likely your life along with it."

"You'd be free of me in that eventuality," he felt he had to point out. "Wasn't that your ideal, to end up a young widow?"

"Yes, but I wanted to be a *rich* widow," she countered, smiling at last. "Which means that you"—she punctuated the word by stabbing a finger into his bare chest—"need to reply to my father. Tell him I belong to you now and that my dowry should be delivered to you immediately. It takes money to make money, and I have big plans for increasing the wealth of House Phel."

"I hear and obey," he replied wryly.

"Surely that's my line," she quipped, softening the stabbing finger to trace his midline down to his belly and the loose cotton pants he'd pulled up again. "Besides, I'd love to get my trousseau and have more than two dresses."

"I'll get you more clothes."

"There are other things I'd like to have, too. Stop being fastidious about this. That money is owed to you, and those things *are* mine. Demand that he send it all."

In truth, he was dreading that particular task. Even at his most ambitious, he hadn't wanted the fortune that accompanied Nic's hand in marriage. He wouldn't have agreed to the dowry in the first place if he hadn't needed it to compensate for the staggering fee he'd had to pay the Convocation for his chance at the Betrothal Trials. He'd practically exhausted House Phel's coffers to come up with that money. Still, Nic's dowry made the whole enterprise feel too much of a financial transaction—something he supposed he should've recognized about the acquisition of a familiar much sooner.

"Maybe we should invite your parents to the wedding," he suggested on impulse, enjoying that he'd surprised her, those raven wing brows arcing as if to take flight. "They could bring the dowry as a wedding gift, and you could reassure yourself of your mother's well-being." Surely Lord Elal wouldn't keep the bride's mother in feline form for that event, and Nic would be reassured to see her mother.

"What wedding?" Now her brows drew together.

"I'd like to have the ceremony, to offer willing vows to each other."

"We're bonded. There's no stronger vow that that. In the eyes of the Convocation, we're more than married. I'm Lady Phel now."

"Nevertheless." He reclaimed her hand, holding it between his. "Will you marry me?"

She rolled her eyes. "This is driven by sentiment. It makes no practical sense."

"Still." He couldn't help smiling at her exasperation. "Will you marry me?"

"I already did," she snapped, waving her free hand at the green landscape outside the window. "Else I wouldn't be living in a swamp."

"It's a marsh. I really need to teach you the difference."

"I'll add it to our ever-growing list of tasks," she replied, sounding not at all enthused.

"So…?" He raised his brows.

"With all we have to get handled, you really want to add a wedding? That's a lot of time, effort, and expense."

"Yes. I have my priorities."

"I'm not going to be able to talk you out of this, am I?"

Privately, he considered that Nic could likely talk him out of anything if she put the full fiery force of her will to it, but he wasn't about to put that particular weapon in her hand. "Will you marry me, Nic?" he asked for the third time, hoping it would be the charm, as in the not-very-accurate tales of magic.

She pursed her full lips. "I suppose it couldn't hurt to have a big social event to counter the inevitable gossip about my ill-advised attempt to escape. And it will help to establish House Phel's position in society, prove that you're not as much of an impoverished bumpkin from the swamps as people believe. Of course, you'd have to raise the remainder of the house from the marshes and bogs if you want to invite guests and have them be impressed."

"Speaking of time, effort, and expense." He grimaced at the daunting thought.

Patting his cheek, she smiled with confidence. "Remember that you have the most powerful familiar in the Convocation to assist you now. Additional incentive for you to demand my dowry immediately: We're going to need the money to dazzle the guests. And tell Papa to send my wedding gown. I had a really pretty one. If I'm going to have the wedding, I want that dress."

"A society wedding, huh?" He'd been picturing an intimate family event, maybe in the peach orchard with the trees in blossom.

"Have you changed your mind?" she asked archly, a challenging glint in her eye.

"Not at all." Though it made his skin crawl to think of those haughty Convocation wizards on *his* lands.

"Then I will marry you, Gabriel Phel." She fluttered her lashes and kissed him. "Redundant though it may be, as you're well and truly stuck with me."

Before she could skip away, he caught her around the waist, indulging in a much longer kiss that left them both breathless. "Get dressed, and I'll show you where the house accounts are."

"Oh, darling," she cooed. "You say the sweetest things."

~ 3 ~

S HE WAS RIDICULOUSLY happy.

And it felt strange. She'd been miserable for so long. Grieving, really, ever since that black day she'd received her final MP scores that finalized the dreaded truth that she'd be forever relegated to being a familiar and never a wizard in her own right. Yes, she'd been determined to control whatever she could of her future, but those years had been powered by bitterness, anger, and a fair amount of dread over what sort of wizard would end up in possession of her. Then there'd been the last few weeks of storm-tossed ups and downs—the terror of flight, loneliness of leaving everyone behind, the chill of fear from her pursuers.

Then dealing with Gabriel himself, which was never straightforward. He made her laugh and want to weep. The way he made love to her had rattled her on a deep level, the intimacy of his regard shattering her careful poise. With a look, he could see right through her, never fooled by her cool posturing. She so desperately wanted to make him happy that a single sincere smile from her brooding wizard made her feel like the sun had burst out from behind clouds.

Worse, she didn't even mind what that meant for her. The

Fascination had been powerful enough that she hadn't been able to face parting from him again once he'd found her in Wartson. With the bonding duly sealed, she felt finally settled and at peace. It was as if a low-level illness had finally relinquished its grip, leaving her filled with vitality and fresh with well-being.

She should probably fret about what this portended for her lack of autonomy, but she was too content. The old Nic had been so fretful and angry, exhausting herself while fighting the bonds of her fate. It was lovely and restful to give up that fruitless struggle.

Plus, starting the day ravishing Gabriel's glorious physique would be enough to put even the dourest person in a perky mood. If she were a familiar from the romantic novels, songbirds would be circling her head, tweeting giddily. Lyndella had been like that when the wizard Sylus finally overcame her resistance and bonded her. She'd danced and sung around his castle, bringing him endless joy. Of course, Lyndella had been astonishingly beautiful, with a golden throat and a dancer's body. If Nic were to emulate Lyndella, she'd only bring Gabriel wincing dismay with her lumbering and croaking. The mental image of him trying to come up with something kind to say had her choking back a laugh.

"It *is* a bit musty," Gabriel said in an apologetic tone, opening the double doors at the end of a hallway on the main level.

She stepped in and surveyed the decidedly musty library. No bits about it. A grand room once upon a time, one large enough to hold several seating areas for reading and conversation, it was sadly lacking grandeur now. The seating areas gaped like missing teeth, the previous furniture no doubt ruined by long submersion. Alcoves set into generous bay window spaces likely once held cozy cushions for curling up on, but now the seats were only warped and peeling wood. The windows themselves had been boarded up with fresher-looking wood, rendering the room dim and the air quite stale. In the shadows, built-in shelves rose from floor to ceiling, holding thousands of books. Ladders made of brass gleamed dully, perched on wheels to be moved into position to access even the highest shelves.

A lone desk sat on a raised area near the one window that hadn't been boarded over, the new-looking glass letting in welcome sunlight, though it didn't penetrate far. Several ledgers sat atop the desk, accompanied by a quill and inkwell.

Gabriel stood back, an odd expression on his arresting face, hands tucked in his pockets as he watched her assessment.

"The books on the lower shelves were ruined?" she asked, noting how the bottom two shelves all around the room stood starkly empty.

"Yes. The house didn't *entirely* sink," he answered, raising one dark brow at her. "At least, this main section didn't," he amended. "But those books had rotted. Though I dried them out as carefully as I knew how, they simply crumbled to dust. And mold," he added with a grimace.

She nodded, unsurprised. Truly, it was miraculous that he'd saved *any* of the books, let alone so many. Wandering to the lone glassed-in window, she tapped the low-quality glass and peered out at the view of the river, the same as from their room, which must be directly above. "And glass in only one window out of economy?"

"Glass is expensive," he acknowledged ruefully, "and I prioritized having glass in our room, as I thought you'd be happier that way."

Glancing at him in some bemusement, Nic considered again all the trouble he'd gone to in order to welcome the bride he'd imagined to be so willing. "How did you know I like to be able to see out?"

"I didn't," he admitted. "I just thought that if I'd been locked in a tower for several months with those metal shutters blocking the windows, I'd feel better having an unobstructed view."

"Can't have your valuable familiars flinging themselves to certain death," she commented wryly. She had hated those shutters. Just another example of his uncanny ability to see through her that he'd noted it. "I suppose you purchased the glass from merchants?"

"Where else?"

"We'll get a far better price negotiating directly with House Byssan." She added setting up an account with them to her mental list. "Buying from a merchant easily doubles the cost, maybe more, way out here. Besides, Quinn Byssan is a good friend from my academy days."

Gabriel looked interested at that. "Wizard?"

"Another familiar." Not many of her friends who'd manifested as wizards had remained friendly after her final status had been announced. She understood. Wizards didn't consort with familiars not their own outside of intimate family circles. It was considered bad form, as the taint lingered from the bad old days when wizards seduced away and even abducted attractively potent familiars. Showing too much interest in another wizard's familiar led to tension between wizards, and tension between wizards led to apocalyptic battles that left only scorched earth behind. Hesitating, she glanced at Gabriel, who was studying her thoughtfully. "I'd like to invite Quinn to the wedding, if you don't mind."

His expression darkened. "What do I have to do to get you to stop asking permission from me like I'm your keeper?"

With a mental sigh, she refrained from reminding him that he *was* her actual keeper. "You could make it an order," she suggested sweetly.

"Not funny, Nic."

"Fine, then. I have a number of friends I plan to invite to the wedding, and I hope they eat you out of house and home."

"Eat *us* out of house and home," he corrected, smiling slightly. "And I think that would be wonderful. I look forward to meeting your friends."

She winced at the prospect of Gabriel being his earnest self, chatting up her familiar friends like they were people and pissing off every wizard master in attendance. She would have to discuss etiquette with him, which could wait. Going to the desk, she opened the top ledger, peering at the carefully penned entries. A schoolboy's handwriting, a clear indication of exactly where Gabriel's rural education had ended. For some reason, the sight of it made her heart melt, imagining younger Gabriel determinedly taking on the duties of the lord of a house. To defuse the sentiment, she flicked the ink pot with a dubious finger, giving Gabriel a deliberately arch look.

"I suppose there's not an actual stylus to be had in all of Meresin?"

"Let me guess," he replied. "House El-Adrel produces magical quills that don't need to be dipped in ink."

It was a good guess, despite the sarcasm. Gabriel possessed a sharp mind, more than making up for his lack of education and experience. "Close. Except that House Calliope holds a special exemption license for the production and sale of the Calliope Stylus, which is self-contained, writes like a dream, and requires no external ink."

"House Calliope prints books, I understood," he said, looking intrigued.

"More than books. It was, oh, at least a century and a half ago that they successfully argued that any device for setting words to paper fell under their aegis."

"A broad interpretation."

"Yes, and good for us because I intend to use that precedent for House Phel's product line. El-Adrel will lay claim to the license on any magically created device or artifact if we don't fight back. Your ever-replenishing water flask will be our test case. I'm going to apply for the trademark on that first, arguing that the water is the key magic involved, not the container. We'll make a fortune on that alone."

Canting his head, he gave her a knowing smile. "I thought you didn't want to fight the Convocation."

"Not the entire Convocation, and not on a question of morality, but another house's license for trade on a product that falls under the aegis of House Phel and that could turn us a tidy profit? Absolutely I will. I'll win, too, or I'm not the first daughter of House Elal." If nothing else, Papa had taught her very well how to consolidate wealth. She would put those skills to good use for House Phel and Meresin. For all those children consigned to rural educations and a lifetime of using magic simply to keep their houses dry. They deserved better, and she aimed to deliver it. "Besides," she added, savoring the incipient victory over the arrogant and greedy tightwads at El-Adrel, "this is about business. That's entirely different."

Gabriel shook his head, laughing softly, though in admiration, she thought, not disdain. "I knew marrying an Elal would be good for our fortunes, but I had truly not expected a warrior of trade."

Something about the words caught her attention. She looked up from puzzling over an entry in the ledger. "Do you mind?"

"No," he answered, sounding completely sincere. "I think you're amazing. I'll just stay out of your way and write my letters."

She glanced around at the ghostly room, absent of any other furniture. "This is your desk, though. I can't take that."

"You'll need to spread out those ledgers." He tipped his head at the miserly surface. "I can work elsewhere."

"Where?" she asked bluntly. It wasn't as if the decrepit manor had a plethora of dry rooms.

"All I need is a table," he replied. "Writing a few letters doesn't require a dedicated space like an arcanium. There's some paper in the drawer there, if you'll give me a stack, and a spare quill and ink pot."

She slid open the drawer and found the paper, low grade

and not nearly adequate for formal missives from Lord Phel. They seriously needed supplies. Perhaps negotiating with House Calliope's subsidiary, House Salis, for better-quality paper should go to the top of her list. There were a number of pressing issues jostling for that position. She was also reconsidering the wisdom of Gabriel penning his own letters. The houses would react to his handwriting the same way she had—and she couldn't bear for them to have another reason to snicker at his provinciality.

"I have a better idea," she said. "Have the servants bring in one of your tables, and we can both work in here. I can advise you on drafting the letters."

He raised a brow. "That would be helpful, to have your advice, but who are these servants you're expecting?"

She gazed at him in consternation. "This is a massive house, even if three quarters of it is still sunk in a swamp, and we plan to remedy that soon enough. How do you plan to run a place of this size without servants or household imps?" She folded her arms. "I might have to serve you in any way you please, but if you make me do housework, I swear to make your life miserable."

Face creasing in irritation, he glowered. "You do not have to serve me, so stop poking at me about it. Everyone here pitches in."

She threw up her hands. "Then order up some brawn to *pitch in* and bring a table in here."

"I can carry a table, Nic."

"You're still healing from the battle with the hunters," she retorted. "Besides which, the lord of a High House doesn't move his own furniture. You need to start acting the part. If you'll round up some workers, you can also ask them to take a few boards off these windows so we'll have more light."

"And when it rains?"

"Is that an inevitability?"

"It rains pretty much every day here, depending."

"Then the workers can put the boards back up again. There's plenty for them to do in the meantime. We'll need an army to clean up this house."

"They'll be out in the cotton fields and orchards this time of day," Gabriel said. "I can hardly ask them to drop those tasks. Which reminds me, I should get out there myself. Remember from yesterday? Mom wanted me to look at the levee that leaked and flooded the orchard. We've been concentrating on produce," he explained, reacting to some expression on her face. "It's one of our strengths, and you're the one all fired up to increase our income."

She attempted to smooth away her exasperation. Seating herself at his desk, she leaned her forearms on it and regarded him seriously. "Gabriel, my only love, I want you to listen closely. You are no longer a farmer."

He gave her a long look, silver intensity swirling enticingly around him. For some reason, it annoyed him when she called him her only love, so she shouldn't persist in it. Something in her, however, took a perverse delight in needling him, in provoking a rise from her brooding wizard. "You're mistaken, my sweet familiar. I *am* a farmer, first and foremost. There's no shame in it."

"Wrong." She slapped a hand on the desk. "The day you

wished for rain and drowned your fields in an unstoppable deluge with your nascent wizardry is the day you stopped being a farmer. You are a wizard, Gabriel. First, foremost, and forever. That's not a choice. It's who you are now, like it or not. What's more," she continued, raising that hand again to stop the protest she saw boiling up in him, "you are Lord Phel. You *did* have a choice there. You could've chosen to wile your wizardry away as a landless rogue, but no. You just *had* to apply to the Convocation to restore House Phel."

"I have a right to restore my family's house and honor," he bit out, reaching the desk and slamming his own hands on it and looming over her. "You have no idea what it's like to grow up under the shadow of coming from a fallen house, from a family that lost its magic. House *Fell*. I hear them make the joke. I'm not that naïve."

"You are if you think you can keep being a farmer."

"What do you call what we're doing with those fields out there?" he demanded, waving a hand at the lands beyond the walls.

Levering up, she leaned on the desk, too, meeting him loom for loom. "I call it *your* lands being farmed by *your* people while *you* act as lord of House Phel."

His eyes glittered, lowered to her mouth. Before she could wonder what he intended, he caught her by the back of the neck and pulled her in for a kiss. For once, he forgot to moderate his strength, kissing her hard, almost bruising, the force of years of struggling with his unwanted destiny in it. She returned it in kind, meeting his disappointed hopes with her own. When he finally broke off the kiss, he leaned his forehead against hers, still gripping the back of her neck. "Our house. Our people. Lady Phel," he said quietly.

"Do you see me out there picking cotton?" she asked lightly, though her voice shook a bit from the rush of passion.

He breathed a laugh. "I assume that falls in the same category as asking you to do housework, which will result in vague but dire vengeance."

She wrapped a hand around his wrist, not pulling away but solidifying the contact. "I didn't mean it. You know I'll do whatever is necessary to rebuild House Phel. I was trying to make a point, and I lost my temper."

Tilting his head, he kissed her again, this time tenderly. "As did I. And I'm not even sure what we were arguing about."

"Let's try this again," she said, easing out of his grip and coming around the desk. Hitching herself up, she sat on it beside him, absently rubbing the back of her neck, which throbbed distractingly.

"I hurt you. Nic, I'm so sorry." Gabriel looked stricken.

"Only a little, and in the best possible way." She pursed her lips in an air kiss. "Next time, try bending me over the desk while you hold me down by the back of the neck and toss up my skirts. That will shut me up longer."

"What?" His face contorted in shock. "No! That's not why I—"

"Gabriel, I'm kidding. Well, not entirely, because it *would* work, and we'd both likely enjoy that method, but I know that's not why you did it."

"Do tell," he ground out, folding his arms. It was ridiculous how the more worked up he got, the more she wanted to climb that big body and rub herself all over him. Or kneel at his feet. Did all familiars plagued by the Fascination feel this way? Probably. The novels didn't capture even half of the true potency of the bonding.

Tempting as it was to fall to her knees and relieve his tension in the most primitive way possible, she patted the desk next to her, waiting for him to sit. "You bonded me only last night and—"

"We bonded each other," he interrupted with an obstinate shake of his head.

"*And* that's a potent connection," she continued. "It will take a while for us to get used to it. A normal wizard would have me restrained in the arcanium, bleeding me for every drop of magic they could wring from me."

He wasn't amused. "We both know I'm not a normal wizard."

"True," she agreed without rancor. "Most wizards have extensive plans laid for the incantations they want to work once they have a familiar. Projects that needed the power boost only a familiar can provide. You, being you, have barely even drawn on my magic."

"I haven't needed to."

"You think you don't need to, but that's your rational brain talking. Your wizard nature isn't a rational creature any more than my familiar nature is."

He considered that, canting his head as he studied her face. "Surely you don't believe that."

"I do believe it. Maman once told me the predator desires the prey—he can't have any mercy in his heart for it."

His expression contorted. "That's revolting."

"That's reality," she replied in exasperation. "There are aspects to our magical natures that are beyond our intellectual control. I know you think the Convocation Academy filled my head with propaganda and misguided convictions of how the world really is, but I'm speaking from experience here. I was sure Fascination was a myth, a romantic idea to persuade familiars that becoming a wizard's slave would be pleasant. Until I met you."

He made an incoherent sound of dismay, and she put a hand on his muscled thigh, enjoying the heated strength there while giving him a bit of comfort. "I'm not saying this by way of recrimination. I'm trying to explain that something beyond my control kicked into force. I think you'll concede that I'm reasonably strong-willed." She cocked a brow at him, then shook her head. "I could not will this away. Much as I tried, I couldn't stop thinking about you. Couldn't stop wanting you." *Wanting to give everything to you,* though she managed not to say that part aloud.

Covering her hand with his, he nodded. "I felt—feel—the same."

"You don't have to look so grim about it," she teased, but he didn't smile.

Instead, he pulled his hand away, knotting his fingers together to rest on his muscular thigh. "I told you from the beginning, Nic: I don't want you unwilling."

She swallowed her immediate retort that she could hardly be any *more* willing. When she'd attempted to escape him, she'd put that doubt in his mind forever. She'd be forever paying the price of that. "Are *you* unwilling?" she countered.

He frowned. "You know I'm not."

"Be honest," she pressed. "You're not battling *any* desires when it comes to me? Not even one or two illicit cravings?"

Guilt flickered in his eyes, along with a flare of dark yearning—quickly followed by shame.

She lowered her voice. "I saw how you looked at the silver bed in the arcanium."

Jerking his gaze from hers, he stared fixedly at his hands, swallowing hard.

"I bet fantasies have occurred to you," she mused. "Things you could do to me."

"Stop." He barely voiced the word, still avoiding her eyes.

"Tell me, are you battling something that feels like hunger? In the arcanium last night, when I asked you if there is any aspect of my magic that makes you feel like you want to consume it, you compared it to red wine, and that sometimes you want nothing more than to drink me up."

"Red wine infused with roses," he corrected hoarsely. "It's specific to you and unlike anything else in the world."

"And you want to drink me up." It pleased her, in truth, that he perceived her that way, and it matched her sense of herself, which somehow shored up some of the confidence she'd lost when she found out she'd only be a familiar. She would never be a wizard, but her magic was an indelible part of her being.

"Something in me does," he admitted, almost without sound, knuckles white. "Which makes no rational sense."

She laid her hand over his clenched ones. "That's my point.

This is about aspects of our magical natures that make no rational sense. But Gabriel?" She paused, waiting for him to look at her. When he did, she met his gaze steadily. "No matter what's gone before this, regardless of how we got here, I'm wholly yours now. There is nothing you can do that would make me want to leave you."

"I'm not sure that's reassuring," he replied grimly.

"It should be, because that's a foundation you can rely on. I embrace who you are. There's nothing you could do that would shock me. You and I are in this together. I know you never wanted to be a wizard, that you didn't truly want to become lord of House Phel, but you are both of those things. And I am your familiar, your partner in all of that. That's a good thing to have. I think maybe you've been very alone all this time, a lone wizard amid a nonmagical family."

A flurry of naked emotions crossed his face as he searched hers. Finally unknotting his clenched hands, he interlaced his fingers with hers. "You have an uncanny ability to see through me."

She nearly snorted, except that this unexpected vulnerability in him had her feeling surprisingly tender. "I often feel the same," she confessed.

He smiled, squeezing her hand. "This is not how I envisioned our marriage." With his free hand, he waved at the dank and musty library. "Though I guess I didn't expect this to magically transform into your Elal castle."

She did snort then. "Well, as you've pointed out, we're not technically married yet, and we've yet to work that transformative magic. This manse will be a showplace by the time I'm done with it. But *you* must embrace the role of Lord Phel."

"How about a compromise?" he suggested, lifting her hand to kiss it. "I'll rally the troops to engage in the battle of Castle Phel, if you won't begrudge me time with the levees. It's water wizardry, and no one else can do it. Surely you agree with diversifying our product line."

"Aha. Someone's been listening. And I do agree, but if you're doing wizardry, you should have me with you."

His brows lowered. "It doesn't require that much magic to—"

"Practice," she interrupted, emphasizing the word. "You and I need to learn to work together. *You*, in particular, need to get over these foolish scruples about using me. It's my reason for being."

"I thought your reason for being was to whip me into acting like a normal wizard and a proper Lord Phel, along with turning House Phel into a thriving business enterprise."

"That too. It's a good thing I'm multi-talented," she conceded with a smirk. "We need a schedule. How about business in the mornings, work on the house and grounds in the afternoons, arcanium practice in the evenings?"

"Arcanium practice?" he echoed dubiously.

"Gabriel," she replied very seriously. "There is a high probability that House Phel is going to end up at war with one or more other houses, if not the entire Convocation if you have your way. You need to be ready. *We* need to be ready."

With a sigh, he nodded. "I suppose you're right."

"I'm going to suggest something else you won't like."

He visibly braced himself, rubbing the back of his neck

with his free hand, a sure sign of agitation. "You might as well hit me with it all at once."

"You should learn to draw Seliah's magic, too." She squeezed his hand when he looked aghast. "It doesn't have to be a sexual connection. Don't look at me like that. I'm not a monster."

"Sorry," he replied with chagrin. "Are you sure it's necessary?"

"Yes. Especially if you don't want to send her to Convocation Academy yet."

"Ever," he corrected firmly.

"I can teach you to drain her magic, which will make her mind less like a *swamp*," she told him sweetly, laughing when he gave her a dry look. "Think of it as a levee against the muck threatening your sister's sanity, saving the blossoms on her orange trees."

Shaking his head, he breathed a laugh. "A valiant effort, but your farming analogies need work."

She wrinkled her nose at him. "I feel quite certain I could live a long and fulfilling life without acquiring that particular skill. Regardless, it would be good to sit down with Seliah and talk. As a first step."

"The first step would be locating her," Gabriel corrected. "She tends to run wild in the marshes."

Probably being away from people helped Seliah's peace of mind, Nic guessed. But that wouldn't save her from the eroding influence of her own untapped magic. "*Can* you find her?"

"I'll put out word," Gabriel replied with a sigh. "We'll find her. I've been thinking about Selly, though, and aspects of wizardry you explained to me on the barge. I didn't manifest as a wizard until I was twenty-two."

"She's already twenty-four."

"She could be still maturing," he argued. "Maybe she will—"

"Gabriel," Nic broke in, her heart aching for him and for herself, for the painful hope and the agonizing shattering of it. "She's a familiar. She'll never be a wizard. That's why her mental health is so poor and degrading over time. The magic is building up in her with no outlet. It will only get worse."

"I had no outlet for my magic until the deluge," he pointed out stubbornly.

"But it also didn't build up in you. There's a reason the Convocation scoring system measures magical *potential*. In wizards, the ability is all in the potential to wield magic. In familiars, it's the potential to store it. I don't know why it is, but familiars are also different from wizards in that we gather magic. Or we generate it. There are two different schools of thought on that. It's ironic in a way, but even the weakest familiar has more magic than the most powerful wizard—we just can't use it."

"Where I do get my magic, then?" he asked, intrigued despite himself.

"Every wizard is different, and some of what makes a wizard weak or powerful is their ability to draw magic on their own. The most commonly accepted theory is that you pull it to you from the sources you have affinity for, water and the moon, in your case. And now, from your familiar." She fluttered her lashes.

"I begin to understand why wizards want familiars so badly," he admitted grudgingly.

"You understood this before, or you wouldn't have applied for me."

He gave her a wry look. "I was just blundering along, grabbing onto any signpost that would guide me. 'You'll need a familiar,' they told me and put me on the subscription list for the Convocation circulars on available familiars." He blew out a long breath, searching her face. "Believe me, if I'd realized… If I'd had any idea what—"

She flicked her index finger against the tip of his nose, making him blink in surprise. "Bad wizard."

"Ow," he complained, rubbing his nose.

"It didn't hurt that much. Enough with the guilt. It's unproductive and holding you back. What's done is done. Let it go."

He eyed her warily. "You did warn me about your practical nature."

"Exactly. And my practical nature is itching to organize my seemingly endless roster of tasks. Go enlist your troops. I have lists to make. I'll also need a complete tour of the house so I can assess what work needs to be done and order supplies accordingly."

"Should I be afraid?"

"Of drowning in the tidal wave of profits to come? Absolutely. As for the house repairs, if you don't want to squander my dowry on your passion projects, I intend to invest it in making this house livable."

Cupping her cheek, he kissed her. Softly and lingeringly. "When I say this isn't the marriage I expected, I should tell you that it's even better."

She raised her brows, surprised—and surprisingly moved. "I told you before, you don't need to tell me pretty lies."

"Strange, terrifying, upsetting, frustrating, enlightening, and oddly twisted," he qualified, lips twitching at what he saw in her face before he kissed her again, "and better than anything I could've imagined." He hopped off the desk and saluted her. "I shall return with brawn."

"You forgot one thing," she called after him. "Expensive!"

He laughed and kept going.

~ 4 ~

All things considered, he felt oddly happy.

He recognized the emotion, though happiness wasn't something he'd had much experience with in recent years. Sure, when he received the missive confirming that Nic had conceived and that he could claim her as his wife and familiar, he'd been ecstatic. But a large part of that had been relief that his gambit had paid off. And that he hadn't bankrupted House Phel before it even got on its feet. That happiness had largely consisted of a healthy dose of self-vindicating triumph.

But Nic was right, as she so often seemed to be with her keen insight into the dark corners of his heart: He *had* been lonely, probably for a long time, without realizing it. Discovering the pleasure of her company, and her complete acceptance of the magic that had taken him by the fist and bent him all out of shape from the young man he'd been, had made that much clear.

His family meant well, and they loved him, but they didn't understand him at all. Something about what Nic said had brought that home with the impact of a thudding arrow. They might want to understand, but they never could. It wasn't their fault, nor could they change that.

Gabriel strode out of the empty house and surveyed the big lawn out front, cleared from yesterday's welcome party. Only his parents and Selly actually lived in the house with him. As far as that went, he suspected his parents often retired to their own cottage, the one he'd grown up in. Selly... Well, as he'd told Nic, though he'd given her a bedroom in the manse, she tended to vanish into the marshes. Everyone else in his extended family preferred their homes in the various villages or near their fields and orchards.

Though much smaller and far less imposing than House Phel, their homes were at least largely dry and in good repair. Nic had a point that the pair of them couldn't rattle around in the big place by themselves. And that they needed daily help maintaining it. He'd been all right on his lonesome, throwing together meals—a great deal from food his mother dropped off—and spending the bulk of his time either in the fields or reading as much as possible from the intact books in the library.

Nic deserved better. He'd put a great deal of expense and effort into preparing a decent bedroom for her, wanting her to be comfortable and feeling it was symbolically important to install the new Lady Phel in the manse. In retrospect, however, he hadn't quite thought it through. Had he envisioned Nic as she'd been in her locked tower room at House Elal, forever tucked inside, reading her books, and gazing out the windows?

To his chagrin, he had to admit there was something to that. He certainly hadn't imagined her demanding a tour of the house, taking over the accounts, and making lists of renovations. Though he should have. He hadn't been in the same room with her for more than a few minutes before he realized nothing would contain her fiery ambition.

As he rounded the small lake before the manse, he studied the serene surface of the water, bright as a mirror this morning, and looked for any sign of the arcanium he now knew lay beneath. No hint of it showed. Perhaps the design of the dome, formed mainly of silver and glass, helped to camouflage the structure. It was amazing, however, that he'd ever been unaware of it. It seemed to call to him, a silvery and seductive song, magical and arousing. Perhaps he simply remembered the powerful coming together from the evening before. Nic, her naked body glowing with moonlight, turning in a slow pirouette beneath the moon window. With a desperate urgency, he wanted to be there with her again immediately, if not sooner. At the same time, he dreaded facing it again, beyond reluctant to confront the dark imaginings that plagued him.

Nic had said the arcanium would have spells laid into the walls to store and focus power, a heritage from a long line of Phel wizards, and that sex magic would infiltrate them, refreshing and reenergizing them. He'd sensed it, the power resonating through his bones and blood, calling to him to use it. Power was more seductive than he'd ever realized, and though the walls of the arcanium whispered of cruelty and twisted desires, he nevertheless craved what they held for him.

He now understood the source of the tales and rumors of various madnesses that had plagued the Phel wizards before the magic died down to insignificant levels in the last several generations. Until it burst back with full force in him. And Selly, too, if Nic was right. Why now? Why them? Worst of all, did the dark and twisted yearning the arcanium stirred in him mean he was destined to follow the same path?

"Ho, Gabriel!" his father called from a distance away, coming from the direction of the fields. His father waved, a strong and hearty man, at home on the land. He looked so… normal, so of the earth and natural things. He wouldn't understand the shadowed imaginings of wizards.

Waiting for his father at the far side of the lake, Gabriel thrust aside the darkly erotic thoughts, focusing on a practical assessment of the regally dilapidated manse. It was a gracious old thing, mostly white—where it wasn't yellowed or coated in green moss—with steps leading to a balustraded porch that ran the length of the main section, though the porch listed noticeably in places, giving the impression of an uneven smile. The columns supporting the several tiers of balconies on the center section, however, had only required a bit of shoring up, as they'd been sunk directly into solid rock, which supported the original core of the house.

If not for that foundation, the entire house would have sunk. The more distal wings certainly had, their gable rooflines barely showing here and there among the marsh foliage, while the more proximal wings lurched at unlikely angles. One was the arcade leading to the sunken north wing, which he'd begun to raise when he received the message that Nic was pregnant. As his parents said, it had indeed sunk again, possibly even more so than it had been before, looking to be creating a strain on the mostly intact part of the house where it was attached.

He should probably have Nic find a place on her lists for that.

It would have been easier, and possibly wiser, to finish sinking the entire decrepit manse and build elsewhere. Start fresh. But sentiment had won out, along with an expensive dollop of pride and stubborn determination. Still smarting from how his life had changed so dramatically, he'd been determined to restore the ancestral manse along with the non-tangible aspects of House Phel.

Despite that determination, the solid farmer in himself had considered the entire enterprise a folly. And yet Nic hadn't thought so. She would have said so if she did, but no, she was throwing herself wholeheartedly into restoring the place. Knowing about the attached arcanium changed everything, and he was grateful in retrospect that sentiment—Nic might call it his wizard's intuition, though he didn't think he deserved that much credit—had won and he'd kept the house in place. The arcanium might be soaked in the blood and cruelty of his ancestors, but that translated to potent stored magic.

He had a feeling they'd need every bit of magic they could gather. He would find a way to control himself and not succumb to the dark needs that whispered to him.

"I thought you'd still be abed, romancing your beautiful new wife." His father clapped him on the shoulder, giving him a broad grin and startling the shit out of him. What he got for brooding and forgetting what was going on outside of his head. "Honeymooning, doncha know," he added with a broad wink for Gabriel's absentmindedness. "Or is she still feeling poorly?"

Gabriel had to quickly suppress a vivid image of taking Nic hard and thoroughly on the floor of their bedroom not an hour ago. There hadn't been any romance to it, giving him a flush of shame in retrospect. He had to search his brain for an answer to the feeling-poorly question, finally remembering the excuse he and Nic had given for retiring early from the welcome party. So much had happened since, though it had been less than a day, that it felt like another lifetime.

"Nic is fine this morning," he answered, unable to help the smile at just *how* fine she was. Apparently his shame didn't last long in the face of his overwhelming lust, which had been his problem all along. "A good night of sleep made all the difference. She's in the library with the accounts. She'll be handling those from now on."

His father grunted in approval. "With her fancy education, she's a good choice for it." Lifting off his broad-brimmed hat, he scratched his head, the hair beneath already damp with sweat from his labor in the fields, though the spring day remained mild. "Cut your hair, did ye?"

He'd forgotten about it, and ran a hand through the disordered mess. "Yes. I need to get someone to neaten it up." Nic's hair, too, though how they'd explain the mutual shearing, he didn't know.

His dad turned to stand beside him, gazing at the house also. "You're thinking about work on the house?"

"Mmm, yes. Nic has plans. She's going to set up agreements with other Convocation houses for us to buy and barter for supplies and services."

Giving him a sidelong look, his father frowned. "You think doing business with those greedy, arrogant bastards is a good idea?"

"No," he replied honestly. "But Nic does, and she knows the Convocation. She made a good point that I can't do things halfway. If we're to restore House Phel as an official Convocation house, then we need to engage in trade and establish alliances."

"We're not like them," his father cautioned. "If you hadn't turned up as a wizard…"

He didn't finish. He didn't have to. Gabriel had turned all their lives upside down with his unwanted magic. The only way to make up for that cataclysmic upheaval was to use that magic to improve all their lives. "Nic and I *are* like them, whether we enjoy the idea or not," Gabriel reminded him. *And Selly, too,* though he didn't say so. Breaking that particular news to his parents would be gut-wrenching. "I'm trying to find a balance that gives us the best of both worlds."

"You know what they say about a man trying to straddle two worlds." His father's grin cracked his weather-worn face. "He gets split up the middle, starting with his balls."

"Thanks for that image, Dad," Gabriel said on a wince.

With a good-natured guffaw, his dad clapped him on the back again. "So what's your plan? I thought you'd raised up as much of the house as you could. I suppose we could saw off the listing sections and salvage what we can. You don't really need such a big house, even after the baby is born." He chewed on his lips, eyeing those wings dubiously.

"We're going to raise it all," Gabriel replied, enjoying his father's surprise. "Now that Nic is here, she and I can work together to perform the necessary magic." He grinned in the face of his father's jaundiced expression. "You'll see."

For the first time since he'd arrived at House Elal to discover Nic had fled rather than marry him, excitement filled him at the prospect of working with her. She was right: They were bonded, and what had gone before was water under the bridge. He needed to set aside his guilt—he would never entirely forgive himself for his role in destroying her hopes for a better life—and focus on building their partnership.

Restoring the house together would be an excellent first project. After he dealt with the fires that needed putting out. Or rather, the water that needed displacing.

It was on the tip of his tongue to tell his father about discovering the old arcanium under the lake when he reconsidered. Nic had said that wizards kept their arcaniums secret. In some houses, apparently, all the occupants knew the location of the arcanium, but couldn't enter. Having the House Phel arcanium as a place no one believed even existed would be even more secure. Still, it felt odd to keep a secret from his father, especially one that implicated their family in unsavory activities. What would his good-hearted, farming parents make of the devices and tools in there?

They'd be shocked, and they wouldn't understand. Yes, better to keep it secret from them. Just one of many secrets, in truth, with no doubt many more to come.

A lone wizard amid a nonmagical family. At least he had Nic now. "Headed to the orchards?" Gabriel asked, and his father nodded. "I'll walk you there."

"Coming to fix the levee?" his dad asked as they turned in that direction.

"I'll take a look at it anyway." Gabriel figured that he'd

promised Nic not to work on the levee. Assessing it wouldn't take much time, and he had to go there anyway to find workers for her. And to set a few people on Selly's trail.

"Your mother's beside herself about those orange saplings," his father noted mournfully. "She's worried about losing that much money."

"Tell her we'll more than make it back now that Nic is here."

"Don't call me a coward, but I'll let *you* tell her that." His dad glanced sideways at him. "You're putting a lot of stock in that new filly of yours."

Recalling Nic's many barbed remarks about being an expensive piece of livestock, Gabriel breathed a laugh. "Yes, I am."

"YOU NEED MINIONS," Nic said without looking up from what appeared to be one of several lists on the desk. "I know you'll want to argue, but there's no getting around it. Hear me out."

"Lady Veronica Phel," he replied formally, "I have brought the assistance you requested."

She glanced up, not in the least embarrassed, and smiled at the group of workers hanging behind him, shuffling mud-caked boots against the parquet floor. Selecting one list, Nic stood and came around the desk, smoothing back her asymmetrical curls and tucking them behind her ears, managing to look elegantly regal anyway. "Greetings to you all, and thank you for coming to help."

They stared at Nic in brash curiosity, far more impressed with meeting a real Convocation familiar than they'd ever been with him. They also eyed the purple and green bruises around her throat, left by the hunter's collar. It looked like Gabriel had throttled her, unfortunately, an impression helped along by a vivid and fresh love bite just under her ear that he must've put there that morning.

"I've made a list of tasks," Nic was saying, smiling warmly at the crew. "I put them in order of my preferred priority and then in what I think is the logical order of precedence, but please feel free to tell me if I'm mistaken. I don't know a great deal about house renovation."

Their mute gaping soon turned to smiles and occasional laughs, as Nic wryly jested with them, charming them into being at ease with her. He shouldn't be surprised that she excelled at this, too. She'd been raised to run House Elal, so herding—what had she called them? "minions"—was no doubt one of the required skills.

Staying out of her way, Gabriel wandered to the desk, perusing the several lists she'd completed. He was reading a dauntingly long list of supplies she apparently intended to acquire, frowning at the inclusion of Elal imps, elementals, and spirits, when she joined him. The workers had begun an industrious and noisy attack of the boards covering the library windows, while another group headed out the door. In search of furniture, no doubt. He wished them luck. "See?" she said, tapping a different list than the one he was looking at. "You need minions."

"I brought you minions."

"No, you brought me barely magical commoners who are earnestly invested in helping and who will be of critical assistance in *this* long list of manual chores." She waved the list that she'd been discussing with the workers at him. "*You* need other wizards working for you. If you had an established house, you'd have a full roster of wizards of various levels—"

"And familiars," he reminded her, not liking the way the Convocation tended to erase the existence of half the magical population.

"In some cases, sure, but not all wizards have familiars."

"Because they can't afford them."

"That's true for some, but not all wizards seek to bond a familiar. Minor wizards can be useful within certain refined skill sets that don't require a familiar's power augmentation."

That coil of cold shame twisted inside him. "Then the Convocation lied to me. I didn't need to acquire a familiar." And ruin Nic's life.

Nic stomped on his booted foot—impressively painful given her small stature and the light slippers she wore.

"Ow," he complained, scooting back.

"No more guilt!" she hissed at him. "And you do need me, stubborn wizard. I specifically qualified my remark as applying to *minor* wizards with a *refined skill set*. That is hugely different from a high-level wizard with MP scores off the charts, no Convocation education, and a lord of a High House with a host of enemies. I'm going to prove to you how much you need me, Gabriel Phel, if I have to beat you over the head to do it."

"That's not what I meant," he protested. "Of course I know I need *you*, I just—"

"Save it." She waved the minions list at him and plunked it on the desk for him to see. "As I was saying, if you'd become Lord Phel through the fullness of time, having grown up in a house full of wizards—*and* familiars—you would have minions already. Right now you have no one, so we need to import some minions."

"I have you, as you've been reminding me so sternly."

"You need *wizard* minions, like any self-respecting head of a house does. For example, Papa has nearly a thousand wizards working for House Elal."

"I don't want to be anything like your father," he ground out.

"Then you shouldn't have acquired his daughter for a wife," she retorted. "You want my savvy in establishing Phel as a High House? You need minions, starting with a House Refoel wizard."

"I thought you planned to set up an account with Refoel, barter for services." He didn't like the idea of any other wizards in Meresin, much less in his house.

"I changed my mind. Once I started assessing what we needed to bring House Phel up to standard, I realized that having in-house wizards with loyalty to you is key."

"How do we know they'd be loyal to us? Seems like they could act as spies for their houses."

She shrugged as if that was of no concern. "There's some of that, for sure, but that can work in our favor, as they can report back that you're not up to anything scurrilous." She raised a significant brow, not saying aloud *like hoping to destroy the Convocation.* "Besides, of all the High Houses, Refoel tends to steer clear of wars and disputes. As healers, they hold themselves to a standard of benevolence over hostility."

"How comforting," he remarked drily.

"Isn't it? Most importantly, we have the control here, so we'll issue the invitations carefully, seeking out people who I believe will be tolerant of... the unusual living conditions, shall we say, in exchange for the opportunity to be first among the wizards of a brand-new High House."

"Which we are not, yet."

"Which we will be."

"You finally said we!" Slipping a hand behind her neck, despite the presence of the workers, he kissed her long and tenderly. "Thank you."

She made a face, but a high flush graced her cheekbones. "A slip of the tongue. Focus, would you?"

Obediently, he studied the list, noting House Ratsiel on it. "I thought one doesn't retain a Ratsiel courier."

"One doesn't. The couriers themselves aren't living beings. But the best houses keep a Ratsiel wizard on site—who keeps a stable of couriers, much as an Elal wizard will have an arsenal of spirits—for speed of communication."

Gabriel suppressed a shudder at the reminder of Jan, the Elal wizard who'd attempted to abduct Nic, and his creepy spirit warriors. "Is that really necessary?" He'd been fine with the previous speed of missives. In fact, he could wish some had arrived more slowly.

"Yes. Unfortunately, we'll have to pay Ratsiel to install a wizard on site."

"Sounds expensive."

"*Looks* expensive," she corrected, "and appearances are important. If we were an established High House, we could make a trade, send Ratsiel a water wizard to keep their wells clean, for example. But you don't yet have junior water wizards, and we're not giving them you."

"Comforting."

"You're much more valuable here," she replied with an impish smile.

"Darling, you say the sweetest things."

"Now, with Refoel, I think we can barter flasks like the healer in Wartson had, with water that purifies wounds. Can you do that?"

"Should be easy, with a bit of experimentation."

She gave him an approving look that warmed his heart. "I wonder who made hers?"

That was a good question. "El-Adrel, of enchanted artifacts fame?"

"Maybe. I wish I'd looked for a trademark stamp. Lost opportunities. It would be ideal to have an El-Adrel wizard work with you to produce the artifacts to hold the waters you enchant, but I doubt they'll want to play—yet."

"Yet?"

She narrowed her gaze at some distant image. "I have ideas for some leverage to use on them."

"You're terrifying in this mode."

"Remember that." She tapped the list. "Given how much

work needs to be done to bring the house up to snuff, I'd also like to invite wizards from Byssan, Ophiel, Hagith, and Ratisbon."

"Glass from Byssan, I understand. Ophiel to replace your wardrobe, but the others?"

"Ophiel for carpets and upholstery," she corrected. "They do fabrics of all kinds. Hagith for metalwork, which seems to be scarce in Meresin, and Ratisbon for furniture and carpentry. From what I've observed, we can supply our own lumber?" She waved a hand at the house at large.

"Yes," he agreed, relieved to be at least not lacking that much.

"Good. That ought to be sufficient for now. With the lower-tier houses, we can get by with offering them less for a wizard, in return for the favor of House Phel. Ratsiel should be the only major expense."

"What about this one?" He stabbed at the line with House Elal, wishing he could do far worse. "I don't want your father's spirit minions on my land, much less an Elal wizard."

"Are you sure? I thought we could invite my cousin Jan," she replied blandly.

He nearly burst out with a furious rebuttal when he caught the dangerous glint in her eye. Stupid him—of course Nic wouldn't want Jan anywhere near her. "I apologize," Gabriel offered on a wince. "I wasn't thinking."

"No, but your protectiveness is charming." She patted his cheek, her smile warm. "We don't need an Elal wizard here, as we can use pre-trained spirits, imps, and elementals. They can handle menial tasks—like dusting—sparing our people for work that requires human intelligence."

"More expense," he grumbled, more because he hated the idea than because of the cost.

"No. Part of my dowry. As an Elal, no matter how lowly my status is as a familiar, I am entitled to a percentage of the family wealth. Or, rather, *you* are entitled to it, as my lord and master." She fluttered her lashes at him, baiting him so outrageously that he held up his hands in surrender, laughing.

"Fine. I don't like it, but far be it from me to deny you what's lawfully yours. I'll finish composing the letters responding to Elal and the others."

Just then, a trio of workers returned carrying a heavy table between them. A fourth followed with a pair of wooden chairs hoisted on her shoulders. Nic directed them to position the table near the newly uncovered windows, though far enough away, he noted, to be clear of any rain that might come in. The day remained clear and bright for the moment, and he had to admit the library looked—and smelled—considerably better with the wall of floor-to-ceiling windows open to the light and air.

Nic was conferring with the workers on their next assignment, so Gabriel obtained a few sheets of paper and a spare quill, setting himself to the unwelcome task. It would help if he hated the Convocation a bit less, but he attempted to channel that long-held rage into the appropriate arrogant disdain. Having dispatched the workers again, Nic sat at her own desk and applied herself diligently to her tasks and lists. She looked happy, gainfully occupied, and even her disparaging mutters about living in a backwater swamp with no resources to speak of lacked any real animosity.

And it was pleasant in a way he'd never anticipated, working with her on the business of the house. She was right: He'd been climbing this mountain for so long on his own that, even though he'd deliberately set out to gain a partner to help him rebuild the house, he hadn't fully imagined how rewarding that would be.

Even when Nic read his letters with pursed lips and a disdainful eye, rather than being annoyed by her criticism, he nearly wanted to laugh. Or throw her over the desk, push up her skirts, and make love to her until she was breathless.

"If you keep looking at me like that, we'll never get these missives out," she said, quill poised over his draft. "May I?"

"Can I stop you?" he asked in a dry tone.

She gave him a brilliant smile. "Well, you could follow that prurient impulse and have me on this desk until my eyes are crossed and I'm too limp from pleasure to say boo, but that won't get glass in the windows."

He stroked the exposed back of her neck, enjoying her shiver of response. He'd loved her long hair, but this cut had its advantages. Pressing his lips to the tender hollow at the base of her skull, he murmured, "How did you know what I was thinking?"

"Your magic," she replied throatily, bending her head in a delicious yielding. "You're all silvery cool until you start thinking sex, then you get... I don't know how to describe it. Spiky."

Reaching beneath her, he cupped her full breast, her nipple taut through the silk, and she moaned as he trailed his lips down the elegant arch of her neck. "Spiky," he echoed.

"For lack of a better word," she replied breathlessly.

"Ah. But as you so practically point out, this won't put glass in the windows." Reluctantly, he stepped out of temptation's reach. "Edit away."

She glanced up with eyes a sensual deep green. "I begin to regret being such a practical soul."

He grinned. "I'm surprised to find how much better this place is with the windows uncovered. Let's get that glass."

"I've created a monster." She rolled her eyes but pointed the quill at him. "*You* make yourself useful and summon a courier."

Hmm. "I thought you wanted to get better-quality paper first."

"I do, for the missives to Papa and the Convocation, and I suppose to Iblis, so they'll think we actually care what they think, for Narlis's sake. But unless you want to walk to House Calliope, we'll be sending them my letter setting up an account and requesting supplies."

"That would be a fair walk, I assume."

She crossed out a line and wrote something in, then looked up with a raised brow. "You don't know how to summon a courier, do you?"

Though he'd resolved to stop touching her, he couldn't resist running his fingers through her silky curls, growing ever more tousled in the humidity. "I thought we'd established that you should assume my ignorance."

With a look of exasperation, she sat back and folded her arms. "How did you communicate with the Convocation before this?"

"Sent a rider to the nearest Convocation city, just over the Ariel border."

Shaking her head, she rummaged for a clean sheet of paper. "I suppose this is as good a segue into the afternoon of working magic as any."

"I thought you determined the afternoons were for working on the house and grounds?"

She pointed the quill at him. "With *magic*. I'm not breaking my nails on manual labor." Grimacing, she surveyed said nails. "Though that's a moot point now, I suppose. They used to be pretty."

Remembering how her nails had sparkled on the night of the Betrothal Trials, he wrapped his hand around her wrist and lifted said nails to kiss them. "Be sure to get a manicure imp in your trousseau of gremlins, then."

"Believe me, I plan to. As you're always being pedantic and telling me a marsh is not a swamp, I'll inform you that a gremlin is an animal, not a spirit, thus not under the Elal aegis."

"So noted."

Pulling her hand away, she sketched a symbol. "This is the crest of House Calliope."

It looked familiar, and he recalled seeing it stamped on covers of the books he'd bought her. "You have it memorized?"

"The advantage of a Convocation Academy education," she replied, neatening a few of the lines. "We memorize all the house crests along with the alphabet. I'm sure there's a book in here somewhere that lists them all."

"There is." He'd found the old House Phel crest in it. The only place he'd found it. Apparently it wasn't included in the newer books, as the Iblis locksmith hadn't recognized it.

"You should learn them. It's good to have them memorized, for all kinds of reasons. Now, touch your finger to the center of the crest. You don't need physical contact, but since you're learning, that will help you to focus." She laid a hand over his. "And draw on my magic to do it."

"Surely this doesn't take much power."

"No, but you need to practice drawing on me with more finesse. Don't look like that. You're learning to be more precise in working with me. Drawing miniscule amounts of power is an excellent exercise. Now extend your wizard senses and request a courier."

He frowned. "Why aren't I requesting the courier from Ratsiel?"

"Because the mercantile houses like Calliope will provide a courier at their expense to fulfill a customer's order, if the customer is promising enough. They'll do it for House Phel."

"Iblis hadn't heard of us."

"Incorrect. That low-level locksmith wizard in a backwater town hadn't heard of us. You can be sure the wizards running House Iblis are paying close attention to the potential rise of a new High House. In fact, we can be sure of it now, since you stole their familiar."

"One they didn't want."

"Not until you expressed interest in her. Quit stalling and make the request."

"I don't know what you mean by extend my wizard senses," he confessed.

"Oh, hrm. I, of course, don't know how that feels." For once too absorbed in the puzzle to sound bitter, she contemplated him. "Feel how the paper is slightly damp?"

"Everything gets damp here," he said apologetically.

"So I've noticed. Without moving your finger, wick the water out of the paper and make a puddle of it on the desk."

That was easy enough. She nodded approvingly. "So, whatever you just did, do the same, only push your intention into the crest and ask that a commercial courier be sent to House Phel."

Only somewhat dubious, he did as she instructed, surprising to feel an answering buzz of magic that felt like an acknowledgment. Nic raised her brows. "Got it done?"

He rubbed his tingling index finger against his thumb. "I think so. Though it seemed too easy."

She gave him that brilliant smile. "You're a powerful wizard, Lord Phel. This *should* be easy. In the future, we'll task a low-level wizard to act as secretary for you, to handle this sort of thing. That's a good job for an apprentice minion." She began sketching a new crest. "For the moment, however, you have a substantial list of requests to send. Apply yourself, please, Lord Phel."

"As you wish, Lady Phel."

~ 5 ~

E VEN BEFORE GABRIEL was halfway through sending the remaining courier requests, the House Calliope courier arrived, giving Nic a lovely sense of vindication. She hadn't been misleading Gabriel—at least, not deliberately so—but she had experienced a frisson of doubt. The other houses *should* accord the new House Phel at least conditional respect, as one never knew who would turn out to be the next power to be reckoned with, but she'd worried that the scandal of her flight might've circulated via gossip, tainting Gabriel's reputation as a fearsome wizard.

After all, it didn't speak well of a wizard to lose his familiar, regardless of the circumstances.

It could be, however, that word of her escape and recapture hadn't made the social rounds. Certainly neither Papa nor the Convocation would want word of her rebellion, failed though it might be, to be commonly known. She'd been secluded in her tower since late autumn, so no one expected to hear much about her. Also, it was winter still in most of the Convocation, making travel difficult, so the real social season wouldn't begin for another month or two.

The written message from Calliope was couched in tones

just short of fawning, extending personal congratulations to the nascent house and providing the account information so that they could supply all of House Phel's publishing needs. Calliope even offered credit terms, in case House Phel wished to pay its account on an annual basis. "No, House Phel does not wish to pay your exorbitant interest," she muttered at the letter she was drafting. "But it's a lovely thought."

She had yet to dig through the house accounts with any thoroughness, but she'd found the most recent sums. Gabriel had kept the finances reasonably updated, at least up until he'd taken off to track her down. Despite her confident assurances to him, she winced as she deducted the cost of setting up a balance with Calliope. If his income numbers were accurate—and she had no reason to doubt them—their expenses would quickly outpace the revenue. They needed to step up their income, fast. Her dowry would be a most welcome addition.

The Calliope courier took her order, carefully grasping the rolled-up scroll in its tiny hands. Spreading its wings, it lifted off from her desk, hovered a moment, trilling that House Calliope thanked her, then vanished.

"The couriers I've seen so far didn't look like... a small person," Gabriel commented from his table.

"I think it's supposed to be an angel, though rendered with considerable artistic license. It was specially designed for House Calliope. Some of the mercantile houses take branding very seriously. Quite some time ago, Calliope paid for House Ariel to collaborate with Ratsiel to create a proprietary courier just for them."

"Fascinating," he commented, though he looked horrified.

"I thought Ariel magic worked on animals, not humans."

"Well, humans do have animal bodies, so there's some overlap. But the Calliope angel is only based on a human shape, with wings. It's an entirely magical construct, with no self-awareness and just enough corporeal form to transport physical objects. They come in all sizes. Just wait until you see our order delivered."

"Oh, joy," he replied, drily enough to make her laugh, and she turned to the next arrival, a courier that was—fortunately for Gabriel's peace of mind—a nondescript cloud from House Byssan with their house crest in translucent, glasslike scrolling.

Gabriel watched her hold out the written request for an account, along with a personal letter to Quinn Byssan, then shook his head when the cloud vanished. "How do they make the material objects disappear?"

"Ratsiel magic," she replied with a shrug. "Nobody knows how they do it. All we know is they scoop up any wizard with an MP score in communication of five or higher."

"Communication magic sounds rather vague," he replied thoughtfully.

"More so than moon magic?" she inquired archly.

"Good point," he conceded.

Before Gabriel had presented himself at Convocation Center, a fully fledged wizard from the swamps of Meresin, the MP scorecards hadn't even included a column for moon magic, though water had been there. Now moon magic would be regularly tested, too. Chewing thoughtfully on her sandwich— since they were still dealing with business, Gabriel had asked someone to bring them lunch, and it had turned out to be a delicious olive-oil-drizzled bread with fresh tomatoes and a mild cheese—Nic considered whether she could add one more change to Gabriel's life, or if she'd pushed him too far already.

"Just ask," he said as he wrote out the third draft of the letter to her father. He lifted his head. "I can feel you thinking at me."

"Can you?" *How interesting.* She could certainly sense the hum of his thoughts as they intensified, but she hadn't expected him to be as attuned to her. Was it a result of the reciprocal bonding? Hard to say. When he just regarded her steadily, she forged ahead. "Speaking of scooping up wizards, you should also begin recruiting young wizards with MP scores in water magic."

He looked unhappy but didn't immediately argue. *Progress!* "I recall your explanation of how this works, that houses bid for wizards with high MP scores in the magic the house is licensed for."

"It doesn't always come to bidding. That's only for the bright young talents of that season. We can't compete for those, and we're not going to try. Yet. I'm going to suggest you want wizards with any potential in water magic, high to low. I'd like to aim in particular for the ones with low MP scores because they'll be grateful for the opportunity."

"To live in a backwater swamp with no resources to speak of?" he asked drily.

She refused to be embarrassed. "It does us no good to delude ourselves about what we don't have to offer. What we *do* have to offer will make up for that."

"Do tell." He sat back in his chair and crossed his long legs, folding his hands behind his neck and giving her his full attention, those wizard eyes black and impenetrable. For all that she'd found him irresistible in his fighting leathers, this laid-back Gabriel at home was oddly enticing also. Of course, that was the Fascination at work. He'd be devastatingly attractive to her covered in mud and swamp water.

She ticked the points off on her fingers, determined to keep her mind on the task at hand. "Exclusive and intensive tutelage by the most powerful water wizard alive. Opportunities to invent new applications for water magic and participate in the development of a product line. And freedom to hone their own skills, rather than owing all their time and energy to the lord of their house." She held her breath, waiting for his reaction. With any other wizard, she wouldn't have dared to suggest such radical ideas, but she'd been thinking a great deal about Gabriel's determination to upset the status quo of the Convocation. If he had any hope of succeeding, he'd need fellow rebels to assist. What better way to attract the malcontents?

Gabriel frowned, however. "Junior wizards normally owe all their time and magical energy to the house that adopts them?"

Letting out the breath in relief, she nodded. "Standard contract. The bright young things can usually negotiate for more latitude, but the moderately talented are expected to be grateful to have room and board. The ones with low scores can look forward to a life that's little better than indentured servitude."

He eyed her. "I find it obscurely comforting to discover that wizards also receive a brutally raw deal from the Convocation."

"It's not all bad. Through diligent application of effort and unshakeable loyalty, they can rise in position and gain more freedom. Their familiars with them," she added, "which gives us incentive to assist our wizard masters with all enthusiasm. Their good fortune is ours."

Gabriel's lip curled in distaste. "There you go, quoting Convocation spin."

"I don't want to fight about this. I'm simply explaining what the average, moderately talented and low-talented wizard faces—and what House Phel can offer both wizards and familiars." Perhaps by emphasizing he'd be helping familiars, too, she could sway him to her concept.

"What all is involved in establishing these contracts?" he asked, an encouraging sign, that he asked after particulars.

"You know, I don't know what other houses do. Something they teach only to wizards, apparently. House Elal has a detailed agreement, plus the tattoo."

His brows climbed. "A tattoo?"

"On the inside of the wrist, inked by a metal elemental. Actually, all Elal citizens receive one. It identifies them as protected by Elal, and allows them to cross the border protections without a wizard present."

"How does that work?"

"I'm not certain of the details, as it's proprietary to wizards, but as I understand it, the metal elemental in the ink passes the information to the spirits guarding that section of the border, and the wizard attending them knows to allow the passage."

"Thereby monitoring everyone who crosses."

"Well, yes," she replied, suddenly uncomfortable. "Papa is zealous about the security of Elal borders."

"Why don't you have a tattoo?"

She looked at the inside of her wrist as if one might appear. "I'm family."

"I see. No tattoos. We'll draft an equitable contract that's fair to everyone involved. Can we offer them a percentage of sales of any products they develop?" he added thoughtfully, surprising her.

"That kind of thing isn't done…" But she trailed off, considering the ramifications.

"All the more reason to do it," he said, leaning forward to prop his elbows on his desk. "The familiars, too. The teams split their share equally."

"Familiars have no way to store wealth," she mused.

"So you're dismissing the possibility."

"No." She glared at him. "I'm thinking through the options. Stop being an ass just because you're prickly on this topic. Familiars have no legal right to property—anything they might receive goes to their wizard, and its incumbent on the wizard to provide for them."

"We can make it legal in Meresin."

"You could. It would give the Convocation one more reason to want House Phel to sink into the swamp again, and the familiars wouldn't be able to spend their income outside of Meresin. We could, however, front for the familiars with the house vendor accounts, provide them opportunities to purchase what they like. But there's a complicating factor."

"There always is."

"Isn't that the truth? The wizards would have to agree to this scheme, and I'm thinking not many will."

"It would be an excellent criterion to eliminate unsuitable candidates. If a wizard won't agree to our basic rules of familiar autonomy, I don't want them."

She contained a sigh of exasperation. "We're not looking for reasons to eliminate candidates. You need to *build* your house."

"Not on the backs of indentured servants," he replied implacably. "I won't bend on this, Nic."

"Do you bend on *anything*?" she snapped back, knowing the answer to her question. She'd known it from the moment he'd walked into her tower room, and she'd despaired, feeling the Fascination click into place for this man who could never be browbeaten or manipulated.

Abruptly, he grinned at her, a wicked slant to it. "I can think of a few things you've gotten me to compromise on."

Absurdly, she flushed at the innuendo, the reminder of how they'd come together. "You're forgetting a key factor in this dynamic."

He sobered. "The bonding."

"Exactly. The wizards might agree on the surface, then tell their familiars to turn over their share of the profits—and the familiar will have to do so. The familiars might even offer that freely, just to keep their wizard happy."

The muscle in his jaw flexing, he fixed her with a deathly black stare that she knew wasn't for her, but for this foolish wizard who might dare to cross him. "I will make it very clear to these wizards that they will abide by the spirit of my rule as well as the letter, or they will pay the consequences."

She shivered, uneasy under that unyielding gaze despite herself. Like the moon, Gabriel had two distinct sides. Having been showered with silvery bright affection from his gentle face, she'd nearly forgotten the ruthless warrior who'd pursued her so relentlessly.

"I'll teach these water wizards you want to attract," he continued in a milder tone, "though it may be a case of the teacher being one step ahead of the student." He essayed a smile, but it came across as a grimace.

"Any number of steps," she assured him. "You're a quick study, and I can promise there is no more powerful or skilled water wizard in the Convocation, even as you are now."

Grunting noncommittally, clearly unconvinced, he eyed her thoughtfully. "Is there any reason I can't draw from the population around here?"

"Not if you can figure out a way to suss out the ones with more than trace abilities. Those won't ever be able to do more than the household spells you mentioned."

He continued to regard her with that intent stare, his thoughts opaque now. "You don't mention moon magic."

"They only just started testing for it again. No one would know if they have it or what their MP score is."

"Would I know?"

She hadn't thought of that. "You might. Testing falls under the aegis of House Hanneil and their psychic wizards. You met one, no doubt, when you were tested."

"Five of them, in fact. Culminating with Lady Hanneil herself."

Nic laughed at his chagrined tone, glad that he was sounding a bit less like he wanted to slice off someone's head with his sword. "They probably couldn't believe the scores and thought there was a false reading somewhere."

"I suspect you're right. At the time it was… bewildering." He let out a sigh, gaze going to the sunny sky outside, and her heart bled a little for the overwhelmed young man he'd been. "I'd like to try testing for it. Moon magic could be even more important to us than water."

She didn't have to ask why. He'd been learning to weaponize moon magic, and he was still thinking they'd be at war sooner or later. She wished she disagreed.

"Are you done here?" he asked, focusing on her again.

"'Done' is a strong word, considering the length of my lists, but this was a good start for today."

"We should go outside," he said, abruptly standing. "Get out of this room and enjoy the clear weather before the rain comes."

She stood also. "Is it going to rain soon?"

He lifted his face, as if testing the air. "In a couple of hours. Enough time for me to give you a tour of the house, such as it is, and our land."

"All of Meresin?" she asked with a lifted brow, taking the hand he held out.

"At least the part that isn't underwater," he replied, so seriously that she nearly swallowed that bait.

"Ha ha. I know Meresin is large enough that we can't see it all in a couple of hours."

He interlaced his fingers with hers, walking her out of the

library and into the hall leading to the grand entrance. That part had been decently restored prior to her arrival, though it would be grander soon. The sounds of hammering and sawing echoed from the adjoining parlors, which were dry, if not exactly livable, and certainly not furnished.

"I don't think of all of Meresin as belonging to House Phel," Gabriel mused, escorting her onto the sunlit porch. Below, the lake glittered, mirroring the house and green surrounds. "I'm sure all of Meresin would dispute any claims of ownership."

"That has to change if Phel is to be a High House."

"Does it? I have no wish to be a governor."

"If it's not yours, Lord Phel, it will be acquired by someone else. Your enemies could nibble up all of Meresin until they have this place surrounded and blockaded."

"We defend the borders and always have, against raiders, scavengers, and greedy Convocation landholders."

"It will get worse," she predicted.

"Such a ray of sunshine."

"Practical," she reminded him, but she laughed, pleased when he smiled down at her. "You could use the income from taxes. Don't look like that. You give them your protection in return—from your army of wizard minions that you'll provide—and that increased security will be an investment in the trade you'll be bringing to all of Meresin, along with magical conveniences. You'll improve their lives, Gabriel."

"*We* will," he corrected. But he didn't sound convinced.

THEY SPENT A pleasant few hours touring the fields and orchards that surrounded House Phel in a fertile spread of glorious colors, like the full skirt of an elaborately embroidered gown. Nic had never imagined such a variety of produce, the mild weather and copious moisture of Meresin yielding a gracious bounty of crops. She revised her earlier dismissal of Gabriel's plan to sell fruit for trade, and began figuring what kind of distribution system they'd need to make the trade cost-effective. With central Elal and the other northern lands still in the grip of winter, Meresin stood to make a fortune selling out-of-season produce.

Her joke about the decrepit barge Gabriel had bought to pursue her to Wartson being the flagship of House Phel's nascent shipping fleet had been more prescient than she'd thought.

"Does Meresin have a shipping port?" she asked Gabriel as their horses circled an unpleasantly fragrant small swamp bordering the bright green of a cotton field. He rode Vale, who pranced and tossed his head as if he'd been stabled and rested for more than a day, and she rode the neat mare Gabriel had bought her in Ophiel, who she'd named Salve.

"No. We have the Dubglass River, which leads to Port Carica."

"That's in Sammael." Though the afternoon sun remained warm before the advent of rain, she had to repress a shiver.

"I'm aware," he replied in that dry tone she'd begun to learn meant it was a source of aggravation for him.

She didn't blame him there. House Sammael dealt in punishment, which made them valuable to the Convocation and unpopular with everyone else. The Sammael heir apparent had been one of her suitors, and he'd been as brusque and unpleasant as you'd expect from that family. He'd also been singularly stupid and nicely aged, so she'd had hopes of running circles around him until he died an early death.

Eyeing Gabriel sideways and placing a hand over her ripening womb, she gave thought to their unborn child. She still wouldn't have had any idea she'd quickened had the Convocation proctor's oracle head not confirmed it. Difficult to imagine, now, that anyone but Gabriel would be the father, and her husband. She could be pregnant with Sammael's child, living in forbidding House Sammael. At least, it looked that way in paintings. It could be that House Sammael encouraged a grim representation, and it wasn't that bad in reality. Still, learning to deal with Sammael as her wizard master would've been leagues worse than her current struggles. Given the way he'd treated her at the Betrothal Trials when she hadn't even belonged to him yet, she doubted even her pregnancy would've given him much pause in extracting all he could from her. That near miss made her shudder. It didn't bear thinking about.

She banished the thought, though not quickly enough to elude Gabriel's keen insight into her mind.

He studied her. "Was *he* one of them?" he asked abruptly, darkness coiling into the underside of his silvery magic.

"One of who?" she asked, making a display of looking puzzled.

"The suitors before me. I know there were three, and I know Sammael heir has been searching for a replacement for his lady wife and familiar, who died last winter. He was one of them, wasn't he?"

"Why does it matter?" She lifted her chin. "It's my personal business."

"Your personal business is also mine now," he practically growled. "Tell me the truth."

"I hear and obey, master," she taunted, but it didn't work to back him off. He simply raised an expectant brow.

"Yes," she admitted, shrugging it off, and offering nothing further.

"Which one?" Gabriel demanded, far from mollified.

"The first one. I can't imagine why that information is relevant to you."

"You know that's not what I'm asking. You said one of them barely spoke to you at all except to give instructions. Was it Sammael?"

The man had a cursed good memory. It made him a quick study, which was to their advantage, but also a tricky opponent if she wanted to conceal anything from him. "Did I say that?" she wondered aloud, attempting to sound vague. *I know you're an innocent,* Sammael's cold voice echoed in her mind, *but no one cares what a familiar has to say. If I want intelligent conversation, I'll talk to another wizard.*

Gabriel reached out with one long arm and snagged Salve's bridle, bringing them close. "You know you did. Quit playing games with me."

"I don't care to discuss this," she replied through gritted teeth to keep her voice from wobbling. She had been innocent when Sammael took her, in more ways than one, and it had been an abrupt degradation to be used so perfunctorily by him. That moment, perhaps more than any other, had brought home the powerlessness of her new status in life. Feeling the prick of tears in her eyes, she determinedly looked away.

Gabriel narrowed his eyes, swore under his breath, and released Salve's bridle. That did not, however, signal a reprieve from the interrogation. He swung down from Vale's back, came over to Nic, and plucked her from the saddle with his easy strength. Instead of setting her down, he held her against him, wrapping his arms around her and holding her in a tight embrace. Despite her resolve to remain regally poised, she dropped her head on his shoulder, surprised to find herself needing the comfort.

"I'm sorry," he said raggedly, and she nodded against his shoulder.

"It's of no matter," she said, her voice coming out small. She'd said that to Gabriel back in her tower, though she'd done a better job then of sounding like she didn't care.

"It is. I asked." Gabriel echoed his own reply, making it clear he remembered, too. Finally, he set her down, though he didn't release her. "I'm sorry," he repeated, "more than you can know, for what you went through."

"It's not your fault."

"In part it is," he asserted. "I took advantage of the same system that exploited you."

"Well, it's turned out fine." She felt better now, less wobbly, not so much on the verge of tears. "What's gone before is gone."

"It will be when he's dead," Gabriel replied with grim purpose.

"Excuse me?" Completely taken aback, she'd nearly stammered in her shock.

"I resolved back then to find out the names of all three of those suitors who brutalized you—and to kill them."

"But… but you *can't* kill the House Sammael heir." Curse it, now she was stammering.

"Watch me." Gabriel's eyes glittered with black hatred. The dark side of the moon. "They will not abuse my wife and live."

"I wasn't your wife then," she pointed out, flailing for an argument to stop him.

He considered that. Came to a decision. "I don't care."

"Gabriel, I never even said it was him." She nearly stomped her foot at her inability to sway him.

"You didn't have to." He touched her cheek, achingly tender in contrast to the roiling shadows under the silver magic. "He made you cry, then and just now. You're a fierce, proud woman, Lady Veronica Phel. Anyone who hurts you enough to draw tears deserves to die."

She was still gaping at him when he lowered his mouth to hers, kissing her with devastating thoroughness, stirring the fire he'd kindled in the library into leaping flame again. Aching with unfulfilled desire, she melted against him, needing him inside and around her, more and more and more.

"Not here," he muttered against her lips, breaking the kiss to nip the tender spot under her jaw that made her shudder with need. "Anyone could come upon us."

"And nobody wants to have sex next to a swamp," she agreed with a wrinkled nose.

He shook his head. "A bog. But your point is taken." Lifting her easily, he settled her in the saddle again and mounted Vale, both horses reluctant to give up the serendipitous grazing opportunity. Moving at a faster clip, they headed back to the manse, perched unevenly on a slight rise in the near distance, between the winding river and the lake.

Slight hills rose gradually on the river's opposite bank. Grayish brown with little foliage, they weren't planted with crops or orchards.

"Gabriel?" She stirred him from the thoughts that had his expression as flinty as those hillsides. He was no doubt plotting how to extract the other two names from her, information she had no intention of giving him. House Phel had enough enemies without Gabriel adding to the roster simply to redress imagined wrongs against her. "Is that the Dubglass River, going past the house, the one that goes to Port Carica?"

He frowned at it as if he'd never seen it before. Yes, his mind had definitely been elsewhere. "Yes, why?"

"Just thinking. And those hills there—why aren't they planted?"

"The soil isn't right. Sand and clay, probably deposited there before the river shifted into its current course. They're actually a problem." He shifted his frown to the unoffending hills. "In heavy rains, the clay gets slick, and we get mud slides, which clog the river. We have to dig it out or the river water floods the marshes there and there." He pointed to the more distant wings of the manse, which were mainly gables showing through the water and grasses, like upturned boats. "Family lore has it that there were several attempts to build the manse on the hillsides originally, as they're the highest point around, but that the structure had to be relocated to the bedrock below, as it kept sliding down the hill with sufficient rain."

He smiled wryly at her. "I've always taken heart from those tales of my ancestors' folly. They put my own failures into perspective." His gaze lingered on the sunken wings of the house. "Sometimes I think I should've razed the house and built it elsewhere."

She'd had the same thought. "Why didn't you?"

"Folly runs in my blood along with the water and moon magic?" He breathed a laugh, shaking his head. "Pride, I suppose. I wanted to prove that the Convocation hadn't truly destroyed my house, that we would rise again from the ashes of destruction."

"Rather, the swamps of them," Nic corrected with a smile.

"That does it." He reined up. "You've been tutoring me in all things to do with magic and the Convocation, including the nature of gremlins. *You* are going to learn the correct terms for wetlands."

She clapped her hands to her cheeks and widened her eyes in a semblance of astonishment. "Can it be that I'll be allowed such sacred knowledge? I'm agog to find out!"

"You think you're funny," he growled, but his lips twitched. "Observe, young pupil." He waved a hand at the sunken wings of the manse. "Do you see any trees or other woody plants in yon wetland?"

Nic pursed her lips and scanned the reedy ponds that merged with the river in places. "The only woody bits I see appear to have once been rooflines."

"Sadly accurate. Also, they are not plants or trees. Thus, this is a marsh."

"That's the definition?"

"Yes. A swamp has trees and the like. Now, turn your scholarly eye upon that low area on the far side of the river."

"The one that looks like a really wet meadow?"

"Not a meadow, but a fen."

"Ah." She nodded knowingly, amused by this whimsical side of him. If nothing else, she'd managed to dig him out of his dark thoughts of vengeance. "Looks like a dense marsh to this untrained dry-lander."

"Exactly. More plant life, fed by a steady source of ground water: the river." He met her gaze, expression serious but dark eyes sparkling. "Remember the bog you didn't like the smell of?"

"Having an excellent memory, I do recall that place from less than a quarter of an hour ago."

"An enclosed depression, without a source of ground water, but instead filled by rain."

"Makes it a bog," she said with a sigh. "I confess I never thought I'd have to know the difference between a swamp, a marsh, a bog, and a fen."

"And now you do." His gaze traveled over the considerable expanse of sunken and partially sunken manse. "It's not too late to raze that heap and start anew."

"Never say it. I'm committed now. Tomorrow, you—with the able assistance of your nubile familiar—will raise House Phel from the marsh of doom."

"Correct usage, but 'doom'?"

"Ignominy?"

"More accurate." He grimaced. "I suppose we should start with the piece I've already raised, see if together we can do more to stabilize it."

"We'll do the whole thing."

Turning his head slowly, he looked at her like he suspected she might have lost her mind. "The whole wing?"

"The whole house." She had to laugh at his incredulous expression. "Correct me if I'm wrong, because I don't know much about house construction, but wouldn't raising just one part while it's being dragged down by the other parts only create strain on the existing structure? I mean, that's one of the things our morning crew reported—that there's ongoing damage in even the dry portions of the core house, because of the stress from the submerged sections."

"Well, yes, of course. There wasn't any way around that, because it's simply not possible to raise the entire manse at once."

"It wasn't possible on *your* own, but that's why you acquired a powerful familiar, isn't it?" She simpered at him.

"I had one or two other reasons in mind," he replied drily.

"Yes, and we'll get to those. But let's just raise the entire structure, stabilize it, remove most of the water—then we can turn the remainder of the restoration over to the worker bees and the low-level water-wickers in the population. That will free us to concentrate on our other pressing matters."

"The entire structure is extensive." He pointed to a far gable, sweeping his hand across to the other distant end in demonstration.

"I can see that. We should spend some time building power for it tonight. Visiting the arcanium was on the schedule anyway."

"Nic." He frowned at her, seeming to be searching for words. "I appreciate your confidence in me, but this is a far more massive undertaking than keeping a barge from wrecking on the rocks. I was barely able to do that."

"It's not any different," she insisted. "You're still tied down to your farmer ways of thinking. Magic doesn't operate according to physical laws. A manse is no different from a barge. It's time you understood what you're capable of doing."

He gazed back at her, uncertain, something of the young man abruptly swamped—and ha to that metaphor—by overwhelming magic in his haunted gaze. "I don't think I can do this."

"That, my only love, sums up your problem." She tried to soften it, to be kind, but he flinched anyway. "You'll see. Better, you'll learn."

"Maybe we need a few days of practice."

"Tomorrow." He'd only build up the endeavor to even more impossible proportions in his mind if she let him stew over it. She would propose doing it immediately, but she wanted plenty of power in reserve. If they tried and failed, he'd only be more predisposed to think of the task as impossible.

She nudged Salve into motion. "I should check for any replies to our messages from this morning before dinner. After we eat, we can spend the night in the arcanium."

"The *entire* night?" Gabriel sounded aghast as Vale trotted briskly to make up the distance.

"Yes, which means we'll need to locate a mattress and blankets for that bed."

"You want to sleep on that… *thing*?"

She could swear, he made it sound like she'd suggested sleeping on a rack studded with spikes. "And use it for some magic-amplifying rituals that will include intense sex." Raising a brow, she gave him a dubious look. "Unless you prefer the floor?"

"As a matter of fact, I would."

"Too bad. The silver bed is made to concentrate your magic. Stop being squeamish about it."

His jaw flexed with irritation. "You have a knack for dragging out that milquetoast word to describe the truly horrible."

She rolled her eyes at him, making sure he could see. "*You* have a knack for the dramatic. It will just be a bit of sex magic, not skinning babies and eating them alive or anything like that."

"I don't want to know if that's something Convocation wizards do."

"Not at all," she reassured him. "What if the baby could grow up to be a powerful wizard or familiar? It makes no sense to run that risk."

He eyed her blackly. "You have such a twisted sense of humor I'm not sure if you're joking or not."

Giving him a bright smile, she dropped that subject without further comment. "You're right, it feels like it's going to rain soon."

"The surprise is that it held off so long."

"Are the winters here cool and rainy, plenty of misty weather?"

"As a matter of fact, they are. Why are you wondering?"

"Perfect weather for grapes," she replied with satisfaction. This would be fun. "Those sandy hills will be ideal for growing them, too."

"Grapes. You want to plant grapes?"

"I want to plant grape vines," she clarified. "A vineyard. We're going to make wine."

He assimilated that. "I suppose you would know how."

"I would—and we're going to give Elal a run for their money with House Phel wines."

"Elal doesn't hold the license?"

"Nope. Grapes are grapes; wine is wine. Not magic, but nature. Elal does supply earth elementals to improve soil and what grows from it. Those could be useful here."

"I'll think about it," he said in a tone that meant he'd already decided he didn't like the idea but didn't want to argue. "I don't know where we can buy grape vines. I don't know much about making wine, but I'm assuming that you can't use just any old grapes."

"Not if we want to make good wine. And we do. So we'll need the very best vines, in several varietals, so we can test which perform best in this climate."

"Sounds expensive," he noted with a sigh of resignation.

"Not at all, except that we'll be forfeiting a bit of income. They're going to be included in my dowry."

Gabriel gazed at her thoughtfully. "Is Lord Elal aware of this plan?"

"Not yet." She tried for a carefree smile but was aware it likely looked more like a baring of teeth. "But he's going to do it. Just you wait and see."

~ 6 ~

WHEN NIC APPEARED to join him for dinner, Gabriel nearly did a double take at the sight of her. In fact, his surprise showed enough that she displayed uncharacteristic hesitation in her usually confident stride, pausing to run a hand over the sleek sides of her closely trimmed hair.

"Do you hate it?" she asked, eyes full of uncertainty. "I had the grooming imp trim it for me, and they only take fairly simple instructions. My hair was lopsided enough that this was the best way to even it up. But it will grow back," she added. "It won't be this short always."

Recovering himself—and chagrined for giving her cause to doubt—he crossed to her and took her hands. "You look more beautiful than ever," he breathed, knowing by the high flush on her arched cheekbones that she received the truth of his impassioned words. Raising one hand above her head, he coaxed her into turning a slow pirouette. The short black hairs defined the elegant lines where her skull met the back of her neck, silky and alluring, tempting him to kiss her just there in that hollow that made her shiver. Sharp points of slightly longer hair curved over her temples, framing her arresting features. Tamed curls atop her head waved in sensual abandon, all of it serving to set off her fiercely intelligent beauty, her deep-green eyes dominating her extraordinary face.

Unable to resist, he cupped the back of her neck, caressing those silky strands as he kissed her deeply, feeling as if he could sink into her and never emerge. "You are so beautiful," he murmured against her lips, "that I want to commission a portrait of you, looking just like this, in case you do decide to grow it long again."

She smiled up at him, arms languidly coiled around his waist, the scent of hothouse roses and fire-warmed wine twining around him with her potent magic. "The first time you called me beautiful, I accused you of trying to manipulate me with pretty lies."

"I remember that accusation well," he replied wryly. He'd been so dazzled by her, astonished at his great good fortune that the loathsome Convocation ritual had resulted in him finding such a gorgeous and fascinating woman to be his life partner. He winced for the naïveté of that self of not that long ago. No wonder Nic had been scornful of his earnest praise. "And I understand why you didn't believe I was sincere."

"I believe you now," she said softly, surprising him. She hastily added, "At least, I believe in your sincerity, though I don't at all understand why you hold that opinion." She arched a raven-winged brow with sardonic humor. "Further evidence of your questionable judgment, no doubt."

He was beginning to understand, too, how she used barbed humor and sarcasm to hold him off, to diffuse any tender emotions between them. "I may have questionable judgment in many arenas, but not in this." He studied her face. "I wish I could describe what I see when I look at you."

"I know what you see, because I *have* seen myself in a mirror," she replied in a very dry voice. "My forehead is too high, my Elal nose is as big as a beak, my jaw too square, and my mouth is way too big for all of it."

"You do have a big mouth," he agreed, kissing those lush lips he couldn't get enough of.

"Ha ha." She nipped his bottom lip, the shock going straight to his groin. "You're the one always asking for opinions you don't actually want to hear."

"I *do* want to hear them," he replied gravely. "Even when I don't like them. That's how a marriage should be."

Restless, she withdrew from him, taking in the long dining table in the partially restored hall, eyeing the planks nailed over the doors to the halls leading to the recently re-sunk arcade, but withholding comment. The dining hall was barely usable, but he'd wanted to have a more formal meal with her. The evening had turned chilly with the advent of a soaking rain, the nip in the air a reminder that winter had not yet fully withdrawn. Two place settings had been laid at one end, with a gleaming silver candelabra spilling warm candlelight.

"Just the two of us?" she inquired, sounding not entirely pleased.

"Yes. Everyone is giving us time to enjoy our honeymoon. They're all taking turns sending over food for us." Taking her hand, he led her around to the end of the table, holding out the chair for her.

She rolled her eyes and slipped into the other chair. "The head of the table belongs to the head of the house, *Lord* Phel."

"Surely we don't need to observe formal manners when we're alone."

"It's good practice for you," she replied, pouring wine for him and handing him the goblet, though he still stood, hesitating. "These things should be become second nature for you. Be arrogant and assume that you are owed pride of place." She pointed a finger at him. "And *don't* ruminate on how acting like that might turn you into it."

"I thought the moratorium on philosophy expired once we dealt with the threats on the breakfast table," he reminded her, irritation rising that she dismissed his concerns so easily, even as he reminded himself that she'd been so thoroughly brainwashed by that loathsome Convocation Academy that she saw no problem with what she recommended he become. He saw the peril clearly, however. Since his magic had manifested, it had felt like he clung to a rapidly eroding slope of what had once been firm footing. With every step he took to embracing his magic and becoming Lord Phel, it seemed he lost sight of one more bit of integrity. *This is how it happens. Give in to the power, and it gradually eats you alive until you have no humanity left.*

Nic glanced up at him, craning her neck more than she needed to in a pointed reminder that he could be seated. "We haven't dealt with them, not fully. Calliope sent a message that our order will be delivered in the morning, at which point we'll have the proper paper to draft your final replies and send them. *Then* you can mope about and mourn the loss of your integrity."

Not entirely certain how he could be both aggravated and

amused by her, he finally sat and sipped his wine as she began filling a plate for each of them. "According to your latest plan, we're raising the entirety of the manse after our missives have been sent."

"Excellent point. We'll have to schedule self-excoriating philosophizing for the afternoon." She handed him the plate and arranged hers before her.

Knowing she wouldn't eat until he did, he took a bite of the steaming baked potato before adding both fresh salted butter and sour cream. Nic observed him keenly, no doubt memorizing his preference. He set aside that irritation, too.

"You could add that to your repertoire as brooding Lord Phel," she added pertly. "Perhaps you can drink heavily as you wallow in self-loathing, then alternate at dinner between sullenness and sudden explosions of anger." Her green eyes danced with wicked mirth over the rim of her goblet.

"Are you enjoying yourself?" he asked, having to fight to restrain a smile.

"As a matter of fact, I am." She slid him a sultry, teasing look. "And in the arcanium at night, you can release all that pent-up fury and passion upon my helpless body."

That killed all humor, along with his appetite. Sliding the plate away, he raked his hands through his unruly curls. He should have gotten Nic to unleash the grooming imp on his hair, too. "I wish you wouldn't say things like that. It's revolting."

Her eyes flashed with shock a moment before she lowered her gaze to her plate. Eating steadily, she focused on her food, not replying. Not meeting his gaze.

"It's not funny to me," he persisted. He'd developed a love-hate relationship with her quirky sense of humor. Her wit surprised and delighted him, but that sharp edge could flay him open with ease, leaving him bleeding. And she used it to deflect any serious conversation between them. She still hadn't replied, so he caught her by the wrist. Stilling, she raised her tumultuous gaze to his, the green dark with emotions he couldn't identify. Except that it was clear he'd hurt her. "I don't know how to explain this to you."

She shook her head as if he'd asked a question. "You don't have to explain. You've made your feelings perfectly clear." Pulling her hand away, she set to eating with determined fervor. "Eat. We don't need to discuss it further."

Somehow he seriously doubted that. "Exactly *what* have I made clear?"

"Your feelings about the arcanium," she replied tersely.

"That's not an answer, Nic. Explain."

With a clatter, she threw down her utensil, then flung herself from the chair and paced furiously away and back again. She'd put on the burgundy riding habit again, he realized. Not appropriate for dinner, most likely, but the velvet would be warmer than the silk or the linen dresses. He'd done nothing yet about getting her more clothes to wear. He looked up from his stricken rumination to find her glaring at him in mute fury, fists clenched by her sides, visibly seething.

"Gabriel," she bit out. "Could we please not do this?"

Carefully, he pushed back from the table, casting a regretful eye over their half-eaten meal, the wine, the candlelight. He'd thought to give her a bit of romance, and he'd been doing all right for a while, he thought, until it went sideways. *Until she deliberately destroyed the mood,* an uncharitable voice in him growled. Keeping his voice even, he attempted a reply to that non-question. "You might understand me perfectly well, but I'm not so fortunate. What am I not to do?"

With a wordless snarl, she looked as if she'd love nothing better than to hurl something at his head. Visibly reining herself in, she straightened her spine and lifted her chin, pulling that regal poise around her like a cloak. "I am aware," she said with impressive coolness, given that snarl, "that you are conflicted about being a wizard, and that I am not what you envisioned for your lady wife."

Uh-oh. This was worse than he'd realized. "That is categorically not true."

"Don't *lie*," she spat, all the fire in her welling up, the scent of rose-infused wine thick as fresh blood. "Everything in this place speaks of the vision you had. I see it everywhere I look. The pretty master suite with its books and view of the river. This dinner with two place settings and polished silver that—"

"Moon magic," he interrupted. "My silver requires no polishing."

"Romance," she spat without pause. "*Honeymooning.*" The way she said the words made them drip with distaste. "You never wanted a familiar, and you still don't."

Feeling his own temper rise, he picked up the eating knife and tapped it on the table. "I want *you*," he said, meeting and holding her gaze.

She laughed, full of bitter scorn. "No, you don't, Gabriel Phel. Not really. You want some ideal of me. The woman you fantasized I'd be when you studied that miniature. A *wife* and *partner*," she sneered, as if those would be the worst things possible.

"And you are those things to me," he replied tightly.

"In your imagination!" she flung back. "Telling me I'm beautiful, and wanting to protect me from the wizards who hurt me, and acting like this is some kind of romantic relationship."

"Nic…" He flailed, completely at sea. She'd been pleased that he found her beautiful, he hadn't imagined it. "I don't understand why you're so upset."

"Because!" she nearly screeched, then swallowed hard. Holding back tears. *Anyone who hurts you enough to draw tears deserves to die.* He'd said that to her not hours ago, and look at him now. "Because at heart you're revolted by what I am."

Unable to sit still for this, he pushed to his feet. "Wrong. I meant that you joking about using you like that in the arcanium is revolting, not that you are."

She laughed, a hysterical edge to it, and briefly dropped her face into her hands. When she met his gaze again, hers was distraught. "That *is* who and what I am. You can't divide the two."

"You are more than a familiar to be used by me," he said on a harsh whisper, to keep from shouting.

"More? That implies that being a familiar isn't enough. That if I'm only that, I'm somehow lacking."

Her tangled logic had him turned around, his head aching from it, the candles smelling too strong. "That's not what I meant. You had ambitions to be a wizard, and you were disappointed that you turned out to be a familiar. I want more than that for you, too."

"But I *am* a familiar! I'm your bonded familiar, which means there are things I crave from you. You might hate that and be revolted by it, but I think you don't realize how *lowering* it is for me to crave something from you that you despise me for wanting and despise yourself for wanting, too." She finished on a harsh sob, pressing her hand to her stomach as if she might be sick. "Do I wish I was a wizard? Yes! With all my heart, but I am not. And it kills me, Gabriel, that you are everything I ever wanted to be, and you scorn it at every turn. I swear, I wish you hadn't cheated in the trials. It would be easier if I'd been bonded to a wizard who at least planned to use me honestly than to suffer this emotional hot and cold from you."

It was as if an arrow had thudded through his chest, ripping his heart out. "You don't mean that."

She lifted her chin defiantly, eyes glittering with unshed tears. "I do mean it."

"You'd rather be cruelly used than treated with respect and kindness," he ground out.

Opening her mouth, she closed it again, but not before her lips wobbled. "I don't know," she finally said. "Maybe it's that I'd know how to do that. I think that… if I were only a pet to you, then maybe it wouldn't hurt so much when you despise me."

Shit. Feeling utterly helpless, he went to her, wanting to reach for her. He stopped himself. She held her ground. "I don't despise you, Nic. I promise. I just want…" Realizing that these words, too, would come out wrong, he let the sentence trail off.

"You want your wholesome Meresin farm girl," Nic supplied for him, her eyes far too wise. "The sweet young woman who grows oranges and feeds the geese, who'd be your loving wife and companion in all things. Who would bed you with sweet affection and bear you children that you could raise together, until they gave you apple-cheeked grandchildren to dandle on your knee. Someone who would never even think of wanting to kneel for you, who wouldn't yearn for the silver chains of your arcanium."

The images she evoked pushed all else from his mind. Nic, kneeling naked but for silver chains, her lush body bound for him to use as he pleased. The wicked tools of the arcanium glinted with dark allure, his imagination wanting to discover what they might do to her. Just envisioning what might pass between them had his magic swelling, pulsing with power— hungering for even more. If the mere thought of such depravity fed his magic, what would the reality do—

"*No!*" he shouted, clapping his hands over his ears, shutting out her words, banishing the possibility that he'd succumb. Dropping his hands, he curled his fingers into fists. "I won't become like Sammael. Not even for you."

Nic gazed at him with wide-eyed and knowing calm. "See?" she asked softly. "You hate the very thought of it. You despise yourself, and me, too."

His jaw clenched so hard it ached, he glared his fury. "You should hate the thought, too."

"I feel I should point out that you are telling me how I

should feel. I told you what I want, and you refuse to take that seriously."

"Because this isn't something you really want. You've just been told to want it. You don't know any better."

She regarded him with something that would be pity if she weren't so coldly furious. "I am not a child, and I am not a fool. I'd venture to say I know—and accept—myself far better than you do."

"I won't do this," he said with vicious determination. "You clearly don't know your own mind, and I refuse to demean you that way."

"I see." She shrugged as if it didn't matter to her one way or the other. "It's your decision, of course. How you use me is entirely up to you."

"Stop putting it that way," he warned her, coming very near to ordering her not to.

"As you say," she replied in a meek tone not matched by her flashing eyes. "But you *are* stuck with me, so I suggest you come to terms with how you want things to be between us."

"I *have* come to terms," he informed her. "And there will be no visit to the arcanium. That's my final decision. We'll work together to raise the manse without that."

"I'll do my best to work within those parameters." She inclined her head as if acknowledging a command, infuriating him further.

"Stop deferring to me," he snarled at her.

She lifted her chin, otherwise bland in expression. "Gabriel, you cannot give me orders, make unilateral decisions about my life, and tell me I don't know what I want while you know better—and also expect me not to defer. You can't have it both ways. You have power over me whether you like it or not, and at this moment, when you are so determined to have things your way, you seem to like it just fine. I can't fight you, and I'm not going to try."

How had this conversation gone so deeply into the bog? He felt mired to the waist in mud, and the more he struggled against it, the deeper he sank.

"May I be excused?" she asked with excruciating politeness.

He nearly said no, nearly demanded that she sit and eat dinner with him. That she be witty and sweet, flirting with him. *You want your wholesome Meresin farm girl.* "Yes, go then."

She curtsied, lowering her gaze demurely, then rose and walked out. If he knew her slightly less, he wouldn't have been able to pick out the stiffness in her gait, the repressed fury and despair tightening the line of her shoulders.

"Nic," he called after her.

When she turned, waiting with polite obedience, he realized he didn't know what to say to her. "I didn't want to fight with you," he said, the words sounding absurd even as he said them.

She softened, ever so slightly, a gleam of something like compassion in her eyes. "I know." Letting out a sigh, she shook her head. "Perhaps you understand now why wizards and familiars can never be partners. It's in a wizard's nature to be commanding, and it's in a familiar's nature to be commanded. The sooner we sort that out, the better off we'll be."

She stood there, saying nothing more. Waiting to be excused, he realized.

"Good night," he told her.

With a polite nod, she left, leaving him alone with their interrupted dinner. With a snarl of pure rage, he dashed the food and dishes from the table, sending the candelabra and melted wax flying. Moon magic burst out of him in a rain of silver, an uncontrolled burst as hadn't happened in a long while.

Perhaps you can drink heavily as you wallow in self-loathing, then alternate at dinner between sullenness and sudden explosions of anger.

Sinking to his knees, he clutched his head, willing himself to control the magic, to draw it back inside. And wished with all his heart that he hadn't driven away the one person who would understand.

~ 7 ~

NIC SPENT A miserable night alone. It didn't help that she didn't know how to light the fire and it was uncomfortably cold without it. She missed having an elemental-heated house with a surprising twist of homesickness. Though she searched through her things, she couldn't find the little fire elemental Missus Ryma had given her in Wartson. She hadn't seen it since they arrived, when it must have been unloaded with the other supplies in their wagon.

She was warm enough under the covers—and still too upset to be hungry—but she woke what felt like every hour to wonder where Gabriel might be sleeping. Then told herself she didn't care. Then reminded herself that this was as it should be: with no more illusions between them that they were anything other than what they fundamentally were. Except that she shouldn't be sleeping in this luxurious master suite—luxurious by House Phel's diminished standards, anyway—while the lord of the manor was… where? Sleeping with Vale in the stables probably, the stubborn oaf.

She didn't care. This was as it should be. The sooner she could reconcile herself to meek obedience, regardless of how wrongheaded and shortsighted Gabriel was being, the easier it would be. Somewhere in all his prattle of partnership and mutual bonding and working together, she'd lost sight of the one thing she'd promised herself to be always brutally honest with herself about. She was a familiar, and as such, she was consigned to a life of powerlessness. It was just a bit of priceless irony that she'd schemed her way out of belonging to the likes of Sammael and his uncaring cruelty, only to bind herself to a wizard who scrupled to use her that way at all.

You clearly don't know your own mind.

Was that true? She didn't know anymore. Which, she had to admit in the dark and restless privacy of her lonely bed, went to prove Gabriel's point. How much of her longing for the sexual magic of the arcanium came from the Fascination driving her to want those darkly tantalizing fantasies? Did she crave Gabriel's chains because it was in her nature as a familiar to want to be controlled, or because it was him? Certainly her body had never ached with this sexual frustration before him. But then, he'd been the first to draw any kind of sexual response from her. Before he'd walked into her tower room, the encounters with other wizards had left her cold at best and feeling filthy at worst. *I refuse to demean you that way.*

What was wrong with her that she thought she wanted that—no, that she knew she wanted and needed it from him— and that it didn't feel demeaning? Sammael had demeaned her with nary a chain or whip in sight. He'd flayed her pride on a profound level and left her bleeding and broken without a mark on her.

Gabriel had hurt her heart, and more the fool she for letting him do it. She'd known better, from the very beginning, than to let herself feel anything more for him than the Fascination demanded. She'd gotten caught up was all, caught up in the dream of raising House Phel—literally and figurative-ly—from the muck and making it into a… what? *Be honest with yourself,* she ordered herself sternly. *This is no time to indulge in denial.*

"Into a home," she whispered into the darkness. The image she'd evoked for Gabriel, of the sweet farm girl with her sunny ways and simple wants, haunted her now. Nic would never be like that. Even at her meekest and most obedient, she couldn't be what Gabriel really wanted. What she honestly didn't blame him for wanting.

She just wished she didn't care.

When the sky finally began to lighten, she got up, deciding that her energy would be best spent on some useful task than fretting and worrying over what she couldn't change. The rain continued to drizzle down, a decided chill in the air, so she donned the burgundy velvet riding habit again. It needed to be cleaned, which meant washing it herself—not a great option, as she wasn't sure of the method—asking someone to wash it for her, or using a cleaning imp she didn't have.

None were going to happen that morning, obviously. She just hoped she didn't stink. Because it made her feel better, she applied the Aratron cosmetics Gabriel had acquired for her in Ophiel, setting the grooming imp to styling her hair. The short sides and back didn't need much, but the looser curls on top had gotten themselves into an astonishing amount of disarray during her restless night. It would've been better to have it all equally short, but she'd succumbed to vanity and a foolish desire to look pretty for Gabriel. *You look more beautiful than ever.* The way he'd looked at her as he'd said that… She sighed for that, and not in a dreamy way.

Setting him firmly out of her thoughts, she went down through the quiet house, feeling quite alone in the chilly dimness. The library windows, save the one glassed-in set, had been boarded over against the rain, plunging the place into gloom, tempting her already glum mood to follow. None of the workers from the day before had shown, probably because Gabriel hadn't told them to. How aggravating that she couldn't round them up and set them to work herself. Of course, it was still early. Maybe they'd turn up later.

Fortunately, several couriers waited for her in the rafters of the library, quietly roosting until her arrival triggered them to deliver their various messages. The Calliope paper shipment had arrived overnight also, along with several decent self-replenishing quills. It was probably just as well that the Calliope courier had simply deposited the order and left, sparing Gabriel the admittedly uncanny sight of a giant angel.

Not exactly happily occupied, but at least busy enough to ignore her misery, Nic set to replying to the accounts-related messages, then to penning the final versions of Gabriel's replies to Iblis, the Convocation, and her papa. She labored the longest over the last, nearly reneging on suggesting that grape vines be sent in lieu of coin. It was part of that dream of making a home, really, to consider cultivating a vineyard to produce wine, not something a new familiar ought to be taking on.

She also knew, however, that Gabriel would think poorly

of her if she backed out of it. There wouldn't be another opportunity like this. Papa refused to sell his precious vines, even grafted ones, to any other house. He wouldn't be happy about giving her a share, but he'd do it. He'd loved her well, and despite his fury with and disappointment in her, Papa would also play fair. He'd said Gabriel deserved a chance to make House Phel succeed, and this would be a good long-term investment.

The sense of fresh water and bright silver alerted her to Gabriel's approach, and she braced herself, neatly stacking the missives awaiting his signature, then folded her hands and waited, back straight. He appeared in the library doorway a moment later, wizard-black eyes landing on her with peculiar intensity. The silver moon magic shimmered molten in him, and the water aspect steamed in the cool air.

Still angry, then. Ah, well.

"I didn't expect you to be up so early," he said, coming into the library and assessing the room. "Why are you sitting here in the cold and dark?"

"That fire elemental I had must be packed away somewhere with the other things we brought from Ophiel, and I wasn't sure how to light a fire manually. Or where to find the supplies." She gestured to the pale light coming through the windows beside her. "I had light enough. These are ready for you to sign, if you approve of the final versions."

He eyed her, the scent of steam more vivid, like a teakettle on boil. "It's like that, then," he said, and came just close enough to pick up the first of the missives. Setting it down with a grunt, he picked up the next, reading them one after the other in rapid succession without comment. Tossing the final one down, he studied her, wizard-black eyes inscrutable. She tried not to squirm under that relentless gaze, tried not to reveal how it aroused her, too.

If only she didn't want him so badly, all of this would be so much easier. Or, if only he wanted her the way she wanted him to have her.

"Any revisions?" she asked, pretending to be calm, even as her heart thudded in her breast.

"No." He fell silent again, and she thought maybe he'd say nothing more. Then he added, "You have an elegant hand."

"Nothing like a Convocation Academy education to drill one in such disciplines," she replied, instantly regretting the words, as the thought of discipline roused her further and made his shuttered gaze go even colder.

"They're excellent, of course," he finally said. "Any reason not to send them off?"

"Not so long as you approve."

His jaw flexed, but he nodded. "I want to say that you don't have to wait for my approval, but you wouldn't listen to that, would you?"

"I do need you to sign them," she said instead of answering, handing him the quill with a lift of her brows.

Looking slightly chagrined, he took it, and—after examining it with interest—signed the stack of letters. She busied herself with sending off the ones she could via the various mercantile couriers, making a stack of the ones he needed to send a signal to send, aware of his eyes on her all the while. Much as she was pleased to have all those tasks off her list, she was almost sorry to finish. Folding her hands in her skirts, she turned back to Gabriel and his burning gaze.

She'd already listed the relevant house crests, so he made quick work of sending the missives. Once they'd cleared the desk, he studied her, thoughts obscure behind his brooding mask, though hints of steam lingered in the air.

"I thought we'd practice working together on some wizardry," he finally said.

"Of course."

Looking annoyed by her agreement, he opened his mouth to say something, then firmly closed it again. "I'll show you what I was trying to do with the wing that sunk again. I've been thinking that if we work piece by piece, it shouldn't require huge expenditures of magic all at once."

Privately, she didn't agree that it would work very well at all that way, but she was also quite certain they didn't have enough magic stored up between them to raise the entire manse at once. "All right," she agreed, waiting for him to lead the way.

He didn't move, glaring at her. "Are you going to be this way from now on?"

Biting back a sigh, she didn't ask "what way?" like she really wanted to. He was teetering on the edge of fury, and she didn't want to fight with him. Abruptly weary, feeling every lost hour of sleep from the night before, she searched for a reply. "I'm trying to be agreeable."

"Like this sweet farm-girl wife you seem to think I want?" he shot back through his teeth.

Reining in her temper, she kept as calm as she could. "I

don't like fighting with you, Gabriel. I apologize for the things I said last night. I'm doing my best to get along with you."

"By being *obedient*," he sneered.

"I don't know what else to do!" she fired back, losing her resolve and nearly shouting at him. "I don't know who you want me to be."

"I want you to be yourself."

No, he didn't, but she couldn't say so without contradicting him, so she set her teeth and nodded. "All right, I'll try to do that."

"Stop being so agreeable!" He took a step closer, hands flexing as if he wanted to seize her. So tempting to taunt him so he would, but that would only lead them back in the same circle.

"Do you even hear yourself?" she asked as calmly as she could, refusing to give ground. "You're yelling at me for being agreeable."

A low sound of frustration snarled out of him, but he took a step back. "Fine," he said through clenched teeth. "I don't want to fight with you either."

Could have fooled her. He was spoiling for a fight. More, he was boiling over with frustration, sexual and otherwise. And the fool wizard wouldn't do what he needed to, for either of them. "Let's go to work on that wing, then," she suggested.

With a stiff nod, he turned, waiting for her to step up and walk beside him.

"Any luck finding Seliah?" she asked as they went down the main hall and turned into the dining hall and scene of the dinner debacle the night before. She raised a brow at the shattered dishes and the floor dusted with silver. Gabriel had told her once how, when his magic had first come upon him, that he'd awakened to find he'd layered the floor silver with transformed moonlight in his sleep. She hadn't asked him what he'd been dreaming about when that happened, but this scene was like looking at her own emotional residue from the restless night, damningly scattered across the floor. She wouldn't care for there to be such glaring evidence of her own rawness, so she refrained from commenting.

"No luck there," Gabriel replied steadily, meeting her questioning gaze as if daring her to say something about the mess. "I have my best trackers looking for her, but she's disappeared into the marshes. It could be days before anyone locates her."

Something there he was leaving out. "Can you find her?"

Slowly, he nodded. "I always could, though over the years I stopped chasing her down every time she disappeared. It seemed to help her, to be away from people. At least, she always came back calmer. Does that sound congruent with what she's struggling with as a latent familiar?"

Nic nearly said there was no such thing as a latent familiar—only someone living among people without the knowledge to recognize her nature—but she and Gabriel seemed to have established a kind of detente, so she didn't want to disrupt that.

"I don't really know," she replied honestly. "All I know about untapped familiars is from stories, and the cautions of my teachers at Convocation Academy." She braced herself for a scathing observation from him on that source of information, but he only nodded thoughtfully. Maybe he was trying, too. "I can tell you that the magic builds up inside, and it can feel like…"

How to describe it? It felt a lot like sexual frustration, like needing to come and not being able to, which was decidedly *not* an analogy she wanted to use with him when they'd managed to find a fragile peace. And he might not react well to thinking of his little sister in those terms.

"You can be honest with me," he said, sounding almost gentle, then raked a hand through his disordered silver curls, the black streak standing out like a lightning bolt made of night. "I realize that I've been asking you to be honest and then punishing you when I don't like the answer."

"Did Vale give you that counsel?" she asked with a smile. It helped more than she'd have imagined to have the tension between them relieved somewhat.

Gabriel cocked his head. "How did you know I slept in the stable?"

"There aren't that many dry places nearby to sleep," she pointed out, then risked edging close enough to pluck a wisp of straw from his sleeve. "And there's physical evidence."

He grimaced. "My clothes are in the master suite, and I didn't want to disturb your rest."

Pressing her lips together, she held back the offer to sleep elsewhere, even though that made the most sense and would fit Convocation expectations. That kind of suggestion would only compound the problems between them, but what else could she say? He wanted honesty, which she realized in that moment, wasn't something she'd been trained to give. She'd learned the ways of power and manipulation, behaviors that were only exacerbating the gulf between her and her wizard. Gabriel wasn't a Convocation wizard and never would be, no matter how she tried to coach him to behave like one.

"You wouldn't have bothered me," she said on impulse, "because I wasn't asleep. I tossed and turned all night, because I was upset also." She waved a hand at the silver on the floor. "I just don't leave as much of a trail," she added with a wry smile.

He huffed out a laugh, quickly swallowed, then fastened his gaze on her, worlds of pain in it. "Vale said I was an ass."

She took the peace offering for what it was, her heart feeling oddly tender, raw and stinging. "I may have behaved badly."

He reached out and set a careful hand on her velvet-clad arm. "I think you had cause. I am brooding and prone to outbursts of anger. And you were spot on that I..." He swallowed, squeezed her arm lightly, searched her face. "I don't like the things I feel sometimes, as if I'm battling some monster inside that I don't dare give into."

"I know that feeling well," she replied softly, putting her hand over his. "Maybe we can work together to figure it out?"

His lips quirked. "That almost sounds like a partnership."

"Yes, well." She rolled her eyes and let out a sigh of the long-suffering. "My wizard is odd and demanding in strange ways. It's incumbent on me to accommodate him."

A muscle ticced in his cheek, and for a moment she thought she'd teased him too far, but then, with a sigh, he wryly acknowledged that. Sliding his hand down her arm until he caught her by the wrist, he lifted her hand slowly enough that she could pull away, bending over it and holding her gaze the whole time. When she didn't resist, he brushed a kiss over the back of her hand, his wizard-black eyes intent on hers. "You honor me with your tolerance," he said very quietly, and she shivered for no good reason, as if he'd said something else, something far more intimate.

"Shall we do some magic, wizard?" she asked with deliberate archness, not entirely comfortable with the emotional intensity.

Gabriel straightened, still holding her hand, his thumb passing over the back of it in a subtle caress, and regarded her with a considering look. No doubt seeing right through her. But he let her off the hook. "Yes, let's try." With a wave of his hand, nails flew out of the boards covering one archway, the planks and nails falling to the floor with a startling clatter.

She managed not to show her startlement and raised a brow instead. "Silver nails. Clever."

"I thought so," he replied with a smug smile, gesturing for her to precede him into the dank hallway that had been revealed. "They're too soft for most uses, but handy for things like that so I can come and go without acquiring brawn." He slid her a smile for that term. "Speaking of which, where are the workers?"

"No one has showed up yet. I assumed because you hadn't told them to."

He looked irritated, his jaw tight. "So noted."

"You should practice using your magic without physical gestures," she said, only partly to divert his attention, hoping the advice wouldn't further annoy him.

He glanced sideways at her, unoffended. "Your father used his fingers to invoke magic, and the Convocation proctor even more so."

"Showing off for you," she explained. The floor beneath her feet gave soggily, but wasn't underwater. They'd entered some sort of salon, probably one that had been used to entertain guests while they waited for dinner to be served. "In the first case, anyway. If Papa didn't want you to see what he was doing, you wouldn't have any warning. What magic did he work?"

"Forcing your mother into her alternate form," Gabriel answered, a note of dawning realization in his tone. "Ah. He wanted me to know he had control of her."

"Very likely. Papa doesn't do anything by accident."

"And the proctor?" They'd crossed the large and distinctly waterlogged salon to another boarded-over archway. Though he made no movement, the silver nails eased out, falling with the boards to reveal a solid door.

"Well done. Proctors tend to be into theatrics, and that one in particular. The ones assigned to monitor the Betrothal Trials and monitor the oracle heads are pretty low-level Hanneil wizards. The oracle heads don't require all that much magic, barely more than a trigger, so their minders tend to eke out as much drama from the position as possible. Mine had guessed I was minded to run, so I imagine she was especially puffed up with borrowed authority."

Gabriel snickered, flashing her a genuinely amused smile. Ah, that was good to see. "You have nailed it precisely, Lady Veronica."

She shrugged a little, embarrassed by how much his approval warmed her. "Should I be concerned about what's on the other side of this door that you haven't opened it yet?"

"A lot of water," he admitted. "I need to concentrate to hold it back."

Holding out her hand, she raised her brows when he hesitated. "First rule of working together: don't wait until you're drained or desperate to use—that is, to call on my assistance," she hastily rephrased when he frowned. "By preserving your own natural magic, you'll be better prepared to handle any surprises, or to handle something on your own should we be separated. You might need to protect me, for example," she added, which was exactly the right note to play, his frown fading into thoughtful acknowledgment.

Taking her hand, he interlaced his fingers with hers, more like a lover than a wizard drawing from his familiar, but she didn't argue, especially when he gave her a quelling look. Some arguments went unsaid, she supposed. "Like I did with calling the couriers?" he asked.

"Yes. Start small, then work your magic, trying to use me as the source instead of your own reserves."

"How do I know if I'm draining you too much?"

She nearly quipped that he'd know when she collapsed on the soggy floorboards, but she could just imagine his reaction to that. Look at her, learning discretion. How to Manage Your Squeamish Wizard 101 should've been a Convocation Academy class. But then, no one else had a wizard unwilling to use them to the hilt. "Maybe that's part of my assignment," she reasoned. "I'll have to let you know how much you're drawing from me—will that work?"

He gave her a considering look. "That's not something that's usually done between a wizard and familiar, is it?"

Relieved not to have to dance around that topic, she smiled. "No, it's not. So, new territory for me, too."

"There's also the reciprocal bonding," he noted. "Maybe I can gauge how much I'm drawing from you."

"Worth a try." Though privately, she doubted it. She doubted that there was any reciprocity to their bonding in the first place. In the second, she'd never heard of a wizard gauging their familiar's reserves, but that might simply sound so unlikely to her because no wizards bothered themselves to try.

Gabriel's magic wound around her like an embrace, most intense where their hands were joined, but also washing over her like a gentle spring rain, like the fall of moonlight on naked skin. Her body responded as if he'd caressed her with sensual intent, but his attention was focused on the far side of the heavy door. She couldn't sense exactly what he was doing, so she concentrated on monitoring the magic draw from her own reservoirs.

It made for an interesting exercise. At Convocation Academy, they'd studied the principles of how a familiar yielded magic to their wizard, as that information was equally valuable no matter how the students manifested. Even in the Advanced Training for Familiars, however, none of her teachers had mentioned techniques for measuring how much magic she had or the rate of drain. All the focus had been on opening up most fully, offering magic without reservation. Very likely they hadn't wanted familiars to get any ideas about resisting the demands of their wizards.

For the first time, it occurred to her to wonder if she *could* restrict that channel of flow. Not now, but Gabriel would probably be willing to experiment with her. Even more likely, he'd probably be over the moon—heh—if they determined she could cut him off if she wanted to. In the meanwhile, she concentrated on monitoring the slow trickle of her magic. He was developing more finesse, but she also wondered if he was accessing enough. He'd been working at the task for longer than he did with most of his magic use. Like all naturally talented types, he tended to be profligate with his magic, blissfully overconfident and unaware of how badly tapped out he could get. Particularly with his dual-magic nature, he'd become accustomed to simply switching to the other when he'd drained one.

Much as she disliked interrupting his focus—and with a Convocation wizard, she'd never dare—she quietly asked, "Are you making progress?"

He grimaced and blew out a breath. "You haven't said if I'm drawing too much, but I think this isn't enough to do the job without augmenting from my own."

She couldn't help the laugh that escaped her then. "Oh, honey, you're not even close to drawing too much. I can barely feel the trickle."

"Seriously?" He raised a dark brow. "Your magic feels so robust to me."

"Take," she murmured with a smile, deliberately evoking their sexual union. "Have. It's all for you."

"It's yours," he corrected.

"I can't use it. You can. Use it for me." The silvery tendrils of magic tightened around her, evocative and deeply stirring, the sense of him drinking from her growing stronger and profoundly erotic. It hadn't felt like this when she'd practiced with wizards at the academy, or even with Gabriel before this, so it must be a result of the bonding. His wizard-black eyes rested on her face, his own expression tight with sexual need, so she knew he felt it, too. No wonder bonded familiars looked to be in the throes of ecstasy at times, even when berated by harsh wizard masters. This felt… amazing. "Yes," she purred, letting him see her pleasure. "That's very, very good."

"All right," he replied, voice hoarse with desire. "That seems to be enough." With his free hand, he turned the old-fashioned handle and pushed the door open, revealing one of the most extraordinary sights Nic had ever glimpsed.

A wall of green water hovered at waist height, tumbling a bit at the top from the force of Gabriel's magic, but otherwise glassy clear. The sun had risen higher, burning through and banishing the misty rain, and daylight streamed through a long row of open arches on either side of the room. The arcade sloped down at a decidedly disastrous angle, but the hall retained a bit of its once-elegant grandeur. The ceiling above rose high with flying buttresses, lovingly detailed with architectural flourishes popular centuries before.

And where the sunlight streamed through the water held back by the invisible wall of magic, fish swam within, brightly gold and cobalt blue. A water snake swam past, rippling with effortless ease. "Amazing," she whispered, at a loss for anything wittier.

"It *has* sunk more than it was before I messed with it," Gabriel said, studying the slant with a frown. "I was hoping they were exaggerating, but apparently not. I don't know if this wing is worth saving."

"I can see why you started here," she replied, aware of the reverence in her tone. "This is a gorgeous arcade. I know of nothing like it still in existence."

Gabriel smiled down at her, a rare, fully delighted expression, nothing brooding in it. "I'm glad you agree." His gaze lifted to roam over the soaring ceiling, the graceful arches that miraculously retained their integrity despite long immersion and neglect.

"Why hasn't all this wood rotted long ago?"

"You know those trees with the big hand-shaped leaves?"

She nodded. They'd passed forests of them, and she'd wondered if they were fruit-bearing trees out of season.

"Tectona trees. The wood is nearly impervious to wet. Most of the house is constructed from it, which is the only reason it's lasted so long. This arcade leads—once led—to a four-story wing of bedrooms. There's another wing, but if there's a way to raise this one…" He trailed off dubiously.

"Then we'll have rooms to offer our guest wizards and your future minions," she filled in firmly. "It's a good plan. How did you raise it before?"

"I wicked water out of the soil beneath, trying to make it firm enough to support the foundation. But I think the slant is too great for that now. And I hadn't at all figured out what to do about the parts that are sunk to the gables."

She nodded, considering. Though he had barely tapped her magic reserves—so far as she could determine without more practice—she felt like she had slightly less magic than before. What she had wouldn't be enough, not without the focusing power of the arcanium, but Gabriel would have to learn that for himself. "The arcade is still connected to the sunken wing beyond?"

"Not anymore. We went in and sawed the two sections apart after my first, quite spectacular failure." He winced. "I had a splitting headache for three days afterward."

Hmm. So Gabriel had learned about the consequences of magic depletion but was still heedless of them. She wasn't sure how to teach him better. "I have a suggestion."

"Please," he replied fervently.

"Remember the barge? Try floating the house up."

"A house isn't a barge," he argued, knitting his brow.

"To water, they are the same thing."

"Water doesn't think."

"No, but you do. Approach this from the other direction. Your magic affects water, not the house. Look at you holding this water back like it's behind a pane of glass." With some irritation, she realized he could be doing that in the library with a low-level spell, no boarding of the windows necessary. They could have kept rain out of the entire manse with fixed enchantments in the windows and saved a fortune in Byssan glass. Maybe they still could if no Byssan wizard applied for the contract. No sense squandering magic if they could outsource to someone who'd also become a loyal minion. "Try moving this water out of the arcade and push it underneath the foundation. Float it like a boat."

"But we're standing on it."

She shook her head. "That doesn't matter. We stood on the barge, too. The water will do what you tell it to do." Circumspectly, she used her free hand to push closed the door to the attached salon. No sense flooding that too, should things go awry.

Gabriel, brow furrowed unhappily, muttered something about easier said than done, but the wall of green water moved away, flowing out through the open arches.

And more water flowed in to replace it. Cursing under his breath, Gabriel drew on her magic more, increasing the speed of the water flowing out—which resulted in water rushing back in at a greater rate. Waves began to form as the ripples fed back on each other, the water growing turbulent, fish swimming frantically through the peaks and troughs. The water snake flew out to land on what had once been an ornamental rug, now festooned with algae, and slithered away rapidly.

With a whoosh of breath, Gabriel abruptly released his hold on her magic, the sudden snap of the connection slapping back at her. His control of the water simultaneously broke. With a roar, all the displaced water rushed back, taking them under and yanking her hand from Gabriel's. She rolled, inadvertently gasping at the shockingly cold water, which most unpleasantly filled her mouth and nose with something that tasted a lot like spoiled lettuce. Her velvet gown dragged her down with its sodden weight, and she shoved against the slimy rug—*eyew*—to struggle up again.

Grasping hands seized her, dragging her up by the shoulders, Gabriel's face panicked. "Nic! Are you all right? Breathe. Talk to me." He shook her a little, and she grabbed ahold of his forearms.

"Stop. I'm fine." She spat water out. Disgusting.

He hauled her against him, embracing her a bit too tightly for comfort. "I was afraid you'd drowned."

"In waist-deep water in less than a minute? I surely hope not. How ignominious a death *that* would be."

"I'm so sorry," he said raggedly, still clutching her tightly. "I failed you. I lost control."

"Yes." Gently, but firmly, she extracted herself. "About that."

"Right. It didn't work." He glumly took in the lake of marsh water filling the room, still sloshing against the walls from the magical tempest. "There's too much water. We should just abandon the house."

She thumped him hard on the chest.

"Ow." Rubbing the spot, he gazed back at her like a wounded puppy.

"Pull yourself together," she snapped. "All that happened is you learned how *not* to do it. Now we try again."

"Again?" He looked aghast, then shook his head. "No. I'm not risking your well-being. You're soaked and shivering."

"And covered with stinking algae crap that I don't want to know what it is," she agreed, plucking something brown and vile from her hair and throwing it far away from her. "But we're both already slimed, so we might as well continue."

"I can't believe you want to try again."

"I can't believe you want to quit after a single failure," she retorted. "Also, if you were so concerned about me, once we were separated, you could've used your reserves to pull the water away from me so I didn't drown."

"I didn't think of that," he admitted with chagrin.

"Start thinking, then," she replied equably. "That's why we practice, to discover our weaknesses and plan around them so if we're in an emergency situation—like a battle against another wizard—we have strategies."

He regarded her with some bemusement. "You weren't exaggerating when you said you're a practical person. I don't think most people would be so sanguine about what just happened."

She shrugged. "Magic goes awry, and we're trying new things. Also, I plan to soak in a long, hot bath after this, as a reward. Now let's talk about what went wrong."

~ 8 ~

"WHAT WENT WRONG is there's simply too much water," Gabriel explained, feeling more than a little churlish. When his control snapped and Nic vanished underwater, the panic had nearly overwhelmed him. Maybe he'd overreacted, but he'd never forgive himself if something happened to her. As it was, she looked like a bedraggled water pixie, the velvet riding habit dripping with algae and swirling in burgundy billows around her, her dark hair plastered against her skull so she seemed be all huge green eyes and temptingly lush lips. He wanted nothing more than to kiss her, to find a way to overcome this tense distance between them.

Distance he'd created through his own blundering.

"You are thinking backwards." She raised one dark brow at his confusion. "You dealt with an ocean when you kept the barge off the rocks in Wartson. This is much less water."

With effort, he dragged his attention to the subject of magic. He was heartily regretting that he hadn't sunk the benighted house long before Nic laid eyes upon it. She wasn't one to relinquish a challenge. "I take your point," he said, attempting to set emotion aside and be logical, "but with the barge you advised me to move the water around the barge itself, not to wrestle the entire ocean. This is a different situation. No matter how fast I moved the water, more flowed in to replace it."

"I noticed," she replied. "And the faster you moved it, the more turbulence you created, making waves like a storm would."

"Exactly." He should feel more triumphant that she understood his point, but she only regarded him blandly.

"So, the solution is…" she prompted.

He scrubbed his hands over his face wearily. The stables had not been comfortable, especially with Vale hogging his stall, displeased at being forced to share. "I don't know, Nic. I suspect the solution is to sink the whole house in a bog and go find somewhere dry to live."

"Wouldn't it be a fen, since it would still be fed by the river nearby?" she asked with an arch look. Then she patted his arm, somewhat awkward with it. "Don't be discouraged. I'm probably a terrible teacher."

"Or I'm a terrible student," he grumbled.

"A perfect match, then." She gave him a rueful smile. "My point is that you were trying to move all the marsh water. Try simply adding to the water beneath this room. As it rises, the water in here will flow out, yes?"

"Right. Why didn't I think of that?"

"You're heavy-handed. Comes of having massive amounts of power. Speaking of which, what happened when you lost control?"

"Hmm. Let me think. Oh! I lost control."

"Ha ha. *Why* did you lose control?"

"Because I'm a shitty wizard," he hazarded.

She didn't laugh, however, instead giving him a fuming glare. "Gabriel Phel. I never once said you were a shitty wizard."

"You called me a lost cause."

"Exactly the opposite. I said you were *not* a lost cause. Now stop sulking and take a step back. What caused you to lose control?"

"It felt like it was all getting away from me," he said with a sigh. "Like a runaway horse."

"All right, then." She beamed at him. "One key approach to managing magic—especially powerful magic like yours and mine—is facing your fears honestly. Fear is the enemy."

He could absolutely see the truth of that—both from what had just happened and from his nonmagical experience fighting off the scavengers that plagued Meresin. "Your magic is a lot to manage." Not something he'd wanted to admit, but that had been the biggest problem.

Not drawing on his own magic and using so much of hers instead had been like gulping red wine, delicious, potent, and going straight to his head. Nic's fire had burned through him, seeming to turn his water magic to steam, making the moon magic reflect brilliantly, even though he hadn't even been trying to use the latter. He braced for Nic's scathing reply, and she did seem to have something to say to that. But she didn't immediately spit it out, instead chewing on her bottom lip, hesitating as she so rarely did.

She'd been walking on eggshells around him since last night. Not that he blamed her, but he was kicking himself for losing all the ground he'd gained with her. He'd managed to establish some trust between them, and he'd dashed it away along with the dishes he'd broken. "Just tell me," he urged. "I can take it."

"You won't like what I have to say," she warned him.

"Then that's my problem." He took her hands. They were cold, a shiver running through her. "We need to get you out of this chilly water."

"Or you could warm it up," she replied pointedly. "At least the water in our clothes, yes?"

"Yes." Using his own magic, he did so, pleased to feel her shivering relax somewhat. "I feel like you've been cold and wet since you met me," he observed.

"It must be more than mere coincidence," she agreed wryly. "The perils of living in a swamp with a water wizard."

The laugh was welcome, loosening his tension. "Tell me."

She shook her head slowly, holding his gaze. "I know you don't like to hear it, but when I tell you that there are good reasons the Convocation teaches wizards to control their familiars, this is one of them. This is a challenge for you more so than for most wizards because you're not as experienced, you don't have rote lessons to fall back on when things fall apart, and because you just *had* to acquire the most powerful familiar you could." She gave him a cheeky smile, but her heart wasn't in it. "Gabriel, in order to use my magic, you have to be able to control it. Otherwise it's as if you've called for rain to water your crops and accidentally ended up with a deluge that washes away all your topsoil."

Never forget that she listened closely to everything he told her. "An excellent farming analogy, if borrowed."

"I'm a good mimic." She continued to regard him seriously, and he knew what she wasn't saying, that it all came back to the cursed arcanium and silver chains. To possessing and controlling her in the way she claimed she wanted, but that terrified him to his bones. Not because he didn't want it, but because he wanted it *too* much. There had to be another way that wouldn't lead him down such a dangerously corrupting path.

"I can understand that I need to control the magic," he said slowly, "but I don't believe that means I must control *you*."

She rolled her eyes. "Fine, then generations of wizards and centuries of study and experimentation are all wrong."

"Finally, I'm getting through to you," he said with a broad smile, and she laughed, albeit with an exasperated shake of her head. It was getting somewhere that he could make her laugh, like coaxing the sun from the clouds. "Can we have this conversation not standing waist deep in cold marsh water?"

"I feel I should point out it's only thigh deep on your ridiculously big body, and we can, yes—*after* you try again."

He groaned at the prospect.

She squeezed his hands, held on to one, and swept the other at the water-filled room. "Get back on that horse, young wizard!"

"I think that's a mixed metaphor."

"Sorry, I don't know any swamp metaphors." At least her eyes danced with humor again, and she was comfortable enough with him to tease. And badger.

Feeling like a youth approaching whiskey again after his

first lethal hangover, he sipped lightly of her magic—and was rewarded with a sardonic sidelong glare.

"The longer you dillydally," she said, "the longer I'm standing waist deep in this nasty water, bracing for one of those water snakes to bite me."

"They're not venomous," he assured her.

"Oh, I feel so much better," she deadpanned. "Now, really draw on my magic. You're so certain you can control it your own way, then do it. Show me these amazing, never-before-seen skills."

With grim determination—and her sarcasm as a goad—he opened himself to the wine-red, rose-red, bloodred torrent of her magic, at least prepared this time for the overwhelming and intoxicating burn of it. As before, she stood quietly beside him, allowing him the silence to concentrate, providing a steadying presence along with her generously potent magic. He'd wanted this, a partner to teach and support him, long before he'd realized the shadow side of his idealistic expectations. He *would* find a way to make this work. He could do this. With the potency of Nic's magic, all he needed to do was apply the skills.

Ignoring the water in the room, he reached for the water outside. The marsh, fed by the river, wanted to reclaim this land. The land wanted to be marsh. Instead of fighting that, he opened the channels for the water to flow into. Water was a force of nature that way. It wanted to flow in, to settle, to slowly carve basins and canyons, to edge out the temporary habitations of the parasitic people on the land and wash them away. Nic had reminded him, perhaps without intending to, that it was always much easier to work *with* water than against it.

So, he went with the flow of the water, giving it the space beneath the arcade, coaxing it to flow in, to take, to have. Nic's sultry invitation echoed in his mind with all its erotic and seductive power, her magic following after, obedient to his command. The rose-infused heated wine of her flowed with the water, all submitting to his will.

The floor moved beneath his feet, surprising him.

"Steady," Nic murmured. "You're doing it. Keep your sea legs and go with the motion. Remember the barge."

Right, the barge. That had been hugely more challenging, the sea raging to dash them upon the rocks, and Nic's magic far less familiar to him then, much less a part of him. How accustomed he'd become to taking from her in such a short space of time.

The predator desires the prey—he can't have any mercy in his heart for it.

It's in a wizard's nature…

The floor shuddered, tilting dangerously, water sloshing around them, startling him.

"Concentrate!" Nic bit out.

"I'm trying," he said between clenched teeth.

"Don't try. *Do.*" Her voice and grip on his hand were remorseless.

No mercy. Devouring her magic, he wrestled the water into submission, making it obey his will, flowing into place beneath the arcade. Dimly, he was aware of the water around them draining away, just as Nic had predicted. Misty sunlight poured in the arches, marching elegantly down either side of the room as they elevated above the water level, plant matter dripping where it hung on ornamental spurs and flourishes.

"Well done, wizard," Nic murmured. "Now stabilize it."

"How?" he whispered, as if speaking too loudly might disturb the delicate balance he'd found. Though the arcade was anchored against the receiving salon wall, the free end where it had once been attached to the north wing allowed the room to bob unnervingly. Because it wasn't a barge and not meant to float. What he was doing wasn't possible.

The room lurched precipitously, dropping through the water like a rock plunging into a still pond. The struts holding the arcade to the core of the house shrieked, popping and rupturing with huge groans. Nic screamed too, swept up by the wave that poured in the arches, her hand ripped from his, her intoxicating torrent of magic abruptly wrenched away.

As if taking revenge, the water caught at him, obstructing his efforts to reach Nic as the cursed waterlogged gown dragged her under, her dark, sleek head disappearing into the depths consuming the hall as it skewed slightly, unanchored, and began sinking as graciously as it had once stood. The whole thing was going under, muddy, algae-green water swirling up to his chest.

Nic was nowhere in sight.

Taking a breath, he dove under the water, swimming through the muck to reach where she struggled against the weight of the velvet gown. He seized her around the waist and struck out for one of the arches. He was a strong swimmer, if nothing else. Belatedly remembering her lecture about using his own magic if he lost the thread of hers, he tried moving the water around them to assist—and discovered he'd drained his own water magic without realizing it. Unable to think of an application for moon magic in the current situation, he determinedly kept swimming. Much as Nic disdained the "manual" method for accomplishing tasks, sometimes muscle did what magic could not. Case in point.

Reaching the reedy edge of what had once been a formal garden, he hauled Nic onto a rise of lawn more mud than grass. She flopped onto her back, pale and drawn, so boneless he thought she might be unconscious. Then her eyes popped open, glaring at the sky with dark-green exasperation. Rolling her head, she transferred the glare to him. "Let me guess. When you went to stabilize the arcade's position, you started *thinking* about how houses don't float."

Glancing over his shoulder, he watched as the pitched roof of the arcade vanished underwater, not even a gable to be seen. Feeling all resolve drain away, not unlike the sinking foundation of the entire manse, he flopped onto his back beside her. "Pretty much," he admitted. "But you have to recognize," he added, not caring if he sounded defensive, "that arcade *wasn't* built to float. I could use magic to shift the water to temporarily lift it, but it's impossible to keep it that way. It's always going to eventually sink."

"Oh, really?" she breathed, managing to sound like a breathless, silly female—something he'd never once heard from her before. Leveraging herself up, she pushed back the muddied, wet tendrils that flopped over her forehead, then pressed a hand to her breast as if her heart was fluttering.

Widening her eyes and batting her water-beaded lashes, she positively simpered at him. "That's so *interesting*, Gabriel. I had no idea! Truly, tis a wonder magic works at all. Maybe it doesn't, and we just imagine things like carriages that move by themselves and couriers that can appear and disappear in an instant."

He glared at her, not even remotely amused to bear the brunt of her sharp wit in that moment. "You're not funny."

Dropping all pretense, she sobered. "Maybe you can tell me what *will* get through your thick skull." She tapped him smartly between the brows. "Your thoughts shape the magic. Nothing more, nothing less. The moment you decide something is impossible, it becomes exactly that."

He looked away from her fierce visage, her sensual beauty striking, even bedraggled and mud-spattered. "The laws of physics don't just vanish because it would be convenient," he ground out. Exhausted, he contemplated simply lying on this muddy bank until he decomposed and became part of it.

"Which laws of physics are those?" she persisted, taking his jaw in her small hand and making him meet her gaze. Unlike his, Nic's determination never flagged; she seemed to possess an infinite capacity to soldier on. She put him to shame, which didn't help him scrape up more resolve. "The ones that say you can't turn moonlight into silver? Tell me, Gabriel—what happens to that silver like you left scattered across the floor of the dining hall?"

"I scrape up what I can and sell it," he admitted. "It's very thin, almost a foil, so it isn't hugely valuable, but it's something."

"Does it turn back to moonlight?"

He frowned. "Not that I've seen."

"So why can't you make flotation permanent too?"

Lifting his hand, he rubbed his forehead, then pushed himself up. Studying the submerged arcade, he tried to make her suggestion seem logical. He couldn't, because it made no sense. "I just don't believe that's possible."

"And that is why you fail." With a heavy sigh, she stood, the sodden velvet hanging heavy on her petite frame. "What do I have to do to get a hot bath around here?"

Something else he'd forgotten to arrange for her. "I'll handle it."

"With all due respect and gratitude, Gabriel, I'd really prefer if you'd teach me to fish. Being able to arrange for my own hot bath would be a welcome level of autonomy."

"Of course." By dint of sheer willpower, he managed to lever himself to his feet, showing her the relatively dry path that would lead them around to the back entrance of the house. He was so tired, his steps were clumsy, his waterlogged boots occasionally tripping on nothing. Nic eyed him, sharply observant.

"Drained your water magic entirely, didn't you?" she asked. When he reluctantly nodded, she tipped her own chin in solidarity. "I'm about empty, too. We really have to work on your control."

"Nic…" He grimaced ruefully at her raised brow. "Could we give discussion of everything I need to learn a brief rest—like for the next hour, perhaps?"

Laughing softly, not without sympathy, she looped her

arm through his, a measure of her natural fire warming him at the contact. "Yes, we can. I apologize. I *do* remember what it's like."

"You do?" he asked, with some surprise, opening the back hall door for her.

"Of course." She shook her head, gaze focused on some memory. "At Convocation Academy, we drilled in all kinds of exercises designed to build discipline and control. All day long, day after day. I started when I was five years old—and we're trying to cram years of training into hours. You're so powerfully talented and ingenious that I forget you never learned the basics." She let out a rueful breath. "And I'm an impatient teacher. You could do far better than learning from me."

Putting his hand over hers on his arm—she was way too cold, having lost the warmth of his spell when his magic failed—he caressed it and smiled at her. "I know I'm a hardheaded student. I may get grumpy, but it's probably good that you're fierce with me."

"*Now* you say so." She smiled warmly.

"Yes," he agreed. "Now that I don't have to be worried that you'll make me wade back into that sunken arcade and lift it again."

She tilted her head thoughtfully, lush mouth pursed as she considered something. "We need to make this fun for you," she decided. "If you're miserable and feeling pressured, that only constricts the flow of magic."

"Most wizards don't look like they're having fun," he noted sourly.

"Because they love the power. They get all their pleasure

from the rush of that, whereas *you*, my ethically tortured wizard, are much too worried about the consequences of power to enjoy it."

She had a point. He was about to reply—probably with something she'd call self-excoriating philosophizing—when he caught the unpleasantly familiar feel of something…

"Hunters!" he yelled, spinning and thrusting Nic behind him. He wasn't wearing his sword, but he'd been practicing for a crisis just like this. Beyond fortuitous that he hadn't thought of a way to use his moon magic. Extruding a silver sword from his own magic, he faced the hunter slinking toward them. A creature of House Tadkiel's ruthless justice and House Ariel's animal-mutating magic, the thing was nothing out of nature. Like an amalgam of a jackal and a weasel in vaguely human shape, it moved with an arching glide, lifting its long snout in the air to sniff in Nic's direction, tilting its head sideways to fasten one eye on them.

"Lady Veronica Phel," it crooned. "You will come quietly."

Behind him, Nic made an incoherent choking sound.

"Lady Phel is going nowhere," Gabriel growled, levering the point of the sword toward the creature's eye. "Go back to your masters and tell them Lady Phel is mine now. She's where she belongs."

"Lord Phel." The hunter dipped its snout, jaws parting to reveal rows of teeth. "You may appeal to the Convocation to have thiss familiar returned to you, eventually, in accordansse with the law. But sshe will be taken into cusstody now. Sstand asside."

"Never. Begone or I will kill you."

The jaw dropped open further, giving the gruesome implication of a grin. "You did not ssucceed sso far, wissard."

With a sinking sense of horror, Gabriel realized this must be the hunter from the barge. He'd blasted a hole the size of a watermelon in the thing's chest, then washed it overboard where it should have drowned. Nic growled in frustration, and he knew she'd realized the same thing. Somehow the thing hadn't died, and instead swam ashore and tracked them here.

The hunter snapped its jaws closed, hissing threats through its fangs. "I cannot be killed. I warned you previoussly that you have made a grave misstake interfering with uss and there would be conssequenssess if you persisted, Lord Phel." A shiver of magic sifted over Gabriel, one he recognized from before. One that had frozen him immobile, rendering him helpless. And prompting Nic to thoroughly lecture him on being such a shitty wizard that he let a canned spell overpower him. *Not this time.* Using the purifying force of his moon magic, he shattered the spell before it could bind him. Huh. Surprisingly simple. No wonder Nic had been contemptuous of him for being caught by it previously.

The hunter sniffed, and its slimy gaze slid past him to Nic. "Learned some tricksss, have we, wissard? Nissse, but you interfere with the Convocation at your peril."

"Blah blah blah," Gabriel growled, keeping himself—and his sword—between the hunter and Nic as it tried to sidle around. "If I slice you into enough pieces, it's the same as death."

"Are you sssure?" The hunter snarled. And Nic screamed.

Gabriel whirled reflexively, cursing at the sight of two

more hunters bearing Nic to the ground. She thrashed and fought, but their unnatural strength was more than she could resist. Mastering himself—because he knew they wanted her intact, along with the child she carried, and so wouldn't hurt her—he turned back to the lead hunter just as it launched itself at him, fanged jaws snapping, curved talons slicing for him.

Fortunately, Gabriel might have shitty wizard reflexes, but he knew how to wield a sword. Better, his muscles knew, moving instinctively from all those years of practice when he thought he'd be only a farmer lad defending his land against the raiders and scavengers. His blade snicked through the hunter, cleaving off one hairy arm at the elbow. The hunter shrieked but kept coming at him, raking at Gabriel's midsection in a taloned swipe that could have disemboweled him if he hadn't jerked himself back in time. The upside was the hunter overreached and Gabriel sidestepped, bringing the sword down in an execution-style, two-handed blow—neatly decapitating the thing.

"Let's see how you do without a head," Gabriel snarled, turning to help Nic.

"You cannot evade the Convocation, wissard," the head answered. "Give up the familiar now and ssave yoursself the devasstashion that awaits you."

Gabriel considered stopping down on those jaws to shut the thing up, but the other two hunters had Nic pinned to the ground, one sitting on her as it tried to wrest a new iron collar around her neck. Without pausing, Gabriel simply beheaded both, sending those heads flying. To his supreme annoyance, the bodies continued their task as if nothing had changed.

Nic's eyes widened in alarm. "Behind you!"

Gabriel grunted, staggering as a weight hit him from behind. The headless body of the lead hunter gripped him, claws scrabbling for purchase on his waterlogged clothes as the head laughed at him, the hyena aspect of the creature coming out in shrilling cackles. Reaching over his head with his free hand, Gabriel grasped a black-blood-soaked hairy shoulder and snapped the bones in his grip. Dragging the beast off him, he methodically chopped off the arms and legs, then yanked one hunter off Nic, then the other, butchering them both.

He and Nic stared at each other a moment, her eyes bright green with emotion, both of them panting. Holding a hand down to her, he asked, "Are you all right?"

"Yes." She paused, then nodded, taking his hand and climbing to her feet, picking her way over the grasping limbs and twitching bodies. "That was a bit startling."

Gabriel stared at her a moment longer, then choked out a hoarse laugh. "I'll say."

"You interfere with the Convocation at your peril, wissard!" the lead hunter shrieked.

He gave in to the savage impulse and kicked the yipping head, sending it sailing through the air to plop into the marsh. Nic watched it for a moment, then turned back to him, brows raised. "You might regret that."

"I wanted to shut it up."

"Indeed you did. But what happens when the head grows a new body and these limbs grow more hunters?" She nudged the limb crawling toward her by dint of digging talons into the muddy ground and dragging the rest behind it.

"Is that what happened? Because I could swear we used the enchanted dagger to melt all but the one that washed overboard."

Nic shrugged. "Probably? Regardless, we need to figure out a way to destroy these completely."

"I'll do that."

"How? No more enchanted dagger to turn them to ooze."

"If nothing else, I'll lock them into something until I figure it out. You go have your bath."

She wrinkled her nose at her blood-spattered self. "And I thought I wanted one before this. Are you hurt?"

He moved his shoulders, testing. "Some stitches might've split, but I'm otherwise all right."

"Hopefully Refoel will show tomorrow and we can get you completely healed."

"You too," he replied, gaze going to her bruised throat and the fresh scratches there.

"I'll be fine. Clean would be nice. Food, as well. I feel I should point out that you have yet to show me how to acquire either."

"Let's do that, then I'll come back and deal with the garbage."

She smiled at that, genuinely amused. "Deal."

Opening the back service door, he gestured her inside. At one time, it had been a kitchen of sorts, meant for assembling meals, even if much of the actual cooking had been conducted some distance away. At present, like most of the house, it was sadly empty, used mainly for staging food brought in. He showed her the flags that could be raised by a pulley system.

"You pick the flag for what you need—food, bath, service, etcetera—attach it to the line and raise it. Someone will see."

"Ah." She eyed it dubiously. "I'm kind of sorry I asked."

"I did warn you that I wouldn't be able to house you in the style you were accustomed to," he said, trying his best not to sound defensive still, and failing at that, too. It rankled that those hunters had gotten the drop on him.

"You're a morose bastard sometimes, aren't you?" She rolled her eyes at him. "I'm not unwilling to deal with the manual method of bath acquisition, but I'm guessing by the time someone sees my pitiful plea by flag, heats, and brings enough water, it's going to be an hour from now."

"Probably longer," he admitted. "It's better to set a schedule for them to simply plan ahead to have a bath ready for you."

"Which doesn't work in cases like this when I'm filthy, sopping wet, and chilled to the bone—and covered in stinking hunter blood." With a determined stride, she headed toward the stairs to the second level. "This is why magic has it all over the manual method, and I'm fortunately bonded to a water wizard. Clever planning on my part, I say."

He followed after her, bemused and mystified. "I warned you that I'm tapped out, and you said you are, too." Thanks to the hunters, he'd nearly depleted his moon magic, too.

She cast him a brilliant smile over her shoulder. "I would explain, but you asked me not to discuss it."

He groaned. "Please tell me you're not planning to teach me something else." Even if he hadn't already been exhausted, the aftermath of the pitched fight left him feeling drained.

"All right, I won't tell you." The moment she stepped into the master suite, she reached behind her neck and triggered the fastening on the Ophiel riding habit, the fabric parting and plopping to her feet in a sodden heap, a trickle of water running from it to a groove in the floorboards. She gave it a disgusted look. "I should've run up the flag for laundry. Oh well, not like it's going anywhere."

Gracefully, she stepped out of the pile of mud-soaked velvet and posed with one hand on her hip. She wore only her knee-high black leather boots and the Ophiel lingerie he'd bought for her. Her long, sculpted thighs rose from the boots like flower stems supporting the blossom of her scantily clad form. The ivory lace lingerie clung to her smooth golden skin as if it had been painted on, the magical fit emphasizing her voluptuous curves, the openings in the lace revealing as much as they concealed. Her dusky nipples showed dark and taut through the camisole, the panties hugging a high arc on her hips, flowing to a point at the vee of her sex, the hair beneath glossy and enticing.

Against all probability, his exhausted and depressed self came to attention with alert interest. Still, he was wary of her agenda. "Nic, what is this about?"

"I don't think you've seen the lovely underwear you bought for me," Nic answered with sensual mischief. "At least, not *on* my body. What do you think?"

Giving him a sultry smile, she lifted her hands into an elegant interweaving above her head, swaying her hips as if in a dance, and turning slowly, showing off the slender line of her waist and lower back, the flare of her hips tapering again into her perfectly rounded bottom. The ivory lace threaded into the cleft of her ass, parting the delicious globes, then disappeared enticingly into the valley between her thighs. Looking at him over her shoulder, she wiggled her bottom—as if he'd perhaps failed to notice it—then she bent over, spreading her legs just enough to show him the shape of her lace-clad mound, her swollen sex barely veiled.

"Do you like it?" she purred, yanking his attention back to her face and her wickedly sparkling eyes.

"Yes," he managed, then had to clear his throat. "Very much. It looks lovely on you."

Like a dancer, she straightened and turned, flicking a long finger against a spot on the camisole so that it fell away, leaving her full breasts naked. Cupping those breasts so they spilled over her hands, she flicked her fingers over her nipples, making them even harder. She moaned a little as she undulated. "Maybe it looks better off?" she asked with raised brows.

"Ah..." He wasn't sure of the answer—or exactly what game this was.

"I know I'm filthy," she murmured with a sexy pout, "but so are you, and you're awfully far away."

"Nic, what are you doing?" But he couldn't stay away. As if of their own accord, his feet dragged him to her, his gaze rapt on the way she toyed with her breasts, so tantalizingly full above her narrow waist. Part of him—the plain farmer boy, no doubt—wanted to be scandalized, but the rest of him rose to the challenge of her provocative behavior, raging to touch, take, and ravage.

She cupped her breasts, lifting them like an offering.

"Please touch me," she breathed.

Realizing he still gripped his sword, as he had no sheath to stow it in, he set it aside, then lifted his hands. "Are you sure?"

"Yes. I'm going to wash soon anyway."

He brushed her hands away, replacing them with his, filling his hands with her full breasts, their soft weight delightfully overflowing his grip, her hard nipples pressing into the hollow of his palms. In a spasm of overwhelming need, he squeezed, desire hitting him hard when she sagged, mouth falling open with a gasp as she writhed against him.

"Mmm." She put her hands behind her neck, arching her back to press more fully into his hands, tipping up her mouth, yet another offering. "Yesss. More."

Unable to resist her blatant invitation, he lowered his mouth to hers, drinking in the heated sweetness of her generous lips, the scent of roses and red wine swirling into his senses. The taste of her settled him, reminding himself on a visceral level that she was all right. Still alive and healthy. Still his. The possessiveness roared up in him, and he slanted his mouth over hers, plundering, her groan scraping through him in answering need.

She twined her fingers into his hair, inclining her nearly naked body against his. Parting her legs, she slipped one slim thigh between his, nudging his aching balls and rolling her hip against his groin, raising herself to straddle his thigh. Deepening the kiss, he released one breast to press a hand against her lower back, pushing his thigh against her sex and lifting her onto tiptoes until she rode him with most of her weight.

She groaned, squirming against him, her sex scorching

through the soaked leather of his pants. "Gabriel," she panted against his lips, "is my bath ready?"

Lifting his head, he frowned at her. "What?"

Like a cat who'd devoured fresh cream, she smiled at him, practically licking her lips. "Be a love and fill the tub with hot water for me. Use my magic if you need to."

"But I—you…" He trailed off in realization, aware that his water magic had begun to replenish itself, and that the rose-red, wine-dark richness of her magic swirled under her skin, waiting to be consumed by his insatiable hunger.

"But you have enough magic again, and so do I." Though he'd stopped kissing her, she still clung closely to him, her heated body soft as she rode his thigh, her eyes half lidded.

Firmly setting her away from him, he rubbed his hands together, abruptly aware again of how filthy they both were. "That was all a pretense?"

Nic propped her fists on her hips, leveling a molten glare on him. "No. Idiot wizard. Give me your hand." She held out hers in demand, holding his gaze with such obstinate determination that he didn't try to argue, laying his hand in hers. She grasped it, stepped up close—and pushed his hand inside the ivory silk panties, his fingers skidding through her slick and scorching sex.

He caught his breath at the feel of her, at the rush of rich magic that flooded him.

"It's very real," she breathed, moving herself against his hand, moaning when he caressed her.

"My hand is dirty," he said, then cursed himself for sounding like the idiot she named him. His brain moved sluggishly, his body full of need for her, seduced and enthralled by her.

She didn't laugh, her sensuous mouth curving in a smile. "Fill the tub with hot water, wizard, and we'll get you cleaned up. Then we can explore just how real this is."

Entirely rapt in her sensual spell, he did as she suggested, willing hot water into the tub in the adjoining chamber, somehow unsurprised at how easy it was. "Your bath is ready," he told her, giving her a long, luscious kiss.

"Excellent. And that didn't take even a quarter of an hour." She extracted herself from his embrace, cocking her head with a grin. "Once you've dealt with the garbage, get naked and join me." With that, she bent over, giving him a breathtaking view as she released the leather boots, then sashayed happily into the bathing chamber, her croon of delight followed by splashing water.

~ 9 ~

THE BATHWATER WAS almost *too* hot, but Nic submerged herself anyway, beyond grateful for the sting of clean water in her myriad scrapes, the heat an anodyne to the scrapes, forming bruises, and persistent chill in her bones. She wanted to scrub herself clean of the hunters' foul touch. She hadn't been all that afraid. Gabriel was right there, and he'd defended her ably. The encounter hadn't been anything like last time. But it had been enough to make her shaky.

She also really didn't like that they'd both been so depleted of magic. They'd won, but the margin had been far too narrow.

Fully underwater, she scrubbed at her scalp with numb fingertips, grimacing at the scrape of grit in her hair interspersed with the occasional bit of unnamable slime. Some of it hunter blood. Ugh. With a sigh, she searched for something to wash her hair with, then realized she'd left her fancy Aratron soaps across the room. Reluctantly levering herself out of the tub, she padded naked and dripping across the bathing chamber, scooped it all up and—shivering in the chill, damp air—ran back to the tub, tossing the vials and bottles on the floor. About to hop back into the water, she caught a reflection in one of the age-spotted mirrors and screamed.

The other woman screamed, too, wrapping her arms around herself and looking about frantically, like a wild animal caught in a trap, her cries escalating in pitch and volume.

"Seliah!" Nic overcame the shock—still on edge from the hunter attack, she'd nearly peed on the floor from the fright—and managed to make her voice loud, calm, and commanding enough to pierce Seliah's ongoing wail of dismay. Gabriel's sister slammed her mouth shut, the sound cutting off abruptly, and she stared at Nic with feral eyes that held little human intelligence. "Seliah," Nic said again, soothingly, holding out her hands. "It's all right. You gave me a start is all."

Seliah stared at her with no hint of comprehension.

"Remember me?" Nic asked, doubting it heartily. "Lady Veronica Elal, Gabriel's… wife. You can call me Nic."

"I know," Seliah said, straightening from her crouch, sanity returning to her amber-brown eyes. They were the same color as their mother's, and Nic wondered if Gabriel's eyes had been that color before the magic turned them wizard black. Seliah tossed her head, looking Nic up and down. "I came here because I wanted to see you."

Nic gestured to her nakedness. "And now you've seen me, all of me."

Seliah, to Nic's great surprise, giggled. "You're—"

"Nic!" Gabriel roared, charging into the bathing chamber, sword drawn, barely skidding to a stop on the water-puddled tiles. Oops. Probably she should've tossed down some towels. "Selly!" Gabriel gasped in astonishment.

"She came to visit me," Nic told him, infusing her tone

with all the cautions she wanted to offer but felt she couldn't say aloud. "Isn't that sweet of her?"

Gabriel didn't look like he thought it was sweet. He looked too pissed for that. With his silver hair mud-matted, slicked and tangled around his face, his wizard-black eyes glittering with determination to protect her, muscles flexing with battle fervor, he appealed to her basest instincts. Though that could be the residual need from what they'd started and now wouldn't be finishing anytime soon. Alas for that. At least the delayed gratification was good for recharging the magic.

He lowered his sword, a resigned line to his shoulders. "Selly," Gabriel said, giving his sister a once-over. She wasn't any cleaner than they were, though she was better dressed for it. Her pants and shirt were stained with mud and other evidence of days spent in the marshes. "We've been looking for you."

Seliah set her jaw obstinately, very like her brother would. "I didn't want to be found."

Gabriel sighed, holding out his hands by his side. "I'm very glad you found us, then," he said gently. "Are you hungry?"

She jerked her chin in a nod, eyes drifting back to Nic.

"I'll just finish my bath," Nic suggested, cold enough to hop into the water without further hesitation. It warmed up a bit more, and she gave Gabriel a grateful smile. Ducking her head to wet it, she began working the shampoo through her hair.

"I sent up a flag for lunch," Gabriel said, gesturing Seliah out of the room. "Why don't we wait for the food out here, give Nic some privacy."

"Why is she here?" Seliah demanded, not budging. "I don't want her here, in my house."

Gabriel set his teeth. "It's our house, and it's Nic's now, too. I explained this to you."

Seliah slid Nic a look of distaste. The girl looked far younger than her twenty-four years, all long legs, knees, and elbows like an adolescent, her skin ravaged by acne, both active and old scars. Her childlike reactions only compounded the impression. She was all out of balance—physically, emotionally, and mentally. The Refoel healer should be able to assist there too.

Though a Refoel wizard would immediately recognize Seliah as an untapped familiar, and Gabriel wasn't prepared to deal with that. They needed to cement the wizard's loyalty first, and she didn't know how they'd accomplish that. It really depended on who answered the call, but House Phel wasn't exactly ready to lay out the charm. They didn't even have a dry room to offer. She'd really been hoping they could raise the entire house today and have the water wicked out of a few rooms, then at least minimally furnished by tomorrow.

Things weren't looking good for that, but at least she wasn't wearing an iron collar and being marched off by hunters. All things in perspective.

"I don't remember you explaining *anything!*" Seliah whined like an even younger child. Was the bouncing about in mental age a side effect of the untapped magic? It must be. Unless the woman had another underlying mental condition. Hadn't there been rumors of madness in House Phel? More so than the standard runaway hubris and megalomaniacal tendencies of most wizards. She and Maman had dismissed those sketchy details as unimportant, but now she wished she'd paid more attention.

"Selly." Gabriel took his sister's arm, not ungently, but black frustration oozed off of him. Taking note of Gabriel's fraying patience, Nic ran some conditioning oil through her hair, using it to detangle the last of the snarls.

"Let go of me!" Seliah shrieked, tugging away from her brother. "You *stink*."

"Gabriel," Nic inserted before he could say anything more. So much for her plans of soaking in the tub and perhaps cavorting with her wizard. Rinsing her hair one last time, she stood again, stepped out of the tub, and grabbed a towel, wrapping herself in it. At least she was clean now. "I'll keep Seliah company while you bathe." When he opened his mouth to argue, she laid a finger over his lips, then kissed him. "You need a moment, and you'll feel better for it. Did you say you ordered lunch?"

"I—yes." He frowned. "It's midafternoon, and you said you were hungry."

"I'm starving." She offered him a warm smile. "Thank you."

"For ordering lunch?"

"For your thoughtfulness." She hesitated. "We can finish what we started later."

With a wistful smile, he lifted a hand to touch her cheek, then curled his fingers and withdrew. "You're clean and I'm not," he noted ruefully.

"And I intend to stay that way. Take your time. Relax a

little. Let me get to know your sister." She kissed him again, lightly but hoping that her pleasure and relief conveyed themselves to him, then snagged her bag of cosmetics, including her comb and the bottled grooming imp. "Come on, Seliah, let's have lunch, and I'll tell you a story."

"What kind of story?" Seliah demanded petulantly, but she went with Nic, a glint of curiosity in her eye.

Nic pulled the bathing chamber door shut behind her. Gabriel, bless him, had lit a fire, and the room was already considerably warmer and drier. She went to the closet containing her meager wardrobe. Dropping the towel, she pulled on the cozily soft bronze robe—all praise for dry clothes—then grabbed up the towel to dry her short curls. Eyeing Seliah, who was exploring the room with an unsophisticated lack of propriety, Nic wondered if the young woman had seen much of what had happened before Nic got in the bathtub. Surely Gabriel would've sensed her presence. But then, somehow Seliah had gotten past him to get up to the master suite.

"Why did you kiss my brother?"

"Because he's my… husband," Nic replied. Calling him her wizard still felt more true to her, but here in Meresin they only seemed to think in terms of marriage. Though that would get confusing fast if they had a wedding. Maybe she should say betrothed? This was why it was easier to just acknowledge him as her wizard master, except that Gabriel took such exception to it. She went to sit by the fire, coming out her curls. "Why don't you sit with me?"

Seliah eyed her suspiciously but sat in the other chair,

perching on the edge. With her snarled dark hair, wary brown eyes, and too-thin body, Seliah reminded Nic of the sparrows flitting about the marshes, skittish and barely glimpsed before they hid themselves in the rushes.

"You know, we're sisters now," Nic said. "That means we can share special secrets."

"Like what?" Seliah asked, curiosity overcoming her wariness.

Nic held up the grooming imp's bottle and waggled it. "Magic," she whispered, and Seliah's eyes grew round.

"My brother is a wizard," the young woman confided.

"Yes, he is. A most powerful one."

"I wish he wasn't."

"Why's that?" Nic glanced at the bathing chamber door, confirming it remained firmly closed. Gabriel didn't need more reasons to regret who he was.

Seliah fidgeted unhappily. "He's always sad now, and he never was before."

Nic bit back a sigh for her brooding wizard. "He'll be happier now," she said firmly, willing it to be true. She might not be a wizard who could shape reality with her thoughts, but she had a powerful will of her own. She was going to make Gabriel happy if she had to drive them both crazy to do it. The absurd thought made her smile, so she widened it for Seliah's benefit. "Did you know we're going to have a baby?" she asked on impulse.

Seliah's gaze went to Nic's lap, then lifted with shrewd distrust. "That's what Mama said, but I saw you naked. You don't have a baby belly."

"It will get bigger," Nic assured her. Something she needed to remind herself of, too. It would be good to have that healer on site, to check that her adventures hadn't affected her unborn passenger. "And then you'll be an aunt! Shall we call you Aunt Selly?"

"All right," she breathed, face lighting. "Now tell me the story. You promised."

Indeed she had. Nic considered what seeds she wanted to plant in Seliah's mind. The young woman had no training in magic, no experience with it besides what she'd observed of her brother—and what she experienced internally due to its corrosive effect. Whether she was consciously aware of that effect or not, part of her would know.

"Once upon a time," Nic began, pleased when Seliah wriggled happily, settling back in the chair, "there was a beautiful princess. Her brother was king, ruling over all the lands anyone could see, and he was a kind and good king."

"Like Gabriel."

"Just like Gabriel," Nic agreed. "And the princess was kind and good, too, beloved by all. But she was unhappy, because all of her best qualities were trapped inside, where no one knew about them."

Seliah touched her fingers to her ravaged face, eyes welling with sympathetic tears. "Why were they trapped?" she asked.

"Because she was cursed," Nic explained gravely. "And when the princess tried to explain to everyone about the curse, no one understood her. Not even her brother. Though the princess spoke the words to tell them, what came out of her mouth wasn't what she planned to say. The curse twisted her meaning, making it into something else. After a while, nothing she said made any sense at all, and people thought she wasn't even trying to be understood. They became annoyed with her, telling her to speak clearly."

Seliah nodded mutely.

"Finally the princess stopped trying to explain anything. Instead she ran away to the forest. The birds and the animals there didn't need her to speak. They accepted her, and she made a life with them. But the curse didn't go away. It only worsened, until the princess found that sometimes she didn't even understand herself, as if her very thoughts had turned inside out, too."

"What happened to her?" Seliah breathed, leaning forward, intent gaze focused on Nic.

What answer to give her? Nic could see herself in this young woman, feel the silvery-cool magic in her, so like her brother's, but stagnant like the marsh water. "Her fairy godmother arrived to save her," she said. "The fairy taught the princess's brother how to break the spell. He did, and they lived happily ever after."

"Truly?" Seliah brightened with painful hope. "Do you think that—"

Knock-knock-knock. The crisp alert on the door made them both jump. Nic let out a huff of a laugh—but Seliah sprang to her feet and ran for the wall of glass doors leading to the balcony. A steady rain slid down the glass, and one door appeared to be slightly ajar, which explained Seliah's unobserved arrival.

"Wait," Nic called, springing to her feet. "It's only lunch!"

But Seliah had dashed out the doors and scrambled with impressive agility over the railing. Nic dashed after her, too slow to do anything but watch as the young woman leapt from handhold to foothold, reaching the back lawn and disappearing around the side of the house. With a groan, Nic tapped her forehead on the railing. Gabriel would not be happy with her.

"Was that Selly?" Gabriel's mother, Daisy, said behind her.

Nic turned reluctantly, then quickly relieved the older woman of the heavy tray she carried. "Yes," she replied with a wince. "She came to see if I was really going to have a baby. We decided she'd be Aunt Selly. Your knock startled her and she ran off, I'm sorry to say." Nic was babbling, but she felt absurdly guilty. Daisy didn't understand what was wrong with her odd daughter, and Nic couldn't explain it to her. Not in a way the barely magical woman from Meresin would understand. Maybe not ever.

Daisy stared toward the balcony and her vanished daughter with a look of disappointment and profound irritation. "I despair of that girl, truly I do. We haven't laid eyes on her since you arrived, Lady Veronica. Not that it's your fault! I don't mean to imply that at all." Daisy wrung her hands together. "Of course, we haven't laid eyes on *you* since you arrived!" She laughed uneasily, wincing. "Which is fine. We've barely seen Gabriel—just the once when he stopped by the levee—so I thought, well, I would bring your lunch myself!" She focused fully on Nic for the first time since entering the room, her eyes going wide. "Oh, your beautiful hair! What happened? You cut it all off."

Nic ran a hand over the cropped hair, glad it was at least

clean and somewhat orderly. What excuse to give? Daisy wouldn't understand about the bonding ceremony either. This living amongst the nonmagical led a person from one lie to another until you were caught in a sticky web of them. "An Elal custom," she said, which was close enough to the truth to give her answer a tone of confidence. "The bride and groom cut each other's hair to symbolically demonstrate leaving their old selves behind to make a new home together."

Daisy's face cleared of one worry, at least. "Ah, that makes a kind of sense. Gabriel telling me he got his caught on a branch sounded just too strange." Daisy considered her. "Why wouldn't he tell me the truth?"

Why indeed? Or why wasn't he a better liar? "I asked him not to," Nic said, freely embroidering on her own tale. "Until I could explain it to you myself." Speaking of too strange… but Daisy seemed to accept that, nodding absently.

"Where is Gabriel?" she asked.

"Taking a bath." Nic tipped her head at the closed bathing chamber door. Though what *was* taking him so long? "I think he might've fallen asleep," she added, hoping that would be in character. Given how much magic Gabriel had spent, the pitched fight with the hunters, along with a restless night fighting Vale for bed space, Nic wouldn't be at all surprised if he had. But Gabriel didn't strike her as a napper. Some people were and some weren't. How little she knew about him still.

Fortunately, Daisy smiled, beaming maternally at Nic's dishabille. "Too much honeymooning, yes? Though you two could go at it more easily." She patted Nic's belly with affectionate familiarity. "After all, the bun is already in the oven."

Yes, but the manse won't raise itself out of the swamp, Nic managed not to say aloud. Instead she smiled and nodded. An all-purpose reply that seemed to satisfy Daisy.

"Well, I'll leave you two to your special time." She turned to go, then paused at the door. "Could we have dinner all together sometime?" she asked wistfully. "Gabriel mentioned planning a wedding, so the family can attend?"

"Yes, of course," Nic agreed immediately. Anything to avoid another awkward dinner with Gabriel in that dining hall. "Tonight?"

Daisy clasped her hands together. "Oh, I would love that. I've made some lists."

Nic found herself smiling in genuine kinship. "I've got lists, too," she confided. "And about more than the wedding. I'd like to share with you some plans for the house renovation, and get your ideas."

"Oh." Daisy put a hand over her heart, going misty eyed, so clearly moved to be included that Nic kicked herself for not thinking of it before. "I would love to be involved."

"Bring your lists tonight," Nic told her warmly, then hesitated. "And probably the food? I feel like a terrible hostess—Maman would be cross with me—but..."

"It's not your fault, dear," Daisy said kindly. "House Phel is a mess, and I know it. How about this? You two come to our house. It's not much, but it's clean and dry, and I can promise the food will be hot. You can bring *your* lists to me."

"That sounds like a perfect solution." Nic only hoped Gabriel would think so, too. "See you this evening."

Daisy gave her a happy wave and slipped out, Nic putting the manual lock into place as silently as possible. She didn't want to offend Gabriel's family, but she'd also had enough of being surprised for one afternoon. Then she went to the bathing chamber and eased the door open, peeking in. Gabriel indeed slept in the tub, his head canted back, face utterly lax, his mouth having fallen open slightly in the lassitude of deep sleep.

He'd at least cleaned up before he passed out, his silver hair sleeked dark against his skull, tanned and muscled arms free of smudges where he'd draped them along the rim of the tub, his elegantly long fingers hanging loose. He looked nearly angelic like this. Not frowning or brooding darkly, not annoyed by or frustrated with her. Not bashing his head against the forces of his magical nature. Her idealist, forever thinking he could change the world. A rush of affection filled her, and she hesitated, wanting more than anything to brush her fingers over his unfurrowed brow, to lick the beads of water from that muscled chest.

She also wanted to keep him just like this, happily asleep and tormented by nothing. She should also probably wake him up, get him out of the cooling water and on to eating lunch. No doubt he was as hungry as she was. Though he also needed sleep.

She was dithering over the decision still when his eyes popped open, staring suspicious holes into the ceiling before he fastened his black gaze on her. "Where's Selly?" he demanded, and Nic sighed for the brief moment of peace, lost now.

Picking up a towel, she sauntered to him. "Your sister left

again. Shall I help you dry off?"

Gabriel frowned at her. At least he looked like his usual self now. That was something. "What do you mean she left—where did she go?"

"Wherever she goes, I imagine," Nic replied mildly. "Your mother was here. She delivered the lunch you sent up a flag for. We arranged for us to go to their house for dinner this evening."

Standing, he snatched the towel from her and tied it around his waist—not before she noted he was still at half-mast from her earlier teasing and looked to be waxing rather than waning—then he stepped out of the tub, taking one long stride to grab another towel from the stack. At least they had plenty of dry towels. Probably a necessity in eternally damp Meresin. It would be nice to put a tiny fire elemental in with them so they'd be warm. Small luxuries.

"What do you mean 'we'?" Gabriel asked, brisking drying himself. Nic didn't mind the show at all, so she reclined on a chaise in the corner. She'd wondered why the pretty antique had been put in the bathing chamber. In case one needed to take a break from grooming? But it served nicely as a soft spot from which to admire her wizard. His youthful collision with moon magic had turned all his body hair silver—except his brows, lashes, and the single lock at his temple—and the paleness of the hair did a lovely job of becoming invisible enough to show all of his skin while highlighting the sculpted lines of his warrior's body with a silvery shimmer.

"Nic?" Gabriel prompted, raising one dark brow.

"Hmm? Oh, 'we' being your mother and me. Don't be

grumpy about it."

"I'm not being grumpy about it," he retorted, quite grumpily indeed. "Why do we have to go to their house? It's a tiny cottage. Not at all what you're accustomed to."

"Honestly, Gabriel," she said on a sigh as she sat up, no longer enjoying the recline, "you make me sound like a snob. I'm interested to see more of Meresin, and it makes more sense for us to go to the hot food than for them to drag it here."

He grimaced. "I know that living in this wreck of a house is little better than being on the road."

"I didn't say that. And we're working on it."

"We're going backwards, if anything," he corrected. Then, before she could reply to that—though combatting his current black mood and defeatism wasn't something she enjoyed bashing her own skull against—he asked, "So, where did Selly go—or should I ask, how?"

"Over the balcony," Nic supplied blandly, figuring there was no reason to hide it from him. "She ran when your mother knocked. I'm pretty sure that's how she got in. She's impressively fast and agile."

"I wanted to talk with her," he grumbled.

"I know, and I tried to keep her here. Ultimately, there wasn't much I could do."

"It's not your fault. I apologize." He blew out a breath and raked his fingers through his hair. "I know I'm irritable and taking it out on you."

"You've had a lousy couple of days, so you're forgiven. Also, sexual frustration is likely a contributor," she pointed out with a sweet smile. "Want me to help with that?"

"I was thinking food," he replied with a half smile, but the tenting in his towel showed otherwise.

"The food is waiting, and this won't take long." She extended a hand to him. "Why don't you come over here?"

She thought he might refuse, but he came to her, taking her hand and then sitting beside her. Running a hand down her back, he kissed her, softly and tenderly. "I'm so sorry about the hunters."

"Why? You dispatched them. That's all that matters."

He grimaced at that. "And I'm sorry I'm being a bastard. Wallowing in self-loathing, then alternating between sullenness and sudden explosions of anger," he quoted her wryly.

"My intense and brooding wizard," she agreed, combing her fingers through his hair, then trailing them over his lovely shoulders. Coaxing him to lie back, she kissed her way down his throat, his skin warm, steaming soft from the bath, spicy from his soap. Working her way down his muscled chest, she tasted him, nibbling at his nipples so he groaned, his hands tightening on her. When she reached the towel, she untied it, feeling as if she unwrapped a special gift selected just for her. Laying the towel open, she unveiled his cock, thrusting from its silver frame of sleek hair to lie against Gabriel's flat abdomen. Delicious.

His hands on her waist, he urged her upward. "Come here," he murmured.

"No," she replied coyly. "You stay there." And she slid between his strong thighs onto the tiled floor, parting them as she went. Gorgeous view.

"Nic, what are you—" He broke off on a choked gasp as

she leaned forward, delicately licking his tightly drawn scrotum, inhaling his musky scent.

"Shh. Lie back and enjoy." Cupping his balls in one hand and wrapping the other around his shaft, she experimented with the silky feel of his skin, how it moved over the turgid tissues beneath. The veins stood out against his skin, and she ran her tongue along one, gratified when he groaned, cock flexing under her lips, his hands delving into her hair.

"Nic, you don't have to do this."

"I want to." To forestall further protest, she pulled the soft head into her mouth, delighted to feel his surrender as he let his head fall back. Perhaps this was the purpose of the chaise; it certainly worked well for it. Savoring the tension in his thighs, at the feel of him in her mouth, she swirled her tongue, seeking the tremors of most intense response. She'd never done this before, but steamier novels described such scenes. It gave her a sensual rush, too, to be kneeling at his feet and tending to him—in a way he'd otherwise object to.

If the wizard wouldn't make her kneel for him, she'd find other ways to experience it.

As expected, it didn't take long, nor did it fortunately require much technique on her part. He tried to stop her in time, ever the gentlemen, but she ignored his hands urging her upward, tightening her clasp on his shaft and sucking him deeper into her mouth. When he came, the rush of magic filled her as his seed filled her mouth, rich and powerful, silver moonlight and seawater, nurturing and fulfilling.

Very pleased with her first attempt, she continued kissing him through the aftershocks, licking the sweet, softening shaft and head, raining soft kisses on his groin and thighs. She could kiss him like this forever, savoring his relaxation and sense of deep pleasure. Gabriel might despise her familiar nature, but she couldn't help it that, at a core level, she wanted to make him happy. At least, in this one way, she could do that, and please herself too.

His fingers flexed on her, and this time she followed the tug and allowed him to pull her up against him. Studying her face, his wizard-black eyes softer and bemused, he rubbed a thumb over her lower lip. "Are you all right?" he asked roughly.

She smiled. "I feel wonderful, yes." She kissed his thumb. "I liked that very much. Ready to eat lunch now?"

"But what about you?" he asked with a slight frown, his hands running down her back. "I need to take care of you."

"Hold that thought for later," she advised, levering herself up. "It's good for me to simmer a bit, to recharge my magic reservoirs."

Sitting up also, he dragged his hands over his head. "I'm sorry I drained you like that."

"Don't be. I recover fast—and so do you, as it turns out—and we need to learn each other's limits, preferably in a nonlethal situation." She held a hand out to him. "But I do want to eat."

Taking her hand, he stood, naked and unconcerned about it now. With one strong arm, he snagged her around the waist, pulling her close against him for a long and lingering kiss. "You are a remarkable woman," he murmured.

"I keep trying to tell you that," she replied with a saucy

smile, unutterably pleased by his praise. When he smiled in return, it was as if the sun had emerged from the overcast, banishing all the chill and rain.

~ 10 ~

IT WAS EVEN stranger than he'd anticipated, seeing Nic in his parents' small cottage where he'd grown up expecting nothing more than to become a farmer someday, to live a similarly humble life. The boy he'd been could never have guessed that someday his wife, a glamorous, high-born noblewoman, boldly beautiful and shimmering with rich magic, would be sitting at the plain wooden table where they took their meals.

And yet, oddly enough, Nic fit right in. She'd brought her lists and had them on the table in the cleared corner between her place and his mom's. The both of them had their heads together over it, discussing guest lists and flowers, the merits of a buffet versus having meals served, as if Nic were any Meresin girl he'd found to marry.

The sweet young woman who grows oranges and feeds the geese, who'd be your loving wife and companion in all things. Who would bed you with sweet affection and bear you children that you could raise together, until they gave you apple-cheeked grandchildren to dandle on your knee. Someone who would never even think of wanting to kneel for you, who wouldn't crave the silver chains of your arcanium. Gabriel flushed at the echo of Nic's scathing words—

and at the equally searing memory of her mouth on him, milking him with exquisite erotic pleasure. Not something he wanted in his mind at his parents' table.

"This rain doesn't bode well for the levee," his father observed, and Gabriel gratefully put his mind on that. The fact that he'd rather think about the prospect of additional flooding ruining the orchards they'd been so carefully nurturing than about the puzzle that was his wife spoke volumes.

"Sorry we didn't make it out there today." Gabriel shook his head. He'd frankly forgotten about it. After he and Nic finally ate, quite late in the day, they'd had to deal with a second round of messages in response to the flurry they'd sent that morning. Then they'd argued, again, about what to do about the house. He hadn't realized that so many of the wizards she'd arranged for would be arriving so soon, and now they had no suitable housing for them. By that point, they'd had to saddle the horses to ride over to his parents' for dinner. Farmer's hours, he'd explained to a puzzled Nic, and she'd cheerfully noted that would leave them plenty of time later in the evening. She had very carefully—and very obviously—omitted what she had in mind, but he knew she thought they should visit the arcanium to build power for another try at raising the arcade and possibly the north wing.

She also very carefully hadn't said anything about the fact that the hunters had caught him flat heeled and nearly out of magic. If he hadn't been able to break that stasis spell and fight manually, things could've gone very differently.

He didn't want to think about any of it.

"Eh," his father grunted. "The levee, she'll hold or she

won't. You can't be everywhere."

"You're a good boy," Narlis said, beaming at him as she handed him a basket of rolls, freshly baked and still warm from the oven. When he took the basket from her, she patted his cheek, then turned back to the baking counter. Taking a roll, he buttered it and bit in, moaning at the way the soft bread melted in his mouth. He had to concede that Nic had been right, yet again, about the merits of them going to the hot food. She had a gift for hedonism that he should stop resisting, as he always ended up enjoying the results of her arrangements.

"Narlis is such a help," his mother said, "and has a gift for baking. Perhaps you'd like to have her help in the kitchen at the manse?"

Gabriel and Nic exchanged a glance. "It would be best," Nic said, "to keep her out of sight for a while. She's safer here."

"Safe from what?" his mother asked with a perplexed frown. "Out of sight from whom?"

"You never know," Nic replied breezily, sliding him a look. Yeah, it was a tangled web of lies and the omission of truths. "And Narlis is still rebuilding her health. What do you think about flowers? If we have the wedding in midsummer, won't they all wilt?"

Daisy launched into an enthusiastic discussion of the merits of various flowers, thoroughly distracted. Gabriel smiled at Nic in admiration, though she ignored him.

"Heard you raised the old arcade," his father said.

"Did you also hear that it sank again?" Gabriel asked, stabbing a piece of meat. Nic glanced up, shooting him an inscrutable green glance before replying to something his mother said.

"I did, as a matter of fact." His father laughed drily. "Perhaps the whole thing is best left sunk," his father continued, shaking his head. "There's a reason she sank in the first place, after all."

"Because there were no longer any wizards in the family to maintain it," Nic put in, proving she'd been listening closely even while carrying on another conversation. She took the buttered roll Gabriel handed her, giving him a warm smile in exchange, and he set to buttering another for himself. "The physical aspect of House Phel is important symbolically as a representation of the metaphorical reincarnation of House Phel," she explained, looking seriously from Daisy to GF. "I absolutely support Gabriel's decision to restore the manse. He's a powerful enough wizard to do it—you should be immensely proud of him—and this project will announce to the Convocation that Lord Phel is a wizard to be reckoned with."

Gabriel wrestled with the twin burns of pride at his parents' pleased expressions and chagrin at the lie. He'd failed embarrassingly and utterly that day, something that Nic continued to blithely ignore.

"I see the symbolism, dear," Daisy said thoughtfully, "but who in the Convocation will ever know? It's not as if any of them visit Meresin."

"They will when we have the wedding at House Phel," Nic assured her with sunny optimism. Her bland glance to him was the only warning he got. "And we'll have visitors starting very soon."

"We will?" Daisy looked to him, and Nic raised a questioning brow, a hint of knowing accusation in her eyes.

He cleared his throat. "We're bringing people in. Wizards specializing in other kinds of magic, and also in water magic, to supplement what Nic and I can do. It will help me with the not being able to be everywhere at once," he commented to his father, who nodded judiciously.

"What other kinds of magic?" his mother wanted to know. "And when are they arriving? You didn't tell me about this, Gabriel."

Nic watched him, eyes jewellike and amused at his predicament. He didn't know when, exactly, he was to have filled in his parents on their flood of plans. "The first arrives tomorrow," he admitted.

"Tomorrow?" his mother echoed, aghast, looking to Nic for corroboration. "Wherever will we put him?"

"They could be a woman," Nic corrected gently, patting Daisy's hand. "A House Refoel wizard, so you'll be very glad to have them here, and we'll figure something out for accommodations. We made it clear that we're in a rebuilding phase, and they will have volunteered for the position."

"Refoel," GF echoed. "I know that's a High House, but what's the significance? What magic can this wizard do that my son can't?" He laid a proud hand on Gabriel's shoulder. "As you say yourself, Gabriel is a powerful wizard. He can do anything he sets his mind to."

The smile Nic gave him was smug, and he knew exactly what she was thinking. *That is why you fail.* Charming.

"Healing," Nic explained to them. "House Refoel specializes in healing, which I think will be most welcome here."

Daisy clasped her hands together, awarding Gabriel with a hopeful smile. "There is healing magic? And we'll have someone right here to do it! This is wonderful news, Gabriel. Thank you!"

"Nic gets the credit for thinking of it, and for setting up the exchange," Gabriel told her. "We'll have other help, too, to fix up the manse. Wizards who can make furniture and put in glass, and so forth. *If* we can lift it out of the water."

"Which we can," Nic said firmly.

"Not by tomorrow," he cautioned the three looking at him expectantly.

"I disagree," Nic countered.

"Disagree all you like," Gabriel said with measured patience, "but even you can't bend reality to your expectations."

She fluttered her lashes. "Want to place a bet on that?"

"You two," Daisy said on a laugh. "I'm so happy yours is a love match. It doesn't always happen under circumstances like yours."

"They're clearly two peas in a pod," GF agreed. "What's for dessert, Narlis sweetie? Let's have some and send these lovebirds on their way."

Narlis came over with a glistening strawberry pie and set it in front of Gabriel, to his father's comical dismay. "You're a good boy," Narlis told him, and kissed him on the forehead.

"NARLIS'S STRAWBERRY PIE is now my favorite thing in the entire world," Nic announced as she mounted Salve. "The entire meal was delicious, in fact."

The pie had been especially good, redolent of spring sunshine and sweet cream, the pastry flaky with butter. "Mom was very flattered that you were so complimentary."

"I wish she wouldn't worry so much about me being a fine lady, blah, blah, blah," Nic said, drawing up the hood of her cloak against the persistent drizzle. "Her food and the other meals people have been sending over are as good as anything ever served at House Elal."

"I wonder if we could get the recipe for that gravy we had in Ophiel?" Gabriel asked.

Nic grinned at him. "And the garlic-infused mashed potatoes. We *need* those recipes. I'm going to investigate."

"I wasn't serious," he protested, realizing belatedly that he needed to be careful about expressing desires of any kind. Between her magically induced desire to please him and her innate determination, she took his least yen as a directive to make it happen.

"I am," she replied, undaunted. "House Phel will serve delicious food if I have anything to say about it, which I do. Why not collect the best recipes we encounter? There are a few I'd like to extract from Missus Ryma back in Wartson, too. I know a few magical conveniences that might tempt her into a trade, too. Hmm."

"Perhaps we should concentrate on the tasks before us?" he suggested.

She sighed. "Are we going to argue about whether or not to try to lift the house out of the swamp again?"

"Well, no, because you took care of that—didn't you?—by enlisting my parents to the cause."

She shrugged, a dim figure in the rainy twilight. "That wasn't my intent. They're proud of you, Gabriel, and they deserve to be. And you deserve to feel good about your wizardry once in a while, instead of forever agonizing over it."

"Ah." Now her ulterior motives became clear. "All of this is by way of luring me back into the arcanium."

She huffed a sound of exasperation. "It's *your* arcanium! I shouldn't *need* to lure you there. It's just a tool, Gabriel. Nothing more or less. A tool is only what you make of it."

There was a cold logic to that, he supposed. Though he wished on one level that he'd never insisted on finding the arcanium. Then it wouldn't pose such a temptation, wouldn't be filling his mind with alluring and perverse images of what could be. He couldn't regret the result—he'd wanted to try a reciprocal bonding instead of making Nic into some kind of mindless and subservient tool in her own right. And that had worked, hadn't it?

"We haven't really talked more," he said quietly, "about the reciprocal bonding and what it means for us."

She didn't look at him, the cowl of her hood creating a still and abstract profile. "We can't know what it means—if anything—if we don't work on magic together," she finally replied.

"We worked together all day today," he pointed out.

"Those are beginning steps. Unbonded wizards and familiars do much of the same at Convocation Academy. Part of the point of having a bonded relationship is taking advantage of that sexual give and take. You experienced that for yourself when we recharged this afternoon."

When she had serviced him, teasing him and then driving him into erotic rapture with her mouth and hands, refusing any pleasure for herself. "Seems to me that was all me taking and you giving." Just like with the magic. He really hated that those exchanges followed the same pattern.

"I was and am perfectly fine with that. I enjoyed what we did together."

"But would you say so if you didn't?" he pounced on that.

She took a beat too long to reply. "Yes."

"No," he said for her. "You wouldn't, because in your twisted-up idea of what our relationship should be, you think you can't refuse me."

"Gabriel Phel," she said tightly. "You may have noticed that I argue with you freely. Some might say constantly."

There was that. "You won't refuse me sexually. That's not the same thing, and you know it."

"Maybe I do and maybe I don't. Let's confine this particular argument to the magic. Yes, I wanted your parents convinced about us raising the manse because I think it is the thing to do and I think we can do it. Most important, however, I strongly believe that if you experience for yourself the kind of power we can brew between us, and if you can see with your own eyes that we can use it to raise and stabilize the entire manse, then you will gain the confidence and ability you will absolutely need if it comes to war."

While she caught her breath, he mulled her points. "You truly believe it could get that extreme."

"Wasn't today enough to convince you?"

"Those hunters were from before," he replied obstinately. "Remnants of the previous conflict."

She shook her head, slowly and firmly. "We're already at cross-purposes with the Convocation. Part of that's my fault. Some of it comes from this historic conflict that brought down House Phel to begin with."

"Regardless of fault or history, we're in this together," he affirmed.

She turned her head and grinned at him, teeth a white gleam in the shadows. "Yes, we are. If worse comes to worst, I want us to be the most effective team possible. And until you unbend enough to truly embrace what you are and what I am—how we can be together—then we're hobbled. Have you considered that, if I were able to take my alternate form, I could've escaped the hunters today?"

That hadn't occurred to him. "You don't know what your alternate form is."

"Maybe I'm a tiger." She bared her teeth in a fierce growl. "Then I could slice and dice those hunters myself."

"Maybe you're a bunny rabbit," he countered to tease her, but the image of her as a defenseless, small bunny at the hunters' mercy made his blood run cold.

"You could not be more wrong," Nic argued, oblivious to

his fear. "I know in my heart of hearts that my alternate form is something ferocious and terrifying to behold."

"That would certainly match your personality," he noted drily.

"Ha ha. My point is, unless we practice together, you will never be able to trigger my alternate form. That's something I want, Gabriel."

And it would be wrong of him to deny her that. He sighed internally. "Does it have to be via the arcanium?"

"Not necessarily, but the arcanium amplifies and focuses your wizardry. It's foolish to reject that tool."

"It doesn't seem all that useful if it only works when we're inside it."

"Aha! But that's not the case. We haven't yet awakened the arcanium and attuned it to your magic. Mine too, which should make you feel better. Once we have, you'll be able to use its focusing power and stored magic from a distance."

"How far?"

"We won't know until we experiment. With your MP scores? I'm guessing quite a ways."

That did sound useful. "How do we awaken and attune it?"

She raised her brows and cocked her head.

"I don't understand why all of these techniques have to be sexually fueled," he said with considerable frustration.

"I know you don't. I didn't before you bedded me, but now I suspect the Betrothal Trials test sexual compatibility beyond simple fertility."

That was an uncomfortable thought. But he knew what she meant—he'd felt that sizzling, sensual connection between them from the moment he walked into her tower room. Maybe even before that, studying her miniature and recognizing something in her that was meant for him.

"I have a basis for comparison," she continued. "You don't because you haven't worked with any familiar besides me." She hesitated. "You won't like this, but one solution would be for you to tap Seliah's magic. Along with helping her, you'd learn to feel the difference."

She was right: he didn't like it. "I'm not doing *that* with my own sister."

Nic blew out a breath, and he vividly picturing her dramatic eye roll. "I told you once before that it wouldn't have to be sexual. Not in this case."

"If that's true, then the magic transference doesn't have to be sexual between us."

She growled in incoherent frustration. "You are the most stubborn wizard in existence."

"No." He set his teeth. "That would be you."

"Wrong. I'm the most stubborn familiar in existence."

He wasn't going to gratify her by laughing, though it took considerable effort. "We'd have to catch Selly again to try that."

"Or at least prevent her from immediately escaping when she turns up again," Nic agreed ruefully. "I am sorry that I wasn't prepared to prevent her from bolting."

"I should've warned you. She's slipped me more times than I'd like to admit."

They'd reached the stables, and he dismounted to light a lantern. "I'll take care of the horses if you want to go in," he said. "The fires are laid and simply need lighting. The strikers are right there, too."

"And then what shall we do?" she asked mildly, as if wondering if he'd like to play cards or simply have a glass wine by the fire.

He lifted the saddle off Vale's high back, the reach and muscle needed for it giving his newly strained injuries a twinge. A good reminder there of how little time had truly passed since he'd found Nic in Wartson. They were still learning each other. Amazing, really, how much they did understand each other already. Most of their arguments stemmed from them not agreeing with what they saw in one another.

Sliding the saddle onto the stand, he studied it as if the worn leather might hold answers. Would he be giving in because he secretly wanted to be convinced to indulge in those darker desires? Either that or Nic had finally convinced him to at least try.

Perhaps both.

"I suppose your first choice would be for the two of us to visit the arcanium and practice building and transferring magic."

"Yes," she replied promptly. Her slim arms slid around his waist, and she nestled against his back, embracing him. "I wish you wouldn't sound like it's a death march through the marshes."

He laid his hands over hers. "I worry about what else I'll discover in myself."

"Like discovering you could make a wall of water fall from

the sky or that a nightmare manifested in reality by covering your bedroom floor in silver," she murmured, cheek pressed between his shoulders.

He turned in her arms, tipping back the cowled hood so he could see her bright face and knowing eyes. "How did you know it was a nightmare?" He was sure he hadn't told her that part. He hadn't told anyone.

"The feeling in your magic when you spoke of it," she answered somberly. "Your moon magic has a bright face and a dark one, like the moon itself. That dream was all dark side of the moon."

"I know you laugh at me for it, but I *am* afraid," he confessed. "That dark side frightens me."

"I only tease you about your fears *because* that dark side doesn't scare me," she replied, the raw honesty clear in her shining eyes. "Does it help to know that?"

"I don't know. I think that maybe you are so fearless that you aren't afraid when you should be."

"I was afraid today, when those hunters attacked."

"Self-preservation."

Her lush mouth tilted in a wry half smile. "I was afraid enough of you and what we might be together that I ran to another country, Gabriel."

He brushed a loose curl off her forehead, then trailed the finger down her smooth cheek. "Fearlessly throwing yourself into a new life rather than chain yourself to a future you dreaded."

Breathing a laugh, she shook her head, then leaned her cheek into his palm, eyes emerald in the low light, and very serious. "I trust you. I realize that my assurances are questionable, because yes, I would have submitted to anything my wizard required of me, regardless of who they were."

"Even Sammael," he said, the name burning his throat.

"I would have *had* to," she replied. "I would've been compelled, with no choice in the matter. *You* have given me the choice, and I choose to give you this. Choose to give it to us both, because I want us to win. Because I want my alternate form."

"Even knowing I could lock you into it without your will?"

"Even so, because I know you would never harm me, not even at your darkest."

"We don't know that," he cautioned.

She snorted, a most unladylike scoffing snorfle. "We do know that," she assured him. "I bet when you were all in a rage after our big fight last night, you were still feeling bad about breaking the dishes."

He frowned at her. "They were expensive dishes, and we don't have that many."

Her face lit with her laughter, and she stood on tiptoe to kiss him. "See? I'm not at all worried about you breaking me."

"Nic…" he groaned, untangling her from his arms.

"We'll start slow," she promised. "You'll be in control, and you decide what we do."

"I'm not sure that's the best—"

She shook her head, a slow and emphatic side to side. "You control the magic, so that's how it has to be. I'll help you with the horses, and we'll go in together. This will be fun."

Aroused, more than a little terrified, and darkly excited, he resigned himself to facing his sinister self.

"ONCE WE RAISE the entire manse," Nic commented, peering unhappily at the flooded tunnel, "we're going to dry out this tunnel."

"I offered to carry you," he pointed out.

"And immediately noted that the water is only ankle deep," she replied tartly. "As if you don't know perfectly well that I am congenitally incapable of backing down from a challenge like that."

He chuckled, no doubt as she intended, as she flashed him a sunny smile. "At least your boots were already wet?"

She waded through the shallow water, holding up the skirts of her gown and screwing up her face in disgust. "That is not the positive you'd think. When are you going to magically waterproof my boots?"

"You should add that to your lists. Then I'll know when it appears on my schedule."

"You laugh, but I'm going to do exactly that." They'd reached the end of the round tunnel, the lantern giving off a meager circle of light. Gabriel stared at the pinch of the stones that finished the tunnel at an apparent dead end, Nic's determined banter fading as the trepidation crawled along his nerves.

Shooting him a stern look, Nic held out a preemptory

hand. "Open the door, Gabriel," she said gently enough, but clearly unwilling to let him back out.

With a sigh, he took her hand, recognizing that it was indeed growing easier to accept taking her magic. Proving a point to himself, he only drew on a small amount, just enough to trip the ancient enchantment on the door, rewarded by Nic's approving smile.

The first time they'd opened the arcanium, he'd had his eyes closed, kissing her to blend their magic, still awkward with their partnering and going on instinct. This time, he observed as his moon magic sifted into the cracks between the stones, the grinding was less pronounced, and the swirling motion of the stones as they spiraled open to make a portal almost liquid.

Nic stepped through, tugging on his hand, but he paused on the other side of the threshold, touching the stones with curious fingertips. "What are you noticing?" she asked with quiet curiosity.

"I'm wondering… the stones moved almost like water. Do you suppose that they could be some sort of solidified water magic?"

She gave him such a pleased and proud smile that he nearly preened. "Now you're thinking like a wizard. And like a Phel. It makes sense to me that you'd guard your greatest secret with a lock that combines moon and water magic. Surely those don't occur in concert outside your bloodline, certainly not in any strength. Now we have an idea of how your ancestors stabilized the foundation of the manse, too."

"By changing water to rock?"

Shrugging cheerfully, she nodded. "Why not? And then, over time and without a wizard to maintain it, the enchantments frayed and the rock turned to water again, slowly sinking those wings." Dropping his hand, she carried the lantern into the arcanium.

"I thought you said the transformations were permanent, like the moonlight to silver."

"I think they can be. It depends on what forces are going counter to that state. If you melt the silver, maybe it turns back into moonlight. It's your magic. You figure it out."

He took a few steps backward, observing closely as the door spiraled shut again, burnished silver on this side, gleaming before the domed room fell into shadow too deep for Nic's lantern to fully illuminate. Beyond the arched glass panels inset in silver frames that formed the walls of the submerged room, the lake water was black with night. Even the great lens of the window at the centerpiece of the curved ceiling was dark, allowing no moonlight through. Too overcast for it.

"No moonlight tonight," he commented.

Nic glanced at him over her shoulder, carrying the lantern around the room, using the flame to light the sconces embedded at regular intervals in the silver frames. "You don't need it."

"But what if—"

"You don't need it," she repeated. "You have me. In addition, not being able to draw on moonlight should help you focus on pulling only from my magic. Also, it might help you distinguish my magic from yours."

As if that was ever an issue. She was the fire to his water, the sun to his moon. "We're still surrounded by water," he felt he should point out.

She curled a lip. "You don't have to remind me, but unless we move to the desert, that's a given. Just don't let the lack of moonlight affect your thinking, all right?"

Oh, right. He tried to clear his mind. Not that he was very good at it. Probably there were mental exercises taught at Convocation Academy that everyone knew but him. Nic moved gracefully from sconce to sconce, adding oil, then lighting them. Almost complete, a circle of warm light surrounded them. "I didn't notice these sconces last time," he said.

"I did, which is good because we'd have been out of luck if I hadn't thought to grab some oil. We can see each other this time."

He'd kind of loved how she'd looked clad only in moonlight. Though tonight they would've been fumbling in the dark. "Maybe once the shipment of elementals arrives, we can put one or two in here for light and heat."

"Are you cold?" she asked, sliding the silver grate over the final flaming sconce.

Oddly enough, he wasn't, though his palms were damp with the chill sweat of nerves. He rubbed them dry against his thighs. "No, I thought you might be."

"I suspect there are spells laid into the arcanium to keep it at a stable temperature." She set the lantern aside and met him under the moon window. Until she stepped into the tiled circle centered under the great lens, he hadn't realized that was where he stood. Something in his magical awareness tingled as she crossed that threshold, the glittering silver-and-blue-tiled border exactly mimicking the boundaries of the moon-window lens above. Tension riffled through him, along with dark desire.

Take, it whispered. *Have.*

Or was that Nic? She tilted her head, observing him with languid, catlike eyes. "Besides," she said, "you never want to bring another wizard's magic into your arcanium. Only your own magic."

"What about enchanted artifacts that I'm supposed to buy from House El-Adrel instead of violating obscure Convocation rules by making myself?" He'd tried to sound lighthearted, but too much tension simmered between them.

"That's an excellent question," she conceded. "And I don't know the answer. I suppose anything you keep in your own arcanium wouldn't be subject to Convocation law. After all, how would they know? But we could ask House Tadkiel for a ruling."

"Let's … not," he ground out, recalling that Tadkiel had helped create the hunters. He was also having a difficult time assembling thoughts beyond plundering that mouth of hers. The way she'd looked that afternoon, with her lush lips wrapped around his cock… Nic's eyes glittered as if she sensed his thoughts. They stood very close, a breath apart, but not yet touching. "What are the consequences of having *your* magic in my arcanium?" he asked, his voice whiskey rough.

Her lips curved in sultry knowing. "My magic becomes a part of yours. That's entirely the point. That's why wizards have familiars, why you take our magic into yourselves and make it into something greater than the sum of the parts."

"Tell me, then," he murmured, feeling as if he could fall into those emerald depths and swim there in eternal contentment, "since we are awakening this arcanium together, attuning it to us—what are the consequences of having my magic become a part of yours?"

~ II ~

HER BREATH CAUGHT audibly in her throat, and she leaned toward him, swaying as if rapt. "It already is. The tendrils of your magic slipped inside my skin long ago, sliding quicksilver through my veins, strumming my nerves to sing just for you. Gabriel," she sighed, "the Fascination bound me to you from that first night. The bonding in this arcanium solidified those ties so no one can take me from you."

"The hunters tried."

"They have no innate intelligence, only followed orders. They wouldn't have succeeded for long. Separating a wizard from their familiar doesn't… go well."

"What happens?"

"Remember the tale I told you of Sylus and Lyndella?"

All too well. He wasn't fond of the tragic story Nic seemed to like so much. "Abducted, Lyndella went mad, and Sylus arrived just in time for her to tragically die in his arms. So he bled off all the untapped magic that drove her insane to begin with and spent it wreaking revenge on his enemy, killing himself, but taking his nemesis with him."

She smiled winningly. "You always listen and remember. It's a lovely trait."

"I'd prefer not to emulate their sad story."

"Then don't. Awaken your arcanium, wizard. Take what is already yours."

Part of him wanted to draw back, to resist those words and their drugging pull, but the rest of him exulted in the knowing and the needing. This beautiful, magical, fierce, and powerful woman was his. His darker nature leapt at the leash, salivating to consume her. "What do I do?" he whispered. Lifting a hand, he caressed her cheek, her flawless skin soft as nothing else in the world.

She held his gaze. "You decide."

"You can't just tell me?"

"I could, but I don't want to spell it out. It's more exciting for me for you to take that lead. More exciting for me is more magic for you and the arcanium. And you are the wizard, that means you must learn to be the guiding force. Follow your wizard's intuition."

Curling his fingers into his palm, he nearly stepped back from her and found he couldn't. She didn't know, couldn't know, what images plagued his mind, the things he fantasized about doing to her. Then her infuriating words from the night before came floating back… *You can release all that pent-up fury and passion upon my helpless body.* He supposed she did know, or somehow guessed at least some of it. But then, how could she look at him so trustingly? He feared breaking that trust more than anything else.

"You said we could start slow," he said, voice barely above a whisper. He'd been avoiding looking at that silver bed, but his gaze went to it, irresistibly drawn. "We didn't get a mattress for the bed."

"Yes, well." Her smile took on an impish tilt. "You and I haven't been so successful with beds. And I figured you weren't ready to think about this one yet."

Those silver chains… No, he wasn't ready to wrestle what that thought did to him. "So… here?"

"Whatever you want. Remember that you're learning to excite and then control my magic. Work the metaphor and do exactly that to me."

"How can I know what's exciting to you?"

Her full lips curved, a hit of ruefulness, a great deal of amusement. "Gabriel, my only love, you've known that from the very beginning. Remember that first meal, how you took control, getting me to eat and drink with you? You seduced me, bit by bit, until I had no ability to resist you."

"I hadn't thought of it that way." Put in those terms, it made him even more culpable.

She laid a hand on his jaw, gripping just enough to get his attention. "Overthinking is a problem for you. Don't think. You followed your instincts that night. Follow them now. You know what you want me to do. Tell me to do it."

Don't think. "All right. Take off your clothes."

Her eyes darkened, a faint tremor in her fingers. "Yes, sir."

Grabbing her wrist before she could trigger the fastenings on her gown, he stopped her. "Don't call me 'sir.'"

She yielded to his grip, inclining toward him. "How shall I address you in here?"

"As you always do."

She shook her head. "It needs to be different, so we both

know what lines of power we're working. Both in the arcanium and outside of it."

He definitely didn't want her calling him anything deferential outside of the arcanium. She waited, compliant in his hold. "Call me wizard, then."

Her lips curved, sultry, perhaps pleased. "Yes, wizard."

He let her go and watched as she stepped back enough to strip off her clothes, a thrill racing through him that she did so at his command. Though he'd seen her naked more regularly the last few days, this was different. When she stood there, naked and so very beautiful, she looked at him through her lashes. "Wizard? Where shall I put my clothes?"

It shouldn't be that arousing that she asked, but it was. *Don't think.* "You won't need them for a while," he answered, surprised at the sound of his own voice, smooth and in control. "Put them in a cabinet."

"Yes, wizard." She crouched to pick up the pile, carrying her boots and gown to a cabinet and shutting them inside, her hips swaying seductively as she walked. He could watch her simply walk around naked for hours. In fact, the thought occurred to him with the bone-deep reverberation of a gong, he *could* have her do that, and she would obey. Everything in him felt as if it came alight, dark excitement flaring in him, Nic the fire that blazed through him, his own magic heating with it, turning to quicksilver and steam.

She stood quietly by the cabinet, awaiting instructions, he realized. *Excite and then control my magic. Work the metaphor and do exactly that to me.* "Come here," he told her, feeling the flare of her arousal in the magic twining between them. She was right, he would and did know. When she reached him, he moved aside enough to point at the exact center of the arcanium, clearly marked by a circle of silver tiles as bright as full moon. Obediently, she stepped onto it, jewel-bright eyes fixed on him, shimmering with magic and desire. "You will kneel for me," he said softly, noting how she shuddered in response. Yes, she'd mentioned wanting that.

Gracefully, she knelt, looking up at him, the threads of connection humming between them. Moved, he caressed her cheek, and she leaned into the touch, warm and yielding. Magic throbbed in him, like he'd never before experienced, hers and his together, a vast ocean of it, feeding into the silver structure and the lake around them, even to the moon, obscured as it was. And from only this much.

"Is this all right?" he asked her.

She narrowed her eyes at him. "Whatever you want is all right, wizard."

Right. Take control. Excite and control.

Caressing her cheek down to the line of her jaw, he grasped her throat, gently but firmly, and tipped her chin up. "Open your mouth."

She trembled under his touch, the pulse point under her jaw leaping against the pressure of his fingers as she complied, opening her lips to him. Following impulse, he slid his thumb inside. Needing no further instruction, she closed her lips over it, the sweet pressure an echo of how her mouth had felt on his cock that afternoon, bringing him to such excruciating completion. He wanted that from her, more and again.

But not yet. *It's good for me to simmer a bit, to recharge my magic reservoirs,* she'd said. All right, then, he could make her simmer. He just needed a few supplies. In the meanwhile… She could inspire him as she waited.

"Clasp your hands behind your neck," he told her, his daker nature thrilling to her immediate compliance. The pose lifted her full breasts, much as she'd teasingly offered them to him. "Arch your back. More. And close your eyes."

On a shuddering breath, she complied. Her nipples were hard, bringing the lush globes to exquisite points, shivering with her breathing and building arousal.

Allowing himself to enjoy this—*don't think; follow your instincts*—he moved around her, making minute adjustments to her pose and touching her as he liked. She responded to his least caress, magic and desire rising beneath her skin, her lips parted slightly, eyelashes like black lace against her skin, the expression on her face rapturous. Feeling like a sculptor graced with the perfect medium, he lifted her breasts, enjoying their sensual weight, then settled them again, sliding his fingers down her spine to arch her even more. There—perfect. "Just like that. Don't move," he told her, brushing her lips with a kiss, and she moaned, a delicious purr of a sound.

Brushing his hands over her thighs, he eased her knees apart. She shifted slightly to assist, still holding the rest of her pose. The skin of her inner thighs was impossibly soft, alluring, enticing. Indulging himself, he traced the sweet stretch up to the hollows framing her sex, the heat from her core palpable as a flame, the slickness of her arousal all the evidence he needed. Trailing his fingers through the damp curls, he watched her expressive face, the rise and fall of her breasts, the tension making her quake as she fought not to move.

She was very good at it, as disciplined as she'd hinted, not moving even when he parted her nether lips and gathered her liquid arousal like harvesting fresh honey, then painted her taut nipples with it. A whimper escaped her, and she pressed her lips closed over the sound.

"Wait here," he told her, and she took a breath, clearly trying to settle herself.

As he prowled through the arcanium, he watched her, the light gleaming on her skin from all sides, making her the focus. A work of sensual art, like an erotic sculpture. She held still, eyes closed, but something in her posture—perhaps her magic—spoke of how keenly she'd trained her attention on him. Opening the drawers and cupboards, he toyed with her, picking up various implements simply to make them chime and arouse her curiosity. The lines of her body strained with interest, her face a picture of barely restrained impatience.

Gathering a few simple things, ignoring some of the more exotic and intriguing tools, no matter how they beckoned, he set them aside and undressed as silently as possible. She was listening for him, so he was quiet, increasing her suspense. Perhaps she knew exactly where he was, just as she stood out like a flame in his mind. The arcanium had become like a silver pond, dense with magic, intensifying so the least tremor from either of them sent ripples that affected them both.

Carrying his selections with him, he moved silently back to her, feeling like a hunter stalking his prey. *The predator can have no mercy in its heart for the prey.* But he did feel mercy, and an infinite tenderness. What she gave him here was the deepest sort of offering. Her absolute trust, giving him whatever he asked. For the first time, he fully understood the intimacy and excruciatingly intense secrecy of the arcanium. Wizard and familiar, this was a relationship of magic and desire, something primal that went to the core mysteries of the universe.

But the Convocation was wrong. The power came from this willing yielding, what she gave up purely out of her own desire. Nothing else would hold as much meaning. No compulsion, no magical bond. Unless it was the Fascination that ensured she submitted to this, rather than her own needs. *Don't think.*

Still, he crouched before her, tracing the line of bruises collaring her throat. She trembled, gasping slightly through barely parted lips.

"Open your eyes," he whispered, and she did, the deep, glowing green illuminating her face, bringing her vividly present to him. Lowering his head slowly, he extended his senses into her more than he ever had, twining tendrils of silver to rest on the pulse points of her soul, sensitive to the least flinch from her, any sense of unwillingness or resistance. There was none.

There was a hint of fear, yes, the edge of trepidation he'd felt from her all along, that she'd told him came from the terror of losing her will to him completely. Perhaps, if they could find a way to ritualize this exchange, they could isolate that power differential to only working the magic. She wanted to find her alternate form. They needed to build the power to defeat their enemies.

It needs to be different, so we both know what lines of power we're working. Both in the arcanium and outside of it. Nic still met his gaze, perfectly unmoving under his hand, yielding utterly as he brushed his lips over hers, her essence thrumming to the touch, her heat rising around him, the wine-dark, bloodred magic suffusing his entire being in turn. He wanted to devour her entirely, and she would let him. The sense of power—and attendant responsibility—nearly made him dizzy. This, everything about this moment with her, encapsulated how he'd felt since the magic cracked him apart in its claws, turning him inside out. This was what he'd needed all along, her, and to learn the control.

With a rush of something that felt like relief, like the release of a fever he hadn't known plagued him, he stretched those silver threads into a rope of control. Releasing her from the kiss, he kept his hand on the back of her neck, pressing her gently and inexorably down until she folded with her forehead resting on the floor. Taking her hands from behind her neck, he moved them to the small of her back, crossing her wrists. She stayed as he arranged her, the only sound her shuddering breaths as he trailed the soft rope apparently made of silver thread over her skin. He let her feel it, wonder at it, before he looped it over her delicate wrists, winding it around and between her hands, binding them there.

So achingly beautiful in her helplessness, she drew him more profoundly than ever. He didn't like to think what that meant, but then, he wasn't supposed to think. She had given him that order, and he could obey at least that. *Your thoughts shape the magic.* So he focused his thoughts on her beauty, her sensual brilliance, her fierce nature turned inside out and offered to him with exquisite vulnerability. On how very much he loved her.

Surely that was a sort of magic too, the passionate love for her that craved both cultivation and direction.

Retrieving his shirt, he tore it into strips, a shiver of reaction rippling over her skin with each hiss of sound. Nothing soft had survived the years of neglect in the arcanium, nothing except that silver rope, which was likely moonlight made solid and softened to a silken fiber. The binding of it on her skin hummed to his magic, a conduit that collected and funneled his magic and hers, amplifying and concentrating. Her knees must surely be growing sore on the unyielding tiles, so he folded his leather jacket, sliding it beneath them, taking the opportunity to spread her thighs wider, raising her full moon ass high above them, her swollen sex parted and offered like the ripest fruit.

Because it seemed to serve to excite them both, he moved around her, making minute adjustments to show off her beauty for him, teasing her with caresses and soft pinches. He'd explored her some before this, finding those sweet spots that enhanced her pleasure. Taking more time with it, he investigated meticulously, adding mouth, tongue, and the occasional edge of teeth to test every bit of her. The nape of her neck, in the hollow revealed by the short, silken nap of black fringe at the base of her skull, proved to be almost more sensitive than she could bear. Her moans and whimpers grew in pitch and frequency, a song played only for him.

Giving her time to calm herself, he smoothed caresses down her spine, then turned her head so her cheek rested on the cool tiles, telling her in a whisper that she could turn it the other direction as she needed to. She blinked at him with languorous eyes, deep as a primeval forest, her face suffused with desire. "Thank you, wizard," she answered, and somehow he knew she meant for all of it, that this was what she'd been asking him for.

Kissing his way down her spine, he positioned himself behind her, shaping the globes of her gorgeous behind with his palms. Then put his mouth on her sex.

She convulsed, a cry of agonized pleasure ripping from her, wine-bright magic exploding in his mind with the flavor of her. He'd thought to tease her with his tongue, but he'd miscalculated the level of her tension, how precariously she'd teetered on the edge of climax, holding herself so still for him, writhing within her skin for completion.

And he… he'd miscalculated the level of savagery in himself, for he was unable to stop himself from rearing up and plunging into that ripe and ready sex. She convulsed around him, her sex as avid as her mouth had been, embracing and massaging his cock, pulling him into her so that he released almost immediately. His roar of triumphant ecstasy bounced off the glass and silver, the water beyond the arcanium shimmering in argent flames as he plunged into her sheath, joining that which he'd been separated from so violently, long ago.

She moved under him, echoing that same wordless frenzy, her guttural cries of climactic need a wine-dark harmony to his silvery magic. It had been like this in the bonding, their magic coiling together like vines, growing, thickening, creating a lattice that couldn't be torn apart.

But this time, the focus wasn't on tying them together. He and Nic were already bonded, with ties glaringly obvious to his magic heightened sight. Taking their melded magic, he poured it into the arcanium, bidding it to awaken, to absorb and reflect their magic. Water and fire. Sun-warmed roses and cool moonlight. The essential *them*.

Emptying the last of himself into her, he collapsed over and around her, wrapping an arm around her waist to snug her against him as he rolled onto his side, holding himself still buried in her, dropping his forehead, sweating silver against the tender nape of her neck, both of them panting raggedly. Exhausted from the distance they'd crossed.

IT TOOK A while for Nic's mind to clear, for the hot haze of blood desire to dissipate enough for her to remember who she was. Gabriel's magic coursed through her, her heart pumping his cool water, her nerves made of singing silver, her very being possessed by him more utterly than her worst imaginings.

It was glorious and perfect. Shattering and satiating.

Leaving her hollowed out and endlessly full.

All a result of their first tentative steps into this realm of working together. Taking things slow. It was difficult to imagine how she'd feel after something more intense. No wonder Maman would collapse for days after an incantation.

She was luckier than she'd known, that Gabriel was the one. This kind of power exchange was not for the faint of heart, or the faintly cared for. Giving herself up so completely, being so rawly vulnerable like this with anyone else might indeed have broken something inside herself. She shuddered at the thought.

"Are you all right?" Gabriel murmured in her ear, brushing the lobe with a tender kiss and gathering her tighter in the circle of his arms.

For once, his solicitude didn't exasperate her. It soothed that part of her still so terribly exposed.

"My hands are numb," she admitted. He pulled out of her with a muttered oath, his nimble fingers that had tormented her so deftly and with such devastating thoroughness loosening the knot on the rope that had bound her so erotically. Though she appreciated the rush of feeling to her hands, she also missed Gabriel's comforting embrace. So, an even greater admission, she added, "But I think I need to be held still."

"Oh, Nic…" He sounded ragged as he gathered her onto his lap, sitting cross-legged and wrapping himself around her. Sheltered in the protective strength of his body, she calmed, the flayed bits of her heart knitting together again. "It was too much," he said.

"No, it was just right," she breathed, becoming aware that the lantern flames had all gone out, replaced by a cooler, silver white, much brighter light. "Look."

He lifted his head, then tilted it back to follow the direction of her gaze, his breath easing out in wonder at the sight. The silver structure of the arcanium glowed, currents of magic running like contained lightning through the struts and bars framing the panes of glass. They seemed to pulse in a regular pattern, streaming up to flow in a circle around the moon window above. The window panes themselves shimmered like water made solid. Perhaps they had been made of water originally, as Gabriel had remarked the stone of the arcanium door seemed to be.

If so, the arcanium had been constructed via an immense wielding of power. More so than even her father commanded. Papa couldn't transmute materials like this. And if the Elal arcanium was capable of storing this amount and intensity of magical energy, well… She just didn't think it was, or she'd have sensed it.

More to the point, if the Phel wizards had been so powerful, how had that magic collapsed so completely that it vanished within a couple of generations? And, why had it appeared again and with such potency in Gabriel and Seliah?

"It's phenomenal," Gabriel breathed. "Though I'm not sure I fully understand what it means."

Her heart fairly burst with love for him, that he could be so masterful in one moment, so deftly commanding her and drawing the magic from her in perfect streams of control— once he stopped dithering about the morality of it—and then so willing to expose his ignorance in the next. Laying a hand on his cheek, she drew his wondering gaze down to hers, brushing the soft silver shadow growing along his jaw. He must've skipped shaving that morning, what with sleeping in the stables, then forgotten after he fell asleep in the bath.

Giving him a long, lingering kiss, she poured her feelings for him into the caress, as if her lips could convey what she didn't have the nerve to speak aloud. And not only because he wouldn't believe her, thinking her mind and will compromised by the Fascination and the bonding.

"What was that for?" he asked with a quirk of a smile.

"A reward," she replied lightly. "What this means," she continued, before he could question her further, "is that we've awakened the arcanium. There is a huge amount of stored magic here. Water and moon intertwined. Do you feel it?"

"Yes," he answered in a reverent tone, wizard-black gaze following the rivers and runnels of sparking magic.

"You know, I've been thinking of the water and moon magic in you as two different categories, but now I'm wondering if they aren't two sides of the same coin. One feeding into the other, a kind of transmutation."

He studied her face thoughtfully. "That could be." Adjusting his embrace so he could look at her more fully while still holding her, as she'd asked him too, he tilted his head. "Tell me truly, though—how are you? Was what we did just now..." He trailed off, not quite able to frame the question.

"It was perfect," she told him, holding his gaze and hoping he'd feel her absolute sincerity. "I won't pretend that it didn't leave me feeling a little fragile, but it was exactly right." He hadn't even caused her any pain, and yet that sensation of being helpless in his control... She shivered, and his arms tightened around her. "I feel a bit hollow," she admitted.

"You're pale," he observed, "and your magic is..."

She tipped her chin at the arcanium. "It's there. Transmuted by you into water and moon magic, stored here so you can use it."

He absorbed that information. "I can access it without touching you?"

"Feels that way to me. Do you disagree?"

"No," he replied slowly, gaze going a softer black as he focused his attention on his wizard senses. "But I didn't know that was possible."

"I'm not sure it is, for any other wizard but you. Maybe all House Phel wizards can do it, but since you're the only one, we can't know. Still, that the arcanium functions this way is a strong argument that they could. I think you should experiment."

"Right." He shook his head, as if trying to clear it. "That's what we intended."

Extricating herself from his embrace, she got to her feet, feeling more than a little creaky. Gabriel watched her stretch, more concern in his eyes than lust, and she went to the cabinet where she'd put her clothes, dressing again. "I think you should raise the manse," she suggested, when he continued to sit there in deep thought, naked and cross-legged, like a sculpture carved in homage to masculine beauty.

"What—now?" His gaze sharpened, a hint of alarm in his expression.

"*Don't think,*" she warned him. "Just do it, while you're in the flow of all this magic, all of it focusing on you in the center of the arcanium. Your ancestors likely sat in that very spot to accomplish the feat in the first place. House Phel wants to rise again. Lift it up and stabilize it. You have a world of magic waiting to do exactly that."

"Without you?" he asked, uncertain.

"You already have me." She gestured to the fiery silver rivers. "This is easy for you, Gabriel. It's been done before. You're simply restoring what was there before. Just do that: put the manse back where it belongs."

He nodded, closed his eyes, and took in a long meditative breath. As he bowed his head, his silver curls fell around his beautiful face, and Nic carved the sight into her memory. This night would be one she would remember forever.

Gabriel's magic streaked through and around her, the water beyond the arcanium illuminating, fine bubbles streaming along the outer glass. The lens of the moon window glowed as if lit from within, a full moon shedding her silver light on her favored child. Beyond the closed door, a quiet rumble throbbed, like distant thunder. The magic quaked, pulsed like a heartbeat, like surf crashing onto shore. Once. Twice. Thrice.

And then quiet.

The arcanium still shimmered, but more like moonlight on water than lightning. Gabriel opened his eyes, fastening them immediately on her. "I did it." His voice was hushed with awe but held no doubt.

"Of course you did." She nearly burst with pride. As much grief as she'd given him, he'd mastered a truly tremendous feat of magic with only a bit of teaching. It was important that he believe how possible it was, but Nic knew full well how few—if any other—Convocation wizards could come even close. It was a relief, too, to have the manse raised and stabilized before any other wizards arrived to witness the difference. Yes, the folk of Meresin would talk about the seeming miracle, but the wizards of other houses would put it down to the exaggeration of common folk. They wouldn't realize how truly spectacular a feat Gabriel had wrought, and that was for the best. Let them underestimate House Phel for the time being. Nic went to Gabriel and held down her hand. "Why don't you get dressed, and let's go see?"

He drew the tendrils of his attention back from the distant spaces, giving every impression of a man setting down a precarious load, watching it settle as he gradually withdrew his support. Using her hand for help, he got to his feet, wincing. "Are you this stiff and sore?"

"It's a hard floor. Maybe you'll listen to me next time when I say a mattress is a good idea."

Sliding an askance gaze at the unused silver bed pushed off to the side, he winced. "I'm not sure I'm ready to escalate just yet." He squeezed her hand, studying her with that concern in his eyes. "I can feel how low your magic is now."

"It will come back," she promised. "That was a major incantation, and, while your control was enhanced by your attention on erotic control, you're still heavy-handed."

He winced. "I apologize."

"No need." She swept a hand at the glowing arcanium. "It wasn't wasted. Look how much is still stored even after you raised and stabilized the entire manse, all at once. Get dressed and let's see what you've wrought."

He didn't move, instead drawing her near and slipping his arms around her waist, snugging her lower body against him.

"What *we've* wrought. I said I did it, but we both know this was a result of our combined efforts. I could never have done this without you, my heart."

My heart. Her own tripped with pleasure—and nerves. It was odd to be dressed while he was naked—and tempting to run her hands over him. But she *was* depleted. If she seduced him into more sex, she might replenish her magic some, but she'd likely sleep through the next day, which would only alarm Gabriel. Besides, she needed to be up and ready to greet the wizards.

Going up on her toes, she kissed him and grinned. "Well, I want to see what we've wrought. If you want to prance around naked, I'm good with that."

He mock growled. "I never prance."

"Could be a sight to see." With nowhere to sit—they really needed to get some furniture down here, too—she plopped herself on the floor, struggling to pull on the disgustingly wet leather boots. "I swear these things shrunk," she complained. "I'll probably get a foot fungus, and then—"

A familiar silver buzz zinged through her, and the leather boot dried, turning supple under her hands. Surprised, she glanced at Gabriel, who was lacing his pants—alas, for that— and watching her with a smug smile. "Nice trick," she acknowledged.

"I can feel that connection to you," he replied. "As if I could use your own water magic through you to do that," he added thoughtfully.

Hmm. That was interesting. She didn't want to get his hopes up about the reciprocal bonding, but this could be a result. Unless other wizards and familiars could do that sort of thing and didn't talk about it, which was possible.

When both of them were dressed, he dialed open the door from the arcanium to the tunnel. Nic whistled in appreciation at the sight. The formerly flooded, dank, and dark tunnel was now dry, even welcoming. Silvery light emanated from almost concealed silver ribs rimming the tunnel all down its length. "So much better," she declared, stepping onto the polished stone floor. "Well done."

Gabriel followed cautiously after. "I didn't do this."

She cocked a dubious brow at him. "Some other wizard, then?"

Shaking his head, he slanted her a dry look. "I mean, this wasn't part of my intention. I wasn't thinking specifically about this tunnel."

"But you *were* thinking about the entirety of the house, about putting it back how it was, dry and stable, yes?"

"Yes," he replied, though clearly unconvinced. "But that was long before my time. I never saw the manse intact, or this tunnel like… this."

"The magic knows. It's embedded in every stone, every silver frame and drop of water in this place. That's part of inheriting a house. Not only does the magic come to you through your forebears, the entirety of House Phel does, too. The material and immaterial aspects."

He was quiet until they reached the door to the main house, opening it into the same dark back room of the cellars as before, though considerably drier. "This hasn't changed."

"I suspect the unprepossessing entrance to the arcanium is

deliberate," she suggested. "No sense advertising its location."

"Except for the glowing glass dome shining through the lake," he noted wryly.

"Aha. I'd put down good money on a bet that no one but us can see it."

"Really?"

"We can test it, but I'm fairly certain." She followed him up the cobwebbed stairs to the unused kitchens, shadowed and empty still, but the walls subtly straighter, the floorboards more solid. "To the arcade or outside?"

"Arcade," he decided, gesturing her to the dining hall. "Nic, I'm thinking about what you said just now, about how I've inherited this whole metaphysical weight of House Phel along with my own wizardry and this rotting heap of a manse."

"Not rotting anymore," she pointed out as they stepped into the dining hall. "We need to light some sconces." She'd be so happy when they got some light-producing fire elementals in her trousseau and dowry goods.

"Allow me," he said wryly, and the room flooded with silver-white moonlight.

"Well done," she said, blowing him a kiss. Going to the door to the receiving salon, she waited for Gabriel to open it, a smile on her face for his obvious reluctance, excitement making her giddy. He doubted still, but she didn't. "Voila!" she squealed as they peered in. The once slanting, soggy room sat square and dry. The carpets hadn't magically unrotted, and no furniture had miraculously appeared—if only!—but it smelled like dry, seasoned wood, and it looked like a place people might not be afraid to occupy. Clapping her hands together, she skipped across to the door to the arcade. "Open it and let's see!"

He hesitated. "Nic, about what I was saying…"

"Gabriel Phel, if you don't open this door right now, I'm going to kick you! This is the fun part of magic. I want to see what you've done."

"What we've done," he said, but the correction sounded automatic. He unsealed the doorway he'd sealed again after their previous failures. Magic stirred as he put his barrier into place, though Nic could tell by the look on his face that he wasn't finding water on the other side to wall off. Cautiously, he edged the door open and peered through, his body going rigid with shock.

Unable to bear the suspense, Nic pushed past him, gasping in delight at the gracious old architecture restored to its former glory. A parquet floor had lurked under the realm of fish and water snakes, now dry and gleaming under the moonlight streaming through the open arches, amplified with Gabriel's help. Nice of the moon to come out and shed her light on Gabriel's feat. Feeling exuberant at the possibilities, Nic broke into a run, dashing down the long arcade. Reaching the center, she stopped and spun, arms flung wide.

"Look, Gabriel!" she sang out. "Look how beautiful it is."

He followed more slowly, almost grudgingly, but at least stirred from his frozen contemplation in the doorway. She met him partway, wrapping her arms around his waist and pulling him into an impromptu dance. He moved with her, though not fluidly, his attention on the flying buttresses, the elegant arches, even the parquet floor as she spun them in a slow circle. "Do you dance? I don't think I've ever asked."

"What?"

"Never mind. A conversation for another time. Enjoy the moment."

"I want to say I don't believe it," he said, his deep voice echoing in the perfect acoustics.

"But you do believe it," she told him. "Otherwise you wouldn't have accomplished this."

"I never saw the arcade like this. I mean, I know I said that already, but there are details here that weren't here before. Pieces that had rotted or broken away."

"The house remembers," she reiterated. "You have it in here." She laid a hand over his breast, firmly reassuring him.

"But what about you?" he asked, stopping their spin, looking at her somberly. "What about the entirety of House Elal's magical legacy?"

A familiar pain twinged in her own breast. "I know I mentioned before—my sister, Alise, has manifested as a wizard. Papa is training her to take over House Elal. That inheritance will be hers."

"How do you bear it?" he whispered. "Giving all of that up."

"I bear it because I have no choice," she replied crisply. "It's that or collapse under the weight of disappointed hopes, and you should know me well enough by now that I'm not someone who gives up without a fight." She tugged out of his arms.

"I'm sorry, Nic. I didn't mean to—"

"You didn't." She'd cut off his words perhaps too abruptly,

but she didn't want to hear his pity for all she'd thought she'd be and have and never would. "I'd rather focus on this brilliant success, Gabriel," she said more kindly. "Let's see the rest of the manse."

"I thought you said you're worn out?"

"Magically, not physically." She held out a hand to him in invitation, in apology. "I'd rather explore the rest of House Phel with you, while we have it all to ourselves."

~ 12 ~

GABRIEL RECOGNIZED THE peace offering—and Nic's deep reluctance to dwell on her disappointments—for what they were. Taking her slim hand, which still felt too cool to him, lacking her usual fire, he walked with her. It bothered him profoundly that he'd drained her of that fire, of her intoxicating rose-infused wine-red magic, leaving barely a flicker of fire within her.

But he didn't say so. He was learning, he supposed, not to lay his qualms on her. Nic, in her characteristically passionate fashion, was all in. No matter what it was or what he asked of her, she gave him everything of herself. Whether compelled by the Fascination, the bonding, or her quintessential self, she simply didn't have it in her to do anything halfway. He couldn't stop her or change that. In all truth, he didn't want to. As much as he'd love to save her pain, he also wouldn't change anything about her.

All he could do, he was slowly beginning to realize, was to do his best to reciprocate. He could right the balance between them by giving her everything of himself in return. So he walked with her down the arcade, joining her in marveling at its beauty both in overall form and its minute details. When they reached the door to the north wing, he hesitated, remembering well how it had been entirely severed long ago.

"Maybe we should stop here," he ventured, "wait for daylight."

"Your moonlight gives us enough light to see. Just look already. You know it's there. You feel it," she replied implacably.

"How do you know?"

"You said so, back in the arcanium."

"You trust me that much?"

She gave him an owlish look. "I obviously trust you with a great deal more than that," she replied, lifting her free hand and rotating her wrist, still bearing the imprints of the silver rope. He flushed at the memory—in chagrin and desire—and had to get a grip on himself. "It's you who needs to learn to trust," she continued. "Trust what your wizard senses tell you."

"Is this part of believing, like my thoughts shaping the magic?"

"Absolutely." She smiled sunnily. "Also, I can feel it through you."

Hmm. Braced for an onslaught of marsh water, he opened the door. On the other side, a huge, high-ceilinged ballroom echoed, empty, the smooth marble floor perfectly dry. "Marble," he observed wryly. "No wonder this was the first wing to sink."

"Was it?" Nic wandered into the ballroom, turning in circles, head tipped back. Moonlight silvered her slim form as it poured in the floor-to-ceiling windows. They were all missing glass but appeared to be framed in the same style as in the master suite, including doors that would open onto terraces. "I think the ceiling is painted, but it's too dark to see exactly what it is."

"According to family lore, yes. The last denizens of House Phel moved out when the north wing sank. The rest of the manse slowly followed."

"You didn't tell me there was a ballroom here."

"I didn't know," he admitted. "It's funny. I never imagined my ancestors having social events like balls."

"Why not? House Phel was a High House. For a time, it was the highest of them all. Seeing the magic you're capable of, what the arcanium can do, I understand that very well now."

He wasn't sure what to make of that remark, so he put it in the back of his mind to mull over as he followed after her exploratory perambulations. "As you've so often observed, House Phel is in Meresin, surrounded by wetlands and far from Convocation Center. This location isn't exactly the center of society."

She was peering at a raised dais in an alcove. "For musicians," she noted. "We could fit an entire orchestra in here."

"What house would I be mortgaging our orange crop to?"

Laughing, she patted his cheek. "House Euterpe, but they're second tier, so it would only take a few trees' worth." She sighed wistfully. "It's an expense that can wait."

"What about the wedding?"

She canted her head. "What about it?"

"Isn't having a ball part of the festivities? I assumed that's why you asked if I danced."

Narrowing her eyes, she studied him. "I assumed your non-reply was a no."

It was, in fact, a no. "I grew up farming, not gracing ballrooms."

"I'm not criticizing," she replied mildly as she continued to the far side of the vast room.

"If you can teach me to raise an entire manse, I assume you can teach me to dance," he said, catching up to her.

"Well, a great deal of *that* was your wizard's intuition," she said, making her doubt clear.

"Dancing can't be that different from sword-fighting."

"I'd prefer not to be gutted at my wedding ball, darling."

"So noted. No sword on the dance floor."

She laughed, a free and musical sound he rarely heard from her. "A wedding ball would be fun," she conceded. "As long as we're dragging everyone out to the marshes of Meresin. So, the ballroom leads onto the terrace above the gardens on the river side, and out to the lawns north of the arcanium lake."

"Only best not to call it that," he reminded her.

"What do you call it?"

"Just… the lake," he told her, feeling foolish, but she only nodded.

She reached a set of several paired wooden doors on the north wall. "If I don't miss my guess, this will be…" With a dramatic shove, she pushed a pair of doors open. "Aha. Yes, a feast hall."

"We need two dining halls?" He followed her into the darker room with open windows only on the river side, so admitting less moonlight. A large fireplace, inlaid with stone, took up most of the opposite wall.

"This one is much larger," she pointed out unnecessarily. "The other is an intimate dining hall, for family or small parties."

He refrained from commenting on the absurdity of calling the other dining hall "intimate."

"We'll use this one for large banquets, feasts we'll host in concord with balls, or on special occasions. The rest of the time, this will be the dining hall for students, contracted wizards, minions, and other assorted guests." She walked briskly from door to door on the north and west walls, opening them and peering in. "Here is a secondary kitchen. And these corridors lead to the guest rooms you mentioned, so the design makes sense. This space is large enough to also serve as a common room. We can set up seating areas near the fireplace on that end, with conversational groupings and also singles for reading and study. A few desks would be nice. There's space for bookcases, too, which might be convenient for the students—unless you'd rather require that all books be stored in the library? There's a good argument for that, too."

That was the second time she'd mentioned students. "I remember agreeing to minions and contracted wizards." As she envisioned the room for him, it came alive in his mind. A cozy room for gathering in the evenings, filled with study and lively conversation. "But students? And assorted guests," he added with a frown.

"Students and guests," she echoed firmly, going to the terrace doors on the river side. "Not marsh rats and water snakes. Don't make it sound like that. This terrace connects to the one for the ballroom. We can have more seating out here. In good weather, it will be like having an additional room."

"For all of those students and guests." He added a grand gesture at the dark and empty hall, the moonlit—and still distinctly marshlike would-be terrace.

"Exactly." She beamed at him. "Let's check out the bedrooms."

The woman was indefatigable. "We should sleep at some point."

"And we will. I just want to see what we're facing with these guest rooms, like will it be possible for a person who is not a swamp creature to live in one. You can go to bed if you're tired, and I'll join you soon."

No way was he leaving her to explore on her own. Not with the possibility of more hunters lurking about. Besides, he wasn't tired, but he worried that she was. "A compromise. We save the south wing for morning."

"Done," she happily agreed, charging into a long, shadowy corridor.

"Tell me about these students and guests."

"Students are like apprentices. Sometimes wizards graduate from Convocation Academy with a mix of mid-level MP scores. They travel around and study with various wizards who are high level in a magic they'd like to explore. Sort of testing out what suits them best. Think of them as protominions. There's three stories?"

"Yes, but I wouldn't trust that staircase."

Ignoring the warning, she traipsed up the wide wooden

stairs that led to a semicircular landing with tall bay windows admitting bright moonlight. She peered at the dark corridor on that level, which he obligingly illuminated. It was almost scary how easily the magic flowed into him, with unimaginable potency.

Nic was already climbing the right-hand flight of stairs to the third floor by the time he joined her. "It's perfectly solid," she informed him. "You do good work, so stop worrying."

"How are these students different from minions?" he asked, rather than argue.

"Minions are already trained and settled in their specialization, or one step away and simply needing a contract with a house to finalize it." She opened the first door and walked confidently into the shadowy room. "Much the same floor plan as the master suite in the main house," she noted. "These will be the best suites up here. Maybe a few like this on the ground floor, for people who don't do stairs well. Otherwise, the grander guests and higher-status wizards will want the view. Second floor will be smaller, student rooms."

Bemused, he followed along as she made her inventory of the third floor. And the attic rooms under the gables. Then the second floor, which indeed held a series of smaller rooms. Finally the ground floor proved her theory correct, with a blend of smaller rooms and grander suites. He nearly remarked that she knew everything ahead of time, so actually going in each room seemed redundant, but he wisely held his tongue.

At the far north end of the ground floor, they came to a set of impressively large and imposing doors. Nic raised questioning brows at him, and he shook his head. "I don't know. Guest suites for the army?"

"Ha ha. Given the amount of water here, we'd do better with a navy."

"Yes, but they can sleep on the boats."

"Wow. Remind me not to enlist in your outfit. These are locked."

"A sign, perhaps, that exploring the barracks can wait until tomorrow."

"You promised the entire north wing. The south wing is waiting until tomorrow. I'm betting it will be a mirror of this wing, sans arcade and ballroom."

"I'm fairly certain I made no such promise."

"We can't stop now. We're having too much fun!" The end of the corridor was decidedly dark, the only light from the moonlight flooding the nearby bedroom, but her broad smile came through in her voice.

Huffing out a laugh, he kissed her, surprised to discover that he was having fun, bizarre as that seemed. Pulling moonlight from the adjoining room, he lit up the unprepossessing cul de sac. "Fine. Unlock the doors and unleash the monster within."

"You laugh, but you never know in a house built by wizards. You'll have to do the unlocking. The lock is magical and not one I can trip. I bet it's some special Phel-magic mechanism."

He gasped theatrically. "What will House Iblis say?"

She snorted at him. "It's over seventy-five years old, so it's not competing. You really need to learn Convocation trademark law."

"I'll pass, thanks." The lock didn't seem to respond to his magic, either water or moon. *Hmm.*

"It might require a physical component," Nic suggested. "It would be inconvenient to summon a wizard anytime someone needed to go through this door. Plus there's a keyhole."

"A magic key?" He could do that much. Scooping up a handful of moonlight, he let it pool silver bright in his palm, holding it near the lock. A silver key formed, rising from his palm and sliding into the keyhole. With an audible click, the lock released, the doors opening inward slightly.

"Nicely done," Nic said, warming his heart. "Your intuition is amazingly well honed, once you get that thinky-thinky brain out of the way. Let's see if I can use the key or if it has to be you."

He handed the key over, observing as she drew the doors together, turning the key in the lock. Nothing. As soon as she removed the key, they swung inward again. "Alas," she sighed, handing him the key again. "A wizard thing. You try it."

The doors locked easily for him, then unlocked again. "That's not fair," he growled.

"Along with life and Meresin weather," she quipped, pushing the doors open and forging boldly ahead into the pitch darkness.

"Hey, we have fair weather," he protested gamely, playing along. If she wanted to joke these things away, then fine. But he'd revisit this lock. "What is this place?" he asked, eyes adjusting to the gloom enough for him to see that it seemed to be a large windowless room. Even his moonlight only penetrated so far into what felt like a vast interior.

"A workroom, I'm guessing," her voice came back to him. "Ouch, shit!"

"Nic, are you all right?" He couldn't see her at all, and her warning about monsters came back with a hair-raising chill. Or hunters.

"Barked my shin is all. I'm coming back your way. This might have to wait for tomorrow.

"I think it *is* tomorrow." Putting an arm around her shoulders, he turned her back to the doorway. "To bed?" he asked hopefully.

"Probably best," she agreed on another sigh, leaning against him and sliding an arm around his waist. "Lock those doors, though."

"To a huge empty room?"

"A huge, theoretically empty workroom, steeped in all kinds of magic, where wizards practice spells, enchantments, and other questionable pursuits. As students, minions, and junior contracted wizards are wont to do."

"And why are they wont to do that?" he asked, only partly in jest.

"Well, you're not letting anyone else use your arcanium, correct?"

Imagining someone else in that space that had become so personal, so intimate—conflicted as he was about the feelings and desires the arcanium stirred in him—gave him an immediate wave of revulsion. Even if Nic hadn't warned him about having another wizard's magic in his arcanium, he wouldn't have wanted to share it. The possessive, even territorial, ferocity took him by surprise. What came of giving free rein to those mercurial wizard's instincts, no doubt.

"Correct," he answered, hearing the growl in his own voice.

"Wizards need a place to practice," Nic continued, so neutrally that she clearly sensed his strong feelings about the arcanium, was amused by them, and was not going to comment. "Practice, especially among students and junior wizards, can mean mistakes. There's a reason that space has no windows and was magically sealed."

He locked the doors.

IN THE MORNING, he woke before Nic did. A rare occurrence—unprecedented, now that he thought about it—and further evidence that the working in the arcanium had exhausted her more than she'd let on. She lay on her back, arms and legs exuberantly flung wide, as restless and abandoned in sleep as she was awake. Sunshine streamed in the windows, warming the room and gilding her strong profile, coaxing red-gold highlights from her dark hair.

Tempting as it was to touch her, he carefully slid out of bed instead, doing his best not to wake her. She didn't move or even alter her deep breathing, so he suspected she might sleep through a hurricane. He'd teased her before about the care and feeding of familiars, a concept she'd firmly rejected, but clearly he'd have to be the one to make sure she didn't overextend in yielding up her magic.

She'd made a caustic remark the evening before about wizards who were too good to avail themselves of grooming imps, so he found her bottled one and had it shave him clean. Then, because Nic had also said the imp had trimmed and shaped up her lopsided hair for her, he tried instructing it to even up his own. It was a bit odd, watching the flickering, amorphous green being move around his head, the hair magically disappearing. Nic said they absorbed the hair and skin cells, delighting in the feast. Something that made him uneasy, which she'd only laughed at.

By the time he emerged from the bathing chamber, Nic was awake, though bleary enough that she barely grunted in reply to his greeting, then bumped her shoulder against the doorway on her way into the bathing chamber. Seeming not to notice, she yawned and corrected course, closing the door behind her. Breakfast had been left for them outside the master suite, so he busied himself fixing plates for them both. Nic emerged, looking fresh and lovely, but with shadows under her eyes. She sat and ate methodically, with none of her usual banter and teasing, so he stayed quiet, too. He was just considering suggesting that she could go back to bed for a while when she lifted her eyes and gave him a long look.

"Stop worrying," she said. "This is normal."

"I didn't say anything," he protested.

"You were thinking I should go back to bed. I'm not going to. There's a great deal to be done today, and I'm perfectly capable of doing it."

"You're reading my thoughts now?"

"I don't have to. You think very loudly," she griped, sounding very like someone who'd imbibed too much wine and regretted it in the morning. "It could be that the pregnancy is making me more tired than usual," she conceded.

He hated to pounce on her slightest mention of the pregnancy, but she'd also made it clear that she didn't like to be interrogated about it. So he had to take the opportunities offered. "How are you feeling that way?" he tendered.

"You can ask about the baby, Gabriel," she replied wryly. "It's yours, after all."

"Ours," he corrected. "And you requested before that I not ask you about it."

She gazed at him blankly for a moment. "Oh! Back on the barge of doom. I rescind that request. I was engaged in some unhealthy denial. To answer your question, I think everything is fine, but it will be nice to have the Refoel healer give an assessment. They should arrive today. I'm just hoping that the Byssan, Ophiel, and Ratisbon wizards arrive first so they can furnish a few rooms." She cocked her head, just as something magical brushed across his senses. He sprang to his feet, seizing his sword and casting about for the source of the disturbance. Nic waved a hand at him. "Wizards," she informed him. "Someone is arriving, so you can almost certainly stand down."

"We'll see," he replied, striding to the suite doors.

"If it is an enemy, you're better off using magic," she said, catching up and descending the great staircase with him.

Not with her so depleted. He wasn't going to draw on any magic—hers or what they'd stored in the arcanium—more than necessary. But he didn't say so, because he was learning, if slowly, how to manage his familiar. "I've noticed wizards don't expect the manual chop-chop method," he said, slanting her a grin as he tossed her caustic assessment of his methods back at her. "Could be effective."

"Not if they melt your sword first."

"House El-Adrel with the enchanted artifacts?"

"House Hagith. Metalworkers."

"Duly noted. Are we expecting a Hagith wizard this morning?"

"No," she admitted, stepping to the side as he opened the great doors to the manse that led onto the long porch that bordered the front of House Phel. Sunlight poured in, making him blink after the interior gloom, and he found himself with Nic on looking forward to having more windows uncovered.

A sled glided around the lake, moving at a speed no mortal steed could match, which meant it was elemental powered. Four people sat within, looking about and occasionally pointing at something. Beside him, Nic let out a soft breath of disappointment, so faint he almost didn't hear it. Sheathing his sword, as the group didn't look all that threatening, he set a hand on her back, giving her an inquiring look.

Giving him a wry smile, she shook her head slightly. "I was hoping it would be my dowry and trousseau. Supplies before people would be optimal, but we get what we get when we get it. How do I look?" She sleeked her palms along the short sides of her hair, then shook out her skirts.

She wore the soft purple linen gown, the one with the neckline that showed off a great deal of her bosom—and the ring of bruises in contrasting green decorating her collarbones. Personally, he was hoping one of their impending guests would be the healer. "You look incredibly beautiful," he told her in perfect honesty, gaze lingering on her tantalizing breasts.

She wrinkled her nose. "Not *do I look good enough to bed*. Do I look presentable for Convocation company?"

"Both," he said decisively, then picked up her hand and kissed it, rewarded with a dry but sincere laugh. "Let's take in the view while we wait." Interlacing her delicate fingers with his, he led her down the broad steps and onto the thick lawn. Reaching the verge of the pond, they turned, taking in the full grandeur of House Phel.

Nic whistled, low and long. "I have to say, I'm impressed despite myself. Goodbye, decrepit manse. Hello, House Phel."

He nodded, not quite summoning the words. A surprising wave of emotion welled up in him, a bewildering tide of grief, joy, pride, fury, and cold vindication. Nic had said he'd inherited the Phel magic. In that moment he wondered if he'd also come into possession of the legacy of those final generations of Phel wizards. The bone-deep love of this house and exhilaration at seeing it intact, rising grandly against the misty blue Meresin sky felt not entirely his.

"We did this," he said in a hushed tone, squeezing Nic's hand. He looked down to find her gazing back with eyes glimmering green with similar emotion. "If nothing else, you and I did this."

"Yes, we did." She transferred her gaze to the manse. "This is a good thing. Special and important."

"The south wing does appear to be a mirror of the north," he observed after a moment, and she giggled.

"What a practical observation, Lord Phel," she accused with a mischievous smile. "I may be rubbing off on you."

He nearly made an off-color remark about her rubbing *on* him, when one of the visitors hailed them. "Hey there, the house," a dark-skinned young man called. "Lord and Lady Phel?"

"Remember," Nic advised under her breath. "Arrogant, powerful, lord of all you survey, including me." She tried to tug her hand out of his, but he held on, suppressing a smile at her muttered imprecations about obstinate wizards.

Probably his impulse to wave in welcome wouldn't fit the arrogant image, Nic recommended, so he straightened instead, inclining his chin slightly as the sled coasted to a stop before them. Three women and one man, all brightly dressed as if for a festival, bowed their heads in greeting. None of them could be any older than Nic. One young woman smiled directly at Nic, a happy glint of friendship in it.

The young man leapt out and bowed fully. "I am Asa, wizard and emissary of House Refoel, submitting my application to be contracted to House Phel." He produced a rolled scroll with a flourish, stamped with the Convocation seal. "My MP scores and other relevant documentation."

Gabriel took the scroll, bemused.

Asa seemed pleased, giving another bow. "I and my house welcome House Phel's invitation for placement. We support and celebrate House Phel's reinstatement, and we look forward to a strong alliance with the Convocation's newest house. My familiar, Laryn." He held out a hand without looking, and a dainty, fair-skinned brunette stepped out of the sled. She curtsied to Gabriel, eyes demurely lowered, then slid a curious glance at Nic, who nodded to her minutely.

"I hope," the Refoel wizard continued, "that I will be an acceptable addition to House Phel."

Gabriel realized—after a slight and awkward pause—that it was up to him to say something to the Refoel wizard's obviously rehearsed speech. Clearly he should have Nic teach him some polite responses to these overtures. *Arrogant, powerful, lord of all you survey.* "House Phel appreciates the good will of House Refoel," he replied. "Lady Phel and I appreciate the long journey you've made to join—" At the hiss of Nic's breath, he hastily revised his words. "To introduce yourselves and apply for the position." He waggled the scroll. "I shall review your documents."

That was the correct approach, because Asa nodded agreeably, and Nic relaxed. Asa's wizard-black gaze did linger on their joined hands, a glimmer of assessing curiosity there. Belatedly, it occurred to him that it might look as if he meant to access his familiar's magic rather than holding his wife's hand out of affection. Ah well, done was done, and he liked holding Nic's hand.

The other two women now alighted from the sled, both golden haired and clear skinned, so alike they could be sisters. The one with black eyes took the lead, bowing to him and giving Nic a nod as well, presenting him with a similar scroll. "I am Sage of House Byssan and this is my familiar, Quinn Byssan." Quinn bobbed a curtsy, smiling widely at Nic, who remained quiet and still, but her hand quivered with happy response. "House Refoel was kind enough to give us a lift, as House Byssan is on Refoel lands." She gave a nod of thanks to Asa, then looked past Gabriel to the manse. "I understand you need some windows."

"Indeed we do," Gabriel replied, far more comfortable with Sage's craftsperson's approach.

"Point us at where you want us to start, then," Sage replied agreeably.

Gabriel looked to Nic, hoping she'd take over. Thankfully, she did. "Welcome to House Phel," she said with a deep curtsy. "Have you all breakfasted? Perhaps you'd like to rest after your journey. I apologize in advance that the manse is still being renovated, so we do not yet have rooms prepared for you. I promise some will be ready by the end of the day."

"Quinn and I are fine," Sage replied, glancing at Quinn and receiving a nod of affirmation.

Gabriel felt some tense part of him release at the obviously easy relationship between that pairing.

"We work best in regular bursts, with rests between, but we can go all day."

"Thank you," Nic replied warmly, and Gabriel began to understand that she could play gracious hostess and solicitous lady of the house in contrast to his forbidding arrogance. "I can show you where to begin. Wizard Asa?"

"I'm fine also," he replied, notably not checking with his familiar. Asa's gaze went to the bruises around Nic's throat. "Laryn and I are early risers, and we all passed a comfortable night not far from here. Once you task Wizard Sage with your lists, Lady Phel, perhaps we can discuss a place where I can see patients. I'm happy to examine your ladyship first, if you like."

"Oh, I don't—" Nic began, tucking her hand in her skirts and Gabriel knew she'd been about to cover her bruises.

"That would be excellent," he interrupted, giving her a quelling look. There were some advantages to playing imperious lord and master. "Lady Phel will be delighted to be your first patient."

Her eyes glittered with some unspoken retort, but she acceded with an excellent pretense of meekness. The Refoel wizard accepted the declaration with a slight bow, his dark face mild. And yet, Gabriel felt judged by the other wizard, who clearly assumed Gabriel had left those marks on his familiar. He opened his mouth to explain, but closed it even before he caught Nic's warning glance. Right. The wizard he was pretending to be wouldn't be sorry for physically abusing his familiar. Likely he wouldn't even notice.

Nic gave him a deep curtsy, not attempting to withdraw her hand from his. "With your permission, Lord Phel, I'll give wizards Asa and Sage a tour of the manse. I know you have correspondence awaiting you in the library."

Appreciating her deft delivery of the appropriate cues, he released her hand, feeling oddly bereft without the contact. And also not particularly thrilled at the reminder of all the missives—and those creepy couriers—likely awaiting his attention. When he'd decided to restore House Phel, he'd imagined more glorious battles and less paperwork. Didn't that just figure?

"Thank you, Lady Phel." He paused awkwardly, hoping it

wasn't apparent. "Join me there after your examination, please."

"As you wish, Lord Phel," she acknowledged humbly. *Arrogant, powerful, lord of all you survey, including me.*

The more he learned about Lord Phel, the more he loathed the guy.

$\sim 13 \sim$

Recognizing Gabriel's rapidly fraying temper, Nic watched with considerable relief as he strode back into the manse. He'd acquitted himself well, much as he loathed the part he had to play, and now deserved some time and space being only himself. The Refoel and Byssan pairings all relaxed as they watched him go, which also gave credit to Gabriel's performance. They'd been suitably impressed and intimidated. Gabriel wouldn't like to hear it, but cold arrogance came naturally to him.

And, maybe it hadn't been necessary, but she'd much rather new arrivals came away from meeting the mysterious Lord Phel reconsidering any plans they might harbor to spy upon or betray him.

"Well," she said brightly, allowing them to think she, too, was cowed by her powerful lord and master and could now speak freely, "let me give you the grand tour."

"Quinn," Sage said, nudging her familiar forward, "go ahead and greet your old friend properly. I know you want to."

Quinn flashed her wizard a grateful smile and flung herself at Nic with a squeal of delight. Nic returned the hug, more moved than she'd expected to see her dear friend. "We have so much to talk about," Quinn whispered in her ear. "There have been so many rumors! And your letter said almost nothing, you bitch. I want to hear *everything*. Will you be able to get away to talk privately?"

"Yes," Nic whispered back, deciding to ignore the implication that Gabriel might keep her on that tight of a leash. Hadn't she just been deliberately creating that impression? "I'd love to catch up." She hadn't heard that Quinn had been bonded to Sage, her older sister, and she was very curious how that had come about. With a last squeeze, she released Quinn. "I'm so happy you're here."

Keeping the smile for Quinn firmly fixed so it wouldn't cool with dislike, Nic turned to Laryn. "It's good to greet you again, too, Laryn."

With her wizard's expectant gaze upon her, Laryn produced a polite smile for Nic. One that Nic knew had to be mostly, if not totally, fake. Laryn had never liked Nic, and she'd been particularly gleeful at Veronica Elal's fall from presumptive heir to House Elal to lowly familiar. How irritating that she would arrive here.

Though it had been a possibility—even a probability, given the relatively small number of unaffiliated wizards who'd be interested in an opportunity like this—that some would be former classmates from Convocation Academy, Nic hadn't been properly braced for it. Inevitably, in inviting junior wizard–familiar pairings to join House Phel, some would also be those who didn't particularly love Nic. They may have all graduated to adult lives, but that didn't mean they'd all matured past petty school-aged squabbles.

"Lady Phel," Laryn replied, smirking enough to make the title a question. "Congratulations on ascending to such an enviably high position. I'm sure House Phel isn't nearly as decrepit as you say."

Nic smiled thinly, having said no such thing. If she'd realized Laryn was a possibility, she'd have worded her message to House Refoel differently. Or perhaps not. She'd been mainly concerned with attracting wizards who would mesh well with Gabriel and his eccentricities. Asa certainly fit the bill there. She turned to Asa, pointedly declining to reply to Laryn's remark. "Asa, I'm so glad you've come. I'd hoped you would answer the invitation."

Asa grinned at her, the genuine smile creasing his dark face. He'd been a year ahead of her at Convocation Academy, and a fine wizard. They'd sometimes speculated that he could find a place at House Elal someday, when she took over for Papa. "It seems our hopes might work out after all, Nic," he said. "Even if somewhat sideways of what we anticipated."

"Isn't that the way of life?" she replied with good humor. She'd been relieved that Asa hadn't applied for her Betrothal Trials, and she'd been prepared to use a summary dismissal against him. Not that he wouldn't be a kind master. Healers weren't necessarily gentle types, especially with some given to thinking themselves omnipotent, holding the power of life and death in their hands, but Asa had a good and generous heart. She just hadn't been able to imagine submitting to someone who'd been a friend. Perhaps Asa had recognized that a familiar with her MP scores would be too much power for a healer, particularly a wizard not in line to head his house.

Now it seemed he hadn't applied because he'd already bonded Laryn. Her face looked fuller than Nic recalled, a lush glow to her skin, her gown loose through the middle. No doubt pregnant with Asa's baby, then. Quinn caught her eye, that familiar glint of pressing gossip in them.

"It is. Keeps life interesting. And I'm glad for this part, at least," Asa was saying, taking in the sight of the elegant, rambling manse. "I hope Lord Phel finds me acceptable. This would be a grand adventure." Laryn smiled at him but looked unconvinced. "You seem to have landed in an excellent position," Asa continued, a lilt of a question in his voice as his gaze returned to the bruises on Nic's neck.

Once again, she had to still her hands to keep from trying to hide the marks. She'd been so groggy when she dressed that she'd only been thinking of something clean, new, and stylish in which to greet their first visitors—not how the low neckline would reveal the hunters' ravages and implicate Gabriel by default. She shouldn't be concerned, as their assumptions would only add to the image she was building of a powerful and ruthless wizard determined to use all of his resources to defend House Phel, regardless of the cost. And yet, she hated for anyone to think badly of Gabriel. Such were the ramifications of harboring such affection for him.

"I'm grateful for my good fortune," she replied firmly. "Shall we?"

AFTER A BRIEF tour of the common areas of the house, Nic left Sage and Quinn creating glass for the windows in the north-wing guest rooms, completing the suite Asa picked out. To her surprise, Asa chose one on the ground floor, saying that he looked forward to being able to go on rambles through the fascinating landscape, and that having a small terrace to sit upon and that allowed him to come and go at will would be ideal. Laryn looked decidedly unenthused at the prospect of nature walks, but her smile for Asa glowed with all the serene acceptance a wizard could ask for from his bonded familiar.

Once Asa chose, Sage and Quinn had leave to pick out their own smaller set of rooms and put in the glass for those once they finished Asa's. Nic felt ever so slightly uncomfortable designating what they were allowed as lower-tier magic workers—she'd clearly been corrupted by Gabriel's radical egalitarianism—but Sage and Quinn accepted the boundaries with good grace, even evincing pleasure at the options Nic presented.

Asa and Laryn then walked back with her to revisit a series of smaller salons in the south wing. Nic, of course, hadn't yet had the opportunity to explore the south wing thoroughly, but it did appear to mostly mirror the north wing, as Gabriel had noted and she'd anticipated. The House Phel architects had been exacting in observing the classical forms, the manse as a whole beautifully balanced in design. As opposed to House

Elal, which had begun as basically a fortress and endured in much the same vein, though with each generation of prideful lord and lady wizards determined to leave their stamp on the edifice. The result was a hodgepodge of walls, turrets, wings, and towers, each attempting to best a similar existing structure in some way.

So far the primary exception with the south wing of House Phel as opposed to the north, was that the south-side version of the ballroom had been subdivided into a series of smaller salons and parlors. Perfect for offices and other kinds of small group gatherings. No doubt they'd been used that way before. Nic didn't have Gabriel's connection to the Phel heritage, naturally, but she found an unexpected pleasure in bringing life back to the house. As if ghosts had lingered in these spaces, pale echoes of what had gone before, and she and Gabriel were coloring them in, room by room, filling the house again with people and magic.

"I'm thinking this salon for you, Asa," she said. The room faced the river and led onto a terrace that could be fenced off for privacy and also used as an entrance for patients who might not care to traipse through the main house to visit the wizard healer. "We could divide it into a reception area and a couple of smaller treatment rooms. As with your suite, we'll have these rooms furnished as soon as the House Ratisbon wizard arrives, so you'll be able to request exactly what you'd prefer."

Asa beamed, nodding along as he envisioned what she described. "That would be brilliant. I hardly dared hope for such an ideal situation. Knowing it would be you here, well, I suppose I *did* hope. Elals have a knack for pulling off everything with class and style." He shrugged, somewhat abashed, while behind him, Laryn glared daggers at Nic. Wonderful. Asa tucked his hands in his loose trouser pockets, ambling around the room. A lone desk sat against one wall, apparently bolted to it. Though dried out, it remained suspiciously green, and Nic only hoped there weren't desiccated water snakes in the drawers or something. She made a mental note to have the worker bees check for such things.

Asa edged a hip onto the desk, swinging one foot thoughtfully. "So, give me the full rundown. What do I have to do to get the contract? Tell me what this Lord Phel is really like. Powerful—I can sense that rumors didn't overstate that. But he's got to be completely ignorant of actual wizardry. Can he *do* anything? And how do I win his confidence?"

It was interesting, as much as Nic had always liked Asa and enjoyed his easygoing nature, she noticed more than ever how much he oozed with that wizard-born arrogance. Laryn might as well be invisible to him, her presence falling out of his mind until he needed her. And he spoke easily with Nic, falling back on their old acquaintance from when their friendship had been based partially on the assumption they'd both be wizards. She understood, actually, his reasoning for asking for inside knowledge, bemused as she was that he was asking her to spill secrets on her wizard master. Was he relying on their friendship or did he think her weak-minded now that she was a bonded familiar?

Regardless, her loyalty belonged to Gabriel, and she wasn't about to violate his trust—or the growing affection between them. She'd grown accustomed enough to Gabriel's unconventional ways that coming up against Convocation attitudes was a bit discomfiting. "I would advise you to be authentic and forthright with Lord Phel," she said in perfect honesty. "As a stranger to the Convocation, he has no patience for posturing or power plays. Be good at what you do, familiarize yourself with the customs and people of Meresin, and..." Her gaze went to Laryn, who was staring out the open windows at something. Or at her own thoughts. Laryn had always been serious to the point of being forbidding. "Treat your familiar well."

If Laryn heard her, she gave no hint of it. Asa raised a brow, gaze going to her neck. "In what way?" he asked, sounding genuinely curious.

This time, Nic did brush her fingers over the scabs and healing bruises, which hardly hurt at all. She considered pushing up her sleeve to show Asa the bite from the hunters, to explain that Gabriel hadn't done these things to her. But she didn't want to discuss her flight and subsequent capture by the Convocation hunters. The less said there, the better. And it wasn't what she meant. She didn't mind at all that Gabriel's rope had left marks on her wrists, nor would she mind other marks from him in the future. How to explain to Asa that what the Convocation saw as appropriate use of a familiar was abuse in Gabriel's eyes?

"Allow Laryn the freedom to follow her own mind when you have no need of her," Nic said, following impulse.

Asa's gaze went to Laryn, who still had her back to them, as if deaf to the entire conversation. "So she could do what?" Asa asked, the question giving Nic a surge of irritation, he sounded so perplexed. No wonder Gabriel chafed at the status of familiars.

"I'm sure she would think of something," Nic replied drily. "For example, to treat my minor wounds and assess the status of my pregnancy, you don't need to access your familiar's magic, do you?"

Asa frowned, his pride pricked. "Not for something so minor, no."

"Then why is she here?"

Asa gazed at Laryn's back, as if suddenly wondering that, too. "Well, I *would* need her for other patients. Say, for a major healing, for grave injuries or a long-unattended chronic disease, which I suspect may be an issue in this backwater countryside. Also if I have many patients in a row, I'd need to recharge or draw on her actively."

"So you don't need her to dance attendance on you constantly."

Giving her an odd look, Asa said, "I wouldn't phrase it exactly that way. I do need her available to me. Quickly, in an emergency."

"It's a big house, but not that big," Nic pointed out.

"True…" Asa snapped his fingers at Laryn, who turned obediently. Nic sighed mentally, hoping Gabriel never saw *that*. "You may be excused, Laryn."

Her suspicious dark-brown eyes went to Nic, a flicker of something angry in them. "What would you like me to do?"

Asa looked to Nic, who had to lock down her eyes to keep them from rolling. "Perhaps you could visit your suite," she suggested, "and make plans for how you'd like to furnish it, including the nursery," she added on a guess.

Laryn gazed back at her stonily. "Yes, Lady Phel." She bowed to them both and left.

"How intriguing," Asa commented, watching Laryn go, and then looking expectantly at Nic. "What did you want to tell me?"

"Pardon?"

"I assumed you wished to have a private conversation, and that's why you wanted Laryn to be sent away."

Well, that didn't go well. "There's a great deal to do here, and Lord Phel doesn't approve of idle hands," she said, wishing that explanation had come to her sooner. "If you want to win his confidence, have Laryn be productively occupied when you're not in immediate need of her."

Asa nodded thoughtfully, then patted the desk beside him. "So noted. And, in light of that, and in lieu of a proper examining table, let me take a look at you."

Oddly self-conscious, she sat beside Asa, lifting her chin as he ran light fingers over the scabs and bruises ringing her throat. "Iron collar, huh?" he asked, though it wasn't a real question. "Ill-fitting, too. If Lord Phel wants a collar that won't injure like this—"

"He doesn't," Nic interrupted firmly. The surest way for Asa to get on Gabriel's bad side would be to suggest any kind of collar for Nic. "I mean," she amended hastily, realizing Asa was getting entirely the wrong idea, "he's not in favor of collars for familiars at all. If you want this contract, you won't be either."

"Hmm." Asa's noncommittal hum invited explanation, but

she offered none. His magic streamed over her skin, itching as the deeper tissues mended. She'd had healing before—for a few minor childhood illnesses, a hefty bout of pneumonia at Convocation Academy one winter, and for a broken arm when she fell off her horse trying a difficult jump—and it never felt like much of anything to her. Magic, yes, but with no particular flavor, scent, or color. Gabriel's magic had been so vivid to her from the first moment that she'd forgotten that other wizards' magic wasn't the same. She'd put it down to Gabriel's truly remarkable level of power; now she wondered. Even with Asa working magical healing on her, it simply didn't feel all that interesting.

"That takes care of that," Asa said with professional neutrality. "Anything else?"

She pushed up the sleeve of her dress, showing him the bite from the hunters. That injury, too, was mostly bruises, the jaws mostly crushing her wrist so she'd drop the enchanted blade that could kill them, the hunter's fangs only puncturing here and there.

"Looks like a dog bite." Asa raised his brows in question, holding Nic's arm but watching her face.

She simply nodded. With a suppressed sigh, Asa healed that, too. "I realize that Lord Phel is not of the Convocation," he said as he worked, "but I can speak with him about the value of familiars—your high value, in particular—and our customs about allowing these sorts of incidental injuries."

Oh, Nic could just imagine that conversation and how well it would go. They'd be lucky if Gabriel didn't blow an artery in his brain and leak blood out of his ears. "None of my injuries are Gabriel's fault," she explained.

"'Gabriel,' is it?"

Nice slip, Nic. "He's more upset than anyone that they occurred."

Asa regarded her gravely. "I'll have to take your word for it."

"Yes, you will."

He cracked a half smile. "As strong-willed as ever. I'm glad to see it, Nic—that being a familiar, bonding to your wizard, hasn't changed that."

She smiled, sticking with declining to comment as the safest course. "And the pregnancy?"

Growing serious, Asa laid a hand over her lower belly, black eyes half lidded in concentration. "It's early days yet," he murmured, half to himself. "Barely a month along, are you?"

"That's right."

"Any tiredness, nausea?"

"Tired," she admitted, "but we've been busy."

"I noticed you're low on magic. I'll talk to Lord Phel about not draining you so completely. Heavy-handed of him."

"Please don't," she begged. She didn't want to explain that Gabriel was still learning, or that the reigniting of the arcanium had been an unusual event. Gabriel would continue to improve in skill and finesse—and in the meanwhile, she didn't want him inhibited in any way.

Asa sighed. "I'll take your wishes into consideration, but draining your magic reserves so dramatically could affect your unborn child, just as it could make you physically ill."

"I know my limits," Nic replied firmly.

"But does he? We both know you won't be able to stop him. His ignorance is a danger to you and his heir, and he needs to know that."

"I need to know *what*, exactly?" Gabriel asked from the doorway. He filled up most of it with his tall, wide-shouldered frame, his silver hair catching the light, except for that night-black streak, as black as his wizard's eyes. Nic forgot sometimes, having grown familiar with Gabriel's innate gentleness and fairness, how intimidating he could be when angered. No pretense needed. Gabriel glared silver daggers at Asa's hand on her belly with those eyes, his magic coiling hard and sharp around him.

Asa sensed it too. Moving slowly, he removed his hand from Nic's belly, holding both up in a gesture of peace that looked much like surrender. "Lord Phel, I was examining your lady to determine the state of her pregnancy."

"And." Gabriel threw out the word like a lance, not asking, but demanding.

"It's not always easy to determine much at this early stage, but all seems to be well, Lord Phel," Asa replied, standing and bowing courteously. "You should have no concerns about your heir."

Gabriel bared his teeth in something that not even the most optimistic could call a smile. "I am not fond of the Convocation's way of reducing people to their useful roles. Our child will be important to me as more than an heir, and my concerns are for Nic, a person who already exists. How is she, how is my ignorance endangering her, and what is it that I need to know?"

"I apologize for any implied insult. It was not intended. Your familiar is in good health, Lord Phel," Asa replied formally. "I've healed Lady Phel of her various *injuries.*"

Asa put a slight emphasis on the final word, and Nic, her watchful gaze on Gabriel, managed not to wince at the flare of anger in his wizard-black eyes. She tried to give him a warning look, but his attention was entirely on Asa. "Mitigate my ignorance," he instructed with quiet insistence. "Quit dancing around and tell me what I need to know about Nic's limits."

"The familiar's magic has been drained excessively," Asa replied. "Dangerously so, as I'm sure you can sense." His tone made it clear he wasn't at all sure Gabriel sensed that, and Nic had to steel herself not to flinch when his gaze snapped to hers, anger, accusation, and—worst of all—guilt in his eyes. She tried to keep her own expression calm and neutral, trying to communicate that this was not an extreme situation. Obviously, she couldn't argue with either wizard, but she hoped Gabriel would reserve judgment for the moment.

"It is, of course, entirely up to you how you use your familiar, Lord Phel," Asa continued with stiff formality. "None in the Convocation would gainsay you. It's likely no surprise to you that I would like to secure this contract. However, I will not compromise my integrity as a healer for it. I won't withhold my opinion and best advice simply to please you."

Though Gabriel visibly fulminated, he considered Asa with a revised opinion. Asa had clearly managed to strike exactly the right note with Gabriel. Perhaps without realizing it, or perhaps in light of Nic's advice. Whichever it was, it had been exactly the right thing to say—and if Asa always spoke so forthrightly to senior wizards, no wonder he hadn't contracted with a house yet and was so eager to gain this position.

"Good," Gabriel grunted, and Asa reacted with a start of surprise, making Gabriel smile mirthlessly. "I'm not interested in hiring sycophants. The job is yours—*if* you swear to always tell me when I'm wrong, and if you'll teach me what I need to know about Nic's abilities and limits—since she clearly isn't going to." His gaze slid to Nic's again, his anger all for her now.

"To be fair, Lord Phel," Asa put in, setting a hand on Nic's shoulder, "familiars are well taught to refuse nothing that their wizards ask. In fact, the bonding won't let them refuse, even if it occurs to them to do so."

Gabriel's jaw flexed, fingers curling into fists, and Asa removed his hand from Nic. "I asked you to give me honest advice, so I won't make a hypocrite of myself and argue with you. But I would appreciate if you wouldn't talk about Nic like she's not right here."

Nic lifted her brows at him, reminding him without words that he was doing the same thing. His mouth twisted in wry acknowledgment.

"I agree to all of your stipulations, Lord Phel," Asa said, then nodded to Nic. "Lady Phel."

Gabriel barely acknowledged him. "Are you done here?" he asked Nic. "Or do you need more healing?"

"I already—" Asa began, but Gabriel stopped him with a flick of his cold gaze.

"I'm much better," Nic assured them both, hopping down from the table. "I would've met you in the library in another few minutes, as you asked. Did something come up?"

He cocked his head slightly, as if considering the answer, some sort of inappropriate retort leaping to his lips before his gaze flicked to Asa, and he squelched it. "Yes," he said simply, holding out a hand to her.

She put her hand in his, obediently going with him as he turned to leave. "You have injuries too, Lord Phel, that Wizard Asa could tend to."

Gabriel glanced over his shoulder at Asa. "Later." He paused. "These rooms will be the healing center, for seeing patients?"

"If it pleases you," Nic replied, lifting a brow on the side of her face that Asa couldn't see.

"It pleases me," Gabriel replied, his tone so dry it sounded sarcastic. "Set it up however you like," he told Asa.

"Thank you, Lord Phel." Asa bowed deeply, his face serious, dimples in his cheeks showing that he struggled to restrain a grin. "I appreciate your confidence in me."

"I'm not sure 'confidence' is the word I'd choose," Gabriel replied, then walked out of the room with such long strides that Nic had to trot to keep up. He held her hand fiercely, magic boiling silver around him, the scent of steam hovering in the air.

"What did you need?" Nic finally asked. After all, she knew what was wrong, so no sense asking that. Even if she was brave enough with him in such a mood.

He slanted her a look, not replying immediately. They entered the library, considerably less gloomy with all the windows open to the bright day, and he released his death grip on her hand to close—and bar—the doors. *All right, then.* Nic shook out her hand while his back was turned, then dropped it into the folds of her gown, composing herself as he turned back to her, folding his arms and staring at her with a forbidding expression.

Nic waited. He said nothing.

"I missed you," he finally ground out, not sounding like meant it.

Feeling as if she was handling a half-feral water elemental, Nic searched for what to say in return.

"And then I saw you, with *him*," Gabriel continued, sparing her that much. "Were you lovers?"

Nic's mouth fell open in surprise, no reply leaping to fill the empty space.

"Not that it's any of my business," Gabriel added hastily. "It's a question unworthy of you and invasive of me. It doesn't matter. Don't answer that."

Was he *jealous*? "I'd like to answer that. No, Asa was a friend, but never a lover. I was a virgin until my Betrothal Trials."

He nodded, stiff, arms still folded. "That doesn't preclude you from having had lovers. And it doesn't matter," he added, sounding as if he was reminding himself, as it clearly did matter to him.

"Gabriel," she said, laying her hands gently on his bulging forearms, the simmering tension popping in his muscles, "I have no feelings like that for Asa. We were classmates and friends, and I was happy to see him. That's all. I'm bonded to you, which means that even if I'd ever had softer feelings for

Asa, I wouldn't have them now."

Huffing out a laugh, Gabriel shook his head. "That does not make me feel any better."

"What would help?" she asked earnestly, massaging his tight muscles with her fingertips.

He frowned blackly, unmoving. "I was jealous," he admitted, sounding like he hated even saying the words. Sighing, he unbent enough to take her hands in his. "I *am* jealous. I hated seeing him put his hands on you. I nearly forbade him from doing so ever again."

"He wouldn't have been surprised. It's in a wizard's nature to be possessive."

Gabriel grimaced. "I really hate when you tell me that what I'm feeling is because I'm a wizard." Despite the strong words, he didn't pull away from her.

Nic pressed her lips together, sorting through various replies to that. "I could resolve not to say that anymore, but it wouldn't make it less true."

Searching her face, Gabriel looked profoundly unhappy. "I wish that…"

"You can be honest with me," she encouraged when he trailed off and didn't continue.

Shaking his head, he blew out a long breath. "What you must think of me."

"I think a great deal of you, Gabriel," she replied with perfect honesty.

"Do you, really, though?" Her breath caught sharply in her throat at the accusation, the very real doubt in his eyes. Before she could answer, though, he went on. "I wish that everything between us didn't come down to wizard and familiar."

She wanted to tell him that it didn't, but would that be the truth? He saw it in her, too, his keen attention on her face, no doubt sensing her emotions, if not the direction of her thoughts. "Gabriel," she said slowly, wanting very much to say whatever might soothe this roiling hurt and anger in him, "while the Fascination draws me to you, and the bonding ties us together, I do care about you. I know you don't want to hear that I love you, because you don't believe it's real or that I don't feel that way of my own free will, but you asked for my friendship and trust. You have that. You are my wizard, which is a permanent bond, but I also don't *want* to be with anyone but you. I like you," she added, somewhat desperately, feeling the inadequacy of the word.

His lips twitched with ironic appreciation, but his eyes held more. A kind of yearning. And a wistful sorrow. "Nic, I don't have your trust and friendship," he said gravely. "If I did, you would have told me that I drained you too much."

"That has nothing to do with trust and friendship," Nic countered. "First of—"

"It has everything to do with that," he snarled, abruptly dropping her hands and pacing away, full of restless anger. "You knew I didn't want to use the arcanium, to do those things to you, exactly for fear of—"

"Yes, I know!" she shouted at him, startling him enough that he paused mid-step, head whipping around in shock. "Now will you *listen* to me instead of telling me how I feel and what my motivations are?"

Dark irritation clouded his face, but he inclined his chin.

"By all means. I look forward to this explanation."

Setting her teeth and refusing to be intimidated by his supercilious attitude, she paced up to him. "First of all," she repeated herself pointedly. "I do know my limits, and I'm not an idiot familiar as Asa, in his wizardly arrogance, assumes. It was easier with him to take the humble approach and ask him not to bring it up with you than attempt to argue with him. I'm a grown woman with exceptionally high MP scores, well-educated, with excellently honed skills. I know what I'm doing. I'm asking *you* to trust in me. I'm not done," she said when he opened his mouth, and he closed it again, firmly pressing his lips together in a stern line.

"Second," she continued, "I suspected it would take galvanizing power to reignite the arcanium like that, and I was willing to do what it takes because that would make everything easier for both of us. A plan that worked, I might add. Third, I didn't tell you because I knew you would worry and that it wouldn't be productive for either of us. *Fourth*," she inserted forcefully when he looked like he wanted to argue, "yes, of course I knew you didn't want to use the arcanium, to do those 'things' *with* me—which I also know you enjoyed just as much as I did—so the last thing I was going to do was tell you anything that would give you an excuse not to do it again." She finished nearly out of breath, the close-fitting bodice tight against her breasts until the Ophiel gown adjusted to accommodate.

Gabriel's gaze flicked down at her excitedly heaving bosom, then up to her face again. He raised one brow sardonically. "Are you done now?"

"I believe so," she replied as coolly as she could, drawing on her best Lady Veronica Elal poise. "Though I reserve the right to add additional counterarguments as they occur to me."

With a sigh, he shook his head. "Of course you do." Then he pinned her with his wizard-black eyes, hard and determined. "*My* counterargument is singular: all of those fine rationalizations come down to one crystal-clear truth. You don't trust me. Not to be given salient information, not to make up my own mind once I have it, and not to use my concern for you in productive ways."

She tried to pick apart his argument. Couldn't. "You have a fair point," she admitted on a sigh.

Gabriel raised both brows. "Did I just win this argument?"

"It's not a competition," she retorted in an arch tone, "but I will take your suggested modifications to my behavior under advisement."

He caught her around the waist before she could step away. Holding her close, he stared into her face, his expression fierce. "Is that Lady Elal speak that you'll try to trust me—or that you'll pretend to?"

She didn't mean to hesitate, but she didn't want to lie either. "It's not easy for me, Gabriel," she confessed on a near whisper. "I come from a world where trusting other people is not a good idea."

"I understand why that's so." But his hands on her only tightened. "What can I do to help?"

"You're doing it." Indeed, in the face of his determined onslaught of her defenses, of her heart, she had little ability to withhold anything that he asked for. "Let me try this. I'll behave as if I trust you, and maybe I'll get used to it. After all, what difference is there between appearing to be a thing and becoming it?"

He laughed softly, but at least without that humorless, bitter edge. "I'll take it." Lowering his mouth to hers, he caressed her lips with his, sweet and tantalizing, a promise of more. The yearning flaring in her, she clung to him, savoring his flavor and his cooling, silvery magic, no longer sharp and steaming, but coiling around her in an affectionate embrace.

Withdrawing from the kiss as slowly as he'd eased in, he leaned his forehead against hers. "This was never easy, between us," he observed quietly, "but it was easier before other people arrived."

"You could always go into a rage and throw them out," she teased.

"Don't tempt me."

"If you don't like Asa, you don't have to keep him." She pulled back enough to study his expression. "There will be others."

"Perversely, I actually do like him."

"So long as he keeps his hands off of me?"

"I suppose it's not practical," he mused as his hands explored her curves, "but I would prefer if you were only mine."

"In point of fact, I am," she reminded him.

He froze. "I didn't mean—"

"It's all right." She framed his face in her hands. "There are reasons for these customs you so despise. I won't say anything about the nature of wizards, but be aware that the magic that runs through you isn't entirely yours. It has wants of its own. Fighting that could tear you apart."

~ 14 ~

I T ALREADY WAS tearing him apart. And with considerable chagrin, Gabriel made note of his own hypocrisy—that he didn't want Nic to know just how much. The wants of the magic, as she put it, pounded through his blood, demanding and possessive. *Familiars don't run around without their wizards,* she'd told him once, and he suddenly and viscerally understood why. He'd been out the door and on his way to find Nic before he even realized he'd decided to. Saying he'd missed her had been such a bland way to describe how profoundly something in him had raged to have her nearby.

And when he'd seen another wizard with his hands on her…

Well, he understood Nic's awful tale of the wizard Sylus and how he'd reacted to the abduction of his familiar. If someone harmed Nic, Gabriel could see himself laying waste to all the world to avenge her. He could've cheerfully killed Asa on the spot, convinced he wouldn't regret it. It was only some appalled remnant of his former self that had stood back, reining in the ferocious desire to destroy. It had only been to prove something to himself that he decided to offer Asa the contract. Gabriel could control himself. He *would* control himself.

And if he failed… well, it would be good to have someone around who would stand up to him if he lost himself in the insatiable craving for Nic. She still framed his face with her slender hands, the essence of wine and roses filtering from her, heady and delicious as she gazed at him with eyes brilliant as emeralds. "What can I do to ease you, wizard?" she asked softly.

Calling him that, as they'd established in the arcanium, had the effect she no doubt intended. That slavering part of himself leapt to answer, images popping into his mind of what he wanted from her, the ways he wished to consume and dominate her. To mark every fingertip of her skin as his. Nic read it in him, too, her lush lips curving in sensual answer. "Take, wizard," she purred. "Have."

This, at least, he could give into without a fight. Picking her up, he carried her to the old desk, setting her on it and pushing between her spread thighs. Then he buried his face in her bosom, inhaling the scent of her skin, the heated flesh in the delicious cleft between the round globes of her breasts. Restraining the urge to bite, he held himself to kissing her velvety skin, laving the newly healed and once-again flawless skin of her throat, even as she whispered encouragements, her fingers twining in his hair as she arched her back to offer him more and more. Pushing up her skirts, he found the enticingly soft skin of her inner thighs—and the slick, heated core of her sex.

She gasped, crying out as he pushed the lacy lingerie aside, sliding his fingers into her. Enjoying her trembles and shudders of need, he stroked a finger into her, tantalizing her with the ball of his thumb. Playing her like an instrument who made music just for him. That thought salved the beast inside, and—with delicate precision—he sipped a bit on her slowly replenishing magic. Not enough to make an impact on her recovery; just enough to give himself a taste. To abate the craving. Not to feast, but to wean himself away from needing it all.

And now that he knew more, now that he was paying better attention, he noticed how the sensual teasing fed the fire in her, her magic intensifying, blooming and growing richer. Caressing her to the point of climax, he backed off, waiting for her to calm before he edged her up to that point again. Never quite letting her go over the edge, though she began to beg for it. Her pleas appeased the possessive need in him, too. Far safer than the other fantasies that occurred to him, darker methods for making her cry and plead with him.

So, despite her entreaties, the growing desperation of her urgent mewls, when he felt the ping of another wizard's arrival, he withdrew his hand, replacing the lingerie to cover her silky flesh and lifting his head to kiss her cheek. "New arrivals," he explained when she gave him a bewildered look.

She clutched at him, fingers fierce as claws. "We can finish first."

Surprised at himself at how much he enjoyed this rush, he kissed her deeply, loving how she yielded so utterly to him. When she melted, he nimbly extracted himself from her grip, shaking his head, hard-pressed not to laugh at her outraged expression. "It wouldn't be polite to make them wait," he explained, doing his best to sound earnest.

"You are Lord Phel," she pointed out. She looked incredibly seductive, perched on the desk with her skirts rucked up around her waist, sex gleaming pink and swollen through the lace of her lingerie. "They can wait for your pleasure."

Unable to restrain the grin, he tapped her on the nose, aware that she'd scent herself on his fingers. "So can you, familiar."

She gaped at him, growing understanding in her eyes. "You left me hanging on purpose."

"Yes." He held out his hand for her. "Arrange your gown and come along."

Lips pressed into a mulish expression, she scooted off the desk, doing as he bade, though she muttered viciously under her breath, "This is not playing fair."

"Isn't it?" he asked blandly. "This is what you've been demonstrating to me, that erotic play between us replenishes the magic. Climax releases it. Therefore arousal without climax builds your magic without releasing it again. I'm following my wizard's instincts, as repeatedly instructed to do. Am I wrong?"

"You are correct," she bit out with a glare. "But you can't tease me like that and not follow through."

"In point of fact, I can. I just did. And you have more magic now." Sensing that replenishing in her made him feel immensely better. She might be irritated with him, but he'd take that over leaving her drained of what made her so vividly alive.

Putting her hand in his, she began walking with him. "I'll just take care of it myself, then. Easy enough."

"No." He halted, giving her a stern look, enjoying the way

her eyes darkened to emerald in response, a faint blush gracing her cheeks. "You won't. You'll wait."

"Until you say so?" She lifted her chin defiantly, but her words were breathy, the challenge arousing to her.

He leaned in, inhaling her wine-dark magic, intoxicating and rich. "Until we're in the arcanium," he breathed against her cheek, taking her earlobe gently in his teeth, so she moaned softly and shuddered in response. His own aching arousal suddenly felt unbearable. Hours and hours until they could dispense with all of these *people* and be alone together.

"I've created a monster," she observed in a hoarse voice, not sounding all that dismayed.

"I am ever your eager pupil," he agreed.

She slipped her free hand between them, clasping his hard cock through his pants, squeezing a shudder out of him in return. "Same goes, then," she said. "If I have to suffer, so do you. It will only build your native magic, and it's good discipline," she added with a sweet smile.

Cupping her cheek, profoundly aware of how her fire billowed in his heart, tender and fierce, he nodded soberly. "Done. Fair is fair."

DESPITE HIS ENDURING sexual frustration—kept at a low simmer by Nic's proximity, her lush figure so gorgeously flattered by the magically fitted gown, her ample breasts tantalizingly displayed—the rest of the day flew past. More wizards, some with familiars, others alone, arrived with regularity. Sage and Quinn worked at a frenzied rate, installing glass in the rooms as the incoming guests selected them.

Nic actually cried out in delight when the Ratisbon wizard arrived to create furniture. An elegant man with an equally well-dressed familiar, he sniffed at the manse, pronouncing it musty but with excellent bones. He immediately rejected the Ophiel wizardling who arrived, saying that he'd personally request an Ophiel friend of his that he happened to know was dreadfully unhappy in her current contract. Managing to be both scrupulously polite to Gabriel and didactic at the same time, he instructed Gabriel on the amount to offer to buy out her contract and that he should do so immediately.

Gabriel nearly refused on principle but caught the lift of Nic's dark brow. When she offered to draft a missive and send it, he did his best to hide his resignation. Nic knew, probably better than he did at this point, what they could afford. Unfortunately, she vanished into the library to take care of the task, leaving him to field the new arrivals and their endless questions. The concept of minions, or this potential secretary he could delegate tasks to, began to sound better and better.

When his mother and father showed up, it was his turn to nearly cry out in relief. His father doffed his cap, audibly scratching his skull at the sight of the restored manse and the considerable crowd of people. His mom shook her head in amazement. "People have been by all morning," she said, "all telling us the house was above water again and looking like nothing we've ever seen before, but I hardly credited it." She stared a moment longer then turned a look on him, a line between her brows—exactly as she'd looked when he created that first deluge, puzzled and a little bit afraid. "I know I said I knew you could do this, but I didn't expect…" She trailed off, biting back the words.

"For Nic and me to do it overnight?" he asked with a smile he didn't feel. What he did feel was a similar aghast astonishment. In the magical moonlit night, exploring the newly raised manse with Nic, he'd grown to accept the presence of the sprawling halls, so infused with the unseen presence of his ancestors, like one accepted the reality of a dreamworld while occupying it. In the bright light of midday, spring in full swing around him with riotous birdsong, his father in his dirt-soiled coveralls and his mother with a few stray orange-blossom petals in her hair from inspecting the blooming orchards, the two worlds collided sharply.

"It is quite a feat," his father acknowledged, carefully situating his hat on his head again. "I'm proud of you, son," he added, though it came as an afterthought and sounded more bewildered than anything.

"I couldn't have done this without Nic," Gabriel explained, not quite sure what he wanted them to understand. "I'm learning a great deal from her." Turning his face away, he wiped a hand over it, hoping he looked flushed from the warm day and not his thoughts of all he was learning from his luscious wife.

"Where did all these people come from?" his mom asked as a group of laughing young wizards burst out of the north wing, turning to point up at the lofty gables. "I mean, I know you two mentioned that healer and a few others, and Nic sent us a message that you needed help sorting guests into rooms, but I didn't expect..."

"People to help us restore the house," he replied, keeping the word deliberately lower case, so they wouldn't think he meant any of these people would become family. Except, they would, wouldn't they? "Nic has been busy."

"Well, she's an organized soul," his mom observed faintly. "And she said she'd have House Phel ready for a big society wedding by midsummer."

"She's well on her way to accomplishing that goal." He noted the rueful twist to his words and wondered at it. "And these are just the highest priority staff on her lists, and the nearest to Meresin. There will be more."

"Well, then," his mother said, brushing at her hair, "I supposed I'd best find Nic and get my assignments."

"You could move back into the house, Mom," he suggested before she could go. "All the windows will have glass soon instead of boards. And new furniture."

She crooked a finger at him, offering her cheek, and he kissed it. "I like my little cottage," she confided. "I suspect it will be quieter than this place."

"Probably true," he agreed.

"What can I do?" his father asked as his mom bustled off, craning her neck to take in the north and south wings.

"How's that levee?" Gabriel asked, the sudden inspiration hitting him with a glow of relief.

"Still leaking like a sieve," his father allowed.

Gabriel clapped his hand on his father's back. "Let's go see to that."

THE SUN WAS lowering when Nic arrived on Salve. She'd freshened up, perhaps even bathed, and looked dewily lovely as a rose in first bloom. She also wore a light-green dress he'd never seen before. Had her trousseau arrived? That would certainly relieve some of her unspoken anxiety about her father's position on her actions.

"You look beautiful," he told her, leaning on his mud-covered shovel.

"I wish I could say the same of you," she replied, arching one brow. "Did you soak in the mud—some sort of rejuvenating spa treatment, perhaps?"

He laughed, stretching his back, aware of the ache of hard work in the muscles there. It had been a good afternoon, grounding to work side by side with his father as he'd done when everyone thought he'd be only an honest farmer. He'd sweated up a storm, worn blisters on his hands, and felt more like himself than in longer than he could recall. Even before he'd gone to Elal to meet Nic, he'd spent far too many days and nights holed up in that moldering library, studying histories and spells, wrestling this magic that possessed him far more than he'd wielded it.

"Do I even want to know about House Magical Mud's healing treatments?" he asked, then lifted a hand to his father's hail from below. "The good news is, I think we've found the weak point in the levee." He pointed with his shovel to the muddy pit he'd just climbed out of. "There was a bit of sinkhole beneath that just kept undermining everything we put on top of it."

Nic eyed the pit dubiously, Salve shifting daintily beneath her. "I'll be irritated with you if you didn't call for me to help because you were worried about draining my magic."

"Nope." He grinned at her. "All manual dig-dig method. Sometimes that does a man good." He reached down to offer his father a hand up the last bit of slippery slope.

"Nic," his father said, doffing his muddy cap. He looked like a child's mannequin made out of mud, so Gabriel figured he didn't look any better. No wonder Nic was giving him the side-eye.

"GF," she replied warmly. "I've been asked to tell you to go home already and that a man your age doesn't need to be working himself to death when younger bodies can do it twice as well in half the time."

His father put on an exaggerated expression of shock. "You look like my daughter-in-law, but that's my wife's voice coming out of your mouth!"

Nic laughed, her heartfelt, musical laugh. "I'm memorizing the lines I should use on your son. Would you like to borrow Salve for a lift home?"

"Ah, no, though it's sweet of you to offer. It's a short walk that will help loosen the kinks. Good work today, son. I think the boys and me can finish 'er off tomorrow."

"Perhaps Gabriel and I could help tomorrow," Nic suggested.

His father glanced at him. "I know you two have important work to do, but…"

"Everything to do with House Phel is important," Nic emphasized. "We'll come to do this tomorrow and demonstrate how we work together to use magic to add to the manual methods." Giving Gabriel a bland look, she invited him to argue.

"See you tomorrow, Dad," Gabriel said, shouldering his shovel and turning his feet toward the manse, new glass windows glittering in the distance as the setting sun hit them. The house looked pretty. Lived in, even.

"I'd offer you a lift," Nic said, "but I already bathed and changed for dinner."

"That's all right." He walked alongside Salve, remembering how Nic had walked beside Vale all the way back to Port Anatole when he'd ridden, too injured to do otherwise. She kept Salve to a slow pace, riding easily, regally even, her seat graceful and her strong profile gilded, dressed like a lady and looking nothing like the bedraggled and collared woman he'd rescued. "It's my turn to walk," he added, and she returned the wry smile.

"At least it isn't pouring rain this time," she replied, clearly remembering that same miserable journey. "Though a good downpour would help to sluice some of that mud off of you before you track it into the house to bathe and dress for dinner."

"There's a bucket outside I can use to deal with the worst of it. Why does this dressing for dinner sound like something more than usual?" Funny that, as if they'd established a usual.

"You're presiding over a formal dinner, Lord Phel," she replied loftily, "which will be attended by your newly contracted Refoel wizard and those hopeful for placement in various capacities, whom you have yet to meet and approve."

He sighed at the prospect. "I needed to get away from the crowds for a bit," he admitted.

The look she gave him was softened with affection—or maybe that was the twilight and his wishful thinking. "I understand," she said softly. "Today was a lot. All of this is."

"True." He gazed at House Phel, the graceful tiers he'd never truly expected to see intact again, the windows blazing with light now, echoing the orange streaking through the high clouds, contrasting with the violet sky behind. "Fire elementals?" he asked. "The Elal shipment must've arrived."

She shook her head, a troubled frown shadowing her face. "Many, many lanterns. We've received no word from Elal at all."

Well, shit. "I'm sorry, Nic," he offered quietly. "Perhaps your father wasn't home or—"

Cutting off his words with a sharp and bitter laugh, she shook her head. "Gabriel, my only love, you do not need to coddle me with rosy optimism. I'm practical, remember? And I know Papa better than anyone, perhaps even better than Maman does, because he taught me how to think like a wizard and the head of a High House. He hasn't replied because he considers my missive unworthy of it. His message is very clear."

"It was a missive from me," Gabriel pointed out. "Likely

it's me he regards as unworthy of a reply."

"No," she replied softly, gazing into the distance. "He knows my handwriting, and he'll recognize my mind behind the words. If you had written the letter, he'd have answered you. This is a slap in my face, a reminder of my station." She sighed. "I gravely miscalculated. You'll have to write the next letter."

Wishing he could touch her, he put a hand on the heel of her boot instead, well below where he might muddy her hem, squeezing lightly so she wrenched her gaze from whatever unhappy vision occupied it and glanced down at him with a sad smile. "Forget him," Gabriel said, shaking her foot a little. "We're not writing to him again."

"We need that dowry. And I want my clothes, and my grapes."

"Is it worth it?" he asked, wanting to make her see that it wasn't. "Surely other places grow grapes. In Wartson, maybe."

"I can't see putting Wartson Summer Red on a label," she retorted without bite.

"Phel Summer Red doesn't sound much better, to be honest."

"I was thinking Gabriel's Blend myself," she mused. "Such a pretty name."

"Veronica's Red," he suggested. "With a hint of roses, just like you."

"Such a romantic." She rolled her eyes, but he thought she wasn't displeased. "Still, I don't want Wartson grapes, though I suppose I could make do. I want what's *mine*. I should be able to make my own summer red wine, whether Papa approves of my choices or not."

He suspected the wine, and the grapes to make it, had become emblematic in her mind of all that her beloved papa had promised, explicitly and implicitly, raising her as his favored child. Nic had lost so much of his regard that the grapes were but a small piece of what she wanted from her father. And the megalomaniacal Lord Elal wouldn't give her even that.

"That's a pretty dress," Gabriel observed, making his own mental list of everything he'd give Nic that her parsimonious family wouldn't. "That's part of why I thought your trousseau had arrived. It's new?"

"Newish. Wizard Wolfgang's Ophiel friend arrived, and I begged her to convert one of the heavier riding habits to something lighter. You don't mind, do you?"

"Of course not." Though he'd loved her in that burgundy velvet. "The wine-colored one or...?"

"The brown one," she reassured him. "And if you approve the Ophiel wizard—Dahlia—then she can make me a new trousseau without taking apart anything else."

"Do I have to approve all the wizards and familiars personally?" he asked. "You know more about them than I do and—"

"Yes, you do," she answered firmly. "I did my part by filtering the invitations to attract the right sort, but you must be the one to decide if you can work closely with another wizard, to the point of having them live in your house and sit at your dinner table nightly."

"Nightly?" he echoed, appalled. "I thought there was this whole plan to sequester that lot to the north wing and feed them separately." Like a kennel, or a stables, but for irritating wizards.

"Perhaps not nightly," she conceded, "but often enough. You'll want to keep an eye on them. Even without dinners, you'll be working closely with these people. Some more than others, but look at how you reacted to Asa."

"I approved him," Gabriel protested.

"Exactly, even though you don't like him. I can't possibly predict that sort of thing."

"I don't *dis*like him."

Nic, very pointedly, didn't say anything.

"I like Sage and Quinn."

"Even a broody and reclusive wizard like you has to like Sage. What did you think of Laryn?"

"I think that *you* don't like her."

Nic glanced at him in surprise. "Was I that obvious?"

He considered the question. "Not to anyone else, I think. I just know you—when you're pretending and when you mean it."

"Hmm. Something for me to remember."

"You should tell me, though, if you dislike someone. You have an equal say in our household." He braced himself for her argument, but she surprised him.

"Thank you. I very much appreciate that consideration. But I don't *dis*like Laryn. I don't," she protested at his dubious glance. "Not really. It's more that she dislikes me, and I react to that. I suspect her feelings have more to do with her own misery than anything I've done. Is it arrogant to say that I think she's always been jealous of me?"

"No, especially since I think it's true." He could see how attractive and well bred but unremarkable Laryn would be jealous of the vivid, spirited Nic.

"Jealousy is a bitter and poisonous thing to live with," Nic said in a reflective tone. "She makes herself unhappier than I ever could, even if I wanted to. Which I don't think I want. What I'd like is…" She trailed off, shaking her head.

"You'd like what?" he prodded, wiggling her foot by the boot heel he still held.

"I'd like to see what the House Phel new regime could do for her," Nic answered hesitantly, almost shyly.

"The 'new regime'?"

"Your whole take on the wizard–familiar dynamic." She waved a hand at the glorious sky like it demonstrated something. "*Partnerships,*" she clarified, saying the word as if he'd made it up. "Someone like Laryn, she has to hate feeling powerless to control her life, carrying a baby she likely resents—she's really not the maternal sort—and dragged off to the swamps of Meresin where she won't even have the pleasures of Convocation society to soothe her."

"With her nemesis as lady of the house she serves in," Gabriel added.

"Yes." Nic rolled her eyes dramatically. "Horrible, arrogant Veronica Elal, familiar to the lord of a High House, running poor Laryn's life. Quelle horreur."

He chuckled. "You're not like that."

"No," she replied in a thoughtful tone, "though arguably I was once quite full of myself. Confident, certain of my rosy future, probably to the point of being insufferable. And people have a tendency to project," she continued before he could say anything to that. "If our positions were reversed, Laryn would no doubt use her power to torment me, so she expects I'll do the same."

"But you're not tempted?"

"No. In fact, I talked to Asa about her already."

"Did you now?"

"Yes, do you mind?"

"Why would I?"

"Just checking. I framed it as a way of working with you, that you don't see things the same as a Convocation wizard and that he'd do well to give Laryn some freedom. Let her have occupations of her own, rather than dance constant attendance on him."

Wonder of wonders. "All true, too," he acknowledged blandly, careful not to show her just how much it meant to him that she was coming to see things his way. "I thought you wanted our incoming wizards to believe we have a traditional Convocation relationship, me all broody and demanding."

"To begin with, yes—but I'd like to wage a subtle campaign with those I think have the mental flexibility to change their thinking, who will then be loyal to you and your new regime. We can't have vipers in our household waiting to strike. This will be a good way of sorting them out."

He had no argument with that. "What did Asa say?"

"He was taken aback, but he's giving it a try. He does want this contract—and to impress you."

And Asa was at least half in love with Nic, though Gabriel didn't say that aloud. She'd only tease him about wizard-borne possessiveness.

They went on in silence for a bit, the walk companionable in an oddly peaceful way. Nic had accused him of wanting that simple farmer girl, and while he wouldn't deny that part of him still longed for that simpler life, this felt meant. His beautiful, fierce, and talented wife understood him like no one else ever had. With both their gazes fixed on the manse, gilded by the purples and golds of a spring sunset in Meresin, the bats emerging to flutter through the crepuscular light, it felt as if this was usual, as if they'd been walking home together all their lives.

He hated to disrupt the peacefulness of the moment, but he felt he had to ask before the opportunity slipped away. "Nic, do *you* resent the pregnancy?" he asked quietly. "You can be honest with me, because I'd understand if you do."

"Because I'm not the maternal sort either?" she asked drily.

"Quite the opposite." He squeezed her ankle. "You are warm, affectionate, nurturing, and thoughtful. You're also fierce, courageous, and believe in building a family. I think you'll be a wonderful mother—but I also know this isn't something you chose."

"But I did," she corrected, gentle but firm. "I went into the Betrothal Trials knowing I'd come out of them pregnant. Unless something went terribly wrong."

"So did Laryn, theoretically."

"True," she acknowledged. "But Laryn and I are very different people that way. She'll do as expected and burn with bitter resentment every step of the way. Whereas I'll embrace the practicality of my situation and make the best of it."

"I can absolutely see that."

"In my way, I'm a sunny optimist." She smiled broadly at him, making him laugh.

"You joke, but you are," he mused. She was the sun to his gloom. Her determination to make the best of everything was a kind of profound optimism, in truth. "I feel I should point out, however, that you evaded the question."

"I didn't evade it so much as I was giving myself time to think about it." She lapsed into thought, and this time he gave her the quiet to consider her answer. "For a long time," she finally said in a soft voice, when they'd very nearly reached the back entrance to the house, "it just didn't seem real to me. Sometimes it still doesn't. I mean, the oracle heads are never wrong, and I can feel certain changes in my body, but it's a lot to wrap my mind around, you know? That there is this whole person, with their own thoughts, feelings, and ambitions, who doesn't yet exist in the world, but who will grow inside of my body and then appear—*poof!*—eight months from now. Isn't it an extraordinary thing, that we just accept this... magic?"

"I suppose so." He'd never quite thought of it that way. "Though we're not surprised when orange blossoms become fruit, or when foals appear in springtime."

"True, though—if you really think about it—those are bizarre and magical transformations, too. Anyway." She smiled down at him, the expression softer than he'd ever seen on her face. "I don't resent it. I'm actually kind of... feeling all fuzzy, warm, and anticipatory. We're going to have a baby, Gabriel. A little person who will be the best of each of us, who will grow up in this beautiful house, surrounded by interesting people. They'll have a good life, familiar or wizard."

"We'll make sure of that," he answered, his voice choked with surprising emotion.

"Yes, we will. And it feels miraculous to me to be able to believe in that." She laughed, almost to herself. "Go bathe and dress. I'll see Salve back to the stables and meet you in the dining hall."

He groaned, having nearly forgotten about that.

"Gabriel," Nic called as she turned Salve toward the stables. "Believing in that kind of life for myself and for our child? That's a gift you've given me, more precious than anything. Even Elal grapes."

~ 15 ~

THE RECEIVING ROOM adjacent to the family dining hall was far from ready, so Nic skipped protocol and had everyone simply convene at the dining table. Wizards and familiars sat or mingled, sipping from the sadly mediocre wine Nic had discovered. She sipped hers and barely avoided wrinkling her nose at the unfinished sharpness. Gabriel flat refused to buy anything from Elal, so she'd have to find a decent alternate source of wine. There was no point in setting up a livable manse and serving excellent food, only to have it accompanied by terrible wine. Something else for the list.

"Nic!" Quinn held out a hand to Nic, squeezing it warmly when Nic took hers. Sage, looking a bit tired—and no wonder with all the windows they'd glassed in—nodded to Nic and wandered off discreetly to chat with Wolfgang and his familiar. Quinn tugged Nic off to a quiet corner. "Do you have a moment to catch up?"

"It might take more than a moment," Nic replied with a smile, "but yes. Lord Phel has some other business and might be some time yet."

"So what is he like?" Quinn widened her pretty blue eyes and mock shuddered. Or maybe the shudder wasn't faked.

"He's terribly powerful, I can sense that much, but is he cruel to you?" Her gaze drifted to Nic's healed throat, and she lowered her voice. "There have been rumors."

"What rumors?" Nic asked, laughing as if entirely amused by the possibility.

Quinn glanced about. "That you tried to run."

"Really?" Nic rolled her eyes. "And how would I have accomplished that?"

With a relieved smile, Quinn relaxed and laughed. "Well, I certainly don't know. And it's clearly not true, because here you are, duly bonded to Lord Phel." Her statement held a hint of a lilt, an unasked question.

"I am," Nic replied firmly. "And most content to serve my wizard in every way possible. Also, I'm Fascinated by him, which means I couldn't have run, even if it occurred to me."

Quinn gave her an odd look. "But Fascination isn't real."

"Are you sure?"

"They said so at Convocation Academy," Quinn replied. "Why would you doubt our teachers?"

"My maman believes it's real."

"Oh, well, Lady Elal." The way Quinn said that had Nic raising her brows.

"What do you mean?"

"Nothing, really," Quinn hastily reassured her. "You know how it with the lords of High Houses, though, especially powerful ones like your father."

Nic did and didn't, but before she could probe more, Quinn continued, speaking rapidly. "So, what's it like? I mean, don't get me wrong, I'm grateful to be working with my sister.

We're lucky to be so compatible, and our bonding keeps everything in the family." In a perhaps unconscious gesture, Quinn ran a hand through her chin-length curls, her gaze going to Sage, whose fair hair was elaborately coiled for dinner. "But I wonder what it's like to be bonded to a wizard who is also your lover," she finished wistfully. Then her gaze sharpened on Nic's face. "Or does that make it worse?"

Nic had no idea how to answer that. "I have no basis for comparison," she offered, but even as she said it, she knew with crystal clarity that she wouldn't change a thing. She loved the partnership she and Gabriel were forming, and she couldn't imagine now dividing their erotic interplay from the magical variety. "He is not cruel to me, quite the opposite," she added, wanting to get that particular question answered. She laid a hand over her belly. "And it is lovely to have my husband, the father of my child, also be my wizard. There's a satisfying unity in that."

"I'll bet," Quinn replied, then made a face. "My family wants me to be bred. Sage has the list of matches for me."

"Oh," Nic said, feeling like she should say more, but what was there to say?

Quinn nodded, as if Nic had said something important. "Sage has promised to pick a man I'll like. She suggested that she pick one who could partner with both of us—our family will want her to produce heirs, too, after all—and that way our children would be more siblings than cousins."

Nic didn't ask Quinn how she felt about that idea. It was clear on Quinn's face, and besides, how a familiar felt wasn't important.

"She's a good sister," Quinn added on a sigh. "And really very considerate of me."

"Does she think that if the pair of you share a lover or husband, it would keep you closer?" Nic asked on impulse. Something she probably would never have asked another familiar before.

Quinn gazed at her in predictable shock. "Why would Sage give any thought to that?"

"She's a good sister," Nic echoed. "Maybe she thinks if she chooses someone for you both, that she's protecting you. And it wouldn't occur to her that you might want to choose someone for yourself."

Quinn blinked. "I don't get to choose someone for myself."

"Not even off the list?" Nic prodded, a part of herself standing back in surprise. "What if you asked Sage to let you meet the candidates, get to know them, and then tell her which you like?"

"How would we possibly do that?" Quinn asked, bewildered. "That's if I even dared ask."

"What can it hurt to ask? Ask when the two of you are alone and find out what she thinks. If she's willing, we could invite the candidates here to House Phel, to court you."

"Nic..." Quinn trailed off, flabbergasted, yet with a glimmer of impossible hope in her eyes. "Would Lord Phel allow that?"

"Yes," Nic replied firmly. "He's not the usual sort of Convocation wizard. He would absolutely be in favor of this."

Quinn gripped Nic's arm. "Do you really think so? I mean, let me talk to Sage."

"You do that," Nic replied warmly. "And if necessary, I'll ask Gabriel to discuss with her."

"No, I'll talk to her. We're close. And she's a good sister."

Nic couldn't help laughing. "So I hear."

Just then, a servant signaled of Gabriel's approach, so Nic rang a bell to ask everyone to take their seats. They rose again as Gabriel entered the hall. He visibly flinched at the sight of the more than two dozen people seated at the long table, but to his credit, he soldiered on, drawing his brooding and forbidding persona around him like a cloak, wizard-black eyes fastened on Nic as he strode to his place at the head of the table. He looked so commanding, shimmering with silvery-cool magic, that she shivered—and she let the gathering see her visceral response to her wizard. All of them had fallen silent when Gabriel entered the room, rising to their feet in deference.

Gabriel reached her position at his left, lifted her hand and kissed it, lips twisting wryly. "Lady Phel."

"Lord Phel," she replied in an equally grave greeting. Tipping her head slightly to their audience, wizard-black and jewel-bright familiar eyes alike studying him with interest, she mentally urged him to welcome them and allow them to be seated.

Turning to the gathering but keeping her hand, he took his time evaluating them, making a show of examining the wizards and familiars he'd not yet met, nodding here and there to the ones he had. "Welcome to House Phel," he told them, his voice like rocks, making it sound like a command rather than a greeting, which worked just fine. "Be seated."

He sat, too, taking the glass of wine she poured him as muted conversation resumed. Servers streamed out of the kitchen, carrying trays with plated dinners. As Nic had instructed, one set a plate before Gabriel first, then her, before working their way down the table. She examined her own plate critically. Not quite as she'd envisioned, but remarkably close given the short prep time. They'd get better.

"So," Gabriel muttered under his breath, "we have a full kitchen and serving staff now?"

"The word 'full' would be a bit of an overreach, but we're getting there. Enough to plate and serve food for the family dining hall, anyway."

"Set out a buffet and let them serve themselves."

"Ah, but then they'd eat more, going back for seconds, and even thirds. This way, they get what they get, they leave once dessert has been served and consumed, and we control the costs."

He considered her a moment, then held up his glass in a toast. "You are a remarkable woman, Lady Phel."

"Remember that," she smirked, even as Asa, to her left, lifted his own glass, echoing the toast, which rippled down the table. "They won't start eating until you do," she said under cover of the cheers.

"Figures," he grumbled, his knowing look reminding her of their first meal together, when he'd begun to outwit her with his game of matching her bite for bite. But he set into eating with gusto, raising his brows at her in surprise.

"Daisy's menu and recipes," she confirmed. "I figured that if I had to torture you with a formal dinner, I could at least arrange for you to have Momma's cooking. And she was happy to have a job."

Under the table, he set a hand on her thigh and squeezed it. "Did they teach that in Care and Feeding of Wizards 101?" he asked, eyes dancing with the intimate joke.

"Did they really have that class at Convocation Academy?" Asa asked in surprise, clearly listening in. He nudged Laryn on his other side. "You should've taken that course," he teased.

Nic schooled her expression but internally winced at Asa's poor joke—and at Laryn's barely suppressed glower.

Wolfgang, across from Laryn, ran a hand over his familiar's hair. "I can vouch that Costa must have gotten high marks in that class. He takes excellent care of me."

Costa blushed and squirmed in his chair, his gaze going to Wolfgang worshipfully. "I try," Costa murmured, leaning into Wolfgang's caress.

Gabriel gazed on the display with some distaste for Costa's submissive behavior, but thankfully didn't comment. Instead he cocked his head at the empty chair on his right. "Are we missing someone?" he asked Nic.

"Seliah sent her regrets," Nic replied for the benefit of everyone listening in. "Your sister had other obligations this evening but hopes to make it in the future."

"Does she?" Gabriel asked, his befuddlement clear.

"Yes," Nic replied firmly. "I expect she'll be able to join us for family dinners very soon."

Whatever Nic was up to, Gabriel figured she knew what she was doing. So, he nodded and grunted, also glad his persona made that kind of response perfectly fine.

NIC'S STRATEGY WORKED well enough that everyone dispersed after the simple but delicious dessert of fresh strawberries glazed with orange-blossom honey, served with newly whipped cream. It helped that she mentioned that brandy would be served in the north-wing common room.

"We're giving them brandy, too?" Gabriel asked blackly as the last of them meandered out of the room.

"Not the best stuff," she soothed, though it wasn't as if they had any that was very good, "and they won't linger, as the common room is far from comfortable yet."

"I'm surprised it's adequate for serving brandy."

"Just barely," she confided.

"You've been busy today, accomplishing amazing feats of hospitality."

Wasn't that the truth. "I don't know about amazing feats," she temporized, "but enough to keep our current roster of residents happy, and happy wizards are productive wizards who will more than earn their keep. And if they don't, we give them the boot."

"I look forward to that part." He put his arm around her, snugging her against his side. "What makes familiars happy?"

"That's easy. Happy wizards."

He slid her a look. "I want to think you're teasing, but I don't think you are."

"Well, there's a great deal of truth in it."

Pausing at the junction where they'd either turn toward the arcanium passageway or toward the staircase to the master suite, he glanced at her. "What would make you happy now?"

It wasn't difficult to know what he was really asking. As much as she'd been looking forward to time in the arcanium with him, Gabriel had clearly worn himself out on every level, between the backbreaking work at the levee and dealing with strange wizards and assorted entourages. His steps had been heavy, and while his magic shone brightly, he looked tired. She was tired too, she had to admit. And her conversation with Quinn lingered in her mind. *I wonder what it's like to be bonded to a wizard who is also your lover.*

"It might be nice to do something really kinky—for us— and have sex in a bed for once," she suggested with a saucy smile. "Unless you're too tired for it."

His black gaze fired, and before she saw him move, he'd swept her into his arms, carrying her laughing up the stairs, taking the steps two and three at a time. "The day I'm dead," he declared, elbowing open the door to their suite, "is the day I'm too tired to bed you, my heart."

"See?" she replied with a purr. "That's how you make a familiar happy."

MORE PEOPLE THAN she'd expected gathered the next morning at the levee, particularly given the heavy overcast. Dark-bellied clouds loomed over them, promising torrential rain even to her untutored eye. That didn't seem to deter the locals or dim their merriment as they turned out in a horde to witness the magical levee rebuilding. More people had gathered, in fact, than she'd realized lived in the vicinity of House Phel. Men and women in coarser clothing suitable for field work, others dressed more for indoor, less filthy pursuits. Children ran about shrieking like it was a festival. The newly arrived wizards and familiars, hearing that Lord Phel would be putting on a practical display of his wizardry, had also made the walk over. They stood in a convivial group, Laryn holding an open umbrella as she scowled at the threatening sky.

Even Narlis had attended with Daisy and GF. The old familiar wore a broad-brimmed hat that partially obscured her face as she looked about with interest, if of a hazy variety. Narlis beamed as she spotted Gabriel, quickening her step to reach up and pat him on the cheek. "You're a good boy," she told him.

"What's going on?" Gabriel asked his parents. "It's not a party."

Daisy made a face and patted his cheek also. "That's where you're wrong," she corrected cheerfully. "Everyone is miffed they didn't get to see you and Nic raise the manse. They're not going to miss this display."

"They're excited, son," GF added. "It's good for your people to see the strength of their new lord." He slid a look to Nic and winked conspiratorially.

Gabriel opened his mouth—to deliver some scathing remark, no doubt—but Nic threaded her arm through his. "It *is* good," she said, tilting her head at the cluster of their guests, including ones who'd arrived just that morning. She had yet to meet any of those, as she and Gabriel had opted to enjoy a private breakfast on their balcony, then went directly to the library to dispense with the most urgent correspondence. No word still from Elal, something she was trying to resign herself to. Nor had the Convocation replied, a silence that began to feel more and more like a sword poised over their necks. It was possible the proctor Gabriel had agreed to host would simply arrive unannounced. Or that that lack of response boded something far worse.

Iblis had counteroffered for Narlis, so Gabriel, on Nic's advice, lowered his own counteroffer. He wasn't pleased, but she promised it was the right move. "A show of power put to productive use makes for a good tale," she explained when Gabriel frowned. "When Iblis hears about the manse and what you demonstrate today, they'll cut their losses."

His gaze strayed to their guests, now representing most of the Convocation High Houses—with a few salient exceptions—along with a healthy smattering of lower-tier houses. "A show, eh?" he mused.

"A showy one," she answered with a sparkling smile, rewarded when he snorted with amusement.

"Better get to it quickly," GF advised, casting a wary eye at the sky, "or yon impending rain will undo all our work from yesterday."

"Come, familiar," Gabriel said in a pompous tone, escorting her to a rise above the levee. "Let's *show* them what we can do."

Though he'd been teasing her, hearing him address her that way gave her a surge of erotic longing that nearly took her breath away. Their lovemaking the night before had been slow and intimate, and lovely in every way, but had only scratched the surface of the need he'd kindled in her with his sensual torments.

"Yes, wizard," she murmured in reply. Catching the flare of his magic, the heat in the wizard-black eyes that pinned her, she realized he hadn't been teasing at all. He knew exactly what he was doing to her. A monster, indeed. And how she enjoyed being devoured.

Unwinding her hand from his arm, he placed her so she rested both hands on his lower back, then raised his hands dramatically to the heavy gray sky, the crowd hushing and growing still. Gabriel drew on her magic, an easy pull, as hers had begun greedily reaching for him the moment he addressed her as "familiar." The sensation tugged at her with a sensual thrill, as if he'd fastened his mouth to her nipples or her sex, feeding from her and caressing in return. Needing more contact, she nestled her cheek against his side, sliding her hands around him to his flat, ridged abdomen and peeking out beneath his muscled arm. Her wizard.

Silver condensed in the air around Gabriel's upraised hands, glittering with argent sparks. The crowd murmured, a surprised ripple growing into cheers. He didn't need the moon magic for the levee work, she suspected, so he'd added that bit for the show she'd requested. Clever.

In the great pit of the levee, mud boiled, turning in a circle as he stirred it with his water magic. Then water began to lift from the viscous mixture, condensing into great, teardrop-shaped globules that rose majestically into the air. Gabriel must have added moonlight to the water, because they glowed from within, iridescent in the gloom. He circled his upraised hands in a sweeping gesture, as if conducting an orchestra, and the assembly gasped as rain began—falling not from the clouds but rising from the ground in a steady, shimmering patter. Even Nic, who was accustomed to feats of mind-bending magic, gaped in astonished delight.

The water chimed cheerfully against the luminescent globes, which increased in size as the tiny droplets impacted their undulating surfaces before merging with them. Gabriel moved his hands in an aerial dance, directing the magnificent globes, each now as large as a person, to float over the levee in ponderous grace, soaking in the upward-falling rain. They hovered over the drying soil lightly as bubbles of soap, in as prodigious a display of power as she could wish for. And still Gabriel only sipped lightly at her magic, winding it deftly with his own as he extracted water from the saturated earthen dam.

Lowering one hand, Gabriel pointed imperiously at his father, as if directing him into life also. At GF's command, workers rushed forward to shovel finely ground stone into the long trench. Gabriel waited for the signal, then crooked a finger at one of the water globes, coaxing it to sail lower, sifting a gentle sprinkle of water over the trench. The mix stirred itself in a figure eight pattern, moving thickly, reminiscent of bread dough. GF held up a hand to Gabriel, and the globe floated up, no longer shedding water. Workers eyed it dubiously as they shoveled in more of the ground stone, which

Gabriel then watered and stirred. Working in stages, they mixed the stone and water until GF pronounced it good.

Gabriel swept both arms in a grand gesture just as thunder boomed above. A final, near-torrential rainfall of water showered upward into the globes—each now as big as a cottage—a glorious ascendence that Gabriel spun a bit of moonlight into so the upward rain shimmered with rainbows and pearlescent light. Sailing the luminescent globes to the nearby river, he burst the bubbles so they exploded with showers of glowing raindrops, falling in prismatic arcs to join the lazily flowing river. The crowd broke into applause, cheering wildly, and Gabriel took Nic's hand, drawing her to stand beside him, holding their joined hands upraised so the jubilation grew even louder—underscored by a thunderous growl of thunder that rumbled over the land.

As if cued by the sound, the clouds released a rain of their own. Children shouted and ran about, holding out their hands as if to catch it, while the field workers seemed to barely notice. The wizards and familiars put up cloak hoods or broke out umbrellas, some walking briskly back toward the manse. GF frowned at the trench and cocked a questioning brow at Gabriel and Nic. "She's not quite set," he worried. "Can you keep it dry for a bit longer, just until we get the tarps in place?"

Gabriel gave her an assessing look. "How are you for mag-ic?"

"Replete," she assured him. "Can't you tell?"

"I wasn't sure if you could fake it somehow."

"I would never fake with you, darling," she replied warm-ly, and GF cleared his throat. "Apologies," she told him, and he waved her off.

"Newlyweds," he replied, shaking his head. "About keeping this cement dry?"

"On it," Gabriel said, drawing on her magic a bit more. He really was getting better at it, not nearly so heavy-handed as in the beginning. The rain soaking her hair and gown abated, and she glanced up, unable to prevent a gasp of awe at the sight. It was as if she stood under a glass dome, the rain hitting an invisible ceiling and rolling down in runnels.

"Good boy," GF chortled, clapping his son on the shoulder, then pivoted to give Nic a hard peck on the cheek. "And good girl." He strode off, calling to the workers who were unrolling long spools of some sort of waxed canvas.

"Can you extend the rain shield enough to give the wizards a dry walk back to the house?" Nic asked.

Gabriel raised a brow, but nodded, focusing in that direction. The group hadn't made it far yet, most of them picking their way fastidiously over the furrowed field and the rapidly forming puddles. Only Asa appeared to be comfortable, ambling along with his hands in his pockets, Laryn only a miserably trudging pair of legs beside him with her yellow umbrella covering the rest of her. They were close enough still for their exclamations of surprise to reach her as Gabriel's shield cut off the pouring rain. Several craned their necks back to study the phenomenon as Nic had, while Asa pointed in their direction, saying something to the group, then bowed in gratitude.

"Wave," Nic instructed, lifting her own hand in acknowledgment, pleased that Gabriel managed a similarly gracious gesture.

"Am I being powerful or generous here?" Gabriel asked.

"Both at once," she replied promptly. "And that was truly impressive. Well done. What was the ground-stone doughy stuff?"

He laughed. "I don't know whether to be flattered or cha-grined that you petted me for a job well done without knowing what I actually did."

She gave him an impish smile. "I don't have to know what you actually did to understand it was good work, but I am curious. Also, if you could keep rain off of us, why didn't you do that in Wartson for that miserable trek back to Port Anatole?"

Wincing, he interlaced their fingers and turned her to walk back to the house, keeping the rain shield over them. "It didn't occur to me," he admitted. "Also, since keeping company with a powerful familiar, I've become considerably more extrava-gant with magic. Keeping the rain off is a steady drain."

She could sense that much, though she wasn't losing magic fast enough that it was a problem. "They'll have those tarps in place soon, I'm sure, and the minions are nearly to the manse," she observed. "You don't need to shelter us."

Giving her an affectionate smile, he squeezed her hand, running a thumb over the back of it. "If we can't use our magic for a bit of comfort for ourselves, what's the point? I don't have many options for spoiling my wife, but I can do this much. I know how you hate getting wet—unless it's a hot bath."

"Thank you." His consideration warmed her as much as the most extravagant gift.

"You're welcome." Lifting her hand, he kissed it, his lips wet with rain and chilly, the stroke of his tongue against her skin hot and enticing, her loins heating immediately.

"Speaking of hot baths," she purred invitingly, "we could go share one."

"With wizard and familiar applicants arriving in droves every hour? I don't think we can afford the time. Three more sets arrived while we were fixing the levee." He shifted his hold on her hand to lightly encircle her wrist, vising gently, but just enough to send another sensual susurrus through her body. "You'll just have to wait until we visit the arcanium tonight," he added with a blandly wicked smile.

She nearly groaned. "It is so not fair that you can do that to me so easily."

He sobered, wizard-black eyes burning into her. "If it's any comfort, I'm suffering alongside you."

"I'm not sure it is any comfort."

"You introduced this method of magic replenishment," he reminded her.

"Believe me, I regret it," she bit out.

He laughed, sounding not sorry at all. "The ground-stone doughy stuff," he said, changing the topic and answering her earlier question, "is a mix of lime, clay, and sand. When you add the right amount of water, it becomes like stone once it sets. It will form a core for the levee that won't wash away like the packed earth does. We should've built it that way to begin with."

"Why didn't you?"

"I only recently found the technique in the library—right

before I came for your Betrothal Trials—and I wasn't sure if I could pull enough water out of the existing levee, and hold the river back at the same time, until just recently."

She returned his grin. "And now you believe."

"This is why I did not fail," he replied gravely, his lips twitching into a smirk.

"Ha ha. You can make fun, but—" She halted in her tracks.

Gabriel tensed, following her gaze to the elaborately gilded carriage powering around the lake. "Who is it?"

"Those are the El-Adrel house colors," she replied through numb lips. House El-Adrel hadn't replied to any of her overtures on a formal collaboration to develop and distribute water-based artifacts. The silence had been of concern, but it hadn't been unreasonable to assume that El-Adrel was simply too busy raking in money to pay attention to a small business proposition from an upstart house.

Gabriel studied her with concern. "Why is this a surprise? I thought you wanted one of their junior wizards to work with us on your product line of ever-replenishing water flasks and waterproof footwear."

"I did," she replied, not tearing her gaze from the approaching carriage. "I do—but a visit from Lady El-Adrel herself doesn't bode well."

Gabriel's eyebrows climbed, his magic bristling silver around him as he spun to face the approaching carriage. His fingers twitched by his sword hilt, and Nic put a staying hand on his arm. "She won't be unguarded, and we don't want to start a war with El-Adrel if we don't have to."

"Seems like we should just declare war on the entire Convocation and have done with it," he muttered blackly.

"Oh yes," she shot back in the same tone. "That's a brilliant idea. Then we wouldn't have to spend all this time and energy rebuilding House Phel. We could simply sink the whole thing ourselves and go live in the swamps like Seliah."

"You say that like it would be a bad thing," he grumbled, but his silver-sharp magic softened slightly, one corner of his mouth twitching in amusement.

She wouldn't reward his behavior by laughing. "Can you keep up the rain shield for a while?"

"Oh yes," he replied softly, grim determination in his voice.

The carriage glided to a smooth halt, the apparent wheels—with gold spokes, no less—a clever device that could roll or glide over watery surfaces as required. Gabriel extended the rain shield to cover the ground between them and the carriage too, and a footman hopped down to open the carriage door. He didn't move quite like a human, his skin a bronze color a bit too metallic for flesh.

"Is that guy a…?" Gabriel asked, trailing off as he searched for the proper term.

"An enchanted artifact, I'm guessing," she replied quietly. "Like an animated doll. I didn't know El-Adrel was doing that."

The footman looked over at them, as if overhearing, a glint of feral intelligence in its gaze that an automaton shouldn't have. Nic caught her breath in shock.

"What?" Gabriel asked *sotto voce*, his magic pricking her with urgency. "Is it a weapon?"

"I won't say no, but I don't think there's any immediate

danger," she whispered back. "It is, however, animated by a spirit, rather than enchantment." Which absolutely meant Elal was collaborating with House El-Adrel. Was it Papa or someone else, and did the Convocation know?

A tall woman stepped out of the carriage. Her glossy black hair, threaded liberally with the platinum of graceful age, flowed nearly to the ground over her simple pantsuit of gold-trimmed ivory. The El-Adrel crest of a lightning bolt—signifying their metaphorical bringing to life of mundane objects—jagged over one shoulder in glittering gilded thread. Her depthless black gaze traveled over House Phel, taking in the manse and surrounds, casually taking in the rain shield with studious boredom, before resting on Gabriel and Nic. With her height and long nose, she appeared to be gazing down from above, a goddess deigning to visit mortals. Nic had met her a few times at Convocation gatherings, but you'd never guess that from the way Lady El-Adrel studied her like an uninteresting species of bug.

Two more guards followed her from the carriage, also bronze-skinned, with alert, not-quite-human intelligence in their eyes. Her familiar followed last, a man of similar age, his auburn hair silvering, his strong body fit and muscular. Nic remembered him too, though not his name, if she'd ever learned it at all. Lady El-Adrel preferred to rule her house alone, so hadn't granted her familiar any rank. His brown eyes sparkled with admiration as he studied Gabriel, then lit on Nic, giving her a saucy wink of solidarity that took her by surprise. Both of them familiars to powerful High House wizards made them comrades of a sort, she supposed. An odd society she'd never before had entrée to and not one she'd ever imagined existed.

"Lord Phel," Lady El-Adrel said as if correctly identifying an unusual bird. "And Lady Veronica Phel, late of House Elal. How the mighty have…" Her black gaze lingered on Nic. "Well, 'fell' doesn't quite work grammatically, tempting though the wordplay might be. Shall we go with 'creatively reinvented themselves'?"

Nic stared back at her steadily, declining to dignify the snide remarks with a reply, nor would she meekly lower her gaze.

"Lady El-Adrel," Gabriel rumbled, not sounding very friendly, inclining his chin just the right amount to indicate polite respect, one equal to another. "What an unexpected surprise."

She arched one thin black brow at Gabriel's less-than-elegant manners. "Are there expected surprises? I suppose I'm to understand from your stilted greeting that my visit is not a welcome one. And yet, you invited us." With a snap of her fingers, she summoned one more person from the depths of the covered carriage. A man with wizard-black eyes, his mother's nose, and his father's auburn hair emerged, an irritated frown creasing his forehead—no doubt for his mother's theatrics. Nic was certain she'd never seen him before and searched the archives of her brain for his identity. An El-Adrel scion, no doubt, but there were at least six, and several of them wizards. And he looked to be about ten years older than she, so they wouldn't have any Convocation Academy friends in common. Still, she should have *some* idea of who he was.

"Our youngest," Lady El-Adrel declared, giving her son an assessing look, as if checking to see that he hadn't smudged himself somehow. "Jadren. He wishes to apply to be a junior wizard at House Phel."

GABRIEL BIT BACK the impulse to immediately refuse and send the lot of them far, far away from House Phel. He also wished very much that he could consult with Nic on the question. She hadn't anticipated any of this, he knew, or she'd have coached him on how to respond. And she couldn't help him now, having assumed proper Convocation demeanor for a familiar, all meek and being seen and not heard. There was an ominous stiffness to her silence, however, her magic very contained, so it seemed likely something wasn't right with this offer. He was tempted to say that nobody else's mommy had brought them to apply, but that would be unnecessarily cruel when it might not be the guy's fault.

Jadren stared back at him unflinchingly, even defiantly. The man, who appeared to be about Gabriel's same age or slightly older, didn't look remotely interested in being a junior anything. "I'll take him into consideration," Gabriel replied, using Nic's trick of a bland regal tone to convey nothing at all. "You brought your MP scorecard, I'm sure." Not a question. This was the first applicant who hadn't immediately presented his papers.

Jadren visibly clenched his jaw, the muscle there ticcing

rapidly. "You can see by my eyes, Lord Phel, that I am a wizard," Jadren replied haughtily. "And if you're any sort of wizard yourself, you should sense my magic. You shouldn't need more assurance than that."

Nic shifted slightly beside him, confirming the rudeness of the interchange. She'd repeatedly assured him that the MP scores of all Convocation members were essentially public knowledge—and she'd reminded him several times that he still needed to dig through the pile of scrolls documenting the scores of all the applicant wizards. Why would Jadren refuse to provide his?

"I'm not much for Convocation laws and customs," Gabriel replied, making his scorn clear, "but I fail to understand why a scion of a respectable High House would disdain those conventions."

"You fail to understand a great deal," Jadren replied, his contempt clear. "Lord *Fell*," he added with a smirk.

Gabriel figured he deserved an award for his remarkable self-control in not running the snotty bastard through right then and there. Well, self-control and those creepy soldier dolls. Nic wasn't giving him any clues, but she couldn't. Lady El-Adrel also simply observed, as if academically interested in how the exchange would play out. It was up to him, then.

"Unfortunately," Gabriel said, making it clear he wasn't sorry at all, "without seeing your MP scores and associated documentation, I cannot assure myself of your compatibility in my house." Nic had been very clear on that. "It seems your long journey is in vain."

"Aha, Lord Phel. It seems you're not as ignorant of Convocation customs as I've been led to believe," Lady El-Adrel said smoothly, her glittering black eyes fixed on him. Potent magic in her, something to guard against, though he wondered if makers of enchanted objects could do much on the fly. She could likely command those soldiers, perhaps more. She deliberately shifted her gaze to Nic, pursing her lips thoughtfully. "Someone has been tutoring you, perhaps. You see, Jadren, why I encouraged you to apply for this familiar? Not only powerful, but useful."

Jadren stared stonily past Nic. "How nice for Lord Phel."

"You have no familiar?" Gabriel asked, more because it seemed like an interesting sore spot to needle than because he cared.

"No," Jadren answered tightly, giving nothing more.

"You've contracted other wizards without familiars, Lord Phel. I have my sources," Lady El-Adrel added with a sly smile. "That clearly isn't a condition of employ."

Though the skin of his face went tight with anger that she so casually informed him he'd been spied on, Gabriel produced a thin smile of his own. "Nevertheless, I will not be offering a contract to your son." *Your spy and plant to undermine my house,* he managed not to say. Nor would he offer them the hospitality of their house. He didn't care what Nic would say about the polite social rules of that.

Lady El-Adrel didn't look bothered by his refusal at all. In fact, her expression sharpened with anticipation, the way a warrior might when presented with the perfect opening in her opponent's guard. "Oh, Lord Phel, I nearly forgot to mention," she purred, extracting a dagger from a pocket of the long white coat she wore. She dangled it between thumb and forefinger, point down. "I believe this is yours?"

Nic made a small sound that likely only he could hear. Of vindication, most likely, as she had to recognize the dagger as well as he did. The silver blade he'd experimented with, bathing in moonlight as he infused it with lethal charms—completely ignorant of the Convocation and its draconian licenses that gave its houses monopolies over certain kinds of magical incantations. Despite Nic's dire warnings of Convocation ire, he hadn't regretted making that blade, since it had been the only thing that fully destroyed the hunters that had so mindlessly pursued Nic.

What he'd most regretted was losing it. Overboard. Into the ocean. Along with that hunter that had somehow survived. He believed the hunter's geas had driven it to survive the drowning and continue to pursue Nic, but someone had to find that dagger.

Lady El-Adrel cocked a brow as if reading his mind. For all he knew, she could. "It was found on a barge that listed you as a previous owner. Naturally, as an enchanted artifact, it was brought to the attention of one of my wizards. Imagine my surprise! No El-Adrel trademark stamp, no maker's mark, *and* it tastes of moon magic." She curled a lip and waggled the dagger so its point ticked back and forth like a pendulum. "Naturally I thought to bring it to House Phel."

Wanting to keep Nic free of the taint of this particular guilt, Gabriel didn't so much as glance at her. "I didn't realize House El-Adrel was in the courier business," he said, making sure to sound as bored as possible. "Does House Ratsiel know?"

A slight change in Nic's breathing and a light aroma of roses wafting against his skin hinted that his sally amused her, and that perhaps it hadn't been entirely the wrong approach. He might not have fancy Convocation manners or Nic's keen understanding of politics, but he'd spent enough of his youth getting into trouble that he knew to never admit to wrongdoing, even if the evidence stared you boldly in the face. Also never outright deny the accusation. You might get punished anyway, but it was always good to leave a door open to potential absolution.

Lady El-Adrel looked off over his shoulder at the manse. "I'll make this quick, shall I, since it appears we won't be offered the basic courtesy of refreshing ourselves."

Gabriel said nothing, and Nic didn't cue him any differently.

"There's no point in you dissembling in an attempt to evade guilt," Lady El-Adrel continued. "Nor for me to mince words. If I wanted to sic the Convocation lawyers on you, I would have the moment my people brought this to my attention."

Ah, here it came. Some sort of blackmail, then.

She passed the blade to her familiar. The man, who shared Jadren's coloring and bone structure, held the knife on open palms, very clearly not prepared to use it as a weapon. "You will offer a contract to Jadren here and now, to be a senior wizard in House Phel, and you will agree to tutor him in such skills as intersect with yours." Lady El-Adrel made that sound unlikely. "And I won't tell the Convocation of your infringement on House El-Adrel's license."

"And in the future?" he asked, well aware she gave no guarantees.

"You proposed a business partnership, and I accept, conditionally. I look forward to negotiating our share of whatever artifacts you and Jadren manage to develop. House El-Adrel will, naturally, produce those objects under our house license. I'm prepared to offer House Phel twenty percent of net sales."

Nic casually slipped her hand through the crook of his elbow. He didn't need her pinch on the sensitive skin there to recognize a shitty deal when he heard one. "I'll contract Jadren as a *junior* wizard in House Phel," Gabriel countered, not above needling Jadren a bit more, though the man showed no reaction. "Given his apparent lack of quantifiable magical potential, however, it's premature to discuss mutual profits that may never come to be. *If* he manages to make something worth selling, we'll be in touch."

Jadren visibly fumed, though his magic remained oddly amorphous. Nic didn't pinch him again, or otherwise seem agitated, so Gabriel must not have gotten it too wrong. Lady El-Adrel drummed long gold nails against her thigh. "I'll have evidence of your license infringement."

"I'll have your son," Gabriel countered. "I wonder which of us cares most about the hostage in the other's keeping."

She smiled coldly. "I wonder."

The chill of that smile gave Gabriel pause. Jadren appeared not to hear.

"Don't cross House El-Adrel." Lady El-Adrel plucked the blade from her familiar's uplifted palms and slipped it back into a pocket. The warning, and searing magic, was clear in her tone. Her gaze lingered on Nic. "You will need allies, not enemies, and House *Fell* has a sorry history of choosing unwisely. Learn from the mistakes of your ancestors, Lord Phel."

Gabriel didn't bother to acknowledge that.

After a moment, Lady El-Adrel shrugged. "No kiss good-bye for your maman, Jadren?"

"Goodbye, Maman," Jadren replied like one of his mother's automatons, not moving to kiss her.

Her lips firmed with annoyance, but she did nothing more than flick her fingers at her familiar. Released, the man gave Jadren a hug. Jadren returned the embrace as the man who was no doubt his father whispered something in his ear before returning to Lady El-Adrel's side, a subservient one step behind her and to the side. She turned back to the carriage.

As she climbed in, she paused with one foot on the step. "Oh, Lady Phel, I nearly forgot. Your papa gave me a message for you." She smiled. "He asked me to tell you to drink water. I don't know what that means, but it seems you have plenty of it here." With a sunny smile so false Gabriel half expected it to crack her face in half, Lady El-Adrel ascended into the carriage. Her familiar bowed to them, waved to his son, and followed after, the guards joining them.

Jadren watched them leave, expression as blank as one of his mother's creations.

DRINK WATER. THOUGH it was hardly the most important aspect of the alarming meeting with Lady El-Adrel, Nic fumed over that message to the point of being unable to process anything else. *Drink water.* Papa wasn't sending her grapes to make wine was the clear message. The other, subtler message was that she'd chosen Gabriel and Meresin over her birth house, so she could live on that. Papa wasn't honoring the dowry agreement either. They would get nothing from House Elal.

If she hadn't been holding onto Gabriel's arm, she might've crumpled to the ground.

"I await your instructions, Lord Phel," Jadren said tonelessly.

Gabriel didn't look to her for guidance, but she could sense he wanted to. "Of course," she replied smoothly, pulling herself together and assuming the role of Lady Phel. "There are any number of suites for you to choose from. Allow me to show you the selection available. As we are in early days of the manse renovation, you'll be able to furnish them according to your taste."

Jadren snorted, not looking at her or otherwise acknowledging Nic's words. He glared at Gabriel. "A nice way of saying I'll be sleeping on the floor tonight."

Tempting. Oh, so tempting to blithely agree, but that would only put Jadren's nose even farther out of joint. And Gabriel seethed with fury beneath her hand. They didn't need to make this already difficult beginning any worse. So, she smiled, adding a breathless laugh as if he'd made a joke. "I think we can drum up a straw pallet," she replied lightly, letting him wonder if *she* was joking or not.

He paused. Then deliberately kept his gaze on Gabriel. "I'm grateful for whatever accommodations you can spare, Lord Phel." He didn't sound grateful, and his jaw was clenched, but he seemed to be sincere. "I will be a willing student, especially if you can teach me this." He gestured at the rain shield.

Gabriel studied him, magic questing cool past her. "Have you water magic, then?"

Jadren grimaced. "I… cannot say."

How interesting.

"Are you a spy?" Gabriel asked bluntly.

For the first time, Jadren smiled. "Of course."

"And you can make enchanted artifacts," Gabriel continued, as if that revelation hadn't been noteworthy.

"That, at least, I can do."

"Hmm." Gabriel grunted noncommittally. He covered Nic's hand with his. "Escort Jadren to the north wing, but find someone else to handle assigning our new minion a room and attend me. I have need of you."

"Of course," Nic replied, not meeting Gabriel's searching gaze. He'd have sensed her distress. Likely he'd understood her papa's coded message as well as she did. "Wizard Jadren, will you come with me?"

Jadren, clearly annoyed at being referred to as a minion, strode up the porch steps beside her, just enough ahead to demonstrate that he refused to follow her anywhere. The new arrivals were keeping either to the living spaces in the north wing or carving out office spaces in the south wing, so this main section was quiet enough that the pattering of rain on the roof sounded steadily from above. It made Nic realize that the rain had made no sound as it deflected off Gabriel's magic overhead. Same as when he'd held the water back in the arcade. It appeared to be some kind of field of force, but that was an illusion. His magic lay in manipulating water, so it was more that he'd been bending the water away. Something to remember.

"This is the main section of the house," Nic said, the tour already becoming rote. "The library is through there, which you may access with Lord Phel's permission, and through here is—"

"Cease your chatter, familiar," Jadren snapped. "If I want information I'll inform you."

Nic shut her mouth, stung. How quickly she'd become used to being treated as an equal human being.

"Elals," Jadren muttered. "The only thing worse than an Elal is a female one."

Tempted to point out the logical fallacy there, Nic nevertheless continued to keep her mouth shut until she passed him off to a cheerful Daisy. Hurrying back, Nic very much hoped Jadren didn't treat her that way in front of Gabriel. Her wizard wouldn't tolerate that, and they couldn't afford to violate the bargain with El-Adrel by harming Jadren or running him off. Gabriel was pacing in the library, hands folded behind his back, a hint of steam in the air.

Sage and Quinn had been busy, and the tall windows that faced over the river had all been glassed in, rain sliding down them in silver rivulets. A fire had been lit and—like a miracle—a couple of cozy reading chairs now sat before it, upholstered in a damask pattern of overlapping silver crescents and full circles over deep blue. A lovely take on the House Phel crest. A matching rug designed on the same theme but predominantly featuring a full moon reflected on water lay between the chairs and cheerful fire. Dahlia had been busy, and was clearly an excellent recommendation. She said as much to Gabriel, who frowned at her.

"What are you talking about?"

"The upholstery, on the new armchairs." Nic gestured toward it, although it wasn't as if there was other furniture she could be talking about. "And the rug. Aren't you pleased with how Dahlia is using the House Phel crest in her designs?"

Gabriel regarded her for a long moment. "Why are you talking to me about furniture and rugs when I know you're upset about your father's message?"

She wound her fingers together, knotting them an extra twist. Then she shook her head for added emphasis. "So he told me to drink water. It's not important."

"Nic."

The grief burbled up in her lungs, wanting to break free in a sob. She refused to let it escape, clamping down hard and holding her breath until it starved for air. Once it sullenly subsided, she dragged in a long breath, momentarily dizzy. "I suppose we'll be shopping for grapes in Wartson, after all," she ventured, attempting to make a joke of it, and failing utterly, her words plopping to the floor, sodden with heartbreak.

"Nic," Gabriel said again, but softly this time. He came to her, gently setting hands on her arms. "He's just angry. Mostly with me."

"Oh, now there you're wrong," she replied on a shuddering breath. "This anger is very pointed. I betrayed House Elal and disappointed him in the worst possible way. He's letting me know that I'm cut off. I'm so sorry, Gabriel." The tears wanted to well up again, so she turned her head to stare into the fire, willing it to burn the sorrow away.

"What are you sorry for?"

"I've jeopardized House Phel. Through my fears and foolishness, I have destroyed your financial future and your strongest bid for status in the Convocation. House Elal will never ally with you. All of this is futile." She tried waving her arms wildly to demonstrate all of their hard work, but Gabriel held her arms tightly, wizard-black eyes intense.

"Listen to me, Nic. None of that is true, and I won't have you say it."

"Gabriel…" She laugh raggedly, that terrible sobbing threading through it, attempting to escape another way. She wouldn't let it. She'd been crying too much lately, being too emotional, and not practical at all. None of this was going how she'd resolved to be. Calm, cool, accepting of her fate and lot in life. "If not for my pride, none of this would've happened. Maman always said my pride would be my downfall and *look*! I'm right here anyway. I accomplished nothing but harm. If I hadn't tried to fight you, fight who I am, then we'd have my dowry, an alliance with House Elal, and Papa would still… He would still… love me." The sob escaped in a great, ugly gulp, the tears breaking like Gabriel's magic giving way, in a torrent of fetid water. Cries of incoherent grief poured out, and she half expected gobs of algae and water snakes to burst out with them.

"Oh, my heart." Gabriel picked her up and carried her to one of the new armchairs, holding her in his lap as he sat, big arms wrapped around her. She curled her fingers into his shirt, burying her face against his chest, unable to fight the tears. What a complete wreck she was. And yet he didn't seem to mind, murmuring nonsense words of comfort, leaning his cheek against the top of her head, enfolding her as if she were something precious. Rain pounded on the roof, pouring down the tall windows in solidarity, and thunder boomed in the distance, an angry counterpoint.

When her internal storm receded, the sobs lessening to stupid little hiccups, shame crawled in to settle cold in her gut. What must her wizard think of her now? "I'm sorry," she managed, her voice small.

His arms tightened. "Don't apologize, not for this."

"But I—"

"I forbid it," he cut in decisively. "There. There's me being a commanding wizard. I will not let you apologize for being justifiably devastated by a tyrant's cruelty."

That gave her pause. Her mind empty of anything else, she stared at the wing of the armchair where it curved past Gabriel's shoulder, as if cupping them in a gentle hand. Lifting her finger to trace the pattern of silver moons on the starless blue velvet, she searched for something else to say. "This is really pretty upholstery, though."

A laugh trembled through him, rumbling under her cheek. "Are those my only options?" he asked gently. "Apologies for events beyond your control or discussions of interior design?"

She smiled, watery though it felt, her nail tracing a tumble of crescent moons. "It's sweet of you to attempt to take that burden from me, but our current circumstances are entirely my fault."

"I don't think anyone has ever called me sweet before," he mused.

Tipping her head back, she met his gaze, his black eyes soft with affection and sympathy. She must look awful, but he gave no hint of it. Reaching up to cup his cheek, she gave him a wobbly smile. "But you are sweet, Gabriel. Far more than I deserve."

"You deserve a great deal more than life has given you," he replied somberly. "And your father's actions are his own. You are not responsible for what he does."

"If I hadn't—"

"You made the choices you did for good reasons," he interrupted. "As did I. We both chose paths that led us to this point, here and now. How other people decide to react to that is on them. What you and I decide to do about it going forward is all we can control."

She considered that a moment. "When did you get so wise?"

His lips twisted wryly. "All that self-excoriating philosophizing."

Snorting a bit at that, she was surprised she could feel humor at all. "Apparently it's more worthwhile than I realized. I should try it."

"You certainly have the self-excoriating bit down pat." He slipped a finger under her chin, lifting it slightly, then tracing light fingers along the sensitive skin under her jaw. "A father's love should never be conditional," he said, spacing his words so she'd absorb the import of them. "And you shouldn't have to earn your papa's regard."

"I had it, once," she whispered. "For a very long time, when we thought I'd be a wizard. Then I failed him and—"

Gabriel put a finger over her lips. "You didn't fail anyone by being who you are."

"Are you going to keep interrupting me?" she demanded, irritation rising.

"Ah, there she is. My spitfire returns. I knew nothing would dampen that fiery spirit for long." He smiled broadly and kissed her.

She leaned into the kiss, extending it beyond what he'd clearly intended, but she needed that from him, needed to feel close to someone, needed to know that Gabriel, at least, loved her like she—Breaking the kiss on a gasp, she stared at him in utter shock. "You're in love with me!"

An almost comical blend of emotions chased each other across his face before he tipped his head wryly. "I believe it's traditional for the person feeling that emotion to make the declaration."

"Since when have you cared about tradition?"

"True." He laughed softly, caressing her cheek, raw vulnerability in his face. "Do you mind?"

"Because it's not done?"

"Yes," he replied in a dry tone. "I'm anticipating the lecture on wizardly behavior and how a familiar isn't worthy of such regard, blah blah blah."

She couldn't quite laugh, as he clearly wanted her to. "It makes me really happy," she confessed in a creaky voice.

"Does it?" He ran a fingertip over her lower lip, a hint of joy lighting his black eyes. "At last I've solved the mystery of how to make a familiar happy."

"Yes, well." She drew his fingertip into her mouth, sucking lightly and teasing the sensitive pad with her tongue, loving the way his face hardened with desire. "Making my wizard happy is still a key part of that."

"You make me very happy, Nic," he whispered, withdrawing his finger to replace it with his lips. He kissed her softly, lingeringly. "Happier than I ever thought possible."

She lifted her hand to comb her fingers through the solitary black lock of hair that streamed back from his temple, black as his eyes. "I'm in love with you, too," she told him, as earnestly as she knew how. "I know you don't believe me, but I do."

"I believe you." He pulled her closer, kissing her deeply, dizzyingly, their kisses a soft music along with the rain and the crackling fire. She wished they could stay in that chair, rapt in each other, for all time. But the world would reach out to them. Likely sooner rather than later.

He seemed to have the same thought, for he gradually broke the kiss, gazing at her ruefully. "I suppose we'll have to wait to commemorate this moment."

"And inaugurate the new furniture properly," she replied

with a solemn nod.

"You're obsessed with this furniture."

"It's pretty," she defended herself, laughing. "And it's really nice to have something to sit on besides your lap." She wiggled her bottom against his hard thighs, and he stopped her with a wince.

"Arguably, I wouldn't have a lap to hold you on without this chair, so I see your point. Nevertheless, up you go." He gripped her by the waist and set her on her feet, adjusting himself with a pained expression.

"Do you want help with that?" she offered, intrigued by the image of kneeling on the new rug and ministering to him with the fire hot on her back, perhaps her skirts rucked up to bare her bottom to—

"Stop that," he warned her. "Or we'll never leave this library."

"You say that like it's a bad thing," she retorted, throwing his earlier words back at him.

He acknowledged the point, then grimaced. "What is El-Adrel up to?"

She sat in the other chair, arranging her skirts and her thoughts. "I don't know," she said slowly.

"I thought you were the queen of Convocation social machinations."

"Ha ha, and I wish." She pressed her lips together, the thought of her papa's rejection still painfully raw. And Maman… who knew what she was suffering? Nic couldn't think about it, not if she wanted to keep from melting down into a puddle again. "Lady El-Adrel had us cold. She could have taken that dagger to the Convocation and done serious damage to you, perhaps forever destroyed your bid to reinstate House Phel. She didn't because she wants something else more."

"Thus Jadren."

"Yes. Jadren is a puzzle." She frowned, trying to dredge up the pieces of memory. "You know, I can list all forty-eight high and second-tier houses, their current lords or ladies, almost all of their heirs and most of their progeny—particularly the wizards—and yet I don't remember anything about Jadren."

"Maybe he didn't attend Convocation Academy."

"That's unheard of."

"Not precisely," he corrected, gesturing to himself.

"*You* are the exception to so many rules that I'm issuing a full present-company exemption."

"You warm the cockles of my cold, cold heart, darling. But seriously, there must be plenty of people who don't attend the academy for one reason or another."

"Sure." She ticked off the reasons on one hand. "Lack of magic, lack of connections, lack of money." She slid him a look. "Lack of sense."

He smirked for her sally, then sobered. "No academy attendance would explain his lack of an MP scorecard."

"No, it wouldn't. The Convocation would *not* let a wizard go untested. I bet it wasn't your idea to go to Convocation Center to get tested."

Tipping his head ruefully, he said, "You are correct, as usual. The Convocation summoned me for testing. Apparently there are no secrets from the Convocation, even in remote

Meresin."

"Keep that in mind, and I'm not surprised. It's far too risky to have rogue untested wizards running around. One of Elal's contracts with Convocation Center is to use spirits to spy out undocumented wizards. A house might try to circumvent that, for one reason or another, but the Convocation would pull El-Adrel's status as a house before they'd allow them to hide a wizard like Jadren. I don't know what was up with them refusing to show us his scores. El-Adrel clearly doesn't want us to see them, but I can promise there is an MP scorecard out there." She tapped a finger thoughtfully on her chin. "I wonder if I can find out through the gossip network."

"Wouldn't El-Adrel fight having their house status removed?"

"They'd try, but they'd be one house against ..."

She trailed off, a terrible thought occurring to her.

"What?" Gabriel prompted, leaning forward to pin his elbows to his knees, steepling his fingers and pressing them to his lips. "Tell me."

"There were signs that Lady El-Adrel has been collaborating with someone from Elal. Those automatons were animated by spirits, and only an Elal wizard of considerable power could do that."

"An alliance for a new product line?"

"If so, it was kept very secret. I would've said before this that I knew everything about Elal business." But then, Papa had been involved in complicated incantations extensively in recent months, retreating to his arcanium regularly, her maman more exhausted than usual. And Nic had been confined to her tower, not exactly in the swim of information.

"Perhaps it's someone else in Elal's employ," Gabriel suggested.

"I considered that, but then there's the message Lady El-Adrel passed along." She had to take a breath to release the tightness in her chest. "That could only have come from Papa. Whatever is behind placing Jadren in House Phel, they're collaborating on it."

"Against the Convocation?" Gabriel's brows rose. "They're already heads of the two most powerful High Houses. They are the Convocation, for all intents and purposes."

"Not truly. There are a lot of checks and balances. You scoff at what you see as the immovable architecture of the Convocation, but those laws are in place for good reasons—and one is to prevent any one house, or alliance of houses, from seizing too much power. There is balance in the current system."

"Hmm." Gabriel tapped his fingers against his lips, brows creased.

"I thought of something else, too. Remember how I told you that Papa encouraged me to accept your application? He made a remark at the time that if you won me, you'd be allied to House Elal, and—without the resources of a full house or experience of your own—forever beholden to Elal."

Gabriel's eyes went hard as obsidian. "Is that so," he said softly, not a question.

She recalled how proud Papa had been of her, how delighted that Gabriel, practically a rogue wizard from a fallen house, had been the one to impregnate her. How Papa had produced that incredible wedding gown and how annoyed he'd been when Maman suggested that Nic's future might be difficult. Of its own accord, her hand went to cover her womb protectively, the child within more vividly real than ever—and more painfully at risk. "He might have thought to control you through me, and through our child."

Gabriel's gaze followed her gesture, lingering there before his eyes rose to meet hers. "He'd be mistaken."

"Well, *I* know that. I knew that the moment you walked into my tower room. But Papa didn't, and then…"

"And then you proved to be too stubborn to be a good tool," Gabriel said, finishing her half-formed thought.

Startled, she stared at him, not quite able to wrap her head around what he was saying.

"You didn't fall meekly in line with their plans, did you?" Gabriel demanded with an amused lift of his brows. "No, you defied the path he laid out for you—with your mother's assistance, I might point out—and you escaped his control. Think about it. All along, his goal has been to get you back to House Elal. He's tried sending spirits after you, having you bodily abducted, playing on your affection, frightening you with implied threats to your mother. And now he's trying to break you by threatening to cut you off from your family and inheritance entirely."

"And working with Lady El-Adrel to plant someone else in your house."

"Our house," he corrected firmly. "Your father would never anticipate that you'd have feelings for me, would he?"

"He might have anticipated the Fascination, but that can't

be induced by…" Aghast, she stopped, as if by not speaking the thought aloud, she could stop it from being true.

"Nic?" Gabriel reached across the narrow space and took her hands. "You can tell me. You're thinking your father somehow induced the Fascination."

"It's largely regarded as a myth," she said faintly, remembering how easily Quinn had dismissed the possibility. "That's what they say at Convocation Academy. That it's not real. That the tale of Sylus and Lyndella is a bunch of romantic nonsense. But then I experienced it, with you, and Maman told me it happened to her too, with…"

"With your father," Gabriel finished grimly. Dropping her hands abruptly, he exploded out of his chair and paced away. Raking both hands through his hair, he clutched his skull, body vibrating with tension. In that posture, displaying his muscular back, spectacular thighs, and tight ass, he looked absurdly beautiful to her. Amazing that she could be so attracted to him, have fantasies of undressing that gorgeous body and losing herself in passion with him, even in a moment of crisis like this. Or, perhaps, especially in a moment of crisis. Somewhere along the way, he'd become the rock she clung to.

Gabriel spun, dropping his hands but still clenching them into fists. "I didn't plan this with him," he said with urgency. "I know you have no reason to believe me, not after I cheated with the fertility spell, but I did not collude with your father to trap you with me. I promise. I swear on anything you ask."

She blinked at him, dragging her mind back from lascivious fantasies of ravishing him, trying to follow the path of his thoughts instead. "It never occurred to me that you might have," she replied honestly.

"It should," he bit out. Then pressed his fists to his temples, pressing his eyes and lips firmly shut. When he opened his eyes again, he came to her and knelt on the rug before her, taking her hands in his. "No one would blame you for coming to that conclusion, least of all me."

"Gabriel," she said very solemnly, then leaned forward to press a kiss between his dark brows, lingering a moment so he'd feel her love in the caress. "You may be willing to skirt—even openly subvert—Convocation law, but you would never stoop to that level of villainy. I would never believe it of you."

He released a breath, his shoulders relaxing. "Thank you. I couldn't bear it if you left me."

"I can't leave you," she chided gently. "More, I don't want to. I can't imagine ever wanting to."

"But if the Fascination isn't real…"

"Even if Papa worked some incantation to create the Fascination, whatever I felt was real. The bonding is very real. You can feel it between us, yes?"

He nodded reluctantly. "I just hate thinking that your feelings for me are the result of magic."

"At some point, you're going to have to trust me to know what I feel. If the Fascination was my imagination, I love you now. If the Fascination was the result of some manipulation of my father's, I love you now. The result is the same, my only love."

He regarded her with a wistfulness that twisted her heart, balanced by a wry twist to his sensuous lips. "Sometimes I'm not sure if you call me your only love because you mean it or because you're teasing me."

"Yes," she replied promptly, and he laughed, kissing her with sweet affection.

~ 17 ~

A KNOCKING ON the library doors interrupted the kiss, so Gabriel stood with a sigh for the ever-growing demands on their time, drawing Nic to her feet. Just as well. They couldn't hide in the library forever, no matter how enticing that prospect.

"Enter," he called. One of the younger local lads, who Nic had apparently conscripted to help out running messages around the manse, edged through the partly opened door. "Lord Phel," he said, the impudent grin making it clear he found it weird to call Gabriel that. "There's a lady wants to see you."

Didn't everyone? "We'll be right out," Gabriel replied. "There are so many wizards all over this place now that I can't tell anymore when new ones arrive," he grumbled to Nic, offering his arm.

"You'll become accustomed to it," she soothed. "And you'll once again know a stranger from your own minions."

"Minions," he muttered darkly. "Vipers at my breast, you mean."

"Jadren is a special case," she conceded as he led her out of the library. The impassive neutrality in her tone gave him pause, and he glanced sharply at her.

"I know that one is particularly full of attitude, but did he say something to you?"

Nic shook her head, so immediately that he knew she was lying. "Not at all, he—"

"Be honest," he reminded her on a growl.

"Not everything is worth discussing," she shot back in the same tone. "I'm not fragile. I grew up in the Convocation, which means I can take a bit of snottiness and…" Her voice trailed off at the sight of the conveyance parked in the light drizzle. Even he recognized that crest, Convocation Center, and the woman descending from it: the proctor who'd presided over Nic's Betrothal Trials.

The older woman's steely gaze landed on Nic, her expression dour with disapproval. She carried herself with far more authority than a wizard of her mid-level abilities deserved to, especially as it was all borrowed.

"Veronica Elal," she barked. "You have been a very naughty familiar."

Nic didn't falter—she wasn't one to crumple under attack—but her magic dimmed. The abundant, rich swirl of fire and roses paled and contracted. "Proctor," she replied in neutral greeting, saying nothing more. Gabriel realized he'd never known the woman's name, only her title.

"And *you*." The proctor transferred her dour, schoolmistress glare to him. "You were told to go home and mind your own business, Lord Phel."

Gabriel made a show of glancing about. "And so I have," he replied mildly enough. Then gathered his magic around him, prepared to fight for his home and his woman. "It seems that *you* are the one sticking her nose into my business."

She smiled thinly. "You invited me, Lord Phel."

Curse it, she was right. And curse Nic and her determination to smooth things over with the Convocation. "I can uninvite you, too," he snapped, seriously considering sending a silver lance of solid moonlight through her chest. The big hole it would make—and the stunned look on her face—would be worth any repercussions. Nic squeezed his forearm lightly, as if sensing his musings.

The proctor shifted uneasily, which gave him a lovely thrum of satisfaction. Yes, be afraid of me. "I meant no disrespect, Lord Phel," she said, far more humbly, her posture turning beseeching. "I'm here to serve and protect you. A rogue familiar is a danger to us all. With her unstable personality, undisciplined nature, and outright rebellion, an improper bonding could allow her to—"

"The bonding has been properly conducted," Asa said, ambling up beside them with hands in pockets. He inclined his head to Nic and Gabriel both. "Wizard Asa of House Refoel," he tossed at the proctor. "I can attest to completed bonding. And Lady Phel is in excellent health, displaying no signs of instability." He glanced deliberately at Nic, raising a brow at the way she inclined herself against Gabriel, arm threaded firmly through his. "Nor of rebellion."

"Thank you, Wizard Asa," the proctor replied sourly, not sounding grateful at all. "But I will be the judge of that." She plucked a case from the chariot, returning her glittering gaze to Nic.

Gabriel recognized the case, the elaborately carved and ancient tabernacle containing the oracle head, and he suppressed a shudder. He didn't care for the horrifying, mummified head—though it probably had no power to harm Nic. The proctor was a different story.

"Make your evaluation and begone then," he bit out.

"I will do so." The proctor, confidence regained, managed to look down her nose at them. "And I will perform my duties to the Convocation at my own pace and at my own discretion. I answer to the Convocation, not to any house, no matter how high. Come with me, familiar. I require a private location where I'll be undisturbed," she added to Gabriel.

Though Nic didn't move to obey, Gabriel clamped a hand over hers to keep her from going. "*Lady Phel*," he emphasized, "will review her busy schedule and send for you when it's convenient for her, at her own pace and discretion," he added.

"That will not do at all," the proctor replied firmly. "I answer to another authority, Lord Phel, not yours. Do not force my hand."

"Try it," Gabriel invited silkily, though Nic dug her nails into his arm.

"I am surprised," the proctor said, after a significant pause, "that a young wizard from a house with such tentative status would flaunt Convocation law."

"Law?" he shot back. "Or custom?"

"I don't advise that you undertake to argue the finer points of Convocation laws and customs with me, Lord Phel," the proctor replied coolly. "It's well known that you have little experience or education in either."

"Mine is quite good," Asa noted almost idly. "On both counts."

"As is mine," Wolfgang said, joining them. "Debate team, Convocation Academy."

"You were a legend, Wizard Ratisbon," Asa said, giving a small salute in acknowledgment. "I was two years behind your championship win. My team also won," he added with a smirk.

"Well met, Wizard Refoel," Wolfgang replied, smiling broadly. "Perhaps we should start a club."

"You should," Sage declared as she and Quinn arrived. "Quinn here was a mock trial champion. No one knows trademark law like she does."

"Oh, now that's a fine idea," Asa replied, his own smile going lethal. "I can think of several test cases for us to try. After, perhaps, we dispense with the current problem."

"Oh, yes," Wolfgang said with an affable wave of his hand. "Though that should be easily handled."

"Exactly what *is* the current problem?" Jadren demanded, striding up and striking an insolent pose. He wrinkled his nose as if smelling something unsavory. "Ugh. One would think traveling to the swamps of Meresin would at least spare one the utter dreariness of dealing with Convocation lackeys."

"Wizard El-Adrel." The proctor burst out with Jadren's title in astonishment that she barely turned into a greeting of sorts. "I didn't expect—"

"No," Jadren cut in. "You wouldn't, would you?" His question was so pointed that the proctor flinched—and Gabriel wondered anew what nefarious plot Jadren represented.

"Of course, Wizard El-Adrel," the proctor nearly stammered, lowering her tabernacle. "I didn't mean to—"

She cut herself off abruptly, staring with goggle eyes past Nic and Gabriel. Then her expression sharpened, fury and triumph blending.

Before he even turned to look, Gabriel knew—by the prickling of incipient doom and Nic's suppressed groan of dismay—what he'd see.

"Lord Phel!" One of the marsh dwellers, a clever tracker nicknamed Rat, called out, "I found yer wayward wildcat. Sorry about the ties, but put up a bit of a fight, she did."

Selly. Rat had trussed her up in soft ropes that bound her arms to her sides. Selly thrashed and wriggled against them, though with little vigor, as she'd clearly been fighting them for some time. Rat tied a good knot, though. Both of them were drenched and mud-soaked.

She took one look at Nic, face contorted. "You *lied!*" she howled. "You didn't teach him how to break the spell. No one believes me. No one understands what I'm saying. I'm cursed forever and now *this!*" She squirmed against the ropes, then broke down, bursting into sobs. Gabriel's heart broke with her.

Gabriel dashed up the steps to embrace her. "Cut the ropes," he said, trying to comfort Selly even as she fought him, going from defeated to frenzied in a blink.

"Ye gotta hold 'er still." Rat had his work knife ready but hesitated. "I don' wanna cut 'er."

"I knew you lot would be uncivilized," Jadren drawled, "but this is beyond the pale. There are much more sophisticated methods for subduing rebellious familiars."

"Familiar," the proctor snarled. "This woman is an untapped familiar."

"What is going on?" Daisy shrieked, pushing past Gabriel to throw her arms around Selly. "My poor girl, what are they doing to you?"

"Mommy," Selly sobbed, collapsing into their mother's arms. "I'm so sorry, Mommy," she hiccupped. "I didn't mean to run away."

"Shh, my darling. You're all right now."

Taking the opportunity, Gabriel snagged the knife from Rat and swiftly cut the ropes while Selly was subdued.

"I can tell you what is going on here," the proctor declared, grabbing a hank of Selly's mud-tangled hair and yanking her head back so his sister squealed like a kicked puppy, the proctor studying Selly's face. "House Phel has been harboring an untapped, undocumented familiar."

"Take your hands off my daughter," Daisy snapped, slapping the proctor's grip away. "Whoever you are, coming to my home and spouting nonsense."

"Here now," GF called, taking the steps two at a time. "What do you want with my wife and daughter? Son, who is this woman?"

The proctor turned her steely, disapproving gaze back on Gabriel. "Your sister, I presume. Has she even been tested? It's a grave crime to hide an untested magic worker."

Jadren muttered something nasty that Gabriel couldn't make out. Gabriel shrugged, trying to appear nonchalant, though Nic's words rang ominously through his head. *A house might try to circumvent that, for one reason or another, but the Convocation would pull El-Adrel's status as a house before they'd allow them to hide a wizard like Jadren.* That probably went for familiars, too. "House Phel will pay the fine, then." He waved that possibility as negligible, though internally he winced at how much that might be. Especially without the Elal money, they were going to be hurting.

The proctor almost smiled—except her face would probably crack apart if she did. "Oh, no, Lord *Fell*, this merits far more than a mere financial penalty. This familiar is clearly insane from neglect, which doubles the crimes, as you've jeopardized a valuable Convocation resource in addition to violating our sacred laws."

"My Selly has never been neglected," Daisy protested. "She's headstrong is all, but she's loved. She's with people who care for her. She's certainly not a familiar."

"Will you compound your crimes with bald lies?" the proctor hissed in astonished glee. Gabriel imagined her totaling up the violations in her head.

He was about to answer that—with what, he didn't know—when Nic thrust herself forward, inserting her body between the proctor and Selly. "They didn't know," she told the proctor, drawing herself up into her lady of manor regal poise. "Until I arrived, Lord Phel's family and the denizens of Meresin lacked anyone with the ability to discern that what they thought was an illness or progressive disability in Seliah actually derived from her being a powerful familiar with untapped magic."

Daisy looked past Nic to him. "What is she talking about, Gabriel?"

He hoped he'd never again see his mother look at him with

such anguish, betrayal, and furious despair. "It's true. Nic told me after she met Selly. She was able to immediately see what we didn't have the wit to understand." He didn't much care to make his house and people look any more unschooled than they already did, but he recognized the advantage of playing up their ignorance in this scenario. "That's why I asked Rat to find Selly for us, so we could have her tested." He nodded at the proctor, hoping he looked coolly vindicated and righteous, not desperately spinning lies.

"When Nic met Selly?" Daisy frowned. "But that was—"

"Yes, just the day before yesterday," he cut in smoothly. "When Selly climbed the balcony and invaded our rooms."

"She told me I was a princess under a spell," Selly wailed softly. "And that she would tell Gabriel how to hel-help me… but she didn't. She lied to me, Mommy."

Nic looked so distressed that Gabriel put a hand on the small of her back, heartened when she lifted her chin. "I apologize, Daisy," she said calmly, though her magic boiled like shredded rose petals in the vortex of a flame. "We planned to tell you, but we knew the news would be difficult, and we wanted to find Selly first."

"Difficult?" Daisy clutched her daughter tightly. "After losing our son to this… *magic*, and now Selly, too—and you call it *difficult*?" Her voice rose perilously.

Nic stiffened under his hand. "Now, Mom…" he began.

"You told her fairy tales!" Daisy flung at Nic. "And then let her run away into the marshes."

"I was trying to offer her a metaphor to understand herself," Nic replied evenly, though her anguish increased.

"What's to understand?" Daisy practically shrieked. "I don't understand any of this!"

"Your daughter is clinically insane," the proctor told her crisply, with not one iota of compassion. "As a familiar, she should have been identified, taught discipline, and been regularly tapped to relieve the magic building inside her. Since that has not occurred, the magic has rotted her mind. I doubt she will ever be sane." She shook her head, tutting. "A shame, really, but that's what comes of willful ignorance." Her scornful gaze dusted over Gabriel and fixed on Nic. "In addition, her existence should have been reported to Convocation Center immediately upon identification. I am certain that you are familiar with Convocation law, familiar."

Nic didn't lower her head, but her magic quailed. "I wasn't certain. That's why we hoped to test her, to be sure—"

The proctor barked out a laugh. "Oh, don't give me your lies. You are Elal to the bone with your sneaking and plotting and prevaricating. Also, you are clearly still in rebellion. Any doubt I've had has been thoroughly destroyed by this development." She turned her scorn onto Gabriel. "I am taking both familiars with me to Convocation Center."

"You and what army?" Gabriel snarled.

"I don't need an army," the proctor sneered. "I have the right of law and the might of the Convocation behind me."

He looked behind her, then made a show of scanning the area. All of their new wizards and familiars, plus a generous share of House Phel workers had gathered around to watch the show. They all met his gaze with steadfast assurance. Bought loyalty, perhaps, but he was relieved Nic had insisted upon gathering these folks. They would back him.

"I don't see any Convocation might," he told the proctor coolly.

"When you do, it will be too late." She said the words so matter-of-factly that the warning gave him a chill of dread. One he refused to reveal.

"This is my house," he said, staring down the proctor, giving his mother a slight nod. "My family, my home. I do not recognize Convocation authority here."

"Gabriel, don't," Nic said, turning to lay a hand on his arm. He might've taken her plea more seriously if she wasn't trembling, fear chilling the green of her eyes. She talked a brave story about taking her lumps from the Convocation, carelessly assuring him that she could withstand any retraining, punishment, and discipline, but he knew her well now, and she couldn't hide her terror from him. Not even to save him.

"Listen to your familiar, Lord Fell," the proctor advised. "It might be your last opportunity."

"Gabriel," Nic said, turning so she could lay both palms flat on his chest. "She's right. You can't defy the Convocation and hope to keep your house status."

"I don't care about the house status."

"Don't you?" she asked urgently. "Because that status protects all of these people. Without it, everyone here will become an outlaw. And the Convocation *will* come in force, believe me." When he hesitated, she continued. "Selly and I will be all right. They can help her at Convocation Center."

"No one is taking my daughter," Daisy declared.

"No, Mom," Gabriel said, wrapping his hands around Nic's

wrists and holding her firmly. "No one is taking either Selly or Nic. Now that we've found Selly, Wizard Asa can treat her. And I'll work to tap her magic."

"You don't know how," the proctor declared, face reddening.

"I'll learn," he replied coolly.

"She must be tested."

"Then test her." He gestured to the tabernacle and its gruesome occupant. "You have the tools. And, I would hope, the expertise."

The proctor glowered, but—pride stung as he'd hoped—nodded minutely. "I can test the familiar, but not like this. The controlled environment of Convocation Center is required. Besides which, the other familiar has crimes to answer for. She is clearly still undisciplined, rebellious, and spiteful. It's my professional opinion that Veronica Elal be remanded into my custody, as was intended from the beginning."

Gabriel tightened his grip on Nic, aware that it steadied her, though she lowered her gaze to stare at his chest. "Nic is my familiar, duly won and bonded. I have the documentation of my ownership." As distasteful as those words were, he wasn't risking anything by discarding the correct Convocation-recognized terminology. "She is mine now, I have need of her, and the Convocation cannot take her from me."

"The bonding has not been confirmed," the proctor reminded him cagily. Her magic flickered over them with spidery invasiveness. "More concerning to me, it appears to be... odd."

Nic glanced up at him through her lashes, a deep-green

warning. Yes, she'd told him the reciprocal bonding might look wrong to an observer. "I can't imagine why," he replied carelessly. "It was duly accomplished, here in my arcanium."

The proctor looked shocked, which was satisfying except that a murmur of surprise and speculation ran through the assembly. Oh well. They would never have kept the arcanium's existence secret for long. And Nic said other wizards acknowledged their arcaniums and still kept them sacrosanct.

"Arcanium?" his father echoed. "What are you talking about, boy?"

"Wizard secrets," he replied, aching at the look on his father's face. *You know what they say about a man trying to straddle two worlds. He gets split up the middle, starting with his balls.* That would explain the sharp pain slicing through him.

The proctor pinched her mouth in sour disappointment. "Takes more than an arcanium to make a wizard, Lord Fell." She managed to slip the insult into the wordplay every time. "And I say your familiar is improperly bonded."

"Examine us, then," he replied, making certain to sound more confident than belligerent. Nic made a slight sound, and he forced himself to relax his grip on her. "We are bonded, and we have nothing to hide."

"Don't you?" She made it sound as if she very much doubted that. "Fine, then. Let's settle this question, in front of all your family, as you insist." Setting the tabernacle on the porch rail, she made a show of waving her hands in a complex incantation.

Now that he'd learned more from Nic, Gabriel recognized the showmanship in the proctor's elaborate gestures. "Mom,

Dad," he said, "you might not want to watch this."

"We're not leaving you, son," GF replied staunchly, and Daisy nodded, though she turned so Selly faced away, still weeping softly in her mother's arms.

The doors of the foot-high tabernacle opened, a gust of foul magic billowing out. Inside the ornate interior, the mummified head opened its lapis-inlaid eyelids, staring at him with soulless eyes. He was prepared for the ghoulish sight this time, knowing its rough leathery appearance for centuries-old skin. Despite the decorations, the eyebrows made of delicately etched gold, the ruby glitter of its lipless mouth, the magic that made its gold-leaf-outlined eyes appear to be living membranes, the oracle head was still utterly revolting. The blast of ancient, twisted magic hit him just as hard, but he was able to discern more, sensing the intertwining forces of Hanneil and El-Adrel skills, with a hint of Ariel mixed in. *Humans do have animal bodies*, Nic had said when he'd mentioned he thought House Ariel worked on animals. Horrifying.

"Oracle," the proctor intoned, and Gabriel set his teeth against her irritatingly officious posture, "has this wizard bonded this familiar?"

The oracle head stared at him, the prickle of its magic making his skin crawl. Nic, who'd turned to face the oracle as well, leaning against him, trembled as if she hated it, too. Gabriel held his breath, willing the thing to confirm their bonded status and end this all now.

"Yes," the oracle head said in its toneless, inhuman voice, and Gabriel let out a relieved breath. "And no," it added.

Behind them, the other wizards and familiars began murmuring, the lilt of surprise and doubt in their voices. Nic went thrummingly tense against him, and the proctor glared at them in thin-lipped triumph.

"Then there is no bond," the proctor prompted.

"Incorrect. There is a bond, of a nonstandard nature."

Nic's groan was inaudible, but he felt it through his connection to her. She'd been right. He should've just done the bonding the traditional way. Except... *No*, the fault wasn't theirs; it was this Convocation and its draconian laws, forcing them out of shape.

"The bond is no doubt faulty, due perhaps to the wizard's inexperience, compounded by the familiar's undisciplined and rebellious nature," the proctor theorized, barely containing her glee.

"Inconclusive," the oracle head replied, and she frowned.

"Analyze the nature of the bond," the proctor instructed.

The oracle did not respond for some time. Around them, people shifted restlessly, sharing muttered remarks. Gabriel's parents stood steadfast, both of them shielding Selly, watching the scene with uncomprehending horror that made his heart twist that it might be partially for him. Beneath his hands, Nic held her breath, and he tried to emulate her.

"Inconclusive," the oracle head finally said, sparking a fresh spate of conversation in their audience.

"Hmph." The proctor nearly spat out the incoherent sound of disgust. "There's nothing for it, then," she declared. "The familiar will be remanded into my custody. They will discover the flaw at Convocation Center."

No! "The oracle head said we are bonded," he argued.

"Heard and witnessed," Asa called out, many of the others echoing him.

"The oracle also determined that the bond is nonstandard," the proctor said, raising her voice so all could hear.

"There is no codicil," Wolfgang said smoothly, "in Convocation law regarding nonstandard bonding. You have no grounds to take custody of Lady Phel."

"Because there's never been a nonstandard bond," the proctor shot back. "This is unprecedented."

"But not illegal," Asa put in. "Lord Phel has bonded his familiar, as verified by your own oracle. That should end the matter."

The proctor fumed, then smiled as some thought occurred to her. Turning her canny gaze on Gabriel, she nodded. "I am willing to leave the familiar with you for the time being, Lord Phel, if you can assure me of her obedience and that she is fully subject to your will. I require a demonstration of your control. To ask less would be irresponsible," she added primly.

Gabriel inclined his head warily. Nic could fake any amount of obedience to him, he was certain. The difficulty would be in controlling himself. But he could do anything for a short time, if it meant protecting Nic.

"A simple demonstration will do," the proctor continued. "Force your familiar into alternate form, and I'll be satisfied."

Behind him, Asa said something to Sage and Quinn, a relieved note in his voice. Nic closed her eyes as if in pain. His parents looked at him in utter bewilderment.

"What is she talking about, Gabriel?" his mother asked. "Alternate form?"

"I'll explain later," he told her, willing them both to be patient. "I will comply with this demonstration," he said to the proctor, "but not here, in front of everyone." Turning Nic in his arms, he caressed her cheek, hoping he looked possessive and controlling, trying to read the message in her eyes. "It's private. Not for the eyes of commoners," he added, desperately hoping that excuse would fly. He hadn't seen any other wizard push their familiar into their alternate form, and Nic had expressed surprise that Lord Elal had done so to Lady Elal in front of Gabriel. He also hoped his parents would forgive him, once he explained.

Nic gave no clue, regarding him somberly. Yes, he knew what she was thinking. If this privacy gambit worked, it would buy them only a little time.

"*Private*, he says," the proctor snorted. "All right, then. As I've requested several times now, take me to a private, quiet location."

"I'll arrange for one," Gabriel told her. "We are under renovation, so I'll require some time. We'll convene tomorrow morning."

"And allow this one to escape again on my watch?" the proctor demanded. "I don't think so. It's now, Lord Phel. Here or in private. I don't care if it's an empty room, but I'll test this unknown familiar to determine her magical potential—and relative sanity—and you can demonstrate your so-called bonding."

"Now see here," GF protested. "What all is involved in this testing? Our Selly is a bit touchy, and I won't stand by and let her be harmed."

Selly looked up then, catching up with the conversation around her. "Harmed?" Then she glared at the back of Nic's head. "You *promised!*" she screamed, loudly enough to crack eardrums and more than enough to startle his mother, who reflexively released Selly to clap her hands over her ears.

"No!" Gabriel yelled, lunging past Nic to grab Selly, who leapt like one of those wildcats from the western marshes onto the porch railing. Rat grabbed for her, but she skipped out of his reach with surprising speed, scampering along the porch rail at top speed. "Don't let her get away," he called out. There were a lot of people standing around and only one, mildly crazed young woman. They should be able to surround her.

But Selly reached the end of the porch, climbed a pillar like it was a tree, and disappeared over the roofline.

"Agile little monkey, isn't she," Jadren commented on a disinterested drawl.

"Stop her," Daisy wailed.

The proctor leveled a grim look on Gabriel, as if he'd somehow planned this. "You will retrieve the familiar."

"Yes," he replied, seizing on the opportunity Selly's flight had afforded. "Come on, Nic." Taking her hand, he pulled Nic into the house.

"Leave your familiar with me," the proctor yelled after him.

He skidded to a stop. "I need her for an incantation to recover my sister. Which order do you want me to follow?"

The proctor worked her mouth in frustration.

"She's getting farther away," he warned the proctor.

"Go, then," she agreed. Gabriel was too busy running

down the hall to make out what else she called after them.

"Where are we going?" Nic gasped as Gabriel practically dragged her down the hallway, his much greater stride leaving her scrambling, his viselike grip on her hand remorseless. "Seliah will be—"

"Selly will be fine," he growled. "For now, anyway. I have no doubt she'll give everyone the slip, and at least out in the marshes she's safe from your Convocation."

"They're not *mine*," Nic protested, though it was reflexive. Her brain wasn't working quite right, still numb from the emotional shock of seeing her Betrothal Trials proctor again. She knew the Convocation would send someone, and she even got the logic of sending the same proctor, but somehow she'd hadn't been prepared for the brutal reality. Those long months she'd spent locked in her tower room, the proctor's regular examinations and caustically patronizing remarks. That had been one world, her previous life. To have that woman appear here, in this place she'd begun to make into a home, sullying a house she and Gabriel had literally raised together from the muck and were building into something truly beautiful… well, it had been a shock.

If her brain were working better, she'd be able to think of a better way to phrase it to herself.

Gabriel wrenched open the door to the cellar, pausing only

to tell her to close it behind them, then careened down the rickety wooden steps. Part of her mind that was keeping the endless lists on house renovations noted that they should fix those. The other part was sitting up and paying attention at the possibility of visiting the arcanium and all of its dark delights.

"We're going to the arcanium?" she panted. "Now? But what about—"

"Whatever you're worrying about, I don't care," Gabriel bit out. "It's you I need to protect."

Nic rolled her eyes to herself. Wizards. At least she could forever throw this back in Gabriel's face if he ever again balked when she mentioned the nature of wizards. "You can't seal me in the arcanium."

He skidded to a stop. "Why not? That might actually work. They're sacrosanct, right? No one can enter another wizard's arcanium."

"True. So when you find my desiccated corpse after I've died of thirst and hunger, no one else will have disturbed my bones," she observed drily.

"I would bring you food. And water, as you've so often observed, is not an issue." He grinned briefly, then strode on.

Since she was a patient and forbearing soul, she didn't point out that he had a grip on her like a constrictor slowly squeezing the life from its prey. "If wizards could get away with imprisoning their familiars in their arcaniums, they no doubt would." Nic drew in a deep breath when Gabriel paused to magically extract a fistful of silver nails from the door leading to the tunnel.

"I didn't want anyone opening this door and finding the

tunnel by accident," he explained to her questioning look, closing the door behind them and sending the nails flying to seal it again. "I know no one can enter the arcanium without us, but better to keep the curious from getting close."

"It's good thinking. Proper wizard paranoia. I'm so proud." She pretended to wipe away a tear.

"You get more sarcastic when you're upset," he noted, charging down the tunnel. "So I'll let that go."

"Do I? And here I thought my sarcasm was all-purpose, wear anywhere, use anytime."

"That too," he muttered, pausing at the final doorway. He already had a grip on her, so he pulled the magic easily, blending it with his own to spiral the door open. "Get inside."

She obeyed, though his high-handedness irritated her. "As much as I love it when you order me around, my only love, I really don't—"

"Have time to argue," he interrupted. "We're going to need a lot of sex magic. Take off your clothes and kneel."

~ 18 ~

THOUGH HER SEX clenched at the command, her familiar nature rousing in eager welcome, her brain was still apparently jogging down the tunnel, perhaps locked outside with silver nails, because she was not catching up to Gabriel's urgency. "Why?" she demanded.

He set his jaw, fulminating silver and steam. "*Now* you balk? All this time you've been wheedling and exhorting me to exert control over you, to take and have, and now, when we have no time to dither, you want to question me?"

"*Dither?*" She raised her brows, tempted to laugh, but he glowered at her. "I just want to know why we're having arcanium sex when there are crises to address. Surely that answer won't take long."

With a growl of impatience, he spun her around and released the trigger on the gown, efficiently stripping it off of her. With a little thrill, she discovered she liked that, too. She might have to refuse to undress for him more often.

"We're going to figure out how to transform you into your alternate form," he explained with exaggerated patience. "How is that not obvious to you?"

Ten different replies leapt to her lips, none of them quite

equal to the moment. Also, Gabriel pulled the gown off over her head just then, muffling any response she might give. He swiftly relieved her of her lingerie too, leaving her naked. She kicked off her slippers, glad she'd changed out of her muddy boots when they returned to the manse. "Gabriel—"

"Kneel," he ordered, cutting her off.

Obeying without thought, she did, aroused excitement flooding her, which did not help to kick her brain into action. Quite the opposite. It would be so easy to yield, to let the eroticism of submitting to his control sweep her away, but that wouldn't solve their very real problems.

"May I speak, wizard?" she asked pointedly, looking up at him. That didn't help the thinking part of her either, as he was so dizzyingly gorgeous standing over her like that, his emotional storm intense and overwhelming. *And in the arcanium at night, you can release all that pent-up fury and passion upon my helpless body.* She'd only been half teasing when she said that. Less than that, because the prospect had her body singing in delight, longing for that very thing with every fiber of her being.

She couldn't believe she was going to stop him.

"No," he said. "We don't have time to talk. Take your alternate form."

Rolling her eyes, she stood. "It doesn't work that way."

"What do I have to do?" he demanded. Before she could answer, he strode across the domed room, seizing the silver bed and wheeling it to under the moon window. "Chain you to this?" he nearly shouted. "Whip you? Force you to submit to my will so we can prove to your precious Convocation that you belong with me? Because I'll do it, Nic. I'll hate myself for hurting you, but I'd rather that than turn you over to *them*. Now get over here and get on this vile thing!" He finished on a near roar.

Oh, he was in a mood.

Taking her time, she sauntered over, shivering under the feral intensity of his wizard-black gaze raking her nakedness. His magic billowed around her, amplified by the arcanium, the silver struts glowing with brilliant moonlight, dispensing the gloom of the lake water under a rain-leaden sky. She paused by the silver bed and looked at it pointedly. "Still no mattress," she noted.

His expression momentarily blanked, then he glared at the offending naked bed frame in betrayed fury. With a howl of rage, he kicked it, sending the thing spinning across the floor to bounce off one thick glass pane.

Nic watched it go with a raised brow, then turned back to her enraged wizard. "Feel any better?"

He glowered at her, fists clenched. "How can you be so calm?" he snarled. "Work with me here."

"Oh, *now* you want me to work with you?" Moving slowly, she closed the distance between them, laying her palms against his muscled chest, his heart thundering beneath. Rigid with tension, he thrummed under her hands. A storm about to break. "Darling," she said smoothly, "this isn't something I ever thought I'd say to you, but you need to calm down. Take a few deep breaths."

He fulminated under her touch, his magic so sharp, so boiling, as he glared daggers at her that for a moment she wasn't sure what he'd do. Seizing her by the waist, he lifted her into the air, and she clutched at his ridged forearms, her feet dangling helplessly in the air. Her sex slick with anticipation, she'd welcome whatever he might do to her. *Take. Have.* She should just yield and let him—*No.* That wouldn't solve their problems.

Maybe he sensed her newfound resolve. Or glimpsed something in her eyes, because sanity returned to his. Setting her carefully on her feet again, he dragged in a long, deep breath. Then another. On the third breath, his set expression crumpled. Very deliberately, he released his grip on her waist. Her body ached, missing him already, but only for a moment because he wrapped her in an embrace, pulling her hard against him as he buried his face against her neck.

"I can't lose you," he groaned, voice breaking, his words muffled against her skin.

"Oh, Gabriel..." Her heart turned over, wrung out, body throbbing with unfulfilled arousal, mind dizzy from being crowded with too many thoughts and feelings. "You won't lose me."

He stiffened, raising his head, fixing her with that wizard-black gaze that penetrated to the most intimate corners of her soul. "Can you promise that?"

"I—" She closed her mouth on the lie. She'd been determined to promise that, but in the face of his earnest vulnerability, she simply couldn't. "Gabriel, I don't know. There's so much stacked against us. If only I hadn't—"

He stopped her with a little shake. "Don't you dare apologize for that again."

"So commanding," she purred, giving him a sultry smile, and he snarled in frustration. "Don't snarl at me. I'm trying to *think*, but it isn't easy for me, being naked with you, here, with your hands on me and your magic coiling through me."

With a curse, he pulled off his long coat and wrapped it around her—it was big enough on her to almost go around twice—then rubbed her arms briskly. "I'm sorry."

"I'm not *cold*," she chided him with a smile. "I just need to clear the erotic haze from my brain."

He smiled in wry sympathy. "I know what you mean."

"All right, let me think." She stepped away from his heady presence, hoping that would clear her head. Glancing around the mostly empty room, she went to the only place to sit, perching on the edge of the silver bed. He frowned at her. "What? There is no other furniture in here, and it's not conducive to rational thinking for me to be on the floor with you looming over me so enticingly."

He raked a hand through his hair. "I never thought furniture would matter so much to me."

Smirking, she crossed her legs, arranging the coat to cover her naked thighs when his gaze fixed there. "You asked how to push me into my alternate form, and the short answer is I don't know. It's in wizard training. Familiars aren't taught it."

He studied her, rationality returning to his fevered gaze. "The proctor knows I don't have a Convocation Academy education. She was betting that I don't know how to do this."

Nic inclined her head. "It was probably her fallback all along. Even if your cursed reciprocal bond hadn't befuddled the oracle head, she would no doubt have required this final demonstration. She wants me back at Convocation Center very badly."

"Vengeance?"

"Probably in part. It galls her that I escaped on her watch," Nic imitated the proctor's pedantic complaint. "But… I suspect there's more to it. The Convocation wants me back for some reason."

"All the more reason not to let you go." Gabriel stalked to her. Then, as if suddenly aware of his looming, he settled his weight onto the bed frame beside her, glaring at the thing when it creaked, as if it offended him.

"Even if we accomplish finding my alternate form, I doubt that will end things in this case. The Convocation won't stop."

He shook his head. "Let's apply the breakfast table rule here."

She blinked at him. Yes, her brain was fogged from arousal on top of the tumult of the day—it killed her to think Selly felt Nic had betrayed her—but she wasn't following. "Breakfast table?"

He smiled and laid a hand on his muscled thigh, palm up in invitation, so she wormed out one of her own to lay her hand in his. "Let's not worry about the next crisis until we at least survive the threat currently before us."

"I'm pretty sure I was asking to forgo philosophy in favor of current threats," she replied with a wrinkled nose, "but point taken."

"You told me that taking your alternate form is something you want?" He made it a question, searching her face for the truth.

"I do want it. It's just not easily done. I wanted us to prac-tice and work our way up to that level."

"Hmm. So not all wizards can push their familiars into alternate form?"

"No. It's one of compelling reasons to bond with a power-ful wizard, beyond wealth and status, if one has a choice."

"That's why you insisted on us using the arcanium, be-cause it takes a lot of power."

"At least the first time, yes. But I suspect some wizards are only able to do the trick while in the arcanium. That's why you don't see it all that often."

"But I saw your father do it."

"Yes." She made a face for that. "Powerful, as I men-tioned."

"And near his arcanium."

"True."

He gazed past her, thinking hard. "You told me once that you didn't know what your alternate form would be, that you might not become a cat like your mother because these things don't run in families."

"Your memory, as always, is excellent."

"That implies that the form is already a part of your magic, that it simply needs to be unlocked."

"I agree with the first part," she replied, thinking it through. "There are multiple theories on why familiars take the alternate forms they do. Some think it's born of the familiar's magic. Others think the wizard's preferences and needs shape the form. Others say it's a combination of the two. I have never, however, heard the process referred to as 'unlocking.' It's always framed as pushing or…"

"Forcing?" he filled in with a raised brow. "How unlike the Convocation to cleave to a metaphor that implies force."

"Now who's employing sarcasm?"

"I'm just trying to speak your language."

"Ha ha. Seriously, I feel I should point out that you not listening to me on traditional methods for magic rituals is, at least in part, what has landed us in this particular problem." She shouldn't have said it, because his face and magic clouded with guilt. But before she could retract or mitigate her words, he shook his head.

"You are, of course, correct," he replied, "but I wouldn't change it. You and I accomplished something special between us, something that even that revolting, but obviously powerful and ancient oracle head couldn't parse."

"We don't even know what we did, if anything," she protested. "It could be just a faulty bonding."

"It seems to me that the oracle head would've been definitive about a faulty bonding."

She wanted to argue the point but couldn't. "Maybe," she said, giving the most ground she was willing to concede at that point.

"Does it *feel* faulty to you?" he persisted, wizard-black eyes full of glittering intensity. "Because I can feel you," he continued when she hesitated, "in my head and in my magic, like you're a fundamental part of me. Like I'd die without you."

"Yes, well," she temporized, a bit breathless from that declaration. "That's because I'm indispensable."

"Nic."

"Fine." *Trust,* she reminded herself. *Behave as if you trust him and you'll get there.* "The bond is real," she agreed. "There's nothing faulty about it. Regardless of whether the Fascination comes from me or some… manipulation." She shook her head when he squeezed her hand, a concerned frown on his face. "You're right. We're connected. I don't know if the bonding feels this way to every familiar, but I know what you mean—in my head, in my magic. In my heart," she added, giving him a tender smile, feeling kind of silly saying that, but rewarded by the warm glow of love surging between them.

"I'm sorry for the bind we're in," Gabriel said slowly, "but I can't regret that our connection is something the Convocation and their tools don't understand. It will make it harder for them to fight us if we're an unknown quantity."

"Unknown even to ourselves," she remarked drily.

"We'll learn. Isn't that what you keep telling me? Practice and learning to work together."

"I don't recall mentioning making it up as we go along." She had to smile, though, for his grand ideas. "Though if anyone has the ingenuity to do this, you do."

"We do," he corrected. "I know you've been going around suggesting radical ideas to other familiars, despite all your Convocation talk."

That actually took her by surprise, reflexive guilt stabbing at her. "Quinn?" she asked hesitantly.

Gabriel nodded, a slow smile spreading across his face. "Sage spoke with me. Stop looking like you're guilty of a crime. I'm proud of you."

She had to roll her eyes at that. "I'm not a puppy."

"Maybe you are," he teased. "Maybe that's your alternate form."

Daniel the Spaniel. She grimaced at how they'd made fun of her awful cousin Jan's pitifully cringing and puppyish familiar. The epitome of everything she never wanted to be. "Alternate forms are always adults," she informed him loftily to cover the very real fear of that eventuality. "Never juveniles."

He nodded, seeing more into her than she'd said. Always understanding more about her than was comfortable. *Trust.*

"We don't have to do this," he offered. "You know I understand any trepidation you might have about your alternate form. I'd understand if you'd never want to take it, to lose control of your very body to someone else, even me."

Even him. Only him, more like. Funny to realize that because she apparently did trust him more than she'd known until this moment. "No, you were right to begin with. We do have to do this."

He shook his head emphatically. "Not if you don't want to."

"We can't stay in the arcanium forever," she pointed out.

"Our bones will lie curled together, undisturbed, for eternity," he replied solemnly, only a hint of a smile curving his beautiful lips.

Unable to resist that mouth, she kissed him. "Such a romantic."

He returned the kiss, the emotion in it quickly turning urgent, and he cupped the back of her neck, holding her close as he drank of her like a man dying of thirst. Breaking the kiss with a gasp, he leaned his forehead against hers. "I will never make you do something you don't want to do. But you're right that we can't stay in the arcanium forever, as romantic as our tragic death would be."

"They'd write novels about us," she agreed. "The new Sylus and Lyndella."

"Spare me that fate," he replied with a dry laugh. "Sylus doesn't come off well in those stories."

"He's brooding and driven," Nic protested, stung into defending the hero of her adolescent fantasies.

"He's an ass," Gabriel declared firmly. "Controlling, self-absorbed, and oblivious to Lyndella's suffering."

Nic narrowed her eyes at him. "Have you been reading my novels?"

"I had to do something while not sleeping in Vale's stall. He has a sneaky tendency to step on you if you're not watching him every moment."

Absurdly touched, Nic trailed her fingers over his cheek. "Then you know Lyndella understood and loved her torment-ed wizard."

Gabriel was silent a moment. "Maybe she shouldn't have."

Nic rolled her eyes at him. "I wonder if Lyndella had to kick Sylus out of his funks occasionally…"

"Lyndella was far too sweet to do anything like that," Gabriel countered.

Nic snorted, and he laughed. Lifting their joined hands, he kissed the back of hers. "What do you want to do?"

"Well, I think we're agreed it's too early in our personal story for the tragic ending to our epic romance, so starving here in the arcanium is a no go."

"We can go out and fight. That proctor should be easy to kill." Gabriel simmered with silvery rage. "I'd enjoy that, in fact."

"And you'd doom House Phel. Murdering a Convocation proctor in cold blood will have them permanently yanking your house status and dividing Meresin up between your neighbors."

Gabriel looked mulish, so she added, "They'd likely kill anyone with your bloodline, to prevent anyone from Phel popping up again to cause them trouble. They probably already regret they didn't salt the earth, which allowed you to appear to dig your thorny self into their sides."

"A daunting thought."

"You've come so far, Gabriel. Don't give up now. Don't give the Convocation an excuse to get rid of you before you accomplish your goals."

He cocked his head. "And which goals might those be?"

"I know you haven't spelled it out, but I assume you want to infiltrate the highest levels of power in the Convocation and either change it or bring it all down."

"Both outcomes have their merits," he admitted.

"All right, then." She could do this. *They* could do this. "That leaves unlocking my alternate form."

He gave her a long look. "Except we still don't know how."

"I think you *make* me do it." It made sense, really. As much as she looked forward to discovering her alternate form, the idea of contorting her flesh into a new body made her skin crawl. Maybe it wasn't something one could make oneself do.

"I haven't had much luck making you do anything at all," Gabriel observed wryly.

"You make me do some things," she purred. "And we both like that."

He didn't take the bait. "I wish we could find a way to make this reciprocal."

"I don't think it's physically possible for us both to be tied up and whipped at the same time."

Not flinching, he gazed at her steadily, but she could tell it took effort on his part not to immediately respond with his usual arguments. "Is that what you think it takes?"

"Maybe?" She thought about all the bits of gossip and innuendo, the romantic tales. "Probably. There are certainly broad hints about interludes like that between Sylus and Lyndella, and others."

"Why whipping? That's a serious question," he said before she could come back with a sarcastic retort.

"Mortification of the flesh? At least the first time, I think you have to take control of my will, then cause me enough pain that I want to leave or change my body."

His expression tight, he considered that. "I don't like this."

"Pain can be erotic, too," she soothed him.

Depthless black eyes on hers, he shook his head slowly. "Causing you enough pain that you want to leave your body isn't erotic. I won't do it."

"What if it's the only way?" she demanded. "I'm willing to do this, so you should be, too."

"Not necessarily," he shot back. "This would be far from

the first time that I've cared more about your well-being and happiness than you do."

Well, that struck her mute for a moment. She had no argument against that. From the moment she met him, she'd known she'd do anything for this wizard. Any amount of suffering, and she'd be happy to offer it to him. And he knew that all too well.

"Care and Feeding of Familiars 101," he said with a grim smile. "I'm going to protect you, even from yourself."

"Fine," she bit out. "Then I'm out of ideas. What are yours?"

"I think that if a familiar can take alternate form without pain, forcing them into it on other occasions—as we've both witnessed is true—then it should be possible the first time. Maybe you wanting it is enough."

"Maybe," she replied, doubt heavy in her tone and heart.

"Let me ask you this: Why don't wizards take alternate forms? If our magic is fundamentally the same, except for that singular ability to activate it, why isn't that in the wizard repertoire?"

"Probably they'd need another wizard to do it to them. That occurred to me also," she admitted. "It would make sense that our connections to our own bodies is too strong to override through our own will. We need someone else to push us there, otherwise maybe some animal instinct kicks in to keep us human. A kind of self-protection."

He nodded slowly. "That makes sense." Then, abruptly, he grinned. "Maybe someday you'll be able to override my animal instincts and push me into my alternate form."

"I'm not a wizard."

"No, but you have a stronger will than anyone else I've known. You make me do things I don't want to all the time."

"Ha ha. Besides, I thought you found the idea of changing form abhorrent."

"I did." He looked thoughtful. "Not anymore. The prospect is interesting." He gave her a wry look. "Part of my decline into monstrosity, no doubt."

"No doubt."

He stood, pulling her to her feet. "I think I know what to do. Give me the coat and kneel."

With a surge of wicked trepidation, she obeyed, handing over the garment, then kneeling naked before him. He nudged her knees with his boot, making her spread her thighs, instructing her to clasp her hands at the small of her back. Tremulous with rising arousal, curious, nerves on a keen edge, she did as he told her.

When he grasped her chin in his hand and lifted her gaze to meet his, he stared her down with all the silver-sharp command a familiar could wish for. "Do you trust me?" he demanded.

Not exactly what she expected. "Yes, wizard."

He tightened his grip, eyes obsidian hard. "Don't lie. I'll know it. Do you trust me?"

"Yes, wizard." She shuddered, realizing it was true. This wasn't compelled, not forced. She was choosing this.

"Do you yield yourself to me?" he asked softly, implacably.

"Yes, wizard." Her body swayed toward him in its own affirmation, yearning.

"Do you submit your will to mine, utterly, without reservation?"

It shouldn't feel so chilling, but the question struck hard. Her will was all she'd had when she lost everything else. She searched his eyes, not knowing what she looked for.

"Do you, Nic?" he urged.

"Yes, Gabriel," she sighed, feeling the deep truth of it. Not always. But here, in the arcanium, with Gabriel, she could submit her will to his and trust him to use it well. Not just any wizard, but Gabriel. Her love.

"Accept my control, then." His eyes, already blacker than a starless night, darkened. His magic swirled around and through her, then settled over her like a silver net. Captive, she instinctively struggled against it, and Gabriel gave her a warning look. "You promised, familiar," he crooned. "Submit. Yield."

"Yes, wizard," she whispered, trembling with need and desire. She let go, giving herself over to his magic, surrendering to his will, and the silver net layered itself into her skin, settling into her nerves, penetrating her muscles, bones, heart, mind, and soul.

"Ah, yes." His black eyes flared with fire, face ridged with his own fierce desire. "You belong to me, don't you?"

"Entirely," she agreed helplessly, yearning toward him, desperate to be taken.

"Not yet," he tsked. "Don't move. I think you'll find you can't." He followed that astonishing declaration with a kiss, hungry, deep, and devastating.

It was true. She couldn't move. She could only receive the

kiss, her mouth opening of its own accord—or of his—the sparks of excitation running wild in her immobile body.

"Wait here," he instructed, chuckling wickedly at his own joke. And she did so, helpless to do otherwise, the sexual tension building with leaps and bounds, pressing against her skin from the inside.

He wheeled the bed to beneath the moon window again, aligning it so the foot of it sat at the focal point, then busied himself with the silver chains. Finished, he pointed a finger at her, then curled it. And she crawled to him, drawn by the invisible leash of his power, trembling with the heightened eroticism.

Drawing her to her feet, Gabriel positioned her against the bed frame, his hands roving freely over her, stimulating and caressing. She wanted to writhe against him, to push her nipples into his stroking palms, to pump her hips in wordless plea, but she could only take what he chose to give, only submit to what he desired of her. It was frustrating and freeing. She could do nothing, so she had no choice but to accept. The sensation of simultaneous constriction and freedom had her mind surging against its boundaries.

She couldn't even moan, in approval or protest, as he stood her against the foot of the bed and chained her arms above her head, outstretched to each bedpost. The silver cuffs fastened around her wrists made contact with the silver net Gabriel had laid into her body, conducting magic through the silver bed to the arcanium, to Gabriel, and back into her own body. By the time he chained her ankles to the bottom of the posts, so she stood spread-eagled and beyond vulnerable, the magic pulsed into, through, and out of her. She'd become a pump, a human-shaped heart circulating magic. Taking in the moon and water magic, heating and growing it with her own and breathing it out again.

Gabriel inhaled deeply, as if sensing it, too. His eyes lit from black to shining silver, his hair flowing in unseen currents of magic, his skin glowing with it. Standing before her, he caressed her body, releasing just enough control to allow her to whimper, to struggle against the chains, to lean her body into his hands.

"Here are the rules," he murmured, sounding as over-whelmed as she felt. The magic gave a resonance to his voice that made her want to drink the words from his mouth. "I'm going to torment you with pleasure. You will not be allowed to climax. When you can't stand a moment longer, I'll release you—into your alternate form."

She cried a wordless plea, not because she couldn't speak, but because she had no words. She only partly understood what he was telling her.

"Shh, my heart." He kissed her softly, lovingly. "Trust me to take care of you. You don't have to understand, because I do. You asked me to take. You asked me to have. Give yourself into my hands."

The giving was a letting go. Untying the final bits of will, she gave herself into his caresses. The sweet torment became an agony that seemed to last forever. Teasing her with lips, hands, nails, teeth, and tongue, Gabriel played her like an instrument, drawing sensation from every fingertip of skin. Though she undulated, writhing and pleading, he paid no attention, his attention focused on her body's responses. The arcanium echoed the ebb and flow, the relentless build of pressure, his magic twining inside her with otherworldly intensity. She went mindless, riding the waves of erotic extremity, aware only of how he touched and tormented her, until she was taut with the need for release, sobbing with raw desire, begging him to let her go.

Framing her face in his hands, he kissed her, the magic churning in a frenzied cycle between them. Pulling his head back, he used his magic to release the chains, taking her wrists in his, holding them in place as his big body pinned her against the bed frame. He stared into her eyes. "My familiar, my lover, my heart. Be released."

The magic seized her all at once, the orgasm ripping through her and tearing her apart at the seams. Her mind fragmented, her identity blown into trillions of silver sparks. She came apart in every way, shivering and shattered.

Then remade.

~ 19 ~

GABRIEL STARED IN awe, not quite able to wrap his admittedly addled brain around what had become of Nic.

She seemed similarly befuddled, cocking her head quizzically, her silver feathers bright, her emerald eyes the same. Shaking her head, she tried to look at herself, startling as her great wings spread wide. Turning in a circle, she tried to get a look at herself but ended up in the same place. She fixed him with a demanding look.

"You did it," he breathed. "*We* did it," he amended when she trilled a contradiction he nevertheless understood.

She trilled a question, listening, as if interested in her own sounds.

"You are a… very large bird," he ventured. "I think you might be a phoenix. I'd have to look it up in the library." A grin stretched his face, a release of its own from the sexual frustration he'd endured along with her. "Given your fiery nature, I'm not surprised. And the metaphor—you have certainly been burnt to ash and reborn a time or two."

She listened intently, then drew a wingtip around, waving it so the silver flashed.

"I'm guessing the silver is from me, from the magic and the arcanium, perhaps. A silver phoenix. Doubly appropriate, yes?"

Trilling again, she cocked her head.

"Yes," he agreed. "Let's put you back and see if we can replicate it. Maybe with a little less sexual frustration. I can see why a wizard would be inclined to go with whipping instead."

She glared green fire at him, and he could swear he heard her *Ha ha* in his head. Concentrating, he found the threads of control he'd woven into her. Could he withdraw them again? He wasn't certain. They felt permanent, but he set that disturbing thought aside. *There are good reasons the Convocation teaches wizards to control their familiars,* Nic had told him. Reasons, indeed, though whether they were what anyone would call "good" was subject to debate. Certainly the power was a heady one. To control another person so completely…

Is the path to becoming a monster, some saner part of himself whispered.

If he wasn't one already.

Yanking himself back from those dark musings, he strummed those threads of control and willed Nic to return to her human form. With startling ease, she did, standing naked before him and holding out her hands in wonder. Her deep-green eyes, huge with residual arousal and the enormity of what she'd done, filled her pale face.

"I have no words," she whispered.

"Maybe take a moment," he suggested, easing closer, but chary of touching her just yet, no matter how badly he wanted to take her into his arms and hold her. "That has to be mind-bending."

She gazed at him, still wide-eyed, but perhaps a little less wild. "It was so strange. I could understand you, but I couldn't quite think like myself." She shuddered and pressed her hands to her face. "When I think about Maman, being trapped all this time…"

He judged it better to act than not, and in two strides, folded her into his embrace. "You don't know that," he murmured. "Don't dwell on speculation over something you can't control."

She lifted a tear-stained face to his. "We have to rescue her."

"All right," he agreed immediately. "We'll find a way—either to ascertain that she's well, or to bring her to safety."

"Thank you," she whispered, huddling into him, pressing her cheek against his chest. "I know that's not the most important thing right now, but…" She let out a long, ragged breath.

"You've been turned inside out, almost literally," he told her softly, kissing her hair, inhaling her scent. Love struck him hard, clenching his heart in a fist and wringing him dry. "Of course it's important. Just one of many important things," he added ruefully.

She sighed. "I really hate that we have about ten crises on the breakfast table and no time in the schedule for self-excoriating philosophy."

He laughed, surprising himself with the bell-deep ringing sound of it. "We will *make* time for that, my heart."

She laughed too, though not as heartily, smiling up at him. "I suppose we should practice the transformation a time or two with my clothes on. I don't fancy parading around naked in front of that prune of a proctor."

"Agreed," he said with fervor. "Let me find your gown."

"First things first," she declared, raking her nails down his chest and undoing the laces of his pants. "Lie down, wizard. You owe me."

Obediently, willingly, he sank to his knees and then to his back. Nic straddled him, outlined in silver fire. And when she sank over him, taking him inside her, the silver web of connection tightened, threading through, in, and around them.

No one could fault this bonding.

Nic and Gabriel's endless list of crises continues in

Grey Magic

Coming December 2021

TITLES BY JEFFE KENNEDY

FANTASY ROMANCES

BONDS OF MAGIC

Dark Wizard

Bright Familiar (July 2021)

Grey Magic (December 2021)

HEIRS OF MAGIC

The Long Night of the Crystalline Moon

(also available in *Under a Winter Sky*)

The Golden Gryphon and the Bear Prince

The Sorceress Queen and the Pirate Rogue

The Dragon's Daughter and the Winter Mage (September 2021)

The Storm Princess and the Raven King (February 2022)

THE FORGOTTEN EMPIRES

The Orchid Throne

The Fiery Crown

The Promised Queen

THE TWELVE KINGDOMS
Negotiation
The Mark of the Tala
The Tears of the Rose
The Talon of the Hawk
Heart's Blood
The Crown of the Queen

THE UNCHARTED REALMS
The Pages of the Mind
The Edge of the Blade
The Snows of Windroven
The Shift of the Tide
The Arrows of the Heart
The Dragons of Summer
The Fate of the Tala
The Lost Princess Returns

THE CHRONICLES OF DASNARIA
Prisoner of the Crown
Exile of the Seas
Warrior of the World

SORCEROUS MOONS
Lonen's War
Oria's Gambit
The Tides of Bára
The Forests of Dru
Oria's Enchantment
Lonen's Reign

A COVENANT OF THORNS

Rogue's Pawn

Rogue's Possession

Rogue's Paradise

CONTEMPORARY ROMANCES

Shooting Star

MISSED CONNECTIONS

Last Dance

With a Prince

Since Last Christmas

CONTEMPORARY EROTIC ROMANCES

Exact Warm Unholy

The Devil's Doorbell

FACETS OF PASSION

Sapphire

Platinum

Ruby

Five Golden Rings

FALLING UNDER

Going Under

Under His Touch

Under Contract

<u>EROTIC PARANORMAL</u>

MASTER OF THE OPERA E-SERIAL
Master of the Opera, Act 1: Passionate Overture
Master of the Opera, Act 2: Ghost Aria
Master of the Opera, Act 3: Phantom Serenade
Master of the Opera, Act 4: Dark Interlude
Master of the Opera, Act 5: A Haunting Duet
Master of the Opera, Act 6: Crescendo
Master of the Opera

BLOOD CURRENCY
Blood Currency

<u>BDSM FAIRYTALE ROMANCE</u>

Petals and Thorns

Thank you for reading!

About Jeffe Kennedy

Jeffe Kennedy is a multi-award-winning and best-selling author of romantic fantasy. She is the current President of the Science Fiction and Fantasy Writers of America (SFWA) and is a member of Romance Writers of America (RWA), and Novelists, Inc. (NINC). She is best known for her RITA® Award-winning novel, *The Pages of the Mind*, the recent trilogy, *The Forgotten Empires*, and the wildly popular, *Dark Wizard*. Jeffe lives in Santa Fe, New Mexico.

Jeffe can be found online at her website: JeffeKennedy.com, on her podcast First Cup of Coffee, every Sunday at the popular SFF Seven blog, on Facebook, on Goodreads, on BookBub, and pretty much constantly on Twitter @jeffekennedy. She is represented by Sarah Younger of Nancy Yost Literary Agency.

jeffekennedy.com

facebook.com/Author.Jeffe.Kennedy

twitter.com/jeffekennedy

goodreads.com/author/show/1014374.Jeffe_Kennedy

bookbub.com/profile/jeffe-kennedy

Sign up for her newsletter here.

jeffekennedy.com/sign-up-for-my-newsletter

www.ingramcontent.com/pod-product-compliance
Lightning Source LLC
Chambersburg PA
CBHW060950190726
48286CB00005B/1504